BELL, BOOK AND CANDLE

Bell, Book and Candle
by
Paul Anthony

The Right of Paul Anthony to be identified as the author of this work has been asserted by him in accordance with the Copyright, Designs and Patents Act of 1988

~

Many of the locations mentioned in this work do actually exist in various parts of the world. But please note that the characters in this book are fictitious. Any resemblance to actual persons living or dead is purely coincidental.

~ ~ ~

First Published 2013
Copyright © Paul Anthony 2013
All Rights Reserved.
Cover Image © Margaret A Scougal 2013

Published by
Paul Anthony Associates

http://www.independentauthornetwork.com/paul-anthony.html
http://paulanthonys.blogspot.co.uk/2011/12/the-paul-anthony-book-shop.html

By The Same Author

~

In Fiction…

~ ~ ~

The Fragile Peace
Bushfire
The Legacy of the Ninth
The Conchenta Conundrum
Moonlight Shadows
Behead the Serpent
Bell, Book and Candle

~ ~ ~

In Poetry…

~

Sunset

~ ~ ~

In Short Stories…

~

Scribbles with Chocolate

~

In Children's Stories
(with Meg Johnston)

~

Monsters, Gnomes and Fairies
(In My Garden)

~

Margaret - Thank you, for never doubting me.
To Paul, Barrie and Vikki - You only get one chance at life.
Live it well, live it in peace, and
Live it with love for one another.

To my special friends - Thank you, you are special.

…… Paul Anthony

~

With thanks to Pauline Livingstone and Margaret Scougal for editing and advising on my work

~

For
S013.

~

Chapter One

~

Southport, Merseyside. Yesterday

Bordering the Irish Sea, Bob Bainbridge patrolled the Coastal Road linking Ainsdale with Southport. His floppy ginger hair stopped well short of his broad shoulders and seemed to strangely compliment the crooked nose dominating his face. A former Royal Marine Commando, lean and mean, Bob was a fairly new addition to Merseyside Constabulary's finest. But he was no stranger to callous streets and violent unforgiving conflict.

Glancing at the mirrored serenity of the Irish Sea nestling close to the road, Bob wondered if the kindly residents of Southport would be peaceful and pleasant today. Would he need his new found policing skills, he contemplated, or was he destined for a quiet shift on a sunny day? Snatching lower gear, Bob guided his patrol car though the bend towards Birkdale Golf Club as a dark blue Nissan 4 x 4 cruised by in the opposite direction.

In a building society on the outskirts of Ainsdale, Shona and Marion were the only two counter clerks on duty. The relief manager was in an office at the back submerged in paper work allowing his two employees to gossip about the latest goings on in their favourite soaps. The queue before them consisted of no more than half a dozen customers and included a retired couple waiting to bank some cheques and an eager group loitering patiently to do their business. Both in their late twenties, Shona and Marion chatted to their customers, smiled at the regulars, and slowly pruned the queue.

Outside, traffic was light with only a few pedestrians gracing the streets. On the Coastal Road, a silver coloured Mercedes sped respectfully along the tarmac and cruised past the Royal Birkdale Golf Club before turning inland towards Ainsdale. When the building society came into view, the driver slid the Mercedes into a lay-by outside the premises and waited.

Peace! The up market, wealthy suburb close to Southport merely basked in the sunshine and ignored the interlopers in the Mercedes. Traffic came and went as did pedestrians, dog-walkers, and a couple of elderly gentlemen heading for a round of golf.

A hand in the front passenger seat of the Mercedes eagerly reached for a walkie-talkie radio and pressed the 'talk' switch. A voice croaked, 'Clear! Come!'

Moments later, a dark blue Nissan 4 x 4 cruised into the street and parked in front of the Mercedes. The two vehicles faced each other when the driver of the Mercedes acknowledged the Nissan's driver.

Two masked men alighted from the Mercedes. Simultaneously, two masked men stepped from the Nissan. They were dressed in dark blue overalls, black leather gloves, black boots and balaclava masks with eye holes cut into the facial area. All four men walked quickly towards the building society. Each man was armed with a black canvas holdall and an AK-47 assault rifle loaded with 7.62 x 39mm cartridges.

At the door, one of the gunmen turned round and checked the street for onlookers. The scene was clear.

Inside the building, Shona was carefully counting out crisp new bank notes to a young customer, 'One hundred and sixty, one hundred and eighty...'

'Pay day!' cracked the happy youth. 'Once a week isn't enough, is it?'

Shona nodded, licked her fingers, refused to be distracted and continued, 'Two hundred, two hundred and twenty....'

Peeling notes from a pile of twenties, she looked up when the front door burst open.

A salvo of gunfire ruined the genteel composure of the day.

Two hundred and twenty pounds in twenty pound notes scattered across the counter and then tumbled to the floor.

The leader of the masked men vaulted a counter, pulled a trigger, and watched the bullet-proof glass disintegrate in surrender to the power of the assault weapon. The sound of the bullet discharging was awesome. Shouting and screaming rent the air when customers dived for cover and staff tried desperately to hide behind the meagre furnishings.

There was another rattle of overwhelming gunfire that reached a deafening crescendo when the deadly cartridges sprayed across the society's walls and ceiling.

Within seconds, the building was a battle zone.

He was over the counter and into the back offices with his colleagues again raking the ceiling and walls with a barrage of gunfire.

A fluorescent light tube exploded and crashed to the floor bursting into a hundred tiny pieces of razor-sharp menace. A streak of gunfire blasted security cameras from their housing and a display stand hosting dozens of pamphlets was shot to pieces.

Customers screamed in terror when a rabid gunman manhandled them into a corner and a second began opening the cashier's tills. Meanwhile, a third ripped the telephone system from the wall sockets and raked a thunderous barrage of fire into the computer screens.

In the back, with a gun to his head, the distraught relief manager opened a safe.

Screaming for all she was worth, Marion eagerly opened the cashier tills and bundled handfuls of banknotes into the holdalls provided. Hiding in a corner, an elderly man punched 999 into his mobile 'phone and then dropped to the ground when another deafening crescendo of gunfire exploded around him.

Then it suddenly went quiet. Silence governed the atmosphere for a moment or two before being challenged by the sound of a woman weeping in fear.

They were gone as quickly as they had arrived leaving only an empty safe; empty tills, shattered glass, splintered woodwork, and Marion and Shona weeping uncontrollably. Dust clouded the atmosphere and part of the ceiling hung loosely from its holding.

The MDF interior structure of the building had taken a beating and lost.

From a rear office, a dishevelled bank manager emerged and whispered nervously, 'Ring the police.'

Ignored, he screamed in anguish, 'For God's sake! Ring the police!'

In the far distance, a lone siren sounded. The Mercedes took off at a steady controlled sprint in one direction whilst the Nissan took off in the other.

Bob Bainbridge lost no time in making the building society and rushed inside to find the mayhem. There he found a group of terrified customers still huddled together in one corner of the room.

'Guns or grenades?' yelled Bob.

'Guns!'

'Where are they?' cried Bob.

'Gone!' cried Shona.

'Which way?' demanded Bob.

There was a shake of the head from the gathering.

'At scene, shots fired. Repeat shots fired,' radioed Bob. 'Offenders made good their escape. Assistance required! Standby for update!'

Rushing outside to find an empty parking area, Bob looked up and down the road but there was no-one present other than a couple of scruffy looking youngsters on bikes.

'Hey, guys,' shouted Bob. 'Did you see anything?'

'You mean the robbers, Mister?' suggested Tom, the slightly older boy poking his nose.

'Yeah, which way did they go?' asked Bob.

'That way,' pointed Tom.

'No, that way,' declared Mickey.

'Very funny,' offered Bob. 'Now tell me again, which way did the robbers go?'

'Tell him, Mickey. Tell the copper,' suggested Tom straddling his bike and picking his nose like there was no tomorrow.

Mickey scowled at his pal but then turned to Bob and said, 'There were four of them. They had guns. Big rifles! Machine guns even! Two of them drove off that way and the other two drove off that way.' Mickey pointed over his shoulder.

'Did you get the car numbers?'

'No, but one was a big Nissan jeep like my dad's and the other was a blue sporty thing with a sunroof.'

'What did the robbers look like?'

'They didn't have faces,' replied Tom.

Perplexed, Bob squinted.

'He means they were wearing masks,' offered Mickey.

'Okay, stay here, boys. I need you to help. Is that alright?'

'Yeah, will we be on the telly?' queried Mickey.

'Of course you will,' suggested Bob.

'Wow!' the kids beamed.

Yelling details of the incident into his radio, Bob pushed open the front door of the building society and approached Marion and Shona.

'Girls, are you alright? Is anyone hurt?'

Snivelling, cowering behind a counter redesigned by gunfire, Shona eventually managed, 'No, I don't think so.'

Turning to the rest of the company, Bob shouted, 'Anyone! Anyone hurt at all?'

There was a shake of heads before Bob updated his radio.

'Thank the Lord for that then,' he laughed. 'Relax, it's all over.' Bob threw open his arms but the faces before him were stone: frozen solid in a moment of terror that would lurk in their minds forever.

'Tell you one thing though,' suggested Bob rubbing a finger through a layer of MDF dust enveloping a computer console. 'You need to sack the cleaner!'

Marion giggled and then began to sob.

Looking at the battle-scarred ceiling above, Bob queried, 'Upstairs? Is there an office upstairs?'

'It's the Benefits Office,' replied Shona. 'It's closed today.'

Shaking his head, Bob offered, 'Benefits office? Pity! Still, you could always borrow their cleaner, I suppose.'

Suddenly, the ice was broken. Shona laughed in relief and Marion's face relaxed.

'Let's start again, shall we?' suggested Bob. 'Does anyone remember anything that might help us find these people: anything at all, folks?'

The relief manager stopped shaking, studied the ceiling and the cartridges littering the floor, and offered. 'I can. I can, officer.'

'And what do you remember, sir,' enquired Bob.

'Their leader, he called me Kafir.'

'Kafir?' probed Bob.

'Yeah, Kafir! What kind of name is that, officer?'

Stunned, Bob Bainbridge felt sick to the bottom of his stomach and shuddered at the very thought of the word. He'd never heard the term as a police officer. But Bob was very familiar with the continent from which the word originated from his days in the armed services.

'Kafir, surely not,' replied Bob, bewildered. 'Kafir!'

'Don't you believe me, officer?' asked the manager. 'It Was Kafir. What does that mean?'

Puzzled, Bob replied, 'If memory serves me well, sir, it means disbeliever.'

Fifteen minutes after the crime occurred, the robbers dumped two stolen vehicles in a layby, switched vehicles, and entered the motorway heading towards the Pennines to make good their escape at high speed.

*

Chapter Two
~

A Conference, Rheged, Penrith.
The same day.

Rheged conference centre, near Penrith, hosted Detective Chief Inspector William Miller Boyd who was due to deliver a lecture to police officers drawn from across the north of England and the South of Scotland. As operational head of the Special Crime Unit part of his remit was to deliver talks relevant to the work of his unit. Boyd's area of responsibility lay within Counter Terrorist Command: the United Kingdom's police response to national and international terrorism. His department is the sharpest tool in the box; one step away from a military reaction, the only police unit in the United Kingdom authorised to carry firearms 24/7 in any part of the country without prior approval of a local chief constable. Consequently, Billy Boyd – as his friends called him – was rather special. He led the best of the best. It was the toughest and most dangerous policing job in the country, and he loved it.

Tall, athletic, with broad shoulders and a finely honed body to match, Boyd was a handsome man. Married to Meg: a Cumbrian nurse, he stood confidently in the wings waiting to be introduced. Checking his wristwatch, Boyd stroked his square chin thoughtfully as his deep blue eyes watched his host walk onto the stage to welcome the audience.

Approximately two hundred and fifty officers waited. Some fidgeted impatiently as they looked down on the stage below them. There was a lectern positioned in the middle of the stage with a large screen dominating the wall behind.

Towards the rear of the onlookers sat Anthea Adams. Married to Raphael, a senior Portuguese detective, Anthea was more than just Boyd's driver and surveillance partner. Detective Sergeant Adams – she'd kept her maiden name - was the lifeblood of the department and second in command of Boyd's surveillance team. A crack shot, Anthea's auburn hair flowed to her shoulders and no further. An intrepid member of the unit, she did not suffer fools gladly and occasionally spoke her mind. Intelligent and extremely competent, Anthea looked forward to a weekend flight to Lisbon whenever she could.

Boyd's host reached centre stage and introduced the speaker to the audience.

Placing one hand on the lectern, Boyd began. 'Thank you, sir, and welcome to all of you. Well, ladies and gentlemen,' Boyd activated his video presentation which flickered onto the screen. 'This is about the work of the Special Crime Unit and our effort to combat terrorism at home and abroad. Now you all know about Counter Terrorist Command and my unit so I'm not going to bore you with a run down on the nuts and bolts of my department. But I am going to acquaint you with the biggest dog in the pack in the hope that we can develop our understanding of the problems we face. We need to defeat this beast but before we can do that we need to know all about it. This is like reading the first pages of a book. You'll never get to the end if you don't appreciate the beginning and what it's all about. I'm going to talk to you about a struggle that has been in existence since the seventh century: Fourteen hundred years of struggle, my friends! I'm going to introduce you to the basics to begin with and then talk to you about Islamic terrorism!'

One detective leaned slightly to a colleague and uttered, 'All the way from Newcastle for a lecture in political correctness; just what I need, Eddie.'

Eddie replied, 'You mean he's going to tell everyone we should respect everyone irrespective of their religion.'

Anthea snarled, 'Shush!'

Boyd announced, 'About five per cent of the population of the United Kingdom is of Muslim religion. That's about 2.7 million people. Here's the basics. Muslims worship in a mosque. Outside every mosque, or just inside, you'll find a place where worshippers leave their shoes.'

'Fascinating,' voiced an officer from the front row. 'I knew that before I sat down.'

'Good,' replied Boyd. 'You're lucky. Some people have never been inside a mosque.'

There was a nod and Boyd continued, 'When visiting a mosque, if I'm on duty and working I keep my shoes on. If I'm a guest and I'm off duty I remove my shoes as a mark of respect. Anyway, everyone is equal and sits on the floor. You'll find a niche in one of the walls. This is the 'mihrab' and reveals the direction worshippers should address in order to face Mecca. Some mosques have a minaret where a muezzin stands at the top of a tower and calls Muslims to prayer five times a day.'

'What about women, sir?' asked a detective

'Women can attend the mosque,' explained Boyd. 'They sit separately from the men but they usually pray at home'

'Thank you,' smiled the officer.

'With immigration control controversial,' stated Boyd. 'The number of Muslims in our country is increasing all the time. It may be true that most Muslims are law abiding but when I finish my presentation today some of you may wonder which law they abide by. At times, I'm not sure.' Boyd added, 'We'll come to Muslim law later. Right now let us consider the daily ritual of a devout Muslim. Each day they make their necessary ablutions before speaking with God. They pray before sunrise, in the early afternoon, in the late afternoon, after sunset, and before midnight. Each time they pray they imagine the position of the Kaaba, in the great mosque of Mecca: the city where Muhammad was born in 570.'

A map appeared on the screen behind Boyd.

'How many times do you pray each day? God was an astronaut wasn't he? Or was he a time traveller? Do you believe in God?' enquired Boyd of the audience.

There was a chuckle or two but Boyd pressed on undeterred, 'How important is God in your life? How vital is it that you must pray five times a day and then for one month of the year you deliberately fast and take no food during daylight hours? But my job is not to dissect their religion. No, I am trying to give you a flavour of the religion. You see, in order to recognise Islamic extremism, I want you to first understand the very basics of Islam.'

A hand shot up, 'So does that mean we are only interested in Muslims who don't eat during Ramadan because they are more extreme than the others?'

There was a burst of laughter and Boyd countered with, 'Actually, you've just touched on how difficult it is to differentiate between ordinary and extreme. Let me explain. During Ramadan Muslims fast from dawn until sunset; throughout that period they cannot eat food, drink liquids, smoke or have sexual relations, and they shouldn't swear either.'

'And what's the payback for being a good Muslim?' asked a uniformed sergeant. 'Free beer for the other eleven months?'

'Well, according to the Koran,' suggested Boyd. 'The rewards are many but Ramadan is one of the five pillars of Islam. There are five principles upon which Islam is based. Firstly, a Muslim needs to believe in the Prophet Muhammad, offer prayers, and recite the Koran. One of the pillars is a concern for the needy and making charitable donations. And there's Ramadan and the hajj. They are expected to make a pilgrimage to Mecca once in a lifetime.'

'Why Mecca?' enquired an interested party.

'Because that's where Muhammad was born,' explained Boyd.

'Why is Muhammad important to the Muslims, Guvnor?'

Boyd replied, 'Muhammad was a religious, political, and military leader. He unified Arabia into a single religious community. Muslims believe Muhammad was a messenger and a prophet from God. Orphaned at an early age, he was brought up by his uncle Abu Talib. Moreover, Muhammad was once a shepherd who regularly retreated to a cave for several nights of seclusion and prayer. At the age of forty he received a revelation from God. He began preaching these disclosures publicly proclaiming that 'God is One' and that complete and total surrender to Him was the only way forward acceptable to God. His followers grew to more than ten thousand despite falling out with neighbouring tribes. I want you all to remember the word 'tribes' because all the problems of the Middle East are rooted in both religion and tribes. They've been fighting across the Middle East on and off for centuries. Anyway, after eight years of fighting with the Meccan tribes Muhammad took control of Mecca and destroyed its pagan idols. By the time of his death most of the Arabian Peninsula had been converted to Islam and one single Muslim community existed. Steadfastly, he reported receiving the word of God until the time of his death and it is the word of God that forms the verses of the Koran which is regarded as the word of God. Consequently, the religion is based on these verses and on the word of God as defined by Muhammad.'

'Isn't that just like the Bible?' someone asked.

'No, the Bible is an assortment of chronicles, texts and writings that are considered sacred in Christianity and Judaism,' explained Boyd. 'But you hit the jackpot there, young man. Muslims will tell you that the Bible is a collection of texts whereas the Koran is the word of God recited by Muhammad and written down by his followers to be taught throughout the centuries as the word of God. You'll hear them say 'Allahu Akbar'. It means 'God is Great'. Muslims will tell you that their God is greater than ours and the Koran is stronger than the Bible.'

'Explain to me, Guvnor,' suggested an elderly detective, 'Why you're just talking about the Muslim faith not Islamic extremism.'

'See me before you leave,' quipped Boyd. 'I have openings for detectives who can follow the plot. You are, of course, correct. You have highlighted the problem we have. For me, the crux of the matter is defining extremism and separating it out from what I will call mainstream religious belief – if that makes sense.'

The elderly detective nodded and rested his chin on a crooked arm.

'You see,' explained Boyd. 'The Koran clearly reveals the Islamic goal of reforming the earth, by armed force if necessary, in order to assume political power and implement the principles of Islam throughout the globe. This is where the origins of Jihad are found. It's an Islamic term meaning 'duty' but in Arabic it means 'struggle'. A person engaged in Jihad is called a mujahid and the plural is mujahideen.'

'Now we're getting somewhere,' voiced the elderly detective. 'Earlier you said Muhammad left one Muslim community but we know there are two: Sunni and Shia. Has this anything to do with the extremism we are trying to separate out?'

'I'll simplify things,' revealed Boyd. 'When Muhammad died there was a split between Shia and Sunni over who was to become leader of the Muslim nation. Sunni Muslims wanted the new leader to be elected from those considered capable of the job. They won the argument. The Shia believe the leadership should have been handed down through the Prophets own family and not decided on by an election. The dispute between these two groups dates back to the death of Muhammad and the argument about who should take over the leadership of the Muslim nation.'

'Who is winning?'

'Put it this way, eighty five per cent of Muslims are Sunni.'

'Where does Al-Qaeda fit into all this?'

More images appeared on the screen and Boyd answered, 'Al-Qaeda is traceable to the Soviet War in Afghanistan. Unlike many other terrorist organisations, it's a stateless army operating a network of mainly Sunni Muslims who are intent on global Jihad and a strict interpretation of sharia law. Al-Qaeda is the enemy and the face of Islamic extremism. Our problem is identifying extreme views. People who preach the spread of Islam by violence and fighting are quite clearly extreme and are therefore our enemy. They have stepped away from religion to embrace violence so when I see someone behaving in an aggressive way I reckon I'm half way to defining extremism. I try not to judge people by the way they look, the book they carry to their place of worship, or what they wear on their head. But I reserve the right to put those with violent attitudes into a separate pigeon hole.'

'What about radicalisation?' asked a female officer. 'Is it a criminal offence to be radicalised?'

'No, not yet,' confirmed Boyd. 'Radicalisation is a process in which an individual adopts extreme political, social or religious views and rejects the status quo of normality. It can be violent or non-violent and although it is not necessarily illegal, it certainly needs to be recognised for what it is — a movement towards the other side — and steps may need to be taken to prevent those who are being radicalised to be reassessed in the light of what they do.'

'And Sharia Law?' articulated a Scottish accent.

'The Muslims want Sharia Law here in Britain and some of them are prepared to go to extremes to get it. In the Arab States they are happy with stoning for adultery, amputations for theft, and death for apostates who turn their back on Islam. In fact, they're quite happy to give the Christians and Jews second class status. This is the kind of law which is practised under the Islamic system in countries like Iran, Saudi Arabia and Great Britain.'

Laughter hit Boyd like a tidal wave when someone shouted, "Great Britain! An Islamic country! You must be joking?'

Boyd offered, 'There are eighty five Sharia courts now operating in this country. We need to understand our own back yard first. We have Islamic Judges ruling on cases here in the UK from financial problems to marital issues amongst British Muslims, and it's all done via the Sharia Courts.'

'But that is outside the law,' proposed a Lancashire officer.'

'Not in the Islamic Republic of Tower Hamlets,' cracked Boyd. 'Tower Hamlets is the epicentre of Muslim activity in London. Residents will tell you that sharia is considered the infallible law of God as opposed to man's interpretation of the law.

Sharia law is drawn from both the Koran and the examples set by Muhammad in the Sunnah. Sharia is interpreted by Qadis – Islamic Judges – who are responsible for the Imams: the religious leaders.'

The mutterings of discontent continued and Boyd broke in with, 'In Britain the Muslim Arbitration Tribunal uses sharia family law to settle disputes. These things are legalised by the 1996 Arbitration Act. Peaceful Muslims worship Allah. Violent Muslims worship the desire to extend the Arab caliphate beyond the boundaries of Arabia with their sharia law. That's the difference between extremity and ordinary.'

The lights dimmed down as Boyd's voice introduced the photo gallery and his video presentation ran its course.

*

Chapter Three

~

The Caldbeck Fells, Cumbria.

Galloping along with a gentle wind swirling her long blonde hair and wafting around her slender figure, the teenager gazed down on a church, its rambling overgrown graveyard, and a stream that meandered like a thin silken ribbon through the picturesque countryside.

The stunning Fells of Caldbeck formed such a magnificent backyard for the youngster. This area of outstanding natural beauty was spoilt only by the third largest structure in the United Kingdom: a radio mast emanating from the nearby transmitting station. Standing over a thousand feet tall, the mast dominated the region and could be seen from virtually the whole of north Cumbria and from across the Solway Firth in the south of Scotland. At night red aircraft warning lights clinging to the structure were visible for miles around. All-pervading, the edifice stood as a silent guardian proudly watching life unfold in this part of the world.

With a sudden snap of the reins, Susie lovingly ordered her white stallion to charge faster as they made the Fell tops and sampled the rich green plateau.

Over the common and along the broad but winding path, Susie took in the breath-taking glories of the Cumbrian countryside: high Fells, deep valleys, severe gullies, and a luscious green meadowland. Riding hard, Susie's free spirit enjoyed the independence of life in the saddle as a bird of prey circled high above her. She heard the cry of a Common Buzzard and knew it was watching over her. Her feathered friend seemed to have adopted her whenever she ventured abroad. Soon, the bird would swoop and display its magnificent finery to her before perching on the highest available point in the area. Susie sensed it was her personal guardian sent from above. Eventually, she tired and began to acknowledge that her horse also needed to rest and recuperate.

Reluctantly, she eased down, turned for home and broke into a canter.

Deep in the valley, close to the stream, Susie brought her steed to a standstill. Raising herself high in the stirrups, she read the sign at the entrance to the farm. It was written in a dull yellow on a large green wooden notice board and advertised the presence of 'The Base – A Retreat and Adventure Base for Young People.'

That's new, Susie thought. It used to be a youth hostel and before that it was a mining centre of some kind. Why do they keep changing these places?

Caressing her horse's neck, Susie wondered what it was like inside the Base. She'd never met anyone who spent time at the location and speculated on whether there really were a lot of young people visiting the site. I bet the local farmers know, she thought, but then reminded herself that a lot of the surrounding area extended for mile upon mile of open countryside. Oh yes, there was a farming community alright but many of the farms in this neck of the woods were quite isolated from one another by the sheer geography involved. Thousands of sheep roamed the high Fells and were cared for by a shepherd or two whose job it was to look after the sheep and nothing else. Whether they had any interest in an adventure centre for young people was another thing. One of the locals would surely know, she decided. The news will get out soon and then we'll know all there is to know about the Base. It'll only be new for a short time, thought Susie. These Fells might seem remote to many but to some of us it's just a big village really.

Susie fed her stallion a lump of sugar loitering in the folds of her jacket.

Boys! Yes, boys, she thought. At sixteen I am allowed to think about boys even if my stuffy old parents say I shouldn't. I'm grown up now. I am an adult even if my Mum and Dad don't think so.

Her eyes followed the narrow lane from the entrance towards the main building. In the distance she could see more structures.

Perhaps they were the accommodation block. She did not know. In the green of the countryside Susie could distinguish a collection of pre-fabricated buildings and a dozen or so log cabins.

Without warning, the rear of a green Land Rover appeared as the vehicle reversed from a brick garage inside the yard.

'Come on, Gabby,' she whispered.

Clicking her heels, Susie yanked the reins and guided the stallion away from The Base, away from the place of promised adventure.

Unperturbed, Susie rode on, stole a glance over her shoulder, but remained unaware of a group of males at work close by.

At The Base a band of men slithered through the undergrowth on their bellies with rifles held in Commando style. Green and black camouflage face-paint distorted their appearance and complimented the coveralls they wore. Like snakes in the grass, they wriggled their way forward until they reached an open ditch.

Raising his arm, the leader signalled the group to divide into two. Immediately, they dropped stealthily into the wet filthy trench, separated, and inched closer to their target. Muddy slime encased them as they encircled The Base.

Standing on a raised wooden decking in front of a ramshackle log cabin, a man, black booted and wearing a black overall, stood with a pair of binoculars scanning the terrain in front of him. The word 'Commandant' was woven in white cotton on the chest area of his coverall. With an olive tinted skin the commanding officer towered over six feet tall. It was difficult to tell from the trenches but he was a giant of a man in some ways, perhaps six feet three tall. He was also quite broad and sported an unkempt ragged moustache and full beard that trailed away below his chin.

Gradually, the surreptitious assailants crawled through the filthy mud-encrusted trench, stumbled onto rough land, and made good their incursion.

25

The commandant suddenly allowed the binoculars to fall to his chest when he pointed and yelled, 'You're out!'

The response was immediate and simultaneous. Breaking cover, the group rapidly discharged their firearms into the chief's body. He fell to the ground and rolled over trying to protect himself. Unruffled, the devil dancing in their eyes, the gang closed with their prey. Tossing grenades and cartridges towards the log cabin, they took great pleasure in the mayhem they caused.

There was another bout of rapid gunfire, a gritty explosion of smoke, an unexpected sound of glass shattering and wood splintering, and a shriek of battle-hardened warriors in their final rush of glory. Then there was an eerie silence save for the barely audible sound of sheep bleating from afar.

Gradually, the commandant regained his feet.

Paint guns empty, hand cartridges devoid of paint, the camouflaged group laughed whilst a coloured liquid dripped from the door of a dilapidated log cabin and the commandant wiped a smudge of paint from his face.

'Again,' he ordered, sliding shards of glass away with his laced-tight boot. 'Reload! Back to the start! You need to be quicker, quieter and stealthier.'

Clapping his hands, the commandant hurried and scurried his pupils. 'Come on! Let's go!' he ordered. 'Make every shot count. We've no room for losers.'

Gradually the crowd of youngsters reformed and made their way back to the start line. Mostly in their late teens or early twenties, the adolescents spoke in the mixed dialect of the West Midlands Asian community.

In the skies above a Common Buzzard detected a morsel on the earth below and plunged towards its first meal of the day.

From the west, the Irish Sea rolled towards the cliffs of St Bees as the tide changed and a surge of dark cloud headed inland towards High Fells of Cumbria. A storm was brewing.

Yet, shrouded by the Fells of North Cumbria, the scenic village of Caldbeck is a hidden jewel in the Lake District's crown. It is beautiful, serene and peaceful, whilst boasting a thriving community and a pounding Lakeland heart.

On the more genteel outskirts of the village, there was a crunch from a heavy shoe on tired embedded gravel when a clergyman made his way steadily along the path through the weed-strewn graveyard. Carrying a dark blue leather-bound bible, tucked in close to his chest, he shivered when an unwelcome breeze bit through the dark jacket and threatened his inner soul. Bald on top, and in his mid-forties, the priest gathered his coat closer and turned up its collar intent on keeping out the cold.

Once inside the ancient church, Matthew donned his cassock and adjusted his white band clerical collar before walking down the nave. He stepped towards the stained glass window depicting Jesus of Nazareth on the Cross. A beam of light penetrated the glass and illuminated Matthew's path towards the altar. From the nave he took the three short steps onto a higher stage and then stepped reverently towards the altar showing great respect for the spiritual presence of his God. As a Christian, he knew the area surrounding the altar was both endowed and enriched with supreme and eminent holiness. In centuries gone by it was at this table that a sacrifice might be made or a religious rite performed. Here, in Matthew's church, the altar was swathed with a deep red coloured cloth that was smooth and velvety to his touch. Upon the hallowed cloth lay a crystal bell, an ancient Bible and an unused white candle.

Placing his own Bible on the Holy table, Matthew made the sign of the Cross and began the service knowing he would not be disturbed. On Sundays they came from miles around to join him in worshipping the Lord. They sang hymns and prayed as a close knit community before dropping coins into the gold plated collection plate at the entrance to the church. Then they shook his hand and shared pleasantries with him and his family before returning to their homes. Such worshippers lived in the numerous villages and hamlets surrounding the house of their God.

Today, he celebrated alone in the cold grey building that lacked colour and verve.

Outside, the wind scuttled through the graveyard chasing the errant leaves into a never-ending circle of despair as the lichen moss clung steadfastly to the old grey neglected headstones.

Inside, the Reverend Matthew Lowther, forty six years old, clean-shaven, balding, and of sober mind and stout body, continued his governance. He lit a candle on the altar before kneeling in prayer.

Matthew took communion with the Lord.

'The body of Christ, the bread of heaven…'

He broke the bread and solemnly devoured it.

'The blood of Christ, the cup of salvation…'

He poured the wine and drank it reverently.

'May the body and blood of our Lord Jesus Christ keep us unto eternal life…'

Closing his eyes, he prayed momentarily aware of rainfall gently tapping on the stained glass window above the altar as a storm brewed in the heavens beyond.

In a far off land, thousands of miles from the Caldbeck Fells and the flight of the buzzard, a guerrilla fighter guided his young horse through a thin copse of cedar trees before climbing to a high point overlooking the brown rocky earth below. Here and there, a nimble goat clung almost miraculously to the side of the mountain whilst a pair of hawks soared on high.

Dismounting, Khalid rubbed fatigue from his eyes and twisted his neck to loosen those aching muscles and help him relax. Tall, broad, Khalid carried an athletic build which gave him a strong and sturdy appearance. He was handsome in so many ways. Yet the two inch scar coursing its way from the high cheek bone of the left side of his face to the corner of his mouth did nothing to compliment his appearance and merely added to his warrior like demeanour. An argument with a Shiite Muslim resulted in the death of his enemy at the cost of a lifelong logo entrenched across his own face. Taking a deep breath, Khalid clambered to a point where a tongue of dark red rock jutted arrogantly out into the sky allowing him to look down on his native land and a multitude of proud hawks soaring above.

The valley floor lay deep below him. In the distance a caravan of mules carrying essential supplies to a far off village laboured gradually along a narrow path. The resultant gathering dust cloud bore witness to an escalating temperature and the passage of creatures across the landscape. Yet from the side of the gorge opposite a sudden torrent of water somehow sprang from the earth and dropped chaotically to a slender watercourse below. Showers of water plummeted into the stream almost masking the opening of a cave into which Khalid's eyes eagerly peered.

Khalid moved his head slightly as he studied the panorama.

My land, he thought. The magnificent diamond in my eye is the country of my heritage. This land is our land and it will always be that way.

Standing tall and erect, Khalid held his arms high and wide in humble salutation and spoke aloud into the wind. 'There is no God but Allah and Muhammad is his Prophet.'

It is his ritual to pray. Each day he made his necessary ablutions before climbing to the high rock to speak with his God. He prayed before sunrise, in the early afternoon, in the late afternoon, after sunset, and before midnight. Each time he prayed, Khalid imagined the position of the Kaaba, in the great mosque of Mecca.

The cave! Khalid watched the water tipple from the gorge and fall across its opening. Silently, Khalid wondered of the cave and the Prophet Muhammad.

Khalid tried to visualise the times of Muhammad. By now, he knew enough English to verify that when translated Muhammad means Praiseworthy. Khalid stood taking in the wild untouched beauty of his land. These are the things that drive me, he thought. It is the Prophet Muhammad and his religion that drives me, underlines me, and subscribes me to follow him in the Jihadist way. I, Khalid, give my life to Islam.

Now, facing in the direction of the Kaaba, Khalid prayed alone and recited the Koran for it was infallible and undeniable in its strength, truth and purity. Passionate, determined, Khalid prayed to Allah and ordered his mind and body to take no sound precautions for his personal safety. Holding no fear of what lay ahead he knew he would not die in vain since his passing would merely ensure a better place for him in his next life. He was prepared for martyrdom and hoped it would be that way. To the intended victim, he held no personal grudge or specific individual hatred. The infidels are from a country corrupted by wealth, power and pride, he considered. The Kafir - the disbeliever – are irrelevant in my mind-set.

For himself, in the final moments of his ultimate glory, Khalid decided to die for his beliefs. His path to Paradise was clear. Enemies instilled no fear in his mind. Blades and bullets are a mere symptom of the eternal war he fought. He prayed again, one last time, before mounting his horse and heading towards the border to a final meeting with his father.

Khalid was many thousands of miles from the United Kingdom.

Nearing his home in Cumbria Boyd first spoke on his mobile to Meg: his wife, and memorised a short list of foodstuffs required from the local supermarket. Turning into the store's car park, he positioned his BMW surveillance vehicle opposite an ATM cash machine and switched the engine off.

A short queue formed behind a man and woman standing at the front of the line for the ATM machine. They argued noisily to the annoyance of those close by.

Taking stock of the situation, Boyd quickly realised they were in their mid-twenties. She was a blonde wearing huge gold earrings. He was a stone or two overweight and looked like a brute.

Boyd's mobile rang and interrupted his train of thought. It was Antonia Harston-Browne from MI5: The Security Service. She'd received a tip-off from the police in Scotland and Boyd was in the right place at the right time to lead a response.

Moments later the call ended with Boyd suddenly aware that life on the Special Crime Unit was not all lectures and laughter. He had a surveillance operation to plan. Opening the glove compartment, Boyd removed an envelope and a ball point pen.

A tirade of foul and abusive language filled the air when the couple's argument intensified and an elderly man in the queue protested shouting, 'Hey, steady on, you two.'

The blonde snapped, 'Back off, it's got nothing to do with you, old man.'

'Yeah!' cried the thug. 'Keep your nose out.'

Boyd stowed his phone in the hand's free on the dashboard, stuffed the pen and envelope into his jacket pocket, and slid from the car.

'Just saying, that's all,' voiced the old man quietly.

'And as for you,' screamed the thug turning his attention to the blonde. 'You can learn to do as you're told.'

Taking a step back, the woman pleaded, 'Careful, Bobby, I just made a mistake, that's all. It's not the end of the world.'

'Really,' came the reply. 'Then you must learn to do as you are told and not as you want?'

The ruffian pushed her backwards and she stumbled into the ATM machine.

'Excuse me,' suggested Boyd joining the queue. 'If you're not using the machine perhaps you can step aside and let us get on with our lives whilst you get on with yours?'

'Mind your own business, pal. I'll push her around if I want. She's my wife.'

As if to prove his announcement, the young hooligan pushed his young wife to the ground again and then grinned broadly at Boyd finishing with, 'On yer bike, pal, before I put you on your arse too.'

'Ahh,' smoothed Boyd. 'Now I'd rather you just stand aside for a moment and let this gentlemen here at the front use the machine. It's as simple as that.'

With the blonde now snivelling and the lout squaring up to Boyd, the elderly gent stepped forward and eagerly inserted his card into the machine.

'Go on, pops,' laughed the thug. 'Be my guest while I sort out big mouth here.'

Shaking his head, Boyd suggested, 'No, you really don't want to say things like that, young man.'

Stepping forward the hooligan launched a vicious right hander towards Boyd who merely moved his head to one side. There was a 'swish' when a clenched fist flew past Boyd's ear into empty airspace.

'Bobby, no!' yelled the blonde.

A left crashed through the air and Boyd met it with his hand, crunched it tight, and forced the limb backwards and to the side.

Screaming in agony, Boyd's assailant felt the full strength of Boyd's upper limb when he suddenly found himself on his knees.

'Now then, young man,' suggested Boyd. 'If you're a nice kind young man you'll just remain there whilst these good people go about their business and use the machine. Otherwise, I'll call security from the supermarket and have them call the police or remove you from the car park. It's your decision.'

Boyd squeezed tighter.

The thug gasped and nodded apologetically.

'Yeah, sorry! Go ahead. Use the bloody machine but let go of me before you break my arm.'

A security guard appeared and ushered the queue forward before saying, 'I've been watching you on the CCTV. Now get off the site or I'll call the police and you can spend the night in the pokey. It's all on video, young 'un. It's up to you.'

Boyd released his grip and watched the hooligan and his blonde partner melt away into the car park.

'Thanks, mister....' queried the security guard trying to get a name.

'I'm just a shopper,' replied Boyd inserting his card into the machine. Just shopping for a few odds and ends but if you've a moment can you make sure he doesn't haven't a go at my car whilst I'm inside? I'll only be a couple of minutes.'

'Of course,' replied the guard. 'I'll wait here until he's well and truly gone.'

A twenty pound note appeared from the machine's outlet. Boyd pocketed the money, nodded to the security guard, and made his way towards the store.

I've no time for this, he thought. Operation Intercept, how many surveillance cars do I need? Removing the envelope and pen, Boyd scrawled a list of names on the back of an envelope before entering the supermarket.

Chapter Four

~

The Khyber Pass, near Peshawar, Pakistan.

The lands of the Mullagori tribe lay to his north when Khalid negotiated an old Silk Road and dissected the Spin Ghar Mountains. Carefully, he followed the ancient route aware that this narrow, barren pass is written in the folklore of a hundred nations. Khalid appreciated that historically a hundred countries had used the Pass to infiltrate these lands. Yet legend revealed they had all failed to conquer the spirit of his people.

On reaching the summit, at Landi Katal, Khalid took one long look back at Afghanistan and then gently guided his horse away.

The horse was young and strong, proud to be carrying its cargo: equally young and strong.

Khalid, an armed guerrilla fighter, rode astride his mount as it trotted steadily from the foothills of the Khyber Pass towards Peshawar: close to the Afghanistan – Pakistan border.

Ahead, in the distance, what appeared to be an abandoned fort eventually came into view. As he drew nearer, strong walls became evident and took on a new meaning. There was no smoke escaping from a campfire into the sky; no tell-tale bleat of goats to reveal the presence of a goat herder or farmer. There was just a high wall forlornly beckoning him forward.

As Khalid approached the fort, the large double wooden doors opened and he entered.

Tethering his horse to a rail, Khalid noticed a satellite dish mounted to the corner of a wall. The concave metal was dull and slightly rusty indicating it was a victim of an aging process. Rolling his neck, he shouldered his rifle, ducked beneath the low lintel, and entered the building.

Armed guards, dressed from head to toe in long grey robes and wearing dark keffiyeh, stood smoking cigarettes. He was expected and, when Khalid advanced towards them, they stubbed out their cigarettes to welcome him with open arms. Respectfully, they led him to an interior meeting room where, in the dim light, a splinter group of mujahideen warriors allied to the Taliban, sat cross-legged on the floor and at tables.

They greeted him reverently, shook his hand, clasped his shoulders, and then waited for proceedings to commence.

Rifles, handguns, and AK 47's, littered the room and more than a dozen laptop computers and mobile phones flickered contemptuously in their bid to gain a hold on the Wi-Fi signal. There seemed to be all manner of handheld technological devices present but Khalid paid little attention to the scientific gizmos.

Setting down his rifle and mobile phone next to a Wi-Fi booster, Khalid took his place at a low table. He removed his keffiyeh and ran his fingers through his hair as if to wash out the dust of his long journey. Crossing his legs, he accepted a drink of water and waited with the others. Whilst swallowing the liquid, he gazed across at a neighbouring laptop and saw the image of a short middle-aged man who was bald and wore dark rimmed spectacles. The image grew and Khalid realised it was his father: Abdul-Ahad who was speaking on a webcam.

Staring directly into the camera, Abdul-Ahad spoke to his followers with the black and yellow flag of Al-Qaeda draped from a wall behind him. Then his image disappeared and was replaced by a picture of bombs exploding in various parts of the world.

Suddenly, there was an inexplicable flicker and the screen went black for no apparent reason. There was a slight murmur of concern before the image returned only this time it was stronger and clearer.

On screen, the Al-Qaeda flag appeared again and then gave way to the reason for the programme. There was a man bent down on his knees and he was jabbering nervously towards the camera in a language that Khalid did not understand. Perspiration clung to his shirt and darkened his underarms whilst tears seemed to trickle

35

from his eyes. The man was petrified, frightened for his life, and he was obviously trying to read from a card held in front of him. In staccato fashion, he spoke aloud the sentences held before him. He did not speak with passion or belief. He merely worked his way through the words in a disjointed faltering fashion. It was not the English tongue of the infidel. It might have been French or Italian, Khalid did not know. He just appreciated that the man who had been kidnapped in the foothills by the mujahideen was of European origin. A ransom had been suggested but had not been paid and now the man who had been shanghaied in Peshawar blubbered uncontrollably as he pleaded for his life. He was spluttering out the words fed to him in a last ditch attempt to appease his captors. What's more, the clip was obviously going out live across the ether.

A sword swung and the victim was decapitated.

A camera followed the flight of the sword then focused on a head rolling amidst a pool of gathering blood.

Khalid was used to the violence of Jihad but was not expecting a beheading. He felt sick in the pit of his stomach and took another cup of water. Drinking liberally, he wondered how close the killing had taken place to where he was sitting.

The film continued for over fifteen minutes during which time Khalid listened to his father's voice amidst the intensity of the audience. It was the voice of an extreme and authoritarian leader callously explaining the reason for a cold-blooded murder and then imploring his fighters to take up arms against the infidel – the disbeliever – the Kafir. The speech of Khalid's father spat hatred and contempt, vilified those who did not follow Islam, and preached a loathing against disbelievers on a global scale.

When the clip ended the gathering closed their laptops and made ready to leave. It was all over.

To everyone's surprise Khalid's father appeared in person.
Cheering!
Chanting!
'Abdul-Ahad! Abdul-Ahad!'

A groundswell of cheering and applause greeted their leader when he magnanimously entered the room to a climax of frenzied unrestrained adoration. Abdul-Ahad was dressed from head to foot in a white robe but his keffiyeh was black adorned with an inspirational yellow flash of cloth.

Standing, Khalid embraced his father and held him close.

Abdul-Ahad returned his son's embrace and then saluted the uninhibited assembly by clasping his hands in prayer and bowing to them.

Adored by his warriors, Khalid's father returned their worship by announcing, 'Allahu Akbar,'

There were repeated shouts of 'Allahu Akbar,' and then Khalid's father declared, 'Allahu Akbar… God is Great… Allahu Akbar…'

The assembly of mujahideen bowed and then rose as one to join the salutation.

'Warriors,' announced Abdul-Ahad. 'We, the Fathers of the Sons of the Shimmering Dawn, are gathered. Come close, feel the warmth of my heart. Smell the nectar of fresh lemons and taste our finest figs upon your lips. Listen to the words of vengeance I speak. Heed my words of attrition. I say unto you… Behold, the Shimmering Dawn is upon us. Allahu Akbar.'

They repeated the phrase; each time growing in strength and volume as the decibels increased and an air of religious fervour seemed to dominate the room.

Within minutes hysteria gripped the building.

'Behold, the Shimmering Dawn is upon us.'

'Behold, the Shimmering Dawn is upon us.'

'Behold, the Shimmering Dawn is upon us.'

And so it continued.

But at the end of the meeting, Khalid, now dressed casually in trousers, shirt and jacket emerged and stood in the centre of the room. He held out his arms to his father who stepped forward and threw his arms around his son.

Abdul-Ahad declared, 'Khalid! My son, I am the Servant of the One but you are the Eternal One. It is time.'

The assembly rose as one to hear their noble leader speak once more.

Abdul-Ahad declared, 'Khalid, you are one of the chosen four. But you, my son, are the special one. You are the Eternal One. You have our message, Eternal One. You are our broad shoulders; our strength, and our heart and soul. Above all, my son, you are our Bejewelled Sword.'

The mujahideen roared in approval again.

'You must follow in my footsteps in the way that you have been shown,' revealed Khalid's father. 'You will fly with the eagles and soar with the hawk and then behold, the gates of Paradise will be forever yours.'

Khalid kissed his father's hands. Then he kissed his cheeks before turning and walking away. At the door, Khalid paused, turned, and proclaimed dutifully... 'For a Shimmering Dawn!'

When Khalid stepped outside into the walled compound, the group follow him chanting, 'Khalid! Khalid! Khalid!'

He did not turn to engage their eye as the mantra grew into an uncontrollable frenzy. He merely heard the incantation of his name as he bypassed his horse and approached the Toyota 4 x 4.

'Khalid! Khalid! Khalid!' recited the crowd.

Two mujahideen shouldering rifles escorted Khalid to the vehicle.

The engine fired. The Toyota wheels bit the dust. Khalid began his journey from the foothills of the Khyber Pass to the hustle and bustle of the thriving city of Peshawar and its International airport in the district of Khyber Pakhtunkwa.

Khalid did not turn to force a wave. He did not turn to throw a last kiss to his father. Neither did he turn to look high into the mountains of the Spin Ghar. Khalid was gone from the mujahideen and the notoriously brave tribe of the Mullagori.

On another continent, vigilant eyes engaged a real time television screen whilst meticulous careful hands fastidiously manipulated the remote controls of a device operating four thousand miles away above foreign soil. Directly above the mountains of the Spin Ghar, an unmanned aerial vehicle – a surveillance drone – flying at a height of seventeen thousand feet took selected video footage of the ground below as it simultaneously gathered electronic data from the atmosphere. Immediately, the product was beamed back to the joint British-American control room in a secure compound in the UK.

In the United Kingdom, later that day, the redheaded Antonia Harston-Browne stood in her office and watched over London.

Biting deeply into an apple, she looked out through her window and studied traffic below and the River Thames meandering its way through the capital.

Tall and slim, Antonia was renowned amongst her male counterparts for her shapely legs and long red hair which flowed down her back covering her shoulder blades. With an hour-glass figure, Antonia wore a dark blue, two-piece, executive-style suit set off with a silver brooch worn on the lapel. The neatly tailored skirt stopped short just above the knee. She called it her office uniform and wore it well. Antonia was one of those individuals who just didn't age. She thrived on adventure and tension. A child of the Sixties, she was every inch a lady: articulate, sophisticated, cultured, educated well above the national standard, and of upper middle class bearing. Indeed, Antonia carried a highly polished professional demeanour wherever she went enjoying two honours degrees and playing a merciless game of squash. At the quintessential exclusive country club she was in her element with the so-called 'county set'. Whilst in the oak-panelled corridors of Whitehall and the highfalutin financial offices of the City, she could wheel and deal with the sharpest of kids on the block. In the City, she wined and dined at expensive restaurants and wore long, flowing gowns that vitalised her sophisticated charms and discarded the facade of her other life. She was privileged, virtually blue-blooded, the daughter of parents since departed: parents who had left her a financial legacy that revealed her to be of comfortable private means. In the City, in the country club, she had no enemies, save those who bitched at her pretentiousness. Moreover, Antonia had connections in every corner of society that one might imagine: the good, the bad, and the ugly.

Today, she was living her other life within the offices of Thames House: the home of Britain's Security Service. The accomplished Antonia was a highly respected member of MI5. As a senior Intelligence Officer, she was a leading member of the controversial Special Crime Unit.

The remnant of her apple core sailed through the air and landed in a litter bin with an audible plonk.

Antonia sank the remnants of a mug of coffee and returned to her desk.

Punching the black and whites on her keyboard, she zoomed into the latest intelligence news feed assigned to her office. Only a senior member of the Intelligence household held such access and she treated her obligations with the utmost respect.

Examining a selection of aerial photographs, Antonia scrutinised bases, compounds and buildings, before realising they were all in a desert or mountainous area far from the shores of the UK. A number of figures cast long shadows on the ground and she wondered upon the origin of the product. She did not know. Presuming the source had been a drone, satellite or spy-plane fly-pass, she tapped her keyboard and accessed the intelligence report where she read a transcript of an intercepted electronic message. Then she studied a computerised note from the originator of the report revealing a link to a website. To preserve the cyber security of her work station, she transferred to a highly encrypted standalone computer on a neighbouring desk and negotiated into the link.

What she saw sickened her.

Antonia unhinged the telephone from its cradle and dialled the pager for Commander James Herbert, the head of the Special Crime Unit.

Sporting a newly grown full white beard and moustache, Commander Herbert had reached a level of maturity where he was beginning to accept the word retirement. It was something he was considering in the future, possibly sooner than many realised. Indeed, the idea of less stress and a more relaxed life style appealed to him at times. At the moment, he had things to do before he made the final decision.

When his pager sounded, Commander Herbert was in conference with the new Director General of the Security Service: Phillip Nesbitt K.B.E.

Phillip's curriculum vitae revealed he had enjoyed a long career in the Service and once handled matters on both the Irish desk and the International Terrorist desk before moving into realms of protective security and organisational administration. He had charted his own career and although, surprisingly, he did not court a strong following it was generally accepted amongst the rank and file that Phillip Nesbitt fitted the seat well. He had wide experience of the Service but had been something of a surprise appointment to many.

Indeed, a good description might be that he was a 'Jack of all trades' and master of none. Sadly, in some quarters his promotion prompted quiet accusations of a 'political appointment'. Phillip acknowledged he had much to accomplish in the days ahead if he were to silence any whispering campaign.

'Well, it's been splendid to meet you, Phillip,' suggested Commander Herbert with a huge grin. 'May I wish you the very best of luck in the future. I'm sure you won't need it but if I can ever help in any way, please feel free to seek me out. Be assured, you have my full support.'

Phillip Nesbitt reached out to shake the commander's hand vigorously replying, 'Thank you, James. I will arrange a regular meeting with your unit – perhaps once a month would suffice - but I should tell you now that I am a little rusty with such operational matters. When last I held such a role there was no such thing as a Special Crime Unit. How things have changed. That said, I note your security clearance is Top Secret Omega Blue. Splendid! I'm looking forward to a presentation of your work from your unit in due course.'

'If I might suggest,' smiled Commander Herbert, 'I'm not convinced that a meeting once a month will be sufficient for your needs.'

'My predecessor, commander, what were her requirements?'

'Once a day!' chuckled Commander Herbert, stroking his moustache.

'Goodness! Well, let's leave it at once a month until I find my feet. I don't want to rush in and find out that I've bitten off more than I can chew. Indeed, you will appreciate that I must not be accused of favouring one department over the other, commander.'

'Quite!' responded Commander Herbert.

'Look, James,' continued the Director General, 'I've arranged for various branches of the Service to co-ordinate presentations for me so if you arrange a date with my confidential personal assistant that would be most satisfactory.'

'A presentation?' queried Commander Herbert.

'Is that a problem, commander?'

'But of course not,' replied Commander Herbert. 'Look, that's my pager still sounding. May I use your telephone, director?'

The Director General swivelled his desk telephone towards Commander Herbert saying, 'Please do.'

Younger, and in his fifties, Phillip Nesbitt was perhaps slightly overweight, of medium height, light brown hair and brown eyes, yet fairly nondescript in appearance. Paradoxically, however, he assumed an air of confidence that had the potential to beguile the unwary and unprepared.

Commander Herbert took the call from Antonia, replaced the handset, and suggested, 'Would you like that presentation now, Phillip? One of our operatives is on to something and requires my presence as a matter of urgency.'

Checking his wristwatch, the Director General replied, 'Yes! Yes, indeed. Why don't I do just that and get this one out of the way so that I can push on with equally urgent matters. Yes, let's do that, commander.'

'Then come with me and I'll take you to our office. It's on the floor below but I suggest we take the lift if you don't mind. My knees are not what they used to be.'

'Of course not, commander, you can tell me all about your unit on the way.'

The two men made their way out of the Director's office.

'The Special Crime Unit!' suggested Commander Herbert. 'How long have you been out of the operational field?'

'Three years! Not counting two with the Americans.'

'I see. In that case, Phillip, you will not be aware that my unit works from a secure area within the Security Service building. My officers only have access to this area within Thames House for obvious reasons relevant to security. They need only know that which concerns them. If it doesn't concern them it's none of their business.'

'Goodness,' suggested Phillip, 'I'm pleased the need to know system now envelops your unit and I'm equally content that the need to know criteria still exists.'

Commander Herbert chuckled and continued, 'The very latest equipment is installed to prevent cyber hacking and we call our floor The Operations Centre. Our unit is three years old this week.'

'James,' probed Phillip sarcastically, 'I don't know whether I should wish you happy birthday or call for a full audit.'

Commander Herbert smoothed his moustache, smiled, and then delivered, 'The Special Crime Unit is a hand-picked team of detectives drawn from Counter Terrorist Command, formerly the anti-terrorist branch. Except to say I have extended the net and drawn in some top detectives from all over the British Isles and added them to hand-picked individuals from MI5 and MI6 as well as other national agencies appropriate to our remit. The officers are all seconded in for three years and then reviewed. We have an office here as well as one at New Scotland Yard.'

The two men entered the lift, selected the floor, and waited for the elevator to deliver them.

'And what is your remit, commander?'

'To win, it's as simple as that.'

'To win what, pray tell?' queried Phillip. 'The war against terrorism, I presume?'

'Peace!'

'So by now you must be accustomed to losing on a daily basis, my friend,' suggested the Director-General with a slight grin.

'Our remit is to defend the State from both organised criminal attack as well as terrorism,' added Commander Herbert. 'The top detectives I speak of are particularly good at their jobs. In fact, they are the elite. They are not selected for their rank but for their ability in a particular field of expertise.'

'Such as?'

'We have surveillance, counter surveillance and anti-surveillance expertise as well as interrogation, investigation and firearms capability!' explained Commander Herbert. 'But we also have the ability to recruit and run informants and agents into all levels of criminality. All manner of skills are present, actually. But tell me, Phillip, perhaps you can answer a question for me?'

'If I can, commander; what's on your mind?'

'You do not precede your status with the title Sir. I noticed you are Knight Commander of the Order of the British Empire.'

'Did you indeed, commander, so you think I should be Sir Phillip in order to impress the masses?'

'It is an award - if that be the right word - usually reserved for both military and intelligence personnel that signifies the holder was involved in matters that might be described as of the most excellent order. I wondered….'

'Keep wondering, James. You are obviously intrigued as to what I did to achieve a Knighthood!'

'It did cross my mind,' admitted Commander Herbert with a pleasant engaging smile.

Chuckling, Phillip replied, 'I won the annual shove halfpenny tournament, James, if you must know. Something at the end of the Cold War, that's all you need to know.'

'Ah, yes, the Soviet Bloc,' laughed Commander Herbert. 'I don't really need to know, do I?'

'Actually, I am the future of the Service not the past and I prefer it that way,' suggested Phillip. 'Ah! We appear to have arrived.'

The lift stopped with a sudden jolt and they stepped into a corridor to enter the nearest office.

Antonia stood to welcome them but Commander Herbert gestured, 'Antonia Harston-Browne, Director! One of our senior operatives assigned to our unit from your organisation.'

'Delighted to meet you, Antonia,' hailed Phillip. 'I can't believe we've not met before.'

'It is a large organisation, sir,' replied Antonia. 'I doubt whether everyone in it knows each other. Things are constantly changing so it's not that unusual to meet new people within the Service. Welcome to the unit.'

'Thank you,' replied Phillip. 'I understand from Commander Herbert that you're onto something.'

'Just something from our American friends that I thought needed to be raised to national level,' revealed Antonia. 'The

Fathers of the Shimmering Dawn have raised their ugly heads once more but this time it affects these shores.'

'I'm all ears,' suggested Phillip. 'Begin your presentation.'

Intrigued, Antonia was immediately drawn to the Director-General. She found him alluring in a way she could not describe. If asked to elucidate upon the encounter Antonia might have proposed that the Director-General's eyes held that certain something that women desired in a man. She could not justify her thoughts beyond that position.

Proficiently, Antonia twisted her computer screen towards her guests and explained, 'I monitor all intelligence news feed from our partners across the globe and within this country on behalf of the unit. I look for things that we, as a specialised unit, ought to be aware of and can do something about. It's a proactive approach as opposed to an attitude that merely notes and records the reports. We don't record history. Someone else does that. I've put this together as a result of collating a number of associated issues.'

Antonia rattled the keyboard and triggered a sequence of events that appeared on the screen.

'It starts with a man called Abdul-Ahad: a high ranking influential member of Al-Qaeda and leader of the Shimmering Dawn and its various offshoots. He's seen here promoting the usual Al-Qaeda propaganda online. These things are picked up in the middle-east and Asia and often televised to the masses across the globe. Then this happens…'

The decapitation followed and the two men gasped in horror.

'Sorry, gentlemen, I should have perhaps warned you,' remarked Antonia.

'Horrendous!' remarked Phillip. 'But this is surely a matter for MI6 and our partners elsewhere, Antonia?'

'I agree, sir,' declared Antonia. 'But the intercepted messages I've put together from various sources reveal references to a large amount of money being made available to fund activity by the four.'

'What four?' queried Commander Herbert allowing his fingers to comb from his high cheeks and trawl through his beard.

'That's why I asked you to take a look at this, commander,' announced Antonia. 'If you accept the veracity and usefulness of this video coverage and associated intercepted messages then you get a taste of the horrors these people can inflict. In addition, you'll see my presentation also includes some intercepts from our very own GCHQ. Read them, gentlemen. They're on screen, for ease of reference, and I suggest there are four members of Al-Qaeda already here in the UK about to begin a terrorist campaign.'

The target?' queried Phillip.

'Not known at this stage,' replied Antonia who then switched to another computer screen and continued, 'You might share the view that we'll never know who or what the target is until it's too late. You know how difficult these types of enquiry can be. Anyway, I used our police counterparts to get hold of some CCTV from a building society in Southport, Merseyside. We have five seconds of imagery and then the raiders knock out the system. There's nothing remarkable about the robbery other than the perpetrators are armed with AK 47 assault rifles and call one of their victims Kafir.'

'That itself is unusual, Antonia,' proposed Commander Herbert. 'I can't ever recall a bank robbery taking place in the United Kingdom involving AK-47's. Where did they get their hands on such high-powered weapons?'

'I don't know,' puzzled Antonia. 'But I do know that your normal Liverpudlian crook doesn't call their victim Kafir.'

'So, if I am to read you correctly, Miss Harston-Browne… It is Miss, isn't it?'

Antonia nodded in agreement.

'Your analysis lacks substantial evidence and, to some degree, is perhaps based on experience rather than fact. You appear to have decided to connect a beheading in the foothills of the Afghan-Pakistan border with footage from a bank robbery in Merseyside.'

'Correct!' confirmed Antonia.

'And then you've twisted it with a blend of electronic message intercepts to make it taste good. Am I right?'

'Yes!'

'Why didn't you get better electronic coverage?' asked Phillip.

Antonia replied, 'The Americans supplied the aerial surveillance shots; MI6 fed the website and electronic intercepts, and Merseyside Crime Directorate provided the robbery video. I think somewhere signal loss from Asia is expected in the circumstances, sir. Something technical, no doubt, I would say. It is over four thousand miles away. On the other hand, Al-Qaeda presumes we are monitoring them. Maybe they were trying to jam us. I don't know.'

'Let us presume we are at war with them for a moment, Antonia,' explained Phillip. 'Unlike conventional warfare, they do not wear uniforms and line up on a battlefield to face the enemy. No, in general, they are unknown and unseen until it's too damn late. My understanding of Al-Qaeda is that they are a multinational stateless army that have a centralised propaganda machine. Such propaganda is thrown out into the cyber world in a decentralised manner and their followers pick it up haphazardly and plan their own attacks. That's how they operate in a nutshell although I could go into chapter and verse to dissect their operations at length - but won't. What you propose is a departure from that stance, Antonia.'

'Correct!'

'You are suggesting, Antonia, that I support you when you have just presented an argument that Al-Qaeda is rewriting their chapter of the terrorist handbook. Unlike the IRA and many other well established terrorist organisations, they do not work in cells or small units of four or six. In fact, they do not have a hierarchical command structure to speak of. Their foundations are embedded in a zealous and dangerous version of religious fervour following the Soviet invasion in Afghanistan. Do you really want me to switch positions and support the assertion they have adopted a cell-like structure?'

'They like to play cat and mouse and lead us on a wild goose chase occasionally. Your guess is as good a mine, sir. It might mean something or it might be meant to distract us,' explained Antonia.

Phillip Nesbitt revisited the presentation and cast his eyes over matters once more.

'To distract us?' considered Phillip carefully. 'Or to attack us?'

The new Director-General reflected for a moment and then announced, 'Is that Chanel number five?'

'Pardon?' exclaimed Antonia surprised at the sudden change of tact.

'Your perfume, is it Chanel number five? I ask because it is a pet hobby of mine - taking in the various odours that abound.'

'You should try my kitchen,' countered Antonia. 'And the herb garden I occasionally tend.'

Phillip smiled, stepped away for a moment, and then resolved, 'I like the way you cook, Antonia. It's a blend worth investigating whether your analysis is right or wrong. Yes, I'm with you on this.'

Antonia felt a wave of pleasure permeate her being when she replied, 'Thank you, sir, but to put the record straight, I seldom cook. I prefer to dine out whenever possible.'

'Me too,' snapped Phillip instantaneously, and then he wondered if there was a hint of interest from the lady. 'We appear to have similar tastes, Antonia.'

'I wouldn't know, sir,' smiled Antonia. 'I'm very fond of Chanel number five, swordfish and Bollinger champagne but not necessarily in that order.'

'I see,' acknowledged Phillip.

Antonia continued, 'I'd like to assign a senior investigating officer to take this enquiry forward and see what can be developed.'

'Commander?' probed Phillip.

'Mmm...,' murmured Commander Herbert. 'You'd better commence a new operational file, Antonia. Find out everything there is to know about this Abdul-Ahad, the Shimmering Dawn, and its various offshoots operating in the United Kingdom. I think we need to decide if there's anything in the revelations that this 'Four' are up to something. Are they already here? Where are they? Do we have any idea who the four are?'

'No, sir!' responded Antonia. 'As I say, these are difficult areas to operate in and gather intelligence from.'

'Indeed,' agreed Commander Herbert.

Interrupting, Antonia offered, 'Mind you, there's more, gentlemen. We already know a little about such a group, or at least what I believe is an offshoot of it. One of our top men is currently looking at the Sons of the Shimmering Dawn. It's a mujahideen offshoot from the Taliban now tied to Al-Qaeda. The police in Paisley, Glasgow, received an anonymous call suggesting a couple of members of the Muslim community up there were raising funds for the group. As you know, raising funds to support terrorism is a criminal offence. Our man is following up the tip-off.'

'Who's on it?' asked Commander Herbert.

'Boyd, sir,' replied Antonia.

'Boyd?' queried the Director-General. 'What's his speciality?'

'William Miller Boyd, sir,' remarked Antonia. 'Detective Chief Inspector Boyd is head of Covert Operations. His speciality is running a stand-alone response team capable of running any major investigation anywhere in the country.'

'Where is Boyd now, Antonia?' asked Commander Herbert.

'Close to home, sir, he's in Cumbria.'

'Home?' queried Phillip Nesbitt, surprised. 'What's he doing at home if he's such a specialist?'

'Of course, I'd forgotten,' revealed Commander Herbert. 'He's been delivering a presentation to an assembly of detectives in the Penrith area. Actually, he's been lecturing on Al-Qaeda and extreme Islamic terrorism.'

'Has he indeed,' remarked Phillip.

On the Scottish border, Boyd sat in the driver's seat of a dark blue BMW surveillance vehicle and watched for his target vehicle to appear. Drumming his fingers on the steering wheel, Boyd eventually radioed, 'Here we go. It's the white Volvo!'

The auburn-haired Detective Sergeant Anthea Adams fingered the ignition key of her high-powered grey Renault saloon and fired the engine before replying, 'Roger, Guvnor. I'm on it.'

The white Volvo sailed past Boyd at high speed.

'Me too,' radioed Janice Burns, a feisty Scottish detective seconded to the unit.

'I'm making ground,' radioed Stuart Armstrong: another Scot.

Boyd depressed the surveillance radio switch and ordered, 'Get it together. Keep it tight. I'm tail end Charlie behind Terry.

At that moment Terry Anwhari motored past Boyd in a silver coloured Saab and joined the team.

Anthea radioed, 'Confirming I have eyeball on the target.... Standby... Guvnor, there's four in the target car and they're approaching the first of three turnoffs for Carlisle. They're in the offside lane of three at seventy five miles an hour.'

'Normal follow, Anthea,' replied Boyd. 'According to the source they should be headed all the way to the Midlands.'

'Where are you planning to strike?' enquired Anthea.

'On the Carlisle – Penrith stretch, Anthea, I'll contact the locals shortly to arrange a routine stop. I'm not expecting any problems. Stop and search and check out the tipoff, that's all we need to do. I must confess I didn't expect the Volvo to appear. I thought it might have been a hoax.'

'Any updates from the source?' enquired Anthea.

'I'll keep you posted,' delivered Boyd. 'Give them plenty of space until we're ready.'

The convoy headed further south into Cumbria with the occupants of the white Volvo unaware they were being followed.

Four miles behind the Volvo, bringing up the end of the elongated surveillance team, Boyd punched a speed digit on his mobile and immediately got through to Antonia Harston-Browne at Thames House.

'Toni! It's Boyd. We're in behind the white Volvo subject of the tipoff. It's a routine stop and search as far as I can see. Is there anything else before we hit it? We're moving in shortly.'

'Boyd, I was just about to ring you. Thank God you rang me.'

'What's the problem, Toni?' queried Boyd.

'Recent intelligence confirms the vehicle may be carrying the proceeds of a collection bound for the Shimmering Dawn grouping. However, intelligence analysis suggests the targets you are following may be carrying the proceeds of an armed robbery from a building society in Southport, Merseyside.'

Accelerating into fifth gear, Boyd chuckled, 'Yeah, yeah, Toni. Intelligence analysis! Good one! You're telling me some robbers stole some money from Merseyside, took it to Scotland, and are now bringing it back to the Midlands. Sorry, that won't wash. I take it there's no change then?'

'I'm being serious, Boyd,' remarked Antonia. 'But I hadn't thought about it that way. The main thing is that the robbery in Southport involved four males armed with AK 47 assault rifles.'

'Four?'

'Yes, four!'

'Four with AK 47's! Now you tell me,' offered an anxious Boyd.

'Why? What are you doing?' asked Antonia.

'About eighty five and gaining,' chuckled Boyd. 'Is that it?'

'Well, you have control, Boyd,' suggested Antonia. 'I thought it wise to give you my analysis.'

'Cheers!' acknowledged Boyd. 'I'll get back to you, Toni.'

The connection closed and Boyd shook his head in desperation. A straight forward routine stop and search had turned into a question of whether or not the suspects might be armed and dangerous. Running his fingers through a mop of wind-blown jet black hair, Boyd considered the options open to him.

Flashing his headlights at a white delivery van encroaching into the third lane, Boyd powered the BMW through and considered his problem. Do I stop and search as a matter of routine or do I arrange a hard stop with a large team of local firearms officers, he pondered. I think it will be okay to do a stop as planned, he decided. But then more cogitation as he scratched his square chin for a fleeting moment before replacing his hand on the steering wheel. I'll never live with myself if Toni is right and I end up getting one of the team shot. What was it Dad once said, lead don't follow? No, it's got to be the hard way. Let's go for it.

Grabbing the radio, Boyd instructed, 'All units, stand by for update.... Trigger.... Trigger... Trigger.... Subjects may be armed and dangerous.... Repeat, subjects may be armed and dangerous.... Watching brief only whilst I arrange assistance...'

The team acknowledged but Anthea countered, 'We are all armed, Guvnor. What are they carrying?'

'Possibly AK 47 assault rifles! Not confirmed! Vigilance required. Standby...'

'Och, man,' intercepted Janice, 'My pea shooter is no match for those guys.'

Chuckling, Boyd instructed, 'Change to channel nine zero nine and maintain follow. Don't get too close, guys!'

Anthea radioed, 'Interchange forty two in the third lane at seventy five miles an hour. The traffic is reasonably light!'

Boyd acknowledged the message and then keyed into the radio with a request. 'Sierra Charlie Zero One calling Cumbria M6 Control. We are southbound from forty two calling a trigger incident.... Repeat calling a trigger incident and requesting assistance on a vehicle stop.'

'Stand by,' transmitted across the airwaves and Boyd imagined a radio operator consulting a supervisor.

In the Cumbria control room, Peter, a young radio operator turned to his Inspector and asked, 'Who the hell is Sierra Charlie Zero One? That's not one of ours.'

'Actually, it is one of ours on secondment, Peter. It's Boyd from the Special Crime Unit in London. I take it you didn't attend the conference on terrorism yesterday?' replied the inspector.

'I heard about it but I didn't go,' responded Peter.

'What's Boyd got into now I wonder,' remarked the inspector.

Peter replied, 'Well I don't know him but whoever he is, he's got some cheek. He just called a trigger on the M6. He wants armed assistance for an unplanned vehicle stop.'

The inspector plugged into the radio channel and sternly advised Peter, 'But now he's planning it, young man, and our Detective Chief Inspector Boyd doesn't suffer fools gladly. Give him what he wants. If Boyd wants an invisible helicopter, a bunch of pink roses, a bucket of steam, and a pipe band playing the national anthem on the hard shoulder that's what he gets. He's the man. Now punch up the trigger routine on your screen and follow it.'

Peter forced a nervous cough, quickly swivelled in his chair, and accessed the keyboard.

Taking control, the inspector radioed, 'Sierra Charlie Zero One, I have your trigger incident. Welcome back! Location, direction, speed and target details required.'

'Sorry to trouble you,' radioed Boyd. 'Recent report indicates the possibility that trigger subjects may be armed with AK-47'S. Not, repeat not, confirmed. Advice only! Exercise extreme caution!'

'Roger! I have control and suggest a take down in one five minutes subject to deployment and location. Fifteen minutes! Concur?'

'Agreed,' replied Boyd. 'You have control. Keep me appraised, speed eighty miles an hour, south.'

Turning to his computer console the inspector followed the trigger routine. Within minutes, a detachment of armed response vehicles were accessing the motorway from east and west.

Boyd squeezed the accelerator to gain ground and checked his rear view mirror. He caught sight of his deep blue eyes, dark eyebrows, and smooth complexion blurring with a line of vehicles and green countryside as he raced by. Drumming his fingers on the steering wheel, his wedding ring reflected his micro image and he felt more relaxed now that he had made his decision. All they had to do now, he decided, was to settle in behind the suspects and wait for assistance. More firepower and more cars would make the job easier.

'Speed eighty miles an hour,' radioed Anthea. 'They have distance on me but I have good vision. We're south of the service station approaching Penrith and…. Oh no!'

A deer suddenly jumped over the fence and bolted onto the carriageway.

There was a squeal of brakes and the rub of burning tyres when the driver of an articulated wagon slewed across the carriageway trying to avoid the bolting animal. A puff of fine white smoke shot from beneath the vehicle when a tyre burst.

Ahead, the white Volvo's brake lights came on and the bonnet dipped violently. A car towing a caravan braked and the combination jack-knifed.

'Watch out everyone,' screamed Anthea into her radio.

Meanwhile, the back end of the caravan sideswiped a three wheel Reliant Robin which disintegrated on impact. A thousand pieces of wood and fibreglass showered the carriageway and a man's body was thrown out of the driver's seat onto the central reservation.

Hitting the brakes, Anthea radioed, 'Accident ahead! Slow down!'

'Where's the target?' snapped Boyd at the rear of the convoy.

'Stand by! I've lost sight of it,' replied Anthea.

'The Volvo has gone straight through,' advised Janice.

When Anthea approached the Reliant Robin's debris, the caravan gradually and bizarrely keeled over before exploding in a cloud of dust. A gas canister detached itself from the rear of the caravan and rolled haphazardly along the carriageway bouncing towards the hard shoulder.

Just ahead of the scene of the accident, the Volvo's front nearside tyre picked up a slice of debris and punctured. The driver lost control at seventy miles an hour and careered towards the hard shoulder. Wrestling the steering wheel, he pumped the brakes before leaving the carriageway.

Seconds later, the Volvo demolished an emergency telephone on the grass verge of the motorway and came to rest with its bonnet facing northwards towards the oncoming surveillance team.

'Crash! Crash! Crash! The target has crashed,' announced Janice excitedly. 'And we have casualties on the carriageway.'

'Ignore them,' screamed Boyd. 'Hit it! Hit the target now! STRIKE!'

'What?' queried Janice. 'Are you sure?'

'STRIKE! STRIKE! STRIKE!' screamed Boyd.

Ploughing through the debris, Janice, Anthea, Stuart, Terry and Boyd pounced on the Volvo and blocked any getaway route.

Anthea was out of her Renault first and, with handgun drawn, shielded herself behind the driver's door shouting, 'Armed police! Hands! Let me see your hands!'

Seconds later, Janice opened the boot of her Seat, produced a side by side double-barrelled shotgun, and screamed, 'Do it! Armed police! Hands! Get those hands up in the air!'

Skidding to a halt, Terry Anwhari rolled from his car and used the car boot as a shield. He was closely followed by Stuart Armstrong in a well-rehearsed drill that blocked in the four targets.

Boyd arrived in the BMW and slung it broadside blocking the carriageway.

An eerie silence descended interrupted only by the sound of steam escaping from a ruptured radiator. Then there was a groan and cry for help from the scene of the accident.

Grabbing the handset, Boyd radioed, 'Trigger Message…. All stop southbound carriageway between Southwaite Services and Catterlen Interchange! Four vehicle accident! Ambulances required! Casualties present! Trigger target contained at scene of collision!'

The radio system went into meltdown.

A car door opened and an Arab looking gentleman stepped from the vehicle to a barrage of instructions from the armed surveillance officers.

'Hands! Show your hands!'

'Freeze! Armed police!'

Boyd's wireless whistled and a voice enquired, 'Confirm you have a firearms situation at the scene of a road traffic collision?'

'Confirmed!' responded Boyd.

'How many casualties do you have?'

Suddenly, they were off. The Arab looking driver was over the fence and into the field running for all his worth with one passenger close behind him and two rooted to the rear compartment of their vehicle.

'No idea,' radioed Boyd. 'Stand by!'

'No!' complained Janice, shouldering her shotgun. 'Not again!'

Levelling his firearm, Stuart took a steady bead and allowed his finger to curl around the trigger.

Anthea and Terry holstered their weapons and set off with Boyd in hot pursuit.

'Are you aiming for the deer or the target?' quipped Janice.

'Damn it, Janice!' whispered Stuart lowering his weapon. 'The deer, of course, I like a bit of venison.'

'Then you'll need a 410 shotgun and an eyesight test, Stuart.'

'Janice,' screamed Boyd. 'Take over. Get the passengers locked up, the ambulances in and the casualties out.'

'Done, Guvnor,' delivered Janice as she made for her radio.

Stuart engaged the two passengers with his firearm. Shaken and shocked from the collision, they offered no resistance and carefully slid from the car onto their knees at Stuart's instruction.

Handcuffing the two passengers, Janice then declared, 'Watch them, Stuart. Don't shoot them. Watch them!'

Nodding, Stuart changed his position and pointed his firearm at the terrified pair.

A white van appeared on the motorway close to the scene of the accident and formed the first of a queue as stationary traffic began to build up.

In a field adjacent to the motorway, Anthea, Terry and Boyd were striding out in pursuit of the outstanding suspects.

There was a sickening thud of clavicle against femur when Terry Anwhari rugby tackled the front seat passenger and brought him down. A couple of ruminating cows looked on from afar when Terry overpowered his mark and pinned him to the ground.

But the driver leapt over a five barred gate with the agility of an Olympic athlete.

Boyd and Anthea climbed over the gate with much less ingenuity but darted after the subject quickly when he got bogged down in the mud infested gateway.

Determined, yet wavering in the slime and losing his balance, the suspect suddenly pulled out a handgun from his trouser belt. He loosed off a couple of indiscriminate shots at the two detectives.

Evil bullets flew wide and high when Boyd nosedived into the gunman's stomach and brought him down.

They entwined unmercifully in the mire before Boyd's clenched fist smashed into his opponent's chin. The wrestling match continued but then Boyd winded the man with a cruel knee to his groin.

Snapping her handgun into position a fraction of an inch from the Arab's face, Anthea shouted, 'Tempt me!'

Disarming the Arab, Boyd dragged the man from the muddy field and pushed him into the gate post where Anthea applied a set of handcuffs.

'Why is it always us, Guvnor?' queried Anthea, breathless. 'We're covered in cow shit and mud, shot at, knackered, exhausted, and lucky to be alive. The troops are stuck to the motorway like bees round a honey pot and we're here. That's not right. Why us?'

'The privileges of rank, sergeant,' chuckled Boyd wiping mud from his face. 'But it could have been worse.'

'How worse?' asked Anthea.

'Our friend has a Smith and Wesson pistol not an AK-47.'

'Why did you shoot at us?' enquired Anthea challenging the Arab driver who deliberately looked away.

Total silence from the tight lipped driver followed.

'Because he's got something in the Volvo that we need to find,' suggested Boyd. 'Come on! Let's get back to the motorway.'

Manhandling the uncooperative suspect over the gate they escorted him towards the M6. On route, they joined Terry Anwhari who uttered a mouthful of Farsi to the two prisoners before hearing Boyd say, 'Well done, Terry. Good take down! Now what the hell did you just say to our prisoners?'

'I told them they were nicked in Farsi, Guvnor.'

'Can't they speak English?'

'Oh, I expect they understand English perfectly,' replied Terry. 'But I think they've got a touch of memory loss at the moment.'

'How surprising,' suggested Anthea.

'Are you guys okay? No-one hurt at all?' enquired Terry.

'No, we're fine, Terry,' responded Boyd. 'Just shit up to the eyeballs, that's all.'

Looking away, Terry whispered, 'You really need to smarten up, Guvnor. Shoes not trainers!'

'What was that, Terry?' queried Boyd.

'Nothing, Guv!' chuckled Terry.

'Funny, I could have sworn I heard you say something.'

'Must have been the wind, Guvnor.'

'The wind, Terry? Wind at the back is for people wearing trainers and not shoes. Ever tried catching anyone in a field wearing platform shoes?'

Chuckling, Terry disclosed, 'You're the only chief inspector in the country that I know wears training shoes rather than leather shoes. Well, I'm glad you're both alright but I couldn't resist it, Guvnor.'

'Why am I not surprised?' countered Boyd laughing. 'By the way, these are new trainers. Don't you like them?'

'Come on,' responded Terry stifling a giggle. 'I'll give you a hand.'

By the time they'd returned to the motorway carriageway, the scene was awash with emergency personnel dealing with casualties amidst the spectre of a dozen flashing blue lights and a score of high visibility fluorescent jackets. Casualties were being tended to on the hard shoulder and the gentleman thrown from a Reliant Robin was being loaded into an ambulance.

Boyd removed the ignition keys from the Volvo and escorted his prisoner to the rear of the vehicle.

Opening the car boot, Boyd asked the prisoner, 'And what have we got here?'

There was no reply. Undeterred, Boyd removed a black blanket draped across the rear of the compartment and revealed a number of black plastic bags. Delving further, Boyd discovered that each bag was bundled with banknotes wrapped in elastic bands.

'Jackpot!' remarked Boyd. 'There's thousands here.'

'And what looks like a couple of laptops and various documents,' mentioned Anthea.

'Is this yours?' enquired Boyd.

'Kafir!' replied the Prisoner.

'That'll do for now,' replied Boyd. 'No-one wants to admit ownership. How strange!' he chuckled. 'Okay, lock them up on suspicion of being involved in the financing of terrorism. It's what we need until we sort out the wheat from the chaff.'

Holstering weapons, the unit separated their prisoners and escorted them into individual police vehicles arriving at the scene.

Without warning, a member of the press appeared favouring a microphone which he thrust beneath Boyd's chin. The pressman turned to a cameraman that was with him and suggested, 'Rolling?'

Oblivious to the microphone, Boyd collided with the reporter and snapped, 'What the hell are you doing here?'

'An opportune moment, that's all, officer. We were travelling down the motorway when the accident happened and the road was blocked. Can I ask you what these people have been arrested for?'

'No, get off the motorway and back into your car,' ordered Boyd. 'This isn't the protocol and well you know it.'

'Yeah, do as the man says,' advocated Stuart.

'Actually, I'm doing my job,' submitted the reporter. 'I know what the protocol is but I have a live beam by satellite straight to the studio. Now can you tell me what's going on?'

Startled, Boyd swiftly snatched a pair of sunglasses from his jacket pocket and perched them firmly on his nose in an attempt to cover his face. Then he announced, 'Okay! I'll make this short and sweet. As a result of information received police today arrested four people on the M6 motorway in Cumbria on suspicion of financing terrorism. Now that's it. Get out of the way and off the motorway.'

The camera followed Boyd as he pushed his way towards a vehicle.

A voice shouted, 'Did the police cause the accident? We heard shots fired. Anyone hurt?'

Stuart Armstrong slid in front of the camera pleading, 'Guys!'

Boyd and Anthea were into the BMW with a convoy of police cars arriving to ferry prisoners away from the scene.

The camera panned and zoomed on the activity of the emergency services.

Allowing his mind to work overtime, Boyd noted the registration number of a white van parked unattended on the hard shoulder and suggested, 'Is that the vehicle the press were in?'

'That's where they came from,' confirmed Anthea. 'But they were lucky, weren't they? Our planned stop was spoilt by a deer running amok on the motorway. No-one could have foreseen that. They were just in the right place at the right time, Guvnor.'

'Do you really think so?' enquired Boyd.

Anthea slammed the car door shut and said, 'This morning you were asking me who our leak might be and how we should deal with it as I recall.'

'Well,' suggested Boyd. 'You don't expect to find corruption amongst so-called hand-picked detectives but one of them is more interested in feathering their own nest rather than doing the job.'

'Or her own nest,' corrected Anthea. 'Have you considered that it might even be me?'

'Yes, of course,' acknowledged Boyd, sarcastically driving away and removing his sunglasses. 'You were first on my list.'

'Gee, thanks!' replied Anthea. 'You're all heart.'

The dark-haired Boyd chuckled, 'But I've been all over Europe with you, Anthea, and we've had more scrapes than I care to mention. No, it's one of the new guys, I'm sure. The question is… Who?'

'It's not good for morale, Guvnor,' advised Anthea. 'And that's the third time in the last few weeks they've door-stepped us at the scene of an arrest.'

'I know. It's a worry,' confessed Boyd. 'But I can't really walk away from the national news media when they turn up at the scene with the excuse they used today. Oh sure, there'll be a proper press conference in due course when the cogs in the machine are acknowledged. Meanwhile, they've got their scoop and so have the affiliate newspapers. Job done!'

'They got your face again,' delivered Anthea.

'Part of it only, I hope,' suggested Boyd. 'It's too uncanny that they just turn up at these things without warning. We were just in the area is the opening remark from these guys. It's bloody ludicrous!'

'Why didn't you just tell them to contact the local police press office and let them deal with it?' enquired Anthea.

'I tried that once,' explained Boyd. 'But they kept the camera rolling and I don't feel like wrapping the camera around the reporter's neck when I'm on live television. It's dangerous ground and I'm on thin ice if I lose my temper in front of a news audience.'

'Who've we got in the frame?' probed Anthea.

'Terry Anwhari!' proposed Boyd.

Anthea pondered the issue for a moment and then offered, 'Terry's parents are from Pakistan but he was born in England. He was brought in because he speaks Arabic - Farsi - and has an excellent record as a detective in the West Midlands. He made significant inroads into the Muslim community and earned their respect and admiration. But there's just something about him that troubles me.'

'I know,' agreed Boyd. 'I can't put my finger on it either. Maybe it's that we just haven't gelled as a team yet. We need a big job or two to mould our team together. What about Stuart?'

'Stuart Armstrong?' queried Anthea. 'Glasgow's finest by all accounts. His CV reads better than yours, Guvnor.'

'Really,' chortled Boyd. 'I'm jealous, Anthea.'

'But he does have a strange sense of humour at times,' explained Anthea.

'He's Scottish as you say,' quipped Boyd jokingly. 'Such people don't have a sense of humour.'

The convoy turned off the motorway, negotiated a roundabout, and headed into Penrith.

'Have you told Commander Herbert about your suspicions?' asked Anthea.

'Not yet, Anthea, I'd rather go to him with the job solved as opposed to presenting him with a problem we can't sort out. In any event, he's planning his retirement as we well know.'

'We've enough to do, Guvnor,' advised Anthea. 'The commander will call in an outsider to investigate so we can get on with the job.'

'Not on my watch, Anthea,' countered Boyd. 'I've too many miles in the bank with the commander to spoil his track record with the unit. No, I'll sort it in my own way and with your help.'

'That's what I was afraid of,' offered Anthea. 'But have you considered an outsider like Janice: Janice Burns, I mean. Do you think she's corrupt?'

Changing gear, Boyd replied, 'They are all new, including Janice and half a dozen back in London. They are especially selected for their prowess in various fields and join us for three to five years. We're supposed to be the best of the best.'

Anthea muttered, 'The best usually return to their force on promotion, Guvnor. If we don't find out who the bad apple is...'

Interrupting, Boyd remarked, 'I know! That's why we need to find out who's taking us to the cleaners. In my mind it could be any of them unfortunately. But corruption!'

'There are different levels of corruption, Guvnor. Someone might be taking a bung for passing information on or they might be just mentioning something in passing to a pal in the press. You know, just a friend helping a friend with no money exchanging hands.'

'If that's the case, Anthea, someone has chosen the wrong friends. This team is a surveillance team often working undercover and in dangerous places. The last thing we need is a traitor blasting our faces all over the television screen.'

'Point taken,' admitted Anthea.

Boyd declared, 'For me corruption is accepting favours in exchange for favours and if we can prove that then I will have no hesitation in pulling the trap door and hanging out the culprit to dry.'

They swung into the police station car park where Boyd jerked on the handbrake and said, 'Let's get these four booked in and the property sorted out. Money, laptops, documents, the works! I'm taking the day off tomorrow. Meg is going to hospital for a check-up and I want to be with her. But ring me and let me know how you get on, Anthea. I'll be training for the London marathon in the morning and at the hospital in the afternoon.'

'And our little corruption enquiry?' queried Anthea.

'I'll check who owns that white van we saw on the motorway. Meanwhile, the unit has police mobile phones. Let's see who's phoning who?'

'You will be popular if that comes out,' suggested Anthea.

'That's the second time today,' delivered Boyd.

'What is?' asked Anthea.

'The privileges of rank!' quipped Boyd.

Detective Chief Inspector Boyd walked into the police station followed by Anthea who offered, 'Tell Meg I was asking after her, Guvnor. I do hope that baby arrives on time.'

'She will, Anthea.'

'You mean it's going to be a girl?'

'Of course,' revealed Boyd. 'I can feel it in my bones. By the way who is bringing your car back?'

'The locals, they blocked it in on the motorway. They're recovering it for me.'

*

Chapter Five
~

The Caldbeck Fells, Cumbria

Broad and athletic in stature, the six foot tall Boyd was dedicated to his sport. Or at least he tried to be. He had planned the day carefully to accommodate a special run. Morning would be a training session for the forthcoming marathon and afternoon would be a visit to hospital with his wife: Meg. They would soon be a Mum and Dad and Boyd had already decided that their little girl was going to be an Olympic running champion one day. Problem was, neither he nor Meg had any idea what gender the next Boyd might be. But that might change in the afternoon if all went well and the hospital staff decided to divulge such information.

Meanwhile, there was a bum bag slung firm around Boyd's waist and a black bandanna tight across his forehead with the ends dangling down his neck. With a slight breeze at his back and rough terrain underfoot, Boyd went running on the Caldbeck Fells.

It was the London Marathon Boyd was aiming for. That was his target. He'd heard about it, watched it, sponsored runners in it, but had never been part of one of the capital's greatest sporting events. He'd decided that would change this year as he strode out across the Fell. Working in London was such that Boyd just had to take the opportunity to run that particular marathon. The good part was that he could also train in Cumbria and there was no better place for building speed and stamina than a pulsating blast across the Fells.

Narrowing those deep blue eyes, Boyd scratched his stubbly square chin, and ordered his body to be victorious. He strode out instructing his mind to concentrate on the path ahead as he held firm across the plateau close to the remains of an old Roman fort.

Marathon running, as far as Boyd thought, was not just about running twenty six miles and three hundred and eighty five yards. Were it that simple, he suggested.

Boyd dug deeper when a steep incline presented itself. Searching for his inner self, he found the determination that made him a leader of men. Grimacing, hurting deep inside, he fought his demons and finally defeated the Fell. Eventually, he turned downhill and made towards the road below.

No, it was about rising to the challenge, he reckoned. The marathon was more than just a run through London from Greenwich Park to the end of the torture chamber. So an early visit to the area and a fifteen mile jog along the Fell tops would do his training regime a power of good. I mean, thought Boyd, Shooters Hill is as flat as a pancake in comparison with these Fells.

Accelerating when the path levelled out, he noticed a five barred gate and the road connecting Mungrisdale to Caldbeck ahead. He was flying like the wind with mind and body in perfect harmony. No, I reckon I'll do the Marathon in about three hours, considered Boyd. Indeed, I can even vault that five barred gate ahead I'm so fit.

Brashly, Boyd placed one hand on the gate stoop, and vaulted over the gate. Catching his foot on the top of the barrier, he crashed down and collided with the tarmac road. Swearing loudly, Boyd rolled over in agony to the sudden screech of brakes and a squeal of tyres. Seconds later, he felt his body slip into the ditch at the side of the road.

There was the cruel sound of a handbrake being yanked on hard followed by a voice expressing the wrath of God.

'You bloody idiot,' screamed a motorist. 'Are you trying to get yourself killed?'

Clambering from the ditch, Boyd began to apologise saying, 'I was miles away, I...'

'Miles away!' snapped the driver interrupting. 'Bloody miles away alright! You're not even on the same planet, you fool! You nearly ended up on the bonnet of my Land Rover and you would not have made a pretty sight, I can tell you. '

'Sorry!' offered Boyd.

'Sorry, you're bloody sorry? You could have killed us all.'

'Hey, steady on. I've said I've apologised.' Boyd snatched a view of the protagonist and repeated, 'Yeah, I'm sorry, vicar.'

Reverend Matthew Lowther, forty six years old, clean-shaven, balding, and of an angry disposition was out of his Land Rover and standing over Boyd with his white clerical band collar brilliant in the sunshine. The vicar's red face inflated in anger by the second and his fists were clenched in annoyance.

A stallion neighed from a horse box drawn by the Land Rover and a teenage girl jumped from the Land Rover, looked scornfully at Boyd, and then offered, 'Easy, Gabby! Easy, boy, it's just some townie being a bloody arse!'

'Susie! ' shouted a woman also alighting from the vehicle. 'Where did you learn such language?'

'From Dad obviously,' countered Susie. 'Who else?'

'I'm sorry, Elizabeth. I lost my temper with this nincompoop,' revealed Matthew. 'Susie, please don't speak to your mother like that.'

'Oh, I see,' snapped Susie. 'It's okay for you to shout and swear but not me. Well, that's fine, Dad. Just fine!'

'Is the horse alright?' enquired Boyd.

'What's it got to do with you?' growled Susie.

'I wondered if the animal was okay, that's all,' offered Boyd still lying on the ground.

'Animal!' screeched Susie. 'Gabriel is a top quality stallion, I'll have you know. He's one of the finest this side of the Pennines.'

'Sorry,' offered Boyd. 'I'm a townie as you say. I'm not really into horses and stuff.'

'Then what are you doing out here in the countryside?' asked Elizabeth Lowther, the vicar's wife.

Offering a hand towards Matthew, Boyd declared, 'Trying to get back on my feet, if you don't mind.'

'I'm sorry. Of course,' replied Matthew pulling Boyd to his feet. 'Are you hurt at all?'

Boyd shook his head and then stretched out his legs before saying, 'No, I'm fine. Just my pride, vicar, that's all.'

'I'd better ring the police,' suggested Elizabeth.

'Why?' asked Matthew. 'Our vehicle isn't damaged and this chap seems to be alright.'

'Oh, I thought you had to ring the police for all road accidents, darling.'

'Not at all, Elizabeth,' smoothed Matthew. Turning to Boyd the vicar said, 'Don't I know you? Your face looks familiar.'

'I don't think we've met,' responded Boyd. 'But I'll be getting along if everyone is alright and Gabriel is fine.'

'Gabby!' growled Susie. 'He's my horse and he's called Gabby, not Gabriel.'

'Now I am confused,' smiled Boyd. 'But I'll be on my way.'

'You're the policeman who was on the television last night,' suggested Matthew. 'The terrorist man!'

'Terrorist,' yelled Elizabeth, alarmed.

'No, Elizabeth,' admonished Matthew. 'He's not the terrorist. He's a policeman who catches terrorists.' Am I right Mister…'

'Boyd! Billy Boyd!'

'The Reverend Matthew Lowther, parish clergyman in these parts,' explained Matthew introducing himself.

Boyd tried to escape offering, 'Now I've detained you people long enough. I'll be gone.' He stepped anxiously to one side.

'Good God, no way,' cracked the vicar. 'Come on, we'll give you a lift into the village. I presume you are headed our way?'

'My car is up on the Common if that helps your geography,' suggested Boyd.

'We're going that way,' smiled Matthew. 'Come on! Jump in. We've not seen a policeman out this way for months.'

Reluctantly, Boyd stepped into the Land Rover and found himself wedged in the middle between Matthew and Elizabeth with Susie in the back.

'No!' cracked Elizabeth, scowling. 'No such thing as police out this way.'

Gazing out of the window at the scenery, Boyd queried, 'What bothers you folks out here then; noisy sheep or disorderly rabbits?'

From the rear of the Land Rover, Susie barked, 'Townies running on our Fells when they should be on their own housing estates sat on their arse watching soaps!'

'Susie!' snapped Elizabeth. 'Language!'

'Point taken, Mister Boyd,' admitted Matthew ignoring his wife and daughter. 'But the presence of a uniformed officer in these parts always helps the community feel safer and more secure.'

'Where's your nearest police station then?' Boyd queried.

'Keswick that way and Wigton the other way,' disclosed Elizabeth.

The chatter continued for a few minutes before Matthew pulled in at Boyd's car and said, 'Well, it's been nice to meet you but I do hope that next time you go hurdling it's not on our roads. Meanwhile, we'll try our best to keep the sheep and the rabbits in order without police help, Mister…'

'Boyd! Billy Boyd!'

'Of course, you've told me once already,' apologised Matthew.

Ratching in his bum bag, Boyd opened his wallet and removed his business card. The card was headed Special Crime Unit and carried a Freephone hotline number to his department.

'If you ever have any problems you can get through to me here,' declared Boyd.

'Wonderful,' remarked Matthew scanning the card. 'You're not even a real policeman.'

'No, but I know someone who is,' delivered Boyd.

'The last time we had a crime in these parts, officer,' said Elizabeth, 'Our church offertory box was stolen. We're still waiting for the police to attend.'

'I'm sorry to hear that,' offered Boyd.

'Oh we got the box back,' responded Matthew. 'A vagrant took it. We found him sleeping in a barn. We fed him, watered him, and sent him on his way.'

'Very Christian of you,' proposed Boyd.

'Oh yes, we are a very Christian family, Mister Boyd. I love my Lord; I love my church, and I love my family.'

'And I love life and my wife,' replied Boyd slightly lost for a proper response.

'Not to worry, Mister Boyd,' offered the vicar sarcastically. 'If I ever meet a terrorist on the Caldbeck Fells threatening either the sheep or the rabbits I'll let you know.'

'Thanks,' offered Boyd trying to force a smile.

'Do keep off the roads,' suggested Elizabeth.

There was a crunch of a gearstick when Matthew forced the vehicle forward and spun it round in the opposite direction.

Boyd waved and was rewarded with Susie's face pressed hard against the glass of the rear passenger compartment.

'Townie!' she mouthed as the vicar and his family drove off. Then she stuck her tongue out like a spoiled child.

Grinning broadly, Boyd spoke aloud, 'Horrible girl! Weird family!'

Boyd's pager sounded.

It was Anthea who briefed him about the latest developments following her enquiries into the arrest of the four men yesterday. Boyd listened intently, asked few questions, and then heard Anthea suggest, 'Commander Herbert wants you back in the office first thing in the morning, Guvnor. We've counted two hundred and fifty thousand pounds from the boot of that Volvo but, more importantly, we can trace another half dozen people involved in its collection from analysis of mobile phones and emails from the computers we recovered. The commander wants you to lead the first of our London raids and meet our latest addition to the team.

Stuart and Janice are leading in Glasgow. Terry and I drew Birmingham.'

'Great! It will be interesting to see if any of them get door-stepped by the press, Anthea. Anyway, I'd better get my skates on,' responded Boyd. 'Home! Shower! Hospital! Motorway! I'll go straight to the office and touch base with Commander Herbert.'

'Yeah,' agreed Anthea. 'We've houses to search! Give my love to Meg.'

'Will do! What new addition to the unit are you talking about, Anthea? I didn't realise we were getting a staffing increase.'

'No idea, Guvnor. I'm just passing on the commander's message.'

That afternoon at the hospital saw Boyd sat at Meg's side as they waited for the results of her twelve week scan. Meg lay patiently on an examination table whilst a young lady doing the scan explained what she was doing and what the images were.

Suddenly she swung the monitor away from Boyd and Meg, stopped what she was doing, and revealed, 'I'm going to ask Doctor Farooqi to join us.'

As she stood to leave, Meg asked, 'Is there a problem, Lucy?'

'Nothing to worry about,' replied Lucy. 'I'll be back in a minute or two.'

Time seemed to decelerate and Boyd studied the wall clock calculating each minute seemed like an hour.

'What's wrong?' he asked the anxious Meg.

Before Meg could manage a reply Doctor Ismail Farooqi entered the room. He wore a neat pair of slacks and a light blue shirt covered by a casual jacket. A tie hung loosely from the open-necked collar of his shirt.

'Ismail, is there a problem?' Meg asked as soon as he walked into the room.

'Lucy has asked me to look at the scan with you. So let's take a look,' he replied.

Lucy re-scanned Meg's abdomen whilst Ismail's eyes studied the screen with obvious interest. Eventually Ismail offered, 'Yes, Lucy, I believe you are right. There and there!'

Dr Farooqi turned smiling amicably to Meg and Boyd and stated, 'Your babies are fine, Meg. There is no problem.'

'Babies!' queried Meg. 'In the plural! You mean there's more than one?'

Boyd tightened his grip on Meg's hand and enquired, 'How many, doctor?'

Lucy replied, 'You are going to be the proud parents of twins.'

Ismail grinned and then shook hands with Boyd saying, 'Congratulations, Mr Boyd. I'm Doctor Ismail Farooqi. Let me point out your babies for you both on the screen. Would you like to know if they are girls or boys?'

'Yes!' exclaimed Boyd

'No!' cried Meg simultaneously.

They laughed.

'It's not obligatory,' revealed the doctor. 'It's parents' choice. You two decide.'

Meg engaged her husband and delivered, 'Well, what do we do, Billy?

'Whatever you wish, Meg,' replied Boyd. 'As long as you're happy, I'm happy.'

Meg considered the matter for a moment and proposed, 'Billy, I think I'd like to know if you don't mind.'

Smiling, Boyd whispered, 'Then why don't you ask?'

Meg turned to the doctor and announced, 'Yes please, Ismail. We'd like to know if we are to be the parents of boys or girls.'

Meditating consciously for a moment, the doctor replied, 'I think you'd better expect a little bit of a shock, Mrs Boyd.'

'Why? What's wrong?' asked Meg suddenly concerned.

'Oh nothing as far as I can tell,' revealed the doctor. 'Except to say that your twins are going to be a boy and a girl.'

'Twins! One of each!' exclaimed Boyd. 'You mean…'

'Oh yes, Mister Boyd,' disclosed the doctor. 'Mrs Boyd is expecting twins: a son and daughter for you both. Congratulations!'

'Twins, Ismail?' queried Meg, at a loss for words. 'Twins!'

'Yes,' confirmed the doctor with a smile. 'I am so very pleased for you, Meg. All your colleagues here in the hospital will be delighted for you.'

'Wow!' remarked Meg. 'Thank you, Ismail. That was so very nice of you.'

Smiling from behind tender brown eyes, Doctor Ismail Farooqi placed his arm on Boyd's shoulder and offered, 'And congratulations to you too, of course, Mister Boyd.'

'Thank you,' responded Boyd. 'Thank you, doctor.'

'Ismail! Please call me Ismail, Mister Boyd.'

'Yes, yes, of course, Ismail,' stuttered Boyd.

Ismail laughed and countered, 'Mister Boyd, I know why you are a little nervous. I have known Meg here for many years. She is not just a colleague but a friend and I am so very pleased to meet you at last. I have heard so very much about you in years gone by.'

'I see,' replied Boyd. 'I apologise. I did not mean to cause embarrassment in the pronunciation of your name.'

'You did not, Mister Boyd. Some of the nurses here just call me 'Issy' and I am happy with that. It is not offensive.'

'Sometimes I just get things wrong,' admitted Boyd.

'Mister Boyd, but it will be an honour to bring your children into the world and watch them grow from babes in arms to youngsters. I just pray that Allah grants me enough time in my life to make mankind happier with the birth of new life.'

A pager sounded and Ismail said, 'My buzzer! I must go now. Good luck, Meg. I shall see you in one month's time. Meanwhile, remember the advice I gave you and follow it.'

'Of course, Ismail,' delivered Meg.

Boyd shook hands and declared, 'Thank you, doctor. Indeed, thank you, Ismail.'

Doctor Farooqi retired and Boyd queried, 'Meg, what advice did he give you?'

Hiding a cheeky sly smile, Meg replied, 'Oh, he thinks the children should have a stay-at-home father. Failing that, he recommends someone who spends more time at home looking after the kids than running around the country on secret missions.'

'Did he, indeed!' offered Boyd.

'I love you,' offered Meg squeezing Boyd's hand.

Boyd kissed Meg tenderly and offered, 'I'm glad I met your colleague, Meg. It is a reminder that I should never pigeonhole people.'

In Sister Meg's office later that day, Boyd sat politely chatting to the nursing staff.

Nothing was going to stop the arrival of the twins, thought Boyd. He squeezed his wife's hand and wondered where he might buy a blue teddy bear - and a pink one!

*

Chapter Six
~

Ibrox, Glasgow.

The source of the River Clyde is located a few miles west of Beattock summit, on the M74 motorway, in Scotland. Formed by the confluence of two watercourses, one tributary is called the Daer Water and the other stream is named the Potrail Water. The Southern Upland Way - Scotland's only coast to coast route - crosses both streams before they eventually meet at Watermeetings. It is here that the Clyde proper is moulded and meanders north into the very heart of Glasgow.

Many grand hotels and fine restaurants vie for business on or close to the banks of the River Clyde, the Paisley Road area, and the famous Ibrox Football Stadium. The stadium is arguably the hub of activity in Ibrox - particularly on match days - and has undoubtedly underpinned the local economy over the years. However, the history, culture and wealth of this attractive area gradually surrender to a feeling of faded sartorial elegance. The recession is biting deep into Scotland's economy and the workforce drifts in search of long-term meaningful employment. A splendid collection of venues and leisure centres do indeed enhance the reputation of the area. Yet next to the apparent wealth, and occasional opulence, there is an awareness of some deprivation and denial. Once removed from the semblance of prosperity, row upon row of broad streets bore either testament to the late nineteenth century Glasgow tenements or a mid-twentieth century terraced structure.

Stuart and Janice knew the area well and were proud of their unique Scottish heritage. Stuart hailed from Kelvingrove and Janice was from Greenock, not far away. Now, appropriately dressed in protective clothing for their operation in one of the terraced streets, they noticed the first signs of dark grey smoke escaping a chimney from an early morning fire. Virtually every doorstep accommodated a milk bottle or two awaiting an exchange delivery and there were few windows that did not present a plant or ornament on display.

Under the shadow of the Mosque, close to Paisley Road, Stuart waited patiently in a blacked out Transit van ready to go.

A liveried patrol car swung broadside into one end of the street whilst, simultaneously, another patrol car blocked off the far end of the terraced row of houses.

Checking his wristwatch, Stuart glanced at his search team who nodded in support. Pressing the talk button on his wireless, Stuart radioed, 'Janice.... We're ready... Situation Report please!'

In a lane, at the rear of one of the terraced houses, Janice eased her bullet proof vest slightly then gently pushed one of the old wooden doors that protected a walkway to the rear of number forty four. She felt it give slightly and held back. Turning to her team, she nodded and watched the thumbs up reply.

Quietly, she whispered into her radio, 'Ready! We're ready, Stuart.'

A milk man casually drove his float towards the top of the road and was denied access to the street by uniformed officers. His rattling milk bottles came to sudden standstill as chimney smoke twirled into the morning sky.

Outside number forty-four, Stuart pressed the talk button and radioed, 'This is Sierra Charlie, I have control... All units standby... Go!'

Opening the rear door of the Transit van, Stuart led five officers onto the pavement and approached the front door. Using the police Enforcer Battering Ram Stuart applied three tonnes of kinetic energy to the front lock and then stood back as the door collapsed inwards and surrendered to the force.

Stuart stood aside as officers rushed in and secured the front of the building.

At the same time, Janice led her team swiftly through the rear lane door and applied the same technique to the back door. She charged into the premises. Within a matter of a couple of minutes, the team had secured all rooms and detained four males of Pakistani origin.

A search began. It soon led to a computer and a list of alleged charities and good causes that appeared to be a front for the collection of money from the Strathclyde region. It would be some hours before Stuart recovered cheque books and bank statements from the rear of a wardrobe in an upstairs bedroom.

'Stuart,' said Janice. 'Do you know what will happen if we dissect these papers and recover the actual cheques and card transactions from the banks?'

'No, what's on your mind,' enquired Stuart.

Janice shook her head and suggested, 'We'll probably end up with a list of hundreds of people in Glasgow who have donated money to the cause. We'll have to open an office here in the city.'

'Very true, Janice,' observed Stuart with a chuckle. 'But it's not the innocent parties we're after. That's one of the problems with the Islamic faith. Muslims are expected to donate whatever they can to charitable causes. It's one of the five pillars of Islam if I remember right, Janice. Problem is Mister bad Muslim persuades Mister good Muslim to give to a certain charity. But it looks like most of these people have been conned into donating money for one thing whilst our prisoners were in the process of diverting it to another. Our problem is that we will probably find that some of this money has been collected from mosques. Some will have been given freely and some will have been falsely extracted by dubious means. That's probably going to be fraud as well as financing terrorism. No, if we keep digging into these papers we'll discover who is straight and who is suspect.'

'I hope so, Stuart, because our friends from Pakistan haven't said a word since we broke the doors down.'

'Yeah, I suspect that when we put them through the system Antonia Harston-Browne will tell us these guys have been to a terrorist training camp in Pakistan or somewhere.'

'A lot to do,' revealed Janice. 'Such a lot to do and this is just the start. It will be months before we have a true picture of what has happened.'

'Then let's get on with it,' suggested Stuart. 'It's just another haystack to take to pieces. The needles are in here somewhere and we've done it before.'

'It's a job for the finance unit,' offered Janice.

'Agreed,' said Stuart. 'That won't be a problem once we've recovered everything for them. They've all the time in the world, haven't they?'

'I think they'd disagree. They like to strike whenever they can. Do we know where the original tip-off came from?' probed Janice.

'Originally a Strathclyde Special Branch officer became suspicious when one or two in the local Muslim community were beginning to think things weren't quite right and decided to involve the police,' revealed Stuart. 'Strathclyde rang the alarm bells on the vehicle. We waited for it, got lucky, and then locked up those four guys on the M6 in Cumbria. Once we'd got into the computer and paperwork in the car boot the Glasgow connection stood out like a sore thumb and supported Strathclyde's suspicions. You know how these things work, Janice. It's nearly always a jigsaw puzzle but finding all the pieces is usually the answer.'

'Good!' responded Janice. 'Maybe there's hope yet then. No-one should support evil whatever their religion is.'

The procedure had been simple and straight forward. It was repeated in Birmingham by Terry Anwhari and Anthea Adams without undue incident.

In Barking, north east London, Boyd, Commander Herbert, Antonia Harston-Browne and Phillip Nesbitt gathered in the coldness of dawn to do their business.

Boyd wore a black leather blouson jacket, thick corduroy jeans and a dark roll neck sweater to keep out the cold. Comparatively, Toni wore a figure hugging sheepskin jacket and denim jeans that accentuated that famous hourglass figure of hers. It was an appearance not lost on the eyes of Phillip Nesbitt.

'All set, William?' enquired Commander Herbert turning the collar of his overcoat up.

'Soon, commander,' replied Boyd. 'I'm just waiting for the latest from the surveillance team. They've been watching all night and we're one short from the three we expect to find in the house.'

'We have surveillance in place, sir,' revealed Antonia to Phillip. 'We're waiting for one of the suspects on night shift. He's a bouncer at a nightclub apparently so we expect him home quite soon. Once he's inside we'll take it down.'

'Thank you, Antonia,' replied Phillip. 'Tell me, what makes your unit unique, Chief Inspector Boyd?'

'The elite amongst our number are trained to some degree by the Regiment – the Special Air Services Regiment – accordingly, for anti-terrorist purposes in the UK, a mix of police and military training makes them the masters when it comes to surveillance and intelligence gathering.'

'I see,' countered the Director General seemingly unconvinced. 'Okay, what do you want me to do, chief inspector?'

Boyd smiled and replied, 'You came to watch our procedures, sir, so I would ask you only to watch our procedures and take no part in them. No disrespect intended but I'm not privy to your specialist operations so if I were you I'd keep my mouth shut and my hands in my pockets and just watch.'

Rubbing his chin thoughtfully, Phillip responded with, 'You don't mince your words, Chief Inspector Boyd.'

'No, I don't,' replied Boyd. 'I've two bosses here watching every move we make and I can do without it. I'm just telling you like it is, sir. Don't take it personally.'

Commander Herbert produced a hip flask and poured two tots of brandy.

'William?' offered the commander. 'Antonia?'

'I'll break with tradition, commander, if you don't mind,' conveyed Boyd. 'Your flask has two cups, sir. I'll miss out and join the team on this one.'

'And me too,' suggested Antonia. 'I decline the brandy, commander, but I might have succumbed to a glass of ice-cold champagne. Bollinger is nice at any time of the day.'

'As you wish,' considered Commander Herbert. 'Phillip, may I tempt you?'

'Indeed, you may,' offered Phillip. 'A small one if you please but only for tradition's sake! Tell me, when did this strange tradition start?'

'When the unit began,' replied Commander Herbert pouring a thimbleful of Spanish brandy into a small silver cup which he delivered to Phillip.

Adjusting his earpiece, Boyd held up his hand and said, 'Here we go, Toni. We're on. Excuse us, gentlemen.' Boyd took a step away and radioed, 'All received White One. I have control. Repeat I have control... Stand by.... Sitreps please...Red Two.... Green One.... Blue Three.' Boyd listened to the updates and then instructed, 'I agree.... I have control.... Hard and fast please. Dominate! Stand By! Wait... Wait.... Wait.... Go!'

Boyd and Antonia were gone from two men drinking brandy from a hip flask on a cold London morning.

Moments later, there was the sound of screeching tyres when the raid took place. The noise of slamming car doors filled the street. Splintering wood could be heard. Breaking glass shattered the serenity of the morning. Shouting! And then there was a welcome silence in the terraces when the search got underway and armed uniformed officers controlled access to and from the neighbourhood.

'Most effective,' observed Phillip Nesbitt. 'Your man enjoys the total respect of his team, speaks his mind, and gets on with the job, James.'

Nodding in agreement, Commander Herbert suggested, 'William never asks anyone to do something that he is not capable of doing himself, Phillip. He's unique in his field actually. William tends to wear his heart on his sleeve and leads from the front. That's why his people respond to him. He is one of them but at the flick of an internal switch he can be one of us.'

'You mean he is a monkey as well as the organ grinder?'

'Something like that,' countered Commander Herbert. 'Another one?'

'No thanks!'

'Good!' suggested Commander Herbert pocketing his hip flask. 'All good traditions should be respected and not abused.'

'Have you told him yet?' enquired Phillip thoughtfully.

'No, not yet, but I will.'

'How will he respond?' queried Phillip.

'Badly to start with but then he'll slowly come round and deal with the problem,' explained Commander Herbert.

'It's very unfair on him,' admitted Phillip

'It was your idea,' countered the commander.

'It needs to be done,' remarked Phillip, with the essence of the Director General of the Security Service. 'We need to know. I asked for your best and you gave me Boyd. I have placed my trust in the Special Crime Unit above other departments I could have approached. Let's hope your judgement is right, James.'

'My judgement?' quizzed the commander. 'My judgement suggests Antonia Harston-Browne will not be amused either, Phillip. She has elements of the Establishment in her pocket and your ruse may backfire on you.'

Phillip Nesbitt gathered his long black overcoat closer to him and disclosed. 'It's a messy business all round, commander! I think I should have had that extra tot after all.'

'It'll keep, Phillip. It'll keep.' Commander Herbert paused and then disclosed, 'I'll do the introductions later today. They'll be short and sweet and then I'll retire to let them find their own ground. The quicker they get to know each other the better.'

'Is that the sum total of your illustrious plan?' enquired Phillip.

'I know my people,' countered Commander Herbert.

Breathless, Boyd and Antonia reappeared. Boyd announced, 'We've found a stash of money in a suitcase on a kitchen table with eight dodgy passports that we found hidden beneath the sink. I think we'll find the jokers we arrested in Cumbria were on their way here via Wolverhampton collecting cash before taking it abroad.'

'There doesn't seem to be much finesse in that, chief inspector,' suggested Phillip. 'At some stage someone is going to wonder why the money wasn't placed in a bank account and electronically transferred to whomever.'

'I agree,' replied Boyd. 'But the enemy know we keep tabs on electronic transfers over a certain amount. Of course, they use such bank transmissions but we know they also prefer cold hard cash in their hands whenever they can. They have multiple ways of moving money around the system, sir. This is just one of them.'

'Technology?' queried Commander Herbert.

Antonia explained, 'We've a couple of computers to examine and a posse of mobile phones, commander. That should keep the tech guys busy for a few days at least.'

'We'll get out of your way then,' offered Commander Herbert. 'I'm sure our new Director General has experienced enough excitement for the day.'

'Agreed,' responded Phillip. 'I'm obliged to you and your team, Chief Inspector Boyd, and to Mrs Harston-Browne as well, of course.'

'Miss!' cracked Antonia mischievously. 'I'm a single person, sir. Haven't you read my personnel file? I'm sure you have clearance in your position but if you haven't perhaps I can pull a few strings.'

'Single like myself! Of course, Antonia.' admitted Phillip with the slightest hint of embarrassment. 'I forgot. A slip of the tongue,

Miss Harston-Browne, and by the way, I do have the necessary clearance.'

'No matter,' replied Antonia with a glint in her eye. 'I must study your résumé when I have a free evening.'

Boyd sensed a certain magnetism attracting the two MI5 officers and intervened with, 'Anytime you want to accompany us on an operation, sir, there'll be no problem at all! No problem!'

'I am obliged,' responded Phillip.

Commander Herbert and Phillip Nesbitt were gone from Barking having witnessed another successful nail in the coffin of the Sons of The Shimmering Dawn.

When their two superiors had left the scene, Boyd turned to Antonia and suggested, 'Toni, do I sense you harbour secret desires for your boss, Phillip Nesbitt?'

Antonia blasted a vociferous reply. 'Don't be ridiculous, Boyd. Where on earth do you get that idea from?'

'Oh, just looking and watching. It's a bad habit of mine.'

'You need to get your eyes tested then,' snapped Antonia.

The two made towards their car but Boyd suggested, 'Pity really, Toni.'

'What is?'

'You could have had me once!'

'You! You had your chance and picked Meg. Remember?'

Boyd grinned and offered, 'I certainly do. I must phone to make sure things are okay with her.'

Relaxing slightly, Antonia proposed, 'Well, give Meg my love and let me know how she is, Boyd. There's a good chap.'

'I will, Toni. I will. We're both so excited at the moment.'

Nearing the BMW, Antonia engaged Boyd and asked, 'You know when you were looking and watching, did you think Phillip was taking a fancy to me?'

Boyd shrugged, pulled the car door open, and snapped, 'Of course not, Toni. Now you're being ridiculous.'

Placing her hands on the car roof, Antonia heard the BMW engine fire and considered Boyd's response. Shaking her head, slightly confused, Antonia climbed into Boyd's car and travelled back to the Yard.

In Glasgow, the operation had been successful. In Birmingham and London, more computers and paperwork had been recovered and would prove to be the foundation of a long and protracted enquiry into fraud and the financing of terrorist activity at home and abroad.

Later that day, in New Scotland Yard, Boyd and Antonia were about to meet the new man on the unit. They were walking down a corridor when Commander Herbert introduced the latest addition to the unit.

'Ah, William, Antonia,' hailed Commander Herbert. 'I'm pleased I've caught you both. Firstly, may I congratulate you both on an excellent operation. I really appreciate you travelling back and taking charge of the operational side of things, William. That said I have someone I'd like you both to meet. He has clearance of course but I wondered if you could firstly update me on how it's gone so far?'

'Stuart and Janice came up trumps in Glasgow, sir,' responded Boyd enthusiastically. 'They're handing everything over to the finance unit for further investigation. It's the same story in Birmingham from Anthea and Terry. As for, Toni, well her analysis seems to improve with age.'

'Cheeky!' quipped Antonia.

'Absolutely,' intervened Commander Herbert. 'My problem is that the Commissioner is absolutely delighted with the outcome. He's so taken with your work he's got it into his head that you've also detected that armed robbery in Southport. The Commissioner wonders if you've recovered the AK-47's yet?'

Boyd and Antonia exchanged surprised glances before Boyd suggested, 'I'll check with Anthea and Stuart but no such recovery has been made, sir, and, as far as I am concerned, we're not expecting to find any evidence to connect our prisoners with that robbery. It's convenient to think it might be the same crew and therefore it's detected but it would be wrong to suppose we've got the right men. Don't you agree, Toni?'

'Yes, I do,' admitted Antonia. 'But something occurs to me. According to that recent intelligence analysis there was mention of a large amount of money being made available to four terrorists working in the United Kingdom. So, here we have a bank robbery committed by four people and then we recover a large amount of money from a car containing four people. Tell me if I'm mad, confused or just making this up, but somewhere in this country there's four terrorists loose. Are we on the right track or is this just a coincidence?'

'Coincidence, I would say, Toni,' voiced Boyd. 'I think we've disrupted a collaboration network working in support of active terrorists. But you're right to keep it on the back burner and remind us.'

'Mmm...' considered Antonia. 'I suppose the reality is that there is no substantial evidence to connect all these silly threads wandering through my analytical mind. Yes, I think your robbers are still at large, commander.'

'I see,' nodded Commander Herbert stroking his wonderful white beard. 'I wonder if the Commissioner is confusing intelligence gathering with evidence gathering. Still, leave it with me. I'll have a word with him. The Commissioner would like to meet you, Boyd. Your reputation seems to have finally made the top landing of the Metropolitan police and for a throw back from Cumbria that's quite an achievement.'

'I'm sure he does, sir,' chuckled Boyd. 'But he'll have to wait until I've filed my reports. 'As you know, sir, we have blanket authority to carry firearms in any part of the United Kingdom provided we report the occasions upon which we draw firearms from the holster or discharge the weapons. I'm up to my eyes in paperwork justifying why firearms were produced in Cumbria.'

'Oh, I'm sure you'll find a way round that one, William,' reflected the commander. 'They could have been the armed robbers from Merseyside for all you knew at the time. Look, can I introduce Mister Ryan to you?'

Sidestepping, Commander Herbert gestured forward a rather slender man, bespectacled, and with a short but thick moustache.

'Mister Ryan, this is Chief Inspector Boyd and Antonia Harston-Browne from the Special Crime Unit.'

There was a moment of polite handshaking then the commander withdrew abruptly saying, 'Mister Ryan is seconded to us until further notice, William. I'm sure you will find he has resources at his disposal that will add great value to our work and I have no hesitation in recommending him to you.'

'I see, thank you, commander,' replied Boyd civilly.

'Well, I'll leave it with you. Touch base later, William, and let me know how the investigation progresses.'

'Will do, sir,' confirmed Boyd.

As Commander Herbert walked away, Antonia queried, 'What on earth has Commander Herbert rushed off for?'

'Beats me, Toni,' suggested Boyd. Then, turning to the interloper, he asked, 'Ryan, is it?'

'It's Albert Charles Henry Ryan, actually, Mister Boyd! I'm with the Treasury Department normally but I've been seconded to you guys for six months.'

'Treasury?' queried Antonia. 'I didn't know Scotland Yard had a Treasury Department.'

'I think he means the government Treasury, Toni,' suggested Boyd. 'That's why the boss scuttled away.'

'Yes, indeed,' endorsed Ryan. 'The Treasury, Whitehall! Well, Horse Guards Road actually but who needs to be precise with such detail!'

'Me,' quipped Boyd. 'I'm about to write out a report for the chief constable of Cumbria Constabulary validating and explaining why I authorised the use of firearms recently. I expect to be precise in my judgement and those reading it will expect it to be accurate in every way.'

'Oh, yes,' enthused Ryan. 'Commander Herbert was telling me about the militants you arrested.'

'Militants?' queried Boyd, exchanging glances with Antonia. 'These were a little more than militant, Albert.'

'I prefer Ryan, Mister Boyd. My parents were exceedingly supportive of the Monarchy and blessed me with the names of numerous Kings of England. But Ryan will do nicely, thank you.'

'Then Ryan it is, sir,' accepted Boyd. 'Now how can we help you and how can you help us?'

'Tell us, Ryan,' delivered Antonia, interrupting and swinging her long red hair onto her shoulders. 'How do the Treasury distinguish between terrorist and militants?'

Boyd shook his head but Antonia persisted with, 'It's your starter for ten, Ryan. How do the Treasury distinguish between terrorist and militants?'

'Toni…' pleaded Boyd, suggesting she might leave it.

Resettling his spectacles on the bridge of his nose, Ryan explained, 'I insist on using the word 'militants' as opposed to terrorists in order to better describe and comprehend the individuals concerned. I tend to use diplomatic speech; it's much more specific.'

Antonia swung her hair anxiously again and responded, 'You'll be calling them ecowarriors or protesters next. A militant may be a radical, revolutionary or downright confrontational. A terrorist is all of those things plus a guerrilla warrior, an extremist, and - in most cases we deal with - a bomber or an assassin. Are you confusing student unrest with international warfare? '

Before Ryan could answer Boyd stated, 'No disrespect intended, sir, but I appreciate why my colleague is forcing the issue.

The fact is I didn't ask for a man from the Treasury to join us and I'm beginning to ask myself why you are here.'

'Absolutely,' reacted Antonia. 'Why are you here, Ryan?'

'I didn't ask to be here,' disclosed Ryan. 'It's a government initiative originating with the offices of the Chancellor of the Exchequer, the Home Secretary, and the Foreign Office. Basically, we're interested in ascertaining if the terrorism laws are fit for purpose having specific regard to the amount of money which is allotted annually to your department. Are we getting our money's worth is the question?'

Antonia and Boyd were astonished, and for a moment speechless.

'I can't imagine why I haven't been informed of this,' suggested Antonia haughtily. 'I would have thought the DG might have discussed it with me at the very least.'

'Well, that confirms why Commander Herbert disappeared so quickly,' offered Boyd. 'And that tells me he may not have known about it either.'

'He didn't,' clarified Ryan. 'My secondment was discussed with the Commissioner's office and the appropriate office in the Security Service. I'm also at liberty to offer you as much government assistance as possible in order to improve your performance where relevant.'

'Improve our performance,' exploded Antonia. 'How dare you breeze into our domain and impose yourself like this? Improve performance? Are you going to give us all multi vitamin tablets?'

'I have much advice to offer on the kind of militants you are dealing with,' suggested Ryan defending his position. 'And, with respect, I'm not imposing myself on your domain; I'm merely answering your questions.'

'Ah,' exclaimed Boyd. 'So, the government will take credit for this wonderful idea of combining civil servants with the police service to save money on actual police officers. Is that it? Refining skills and combining resources?'

'I know my job, Boyd,' countered Ryan, aggressively. 'And what is expected of me. I've served with the Foreign Office in Tehran, Baghdad, and Kabul providing information on Arabic culture, religion and traditions to our government officials searching for a peace solution.'

'You haven't done very well so far then,' suggested Boyd. 'Our soldiers are still fighting.'

'I resent that remark, Boyd' seethed Ryan. 'It's not for the want of trying and how dare you comment on Afghanistan. What do you know of the situation? You've never been on the front line there.'

'No, we're on the front line here,' replied Boyd smoothly.

Continuing angrily, Ryan snapped, 'And I'll remind you both that I am the government expert on the tribes of Arabia, politics and culture in the area. I can tell you everything you need to know about the culture and politics of Iraq, Afghanistan, Pakistan, Syria, Egypt...'

'Excellent,' remarked Boyd. 'I spend my free time reading newspaper reports about Turkey, Egypt, and Chechnya – places like that – keeps me busy.'

'And what do the journals tell you?' asked Ryan.

'That religion is replacing politics in various parliaments here and there across the globe. I call it the march of the Arab caliphate and the extremities of Sunni Muslims are in the lead.'

'An interesting observation,' remarked Ryan.

Smiling, Boyd enquired, 'But can you tell me why we're still fighting terrorism at home and abroad, Ryan?

'Yes, if you have the time and the inclination.'

'Then be my guest,' invited Boyd. 'Come on, my office.... Antonia?'

'Oh yes,' revealed Antonia. 'I can't wait to hear what you two guys think of that one.'

Moments later, the trio were sat in Boyd's office behind closed doors.

Boyd opened with, 'Over to you, Ryan. Impress us.'

'Is this a job interview?' cracked Ryan.

'No, but it will tell me how passionate you are about your subject,' delivered Boyd. 'Now fire away.'

Ryan cast his eyes around the framed photographs of various terrorist incidents occupying the walls of Boyd's office. In amongst the photographs of global events there was a rather strange crest that caught Ryan's eye. There was nothing special about the crest other than it was the image of a bell, book and candle intertwined. The crest occupied the centre of the display next to the photograph of the twin towers attack in New York, in September, 2011. But the wall was festooned with images from 1970 onwards of Northern Ireland, the Middle East, and dozens of other locations. The wall itself was a history lesson.

'Well,' declared Ryan. 'The problem for governments like ours is that they do not recognise the causes of terrorism. They counter the phenomenon with more terrorism by issuing an instinctive physical response from the state.'

'Do they indeed,' remarked Boyd. 'What would you think of such governments if they just capitulated and let everyone walk over them, Ryan? Maybe they do recognise the causes but choose to react in the way they do since they want to eradicate the problem of bombers and assassins before them? Generally speaking, the government of the day cannot change things overnight in the way fanatical extremists want. '

Ryan shook his head and suggested, 'All terrorist acts are motivated by two things: social and political injustice. People choose terrorism when they see something they think is historically, socially, or politically wrong. They get upset when they are stripped of their land or their rights or when they are deemed no longer entitled to these. You see, Mister Boyd – Antonia – Such people really think that violence, or the threat of violence, will bring about change. So my job is to try and lower the tone of those causation factors in political circles.'

'You mean your diplomacy function in Kabul and Iraq, places like that?' queried Boyd.

'Correct, that's it in a nutshell really,' suggested Ryan. 'You see terrorists believe that violence justifies the end. They've no choice. No-one wants to listen to them. Nobody believes them. They're on their own so they go their own way.'

'Analytically speaking,' suggested Antonia. 'You are correct. You can pull out all the bits and pieces that make up the causation factors but at the end of the day, you will always be left with social and political injustice as the primary factors.'

'Religion?' queried Boyd.

'Under the banner of social injustice, Boyd,' decided Antonia.

'I see,' remarked Boyd. 'Ryan, I'm with you - so far - and agree that such things like the Zionists who bombed British targets in Palestine in 1930 did so because they felt it necessary to create a Jewish state. In the 60's and 70's the Popular Front for the Liberation of Palestine believed armed attacks on Israel were a justifiable response to the occupation of their lands. And the IRA bombed English targets in the 80's to make the point that their land was colonised by what they termed British Imperialists. Personally, historically, they are probably correct but I sometimes wonder why the leaders of these organisations take on responsibility for the actions of their various groups. Is to feed their ego and ensure their own power base? Or is it to challenge social and political injustice? Sorry, but in my job, Ryan, I'm not paid to make political or diplomatic decisions. I'm paid to uphold the law. That said, sadly, despite the passage of time these problems still exist. Today, our biggest challenge seems to be Middle Eastern religious ideology.'

Nodding, Ryan replied, 'When Osama bin Laden declared war on America he believed that American troops based in Saudi Arabia represented an abomination to the Islamic state he wanted in the Arabia peninsula.'

'Did he really?' noted Boyd.

'Yes,' responded Ryan tilting his spectacles back onto the bridge of his nose. 'Where you agree the IRA were historically correct in claiming England subjugated the Irish people I believe there is merit in Osama bin Laden's argument.'

'My comment about the English suppressing the Irish is based in the history of King James 1st and the Plantations. He sent specific English and Scottish families of the Protestant religion to occupy the lands of Irish catholic families. It just seems so wrong to me and perhaps explains the Irish problem as we know it today. That said I'm sure if I go back further in Irish history I'll come up with a reason to deny Irish Republican terrorists any credence. And that's the problem, Ryan; humankind can't go forward for looking back.'

'I disagree,' replied Ryan passionately. 'You can't moderate your beliefs in the way that you've just explained, Mister Boyd.'

Boyd leaned forward and demanded, 'Yeah, well I'm living today and I'm working my patch in the way that I know how. Now tell me, Ryan, do you support Osama bin Laden's principles?'

There was a pause too long for Boyd and he repeated, 'Ryan, do you support the beliefs of Osama bin Laden?'

'Of course not, Boyd,' replied Ryan.

'Coffee?' suggested Antonia interrupting. 'You two seem quite immersed in the sociological aspects of historic terrorism. Give it a rest, guys. I'll put the kettle on whilst you two talk about football or something really much more important.'

Taking the hint, Boyd leaned back and relaxed into his chair as Ryan smoothed a handkerchief across his brow and wiped away a smidgen of perspiration.

Chapter Seven

~

Sana'a, The Yemen.

The Republic of Yemen occupies the Arabian Peninsula and a strategically important position for the United Kingdom, the United States of America, Russia and China. It is ideally situated as the guardian of the Red Sea. Oil rich Saudi Arabia lies immediately to its north; the Red Sea to the west, the Gulf of Aden and Arabian Sea to the south and Oman to the east.

Yemen is one of the oldest centres of civilisation in the world and is the only state in the Arabian Peninsula to have a republican form of government. It was the first country in the region to grant women the right to vote when, in 1990, North and South Yemen amalgamated to form the present republic. The country is occupied by many different and varied tribes who rule over large parts of the republic. Government forces, influence and supremacy, cluster to the south whilst competing tribes overshadow the rest of the jurisdiction.

Since the State of Israel was declared in 1948 over fifty thousand Jews have been safely airlifted to Israel leaving less than one hundred Jewish families living under government protection in the south of the country. Significant areas of the republic have developed into a virulent and venomous territory with a strong hatred of America and its western allies prevalent throughout.

As the demographic make-up of the republic evolves it is perhaps not surprising that the area is also home to one of Al-Qaeda's Islamic Emirates.

Saleem stood on the high mountains seven thousand five hundred feet above the Sunni town of Sana'a: the capital of the Republic of Yemen.

Looking down into the old city of Sana'a Saleem clearly understood why his home was a World Heritage Site. He marvelled at the splendour of the ancient city. Before him stretched mile upon mile of traditional red-brick skyscrapers that had been embedded in the land for over a century. Such an intriguing sight fashioned an unforgettable skyline featuring whitewashed friezes and similar window frames. Yet there was a remarkable almost chocolate-box look about the shape of the place with its variously coloured brown square buildings, narrow lanes, and compact public squares.

But what struck Saleem most was the number of domes, mosques and minarets on display.

Closing his eyes, he tried to imagine how it might feel at the top of a minaret He tried to visualise how he would feel at the top of such a slim structure. The minaret seemed to emerge insipidly from the ground like a piece of straw before subsequently dominating its neighbourhood. From such a vantage point the call to prayer was made to the Muslim community. Known as 'adhan' the call invaded the district five times a day: at dawn, noon, mid-afternoon, sunset and night.

Genial in his inner being, Saleem quietly recalled how the very first call to prayer was made from the roof of the Prophet Muhammad's house in Mecca.

What a beautiful city, he thought. What a haunting and impressive sight to commit to his memory and accompany him on his journey. Indistinctly, from the streets below, he heard the call to prayer and duly undertook his duty.

Eventually, bringing down his hands to his side, Saleem finished praying. Alone, and deep in thought, he climbed into his jeep, fired the engine, and began the long descent to Sana'a where the Sunni Muslim population was dominant and increasing.

Saleem did not wave at his friends as he drove through town. He did not pause for food or drink and he paid no heed to the Mosque on the corner. He drove past the domed mosques, minarets, and chocolate-box skyscrapers as he turned over in his mind the flight number and the window seat that would convey him away from the Yemen. Then he repeated the things that he must do in the future. His brain rehearsed the conversation he would have when his false passports were collected, and where he would hide them. Concentrating on the road ahead, he was aware of an aircraft overhead flying off to who knows where.

Saleem felt no remorse, no pain. In his mindset, he was going on a holiday - of a kind - He was going to Paradise. The son of a farmer, he was also a guerrilla fighter who was skilled in the art of murder. Saleem was the sharp end of a blade: a killer of men

Steering the jeep quite deliberately away from his home, he took the highway for Sana'a International Airport, close to Aden, and a crucial flight to the western world.

Back in New Scotland Yard, there was a heated discussion still underway.

Ryan countered with, 'People have got Osama bin Laden down as a religious fanatic. It isn't true, Boyd. He was a religious leader not a fanatic.'

Considering the remark carefully, Boyd suggested, 'Religious fanaticism creates conditions that are favourable for terrorism. We know religious zealots do not cause terrorism. History is littered with individuals who have led various religious factions all over the world – From Waco to India – and back again: People who have organised sects and factions on the basis of some trumped up belief that the world is about to end next year or having ten wives is good for the propagation of Christianity. And then, would you believe, getting together thousands of people to follow them. No, terrorism, for me, is much more complex than that. In my experience it's a specific kind of violence or threat used by people who do not have an army at their disposal but wish they did. They try to create such armies by various means. When not successful they sometimes act alone. There's one dominant factor in all of this, Ryan. They do not have to choose violence but they do.'

'Yes, I know all that,' sighed Ryan. 'As it says in the Koran – And whatever the Messenger gives you, take it, and whatever he forbids you, leave it. And fear Allah: truly Allah is severe in punishment – Okay?'

'The Koran! You know it well it would seem,' remarked Boyd. 'Why do you read it?'

'I'm interested that's all,' remarked Ryan.

'My guys don't know the Koran backwards, Ryan, but they sure as hell know what it means and what problems extremism brings.'

'Yes, well, my experiences are similar in Iraq and elsewhere,' explained Ryan suddenly adopting a somewhat arrogant attitude.

'But my team do not operate in Iraq - and elsewhere - as you put it, Ryan,' stated Boyd. 'We operate on home soil and need to be aware of what's going on our streets. Millions of Muslims live happily ever after in our country. It's our job to find the protesters, the militants as you call them, and the bombers. That's why we need to know and understand the trivia of life, Ryan, so that we have an understanding how the other half live.'

'Jolly good,' responded Ryan. 'I'll look forward to working with you and advising you along the way, chief inspector.'

'I'm sure you will,' quipped Boyd, slightly annoyed.

'By the way, I found an empty office, Mister Boyd.'

'Good,' responded Boyd. 'That's settled then. It's a bit open plan, I know, but I hope the guys will look after you.'

'Oh it's not open plan, chief inspector. My office is next to yours.'

As Ryan got up and strolled away from the office, Boyd exhaled loudly, turned to Antonia, and said, 'This is going to be fun, Toni.'

'You're telling me,' offered Antonia.

Boyd watched Ryan turn a corner and head towards the canteen. Engaging Antonia, Boyd commented, 'Mister Ryan, Toni, he's not of our kind. I don't like him and I don't know why. Here's something wrong there. Check him out.'

'Do me a favour. He's with the Treasury, Boyd. He'll have Ministry of Defence clearance and listening to him talking about Iraq and Afghanistan I expect his access and accountability is far in excess of our little cosy world.'

'Maybe, Toni, but Mister Ryan is not having direct access to my pen, my pencil, my office, my telephone, my diary, my spare socks, my coffee mug or anything until I know what makes him tick and why he's been planted amongst us. You do know I have trouble in trusting a system that handpicks the best detectives in the country and then infiltrates an unknown into them!'

'Oh, I'm sure Commander Herbert knows what's going on,' insisted Antonia.

Nodding, Boyd countered with, 'Maybe, but we've enough with a leak in the department without Ryan sniffing about.'

'Why don't you tell the commander about the leak, Boyd? Only you and I and Anthea know about your suspicions. Hand it over to the commander and he'll bring a team in to investigate.'

'He's retiring soon, Toni. No! He's going to walk away with all his badges shining and no chance of someone tarnishing his career. I owe him a lot and I'll sort it.'

'Are you sure?'

'I'll deal with it, Toni. I'll put Anthea on the case.'

'Good choice!' delivered Antonia.

Continuing, Boyd demanded, 'I want to know everything there is to know about Ryan as soon as possible. Car; telephone numbers, blood group, sexual preferences, education, hobbies, social media, likes and dislikes, regular haunts, favourite colour, favourite football team, golf handicap, number of suits in his wardrobe, usual lottery numbers, everything there is to know.'

'I get the picture. Full profile!' clarified Antonia.

'I want to know what his pulse rate is and what makes his heart beat. I want to know who he telephones, when and why! Eco warriors, militants, protestors, anyone like that, I need to know.'

'The MOD will probably have already done that it in the course of vetting the man and assigning clearance to him,' advised Antonia.

'Do it again! Do it your way, Toni. Think outside the box!' suggested Boyd.

'Okay! I'll make a start and deliver the product to Anthea. But if the wheel comes off how will you explain our unauthorised covert enquiry to the politicians?'

'You want me to trust a politician, Toni?'

'Point taken,' chuckled Antonia.

Squeezing Antonia's hand, Boyd whispered, 'Thanks, Toni.'

*

Chapter Eight
~

Cairo, Egypt.

Cairo International Airport consists of four terminals and is located at the tip of the Red Sea in Egypt. After Johannesburg it is the second largest airport on the continent of Africa

Two men arrived on separate flights from Iran and Aswan.

Al Harith had travelled from Iran and Rafid had flown from Aswan, in the south of Egypt.

Separately, they studied the departure board waiting for the European flights to appear before refreshing with a light meal and seeking their God.

Close by, the travel industry aspired to deliver more and more tourists intent on sampling the history and culture of the Egyptian people. This was witnessed by the comings and goings of hundreds of flights every day. Ignoring the roar of jet engines and the hustle bustle of international travel, the two men sought privacy.

In the prayer area, they carried out their ablutions independent of each other and then worshipped Allah with a dozen other passengers waiting for a travel link.

Rafid and Al Harith were bound for Great Britain doing the work of Al-Qaeda. The journey would be long and indirect as they laid a false trail. This was their first leg. They knew their final destination would not be reached for some time yet. Irrespectively, they were off to meet their maker and there was no going back.

They produced one-way tickets at check-in.

The stallion was full steam ahead over Caldbeck Fells with Susie Lowther low in the stirrups and enjoying the freedom of a uniquely sunny day and a light breeze. Only the nearby radio mast bore witness to the teenager's antics.

'Go on, Gabby,' she cried. 'Show me what you can do.'

Striding out, Gabby galloped along at a tremendous speed tearing up the land with Susie hanging on tight enjoying the exhilarating journey. Yet she was caring of her horse and after a mile or so Susie reined the stallion in. She settled onto the saddle bringing Gabby to a canter. Ahead lay Skiddaw and the nearby glories of the stretch between Mungrisdale and Saddleback.

But Susie had other plans.

Bringing her charge to a walking pace, she guided Gabby between two large oak trees and then crossed a makeshift wooden bridge that spanned a narrow stream into the rear of The Base: an adventure Retreat for young people.

Careful now, she thought. Nice and easy does it but I will find out where the boys are. They stay here, don't they? At least, that's what the signs say at the entrance. It's a Retreat: a place where they come on holiday for a week and enjoy themselves paintballing and stuff. Susie thought it was about time they knew about the village youth club and the community centre. And the girls, of course! Apart from that, why couldn't her friends from the village and surrounding area use the paintball site? It might be fun.

Dismounting, Susie tethered Gabby to a low branch, nuzzled her, and then crept stealthily towards the Base and the accommodation complex.

There was nothing special about the place at all, she decided. In fact it was a bit of a dump in some ways. Everywhere seemed to be rather rundown and unassuming; even the entrance to an old mine shaft required maintenance of some kind. Narrow gauge railway lines drifted to the wooden gate that barred entry to the mine and then stopped for no reason at all. The gate bore a heavy close coupled padlock on a bright new hasp attached to a substantial wooden frame. Yet rock and earth surrounding the wooden frame was crumbling and seemed hazardous. There were gaps between the frame and the rock giving an impression of vulnerability. Was it dangerous in there, she wondered. Maybe that's why the gate was padlocked, she did not know. No wonder the locals didn't know much about the place. It had deteriorated into a dump, as simple as that.

Dismissing the mine, Susie made her way further into the Base.

A long and narrow well-trodden path meandered through the complex stopping off at various outbuildings that seemed to have no rhyme or reason attached to them. What purpose did they serve? They were just wooden huts of various shapes and sizes and some of them were covered with splashes of paint boasting broken windows and doors hanging from their hinges.

Susie decided the Base was similar to one of those film sets used in cowboy westerns and she stifled a giggle.

Of course, Susie concluded, this part of the Base was part of an assault course. She'd heard of such places and once enjoyed a school trip to an army camp at Warcop, near Appleby, where the schools in the area took part in a competition.

As Susie crept slowly though the complex, she realised how quiet it was and what similarities there were to Warcop's assault course. She studied the brick wall standing in the middle of the lane. Guessing, she presumed it was perhaps nine feet tall. She did not know. Then her eye caught sight of a rope attached to the top of the wall and she knew it was positioned there so that a person could grasp it and pull themselves over the obstruction.

Deeper inside the grounds, Susie heard the slight trickle of the stream and followed its course towards some more significant buildings. Making towards the brick buildings, she took in the windows and the substantial doors that made this area stand out from the rest. This is the accommodation centre, she decided.

Creeping very slowly and quietly towards the low windows, Susie stretched upwards onto her tiptoes and looked inside.

Bunk beds were present, along with metal lockers, a rusting refrigerator, a washing machine, and a couple of old sinks. Then she saw the television in the corner. It was the accommodation block alright but it was very quiet. Where were the people? Should she not tell someone she was here? Susie was unsure of herself.

In any case, what was wrong with finding young people on the site and letting them know about the Youth Club and the Community Centre? It was a great idea and they would make new friends and enjoy themselves, wouldn't they. Apart from that, it might benefit Susie's street credibility if she managed to invite a few of the boys from the Base to come to the village dance at the weekend. She would be a legend in the village.

Moving further along to the next building, Susie realised the door was bolted and secured with another fresh padlock. The ageing windows were also covered in a fine metallic mesh.

Susie's heart seemed to beat out like a drum in her chest. The sound dominated her very being when she felt it beating faster and faster. On tiptoes, she reached as far as she might and then peeked above the window sill. Gradually, she raised her chin to get a better view.

Suddenly, an arm grabbed her from behind, spun her round, and pushed her hard against the wall.

Susie screamed but a man wearing a black coverall grasped her throat and demanded, 'Who are you? What are you doing?'

Gasping for breath, trembling with shock, Susie couldn't speak but read the word 'Commandant' printed in white cotton on the man's coverall.

Visibly choking, her eyes watered as his hand tightened its grip and she felt his fingernails biting into her flesh.

He released his grip slightly and again demanded, 'What are you up to? You are a thief!'

'I'm no thief,' Susie wheezed. 'I'm looking for the boys.'

'Boys?' probed the commandant, confused. 'What boys? There are no boys here. You are trespassing on my land.'

Brutally, he pushed Susie down to her knees using the strength of his massive shoulders and demanded, 'Tell me! What are you doing here?'

'I told you,' she panted. 'Boys! There's a dance in the village. We need to get them to come to the dance at the weekend.'

Annoyed and angry, the beast released his grip and threw her backwards away from the building.

Stumbling, Susie rolled in the dirt again and began to cry. Looking up, she took in the chilling image of a man with an olive tinted skin. He was over six feet tall, broad, and sported an unkempt ragged moustache and full beard. The man carried an angry scowl on his face and seemed to have no compassion.

'Away with you,' the commandant cried. 'Never let me see you again in this place. There are no boys and this is no place for the likes of you. Be off with you, girl.'

Regaining her feet,' Susie glanced once more at the man and thought she saw the devil dancing in his eyes,

Susie took a step back.

'Go on!' He shouted, advancing towards her. 'I never want to see you here again.'

Susie turned and ran as fast she could.

In the squad office of the Special Crime Unit in New Scotland Yard, a red, white and blue coloured telephone rang. It was one of the hotlines into the office from the Unit's numerous informants and agents that it employed all over London. It wasn't just a telephone; it was a direct link to London's criminal underworld.

No-one used the phone to dial out. It was incoming only.

Jim Young's body darted across the room and his hand reached out to take the call.

'Jonah's Takeaway,' answered the detective. 'What can I do for you?' Cocking an ear to the phone, Jim indicated thumbs up to Boyd and said, 'I'm all ears, pal. When and where?'

Boyd watched Jim form the shape of a gun with his right hand and then imitate a trigger with his fingers.

Turning to the body of the office, Boyd engaged the squad and instructed, 'Response Unit, stand by! It looks like a trigger message coming in.'

There was a quiet but controlled movement of a dozen or more detectives closing files, diaries and drawers before donning various items of apparel and reaching for shoulder holsters. A stack of comments followed as the tension grew. They knew whoever it was on the phone had decided to make an urgent call instead of waiting for a scheduled meeting with their handler. The telephone was a powerful instrument. Potentially, it could take them anywhere.

Jim ended the conversation, began scribbling notes, and said, 'That was one of our sources - Codename Billy Bunter - It's the Bellagoni job! The painting is changing hands today. Bexleyheath! A van and a blue Mercedes are meeting on the car park of The Bent Daffodil in an hour's time. Tall bald headed guy is the carrier in the van and a French guy in the Mercedes is the money man.'

'Is the money man the buyer or the go-between, Jim?' asked Boyd. 'Or didn't Billy Bunter know?'

'Not known, Guvnor,' replied Jim. 'But he reckons the French guy is always tooled up. Handgun for protection against getting ripped off.'

'Okay, good work. That sounds like he's picking it up for someone and looking after himself in the process. There's a big fish somewhere in the art world buying this and they don't want their fingers burnt. And Billy Bunter?' queried Boyd.

'My source, Guvnor, you know who I mean. He got The Death of a Philistine back for us last year, if you remember,' explained Jim. 'He's been chasing the Bellagoni for six months.'

'Good! I remember him, Jim. Okay, have we got time to put our own Frenchman in and buy the painting? Have we got time to let the show go down and then follow the Frenchmen to wherever? Have we got the manpower to throw an unplanned surveillance operation together? Not in an hour, I reckon. Just a moment, Jim.'

Boyd snatched a phone and dialled Commander Herbert. The phone was answered instantly.

'It's the Bellagoni, Commander! A trusted and proven source - Billy Bunter - has pointed us at the when and where the stolen painting is being swopped for money. It's going down in an hour. Bexleyheath! The point is we don't have time to mount a proper operation to take the team down. I'd want to follow the buyer and see where he goes but the information is loose and we don't have time to firm it up.'

'Billy Bunter?' queried Commander Herbert. 'Oh yes, I recall the individual. What's on your mind, William?'

'Call it a draw and recover the painting in the first instance and then take it from there,' suggested Boyd. 'If the source is correct we'll recover the painting but whether we get the real thief and the fence is another thing. They may just be the go-betweens paid to move the painting and transport the cash. The actual thief and intended recipient of the stolen painting may not figure at Walthamstow.'

'What value is the Bellagoni again?' asked the commander.

'One and half million pounds according to the Arts and Antique Squad.'

'Have you informed them, William? It's their baby. Maybe they'd like to cover the operation?'

'They'll ask the same questions, commander, and it's our source. Get it right and recover the painting and the top landing will love us. Get it wrong and they'll hang us out to dry and say we should have done this and we should have done that. You'll get the flak, commander; that's why I'm ringing you. The clock is ticking and I'm covering the bases with you. I say recover the painting if we can unless you can give me a miracle and a sack full of surveillance officers. Put simply, an hour isn't enough time to follow the advanced detection text book – if there is such a thing. It's a forty minute drive to Bexleyheath.'

There was silence at the other end of the phone before Commander Herbert replied, 'I agree, William. Time is the enemy. Hit it now with what you've got but if you get the opportunity to be open-ended then do so. It occurs to me Bexleyheath is close to both the M25 and M20 motorways. The French connection might see you taking the M20 towards Dover whereas the M25 might take you in the direction of Heathrow airport. See how it pans out, William, and jump the hurdles as you come to them. You have ground control. I will support you. I'll speak with the commander of Arts and Antiques. Good luck!'

The phone went dead.

Boyd shook his head in admiration for the man who would walk over a coal fire for him. Commander Herbert will support me as long as he knows what the score is and what the options are, thought Boyd. A boss able to decide what we should do and how to play the cards in his hand, and they wonder why I won't upset his retirement by calling in a team to investigate the internal workings of the Unit. No way, thought Boyd. This is how we do it. Our way!

Replacing the handset, Boyd called, 'Okay, everyone, we're on. Firearms authorised! Standard operating procedures. Briefing on the way. Let's go. Bexleyheath!'

An armoury door was unlocked and ammunition, bullet proof vests, and various necessities were issued. There was a swift movement to the door as the Special Crime Unit's Response Squad went into action.

Elsewhere, the Reverend Matthew Lowther tended his flock by visiting and befriending people in his parish. He offered help and comfort to the elderly and infirm whilst supporting and advising the young on his patch. In his mind, they were all God's children and it was his job to help those who were in trouble and comfort those who needed assistance. With a smile and a firm handshake, the former army chaplain strolled through the village with his wife, Elizabeth, and his daughter, Susie. The vicar knew everyone and a short stroll might often take much longer than necessary by the time he had stopped to chat to his parishioners.

Passing the window of a local pub, Matthew resisted a hand beckoning him inside and shouted, 'Not today, Isaac, but thank you. Regards to Emma!'

There was a muffled reply and the trio walked on.

Matthew held his Bible closer to his chest and exhaled loudly.

'If you'd like to have a drink then just go and join them,' suggested Elizabeth as they climbed a gradual incline. 'It's not against the law for a man of the clergy to drink with his flock. I can make the top of the hill and reach the shop quite easily, Matthew. In any event, Susie will help me. I'm just going to top up on one or two items that we need.'

'I'm enjoying the walk actually, Elizabeth,' revealed Matthew adjusting his white collar band in the heat of the day. 'I'm just finding the hill a little steep today. It must be old age.'

'Goodness me, Matthew, in your army days you surely trekked much further?'

'A long time ago, I'm afraid, Elizabeth. I was a lot younger then.'

'You won't mind carrying a few things back, Susie,' asked Elizabeth.

'Of course not, Mum,' Susie replied.

'How did your ride go today?' asked Matthew.

'Fine thanks!' snapped Susie. Abruptly changing the subject, Susie asked, 'What time is the dance on Saturday, Dad?'

'Half past seven, Susie,' advised Matthew. 'I thought you knew?'

'Did I? Oh yes, half past seven, of course,' replied Susie.

'Are you sure you're okay, Susie?' fussed Elizabeth. 'Perhaps you caught a bit of a cold whilst you were with Gabby.'

Chattering, the three made their gradual way to the shop close to the top of the hill.

A dark green Land Rover pulled up by the kerb and a tall man got out of the vehicle and entered the shop.

Susie immediately recognised the commandant of The Base and began to straggle behind.

'Keep up, Susie,' proposed her mum: Elizabeth.

'Mmm…' muttered Susie, switching herself off from proceedings.

'Morning!' shouted the postman from the other side of the road. 'How are you all?'

'Fine thanks, Reg,' replied Matthew.

The commandant exited the village shop carrying half a dozen parcels and promptly bumped into Elizabeth Lowther. A couple of parcels fell to the ground and Matthew rushed to catch one in his arms before it hit the pavement.

'Hey, steady on,' proposed Matthew. 'Not so fast.'

'I was not my fault,' delivered the commandant. 'The woman should have been watching where she was going.'

Matthew stood upright and challenged the commandant saying, 'Is that a fact? I disagree. You are carrying so many parcels that it is you who can't see where you are going.'

The commandant swung towards Matthew in a manner suggesting that he was about to throw down a gauntlet. Then the olive skinned adult took in the vision of a man of the cloth and his family and softened his attitude. 'Yes, yes of course. I think you are right. I am sorry.'

'No problem,' returned Matthew. 'I say, your English is good for a …. Syrian?'

The man smiled nervously and replied, 'Syrian, yes, Syrian it is.'

'Where did you learn to speak our language?' asked Elizabeth.

'Syria!' replied the commandant. 'Yes, I learnt to speak English in Syria.'

'How unusual,' commented Matthew unaware that his daughter, Susie, had slid out of sight behind her mother's back. 'But that would explain why we haven't met before. Have you just moved to the area?'

Reluctant to answer, the commandant tried to shuffle past the family but Matthew persisted saying, 'It's just that I'm the local vicar in these parts should you ever need my help or assistance. I expect you might still have some occasional problems with the local culture seeing as you come from Syria.'

'Yes, yes, of course. A vicar, of course,' stuttered the commandant opening the rear door to his Land Rover.

'Here let me help you with your boxes,' offered Matthew placing his Bible on the back seat.

Together they managed to load the rear of the Land Rover with the man's packages and then Matthew stuck out his hand and said, 'Lowther! The Reverend Matthew Lowther! I'm pleased to meet you, Mister…'

'Azzam! My name is Azzam,' revealed the commandant. 'I am sorry to have bumped into your woman.'

Taken aback slightly, Matthew declared, 'This is Elizabeth and she is my wife actually, Azzam. She is not my woman.'

Flustered and perhaps caught off balance, Azzam offered, 'Of course, your wife. Forgive me, Vicar Lowther, I am making a mess of things. Your wife!'

Azzam turned to acknowledge Elizabeth and suddenly beamed an incredible smile. 'I am very pleased to make your acquaintance, Elizabeth,' he said. 'And you too, Vicar Lowther.'

'The Reverend Lowther!' corrected Matthew

'And I'm pleased to meet you too,' revealed Elizabeth. 'This is my daughter, Susie…' Elizabeth swivelled round but could not find Susie who had merely moved behind her father's back.

'Susie!' snapped Matthew. 'Stop playing games and grow up.'

Hesitant, Susie stepped to one side and glanced at Azzam who pretended not to recognise her.

Deep inside, Susie breathed a sigh of relief. The last thing she wanted was to be admonished by her parents for snooping on the commandant's property. And the boys? No, please don't mention the boys, she thought.

'Delighted to meet you all,' disclosed Azzam consciously aware of his previous meeting with Susie. 'Now if you will excuse me I must get back as soon as possible.'

'Get back?' probed Matthew with a smile. 'You're not going back to Syria today are you, Azzam?'

'No, I am not. I am going home,' replied Azzam.

'Where do you live?' queried Matthew.

Catching sight of Susie for a brief moment, Azzam admitted, 'I run an adventure Retreat for young people. It is the other side of Hesket Newmarket.'

'Do you indeed, splendid!' remarked Matthew. 'I know exactly where you mean. It's near the old mine shafts which were closed over a decade ago. Well, that's really wonderful news. Azzam. I'm so pleased. It puts you firmly in my parish. I'll look forward to welcoming you to church unless, of course, you are not of our faith.'

Pulling open his car door, Azzam replied, 'I follow the way of Islam, Vicar Lowther. I shall not be at your church.'

'You must be Muslim?' probed Matthew politely.

Seating himself in the driver's seat, Azzam fired the engine and replied, 'That is right, vicar. I do not worship your God.'

'Then I shall look forward to discussing how Islam and Christianity might survive together in a better world, Azzam,' declared Matthew.

Astonished at the remark, Azzam pulled the door closed, revved the engine, and said, 'I do not have time to talk about such things.'

Matthew persisted with, 'That is a great pity, Azzam, because I believe it is the wish of the Lord that the world will one day come together in harmony. I know that Muhammad was a prophet, Azzam, but did you know that Jesus of Nazareth was the Son of God. We refer to him as Jesus Christ and I do know that your faith regards Jesus as a very important Prophet in the scheme of things. There is so much commonality in our two faiths, Azzam. We must discuss them properly sometime.'

'Nazareth!' barked Azzam depressing the clutch. 'It is the Arab capital of Israel. It is Muslim now.'

'Yes, but…' attempted Matthew.

Scowling dispassionately, Azzam selected a gear, and drove off without another word. At the summit of the hill, he spun the vehicle round with surprising skill and drove past Matthew and his family with a reluctant smile and a carefree wave.

'Well, I never,' announced Elizabeth. 'That just shows you, Matthew. You ought to preach only from the pulpit and not when you bump into someone in the street.'

'Yes, I was rather pushy, Elizabeth. I'll remember next time. It's just that we rarely see many of his ethnic group here.'

'A Syrian!' expressed Elizabeth. 'I know we've got Polish and Chinese people but a Syrian. Well, I never.'

'He's no Syrian,' delivered Matthew. 'An Arab, yes, but not of Syria. Not if my army days are anything to go by.'

'But he's rather handsome in a bizarre kind of way,' remarked Elizabeth. 'Tall! Nice suntan and an extremely polite gentleman considering he's not from around here.'

'That sounds almost racist,' suggested Susie. 'And he's certainly not polite. He's evil.'

'Susie!' scolded Matthew. 'That's a fine thing to say. You did your best to keep out of the conversation from the very start. You're not a child anymore, Susie. You must learn to interact with other people, particularly strangers.'

'Strangers! Oh he's strange alright,' delivered Susie.

'What do you mean by that?' queried Matthew

'Oh nothing, nothing at all, Dad,' snivelled Susie.

'Tell me!' instructed Matthew. 'Why do you call this man strange when you have only just met him?'

Susie did not reply and looked away.

'See what we mean,' explained Elizabeth. 'Your father is trying to discuss something with you as if you were an adult, not a silly little teenager who is sometimes an embarrassment to her family.'

'Promise you won't be angry, Dad,' demanded Susie. 'Promise!'

Sighing deeply, Matthew agreed, 'We promise, don't we, Elizabeth?'

'Of course, now what's all this about, Susie?' queried Elizabeth.

Head down, a little truculent to begin with, Susie explained, 'Well, I am nearly seventeen and I deserve to be heard. I am getting quite old now.'

'Yes, yes, yes,' fussed Elizabeth.

'It was when I was riding. I sneaked into the Base by the back entrance and he caught me.'

'Who, the Syrian chap?' asked Elizabeth.

'Yes,' Susie replied. 'He pushed me around and then I fell on the ground. He told me never to go there again. The man is horrible.'

'Azzam pushed you to the ground?' queried Matthew.

'Yes, he's a horrible man, Dad.'

'Why did you go there?' asked Matthew.

Susie looked away and gradually admitted, 'I fancied having a go paintballing.'

'Really?' queried Matthew disbelieving. 'Funny, you've never mentioned paintballing before. I don't believe you, Susie. Now would you please tell me the truth?'

'Well, I really wanted to get some young people - teenagers - to go the dance.'

'And did you find any youngsters at the Base?' enquired Elizabeth, intrigued.

'No! That man just told me I was trespassing and pushed me away.'

'Actually, Susie,' explained Matthew, 'He was quite entitled to tell you off. You were trespassing and he is within his rights to look after his property. You really should know better and cannot behave like a little girl and then expect to be dealt with as an adult.'

Susie bowed her head and studied her feet for a moment.

'That may be the case,' snapped Elizabeth. 'But by the same token the Arab chap is not entitled to push our daughter around. Who does he think he is bullying people like that?'

'As an Arab and a Muslim, Elizabeth, he has been brought up in a culture where women are considered differently to how we respect women here in England. Muslims have a habit of dressing their females from head to toe in the Burka – or niqab – because the woman feels safer if she is covered up. She may be in fear for herself or others because of her beauty. Yet bizarrely Muslims have a reputation of treating their women like cattle. They seem to have very little respect for women and I suspect Azzam dealt with Susie in the way he has been brought up to treat a woman. He probably didn't give the matter the slightest thought.'

'Oh, that's okay if it's a cultural thing then,' retaliated Susie. 'You defend the Arab man but don't stand up for me, Dad. I'm only your daughter. Oh yes, he was all smiles when he wanted to be when he was talking to you two just then but he was nasty to me at the Base.'

Elizabeth and Matthew exchanged worried glances before Matthew carefully reassessed the circumstances and declared, 'Well, if you agree to behave like an adult in future, Susie, I'll arrange to go and see Azzam and give him a piece of my mind.

'Cool! That's a deal, Dad,' smiled Susie.

At Thames House, overlooking the river, Antonia Harston-Browne and Anthea Adams were behind a door marked 'Special Crime Unit'. Upon the table, scattered into neat piles, lay bundles of documents.

Pointing at the various packages, Antonia revealed, 'Rather you than me, Anthea, but this is what your Mister Boyd wanted. Right, here we have Ryan's Ministry of Defence Profile. It covers his appointment to the Treasury and the various committees and sub groups that he's been involved with over the years.'

Moving her hand to another pile, Antonia said, 'And these are details of phone calls he's made from both his mobile and his landline during the last twelve months. You'll also see we've obtained details from his home telephone as well and, in this file,' Antonia indicated a buff folder, 'You'll find a photograph of him as well as images of his house, car and family.'

'All I have to do is find out what he's up to then,' sighed Anthea. 'Come on, Antonia. You're the expert. What do you think?'

Tapping her fingers on the table, Antonia then pursed her lips and revealed, 'I think I've taken a cursory glance at this and can't find anything out of place. Or to be more precise, Anthea, I can't find anything that would lead me to think Ryan cannot be trusted.'

'That's not what I wanted to hear,' offered Anthea.

Antonia continued, 'Between you and me, Anthea, I sometimes wonder if Chief Inspector Boyd sees skeletons in his cupboard when there are no skeletons to find.'

Leafing through a file in her hands, Anthea mused, 'Boyd is a rather unique individual as you know, Antonia. In fact, you probably know him better than I but I work with him day in day out and see a different side to him than others. It's hard to explain but when we were on the motorway the other day, rather than stop and deal with the immediate aftermath of an accident, he instructed the team to hit the target car and ignore the accident.'

'Was that wrong?' probed Antonia.

'Many would have stopped to help at the scene,' explained Anthea. 'But Boyd just told us to hit the car. I think he had a hunch. He's like that. But by hitting them at that precise time he affected their arrest and prevented them from hitting back at us or escaping.'

'I thought they were shooting at you.'

'One of them was. That's my point, Antonia, if we'd given them time they might have realised we were following them and caused us much more serious problems. Boyd just gets so focused at times. Everything goes out the window and he can only see the target and not the bodies strewn across the motorway.'

Intrigued, Antonia offered, 'Well, I wish you luck. Part of me thinks he might have personalised this enquiry because he just doesn't want Ryan looking over his shoulder. He's like that too. Our Mister Boyd likes thing done his way or not at all and he doesn't suffer fools gladly. By the way, the file you are holding contains details of your team and their phone calls as well as financial transactions. It's the first step in looking for a leak.'

Shaking her head sadly, Anthea asked, 'Why me? Why did I get this to do here?'

'You mean you haven't worked that out, Anthea,' remarked Antonia. 'He's selected you as his next inspector, that's why.'

'What?' Anthea was astonished.

Antonia explained, 'There's the commander who is due to retire. He should have a superintendent in the Unit but he won't appoint one because – as he puts it – he hasn't found the right one yet. Commander Herbert really means that he can't find a superintendent who is not only qualified but is able to move to London lock, stock and barrel and display total commitment to the job in hand. Then there's Boyd who should have four inspectors running four sections. Your section doesn't have an inspector that's why Boyd is always with you guys whenever he can be. Each section has a sergeant and ten constables. Total police strength, not including civilian support, is forty nine of Britain's best. It should be fifty one. You're running a superintendent and an inspector short, Anthea.'

'So where do I fit?' enquired Anthea.

Erudite, Antonia replied, 'Put it this way, the commander retires and someone moves sideways in the Yard to fill his position. Boyd is promoted to superintendent and you get Boyd's job. That's why he wants you to crack this to add to your credentials. It's a no brainer. Think about it!'

Studying a computer screen, Anthea commented, 'I'll try not to otherwise I'll never wade through all this lot. Thanks for banging it onto the computer by the way.'

'No problem,' replied Antonia. 'The folder in your hand is all related to Special Crime Unit officers. You've got the whole world in your hands, Anthea. The only people privy to that information is the commander, Boyd and I. That's how much he believes in you and trusts you.'

Sitting down at the desk, Anthea declared, 'Oh boy! What have I let myself in for?'

A computer powered into life, a mouse moved and a keyboard was engaged as Anthea began a preliminary investigation into the department's leak and an intruder named Ryan.

Moments later, shortbread and a percolator of coffee appeared along with the makings. Antonia sympathetically offered, 'You're in for a long spell. This might help.'

Without taking her eyes from the screen, Anthea replied, 'Thanks, Antonia. I have a feeling I'm going over old ground that's been raked over before. It's going to be a long night. By the way, who's manning the intelligence newsreel in your absence?'

'You!' revealed Antonia.

'Me? What do I do?' queried Anthea.

'Don't worry,' smiled Antonia. 'My deputy looks after it when I'm not here but I've arranged to link anything relevant to our enquiry straight through to your computer.'

'You're so kind,' responded Anthea with a smile.

'I know,' laughed Antonia. 'Oh, by the way, Boyd gave me a note to give to you.'

Taking a slip of paper, Anthea unfolded it and responded, 'Typical! He wants a timeline of movements on Ryan.'

'What exactly is a timeline movement?' enquired Antonia.

'Basically,' explained Anthea, 'It's a chronological analysis of every action an individual undertakes in a twenty four hour period. Day in and day out, it will reveal Ryan's habitual movements and what he does every hour.'

'Good God!' remarked Antonia. 'Lucky you!'

Anthea placed Boyd's note on the pile of papers and engaged the computer screen.

There was the whispered clunk of a door catch when Antonia left Anthea to her own devices.

In Bexleyheath, Boyd and Jim Young swung into a row of detached bungalows and swung the car round in someone's driveway. Coasting to a standstill by the kerb, Boyd flicked the gearstick into neutral and offered, 'That was some drive, Jim. Do you think we're too late?'

Checking his wristwatch, Jim suggested, 'If our little Billy Bunter is correct the meet should be going down in seven minutes.'

'And we've got four cars containing eight men.'

'Where's Anthea?' asked Jim.

'Busy putting a crown court file together,' remarked Boyd engaging the radio. 'All units, seven minutes to show time. Be advised, no surveillance. If there is a meet and the two vehicles show up, we'll take them down. Remember, watch your backgrounds, arcs of fire, range to target and only shoot when life is endangered. I have control.... Stand by.'

'Pity we can't take the Frenchman back to Dover and onwards,' suggested Jim.

'Not enough staff, Jim,' declared Boyd. 'A man carrying a gun and a painting worth one and a half million pounds usually checks his mirror and takes you round the houses first. No, if we had a full team and a day to plan it professionally I'd agree with you. As it is we're too stretched. These bloody counter terrorist enquires are....'

'Echo One to Boss car we have a white van moving onto the plot.'

The radio call interrupted Boyd who acknowledged the signal and then said to Jim, 'What's your vision like, Jim?'

Jim Young moved his head slightly to the left and replied, 'Perfect! I see the van. In fact... Wait one... Yeah, we have a blue Mercedes scouring the area probably checking the patch out.'

Boyd relayed the message on his radio and then hit the digits on his mobile phone. Moments later, he spoke to the control room and said, 'Trigger situation Bexleyheath confirmed. Clear unarmed uniforms from the area. Code Red!'

'I sure hope we've no loose community officers in the area, Guvnor,' suggested Jim.

'Community officers? You mean we've still got them?'

The radio whistled and reported, 'Echo One to Boss car we have the blue Mercedes parking next to the van. The drivers have acknowledged each other.... Wait one... The Mercedes driver is going to the boot of the car..... Wait one..... The van driver is with him.... Wait one....'

'We'll take closer order, Jim,' replied Boyd firing the engine. 'And steal a hundred yards.'

'Echo One.... The van driver is nodding his head.... They're at the back of the van.... The van door is open....'

Inside Echo One, a photographer was hard at work snapping the pictures.

'Echo One.... I have a transfer of packages.'

'Can you call it?' instructed Boyd. 'Echo One you have control. You have ground control, over!'

Just a short sentence or two, thought Boyd, but he'd just put the final decision regarding a million and a half pound heist into the hands of a lower rank detective with eleven years' service, and he knew it. He was asking Echo One if there was enough evidence to justify an arrest. Did Echo One believe the painting and cash were being exchanged? Could Echo One lead or would he always remain a follower? But that's why he was there. Tomorrow that man might be out on his own in the sticks down at Newquay calling the shots on a boat load of illegal immigrants or illegal drugs coming into the country. That's why Echo One had been selected; why he'd made the grade, and why he was in the Unit: To make a decision, to be the best of the best.

'Echo One I have control….. Transfer complete… Stand by…. Echo One I have control…. Strike… Strike… Strike…'

Boyd was already in low gear when he hit the accelerator and thrust the BMW into the main road. Swinging the vehicle into the traffic flow, Jim had no option but to cling to a roof strap when Boyd urged the car towards the car park.

'Shots fired… Shots fired…. I am engaging…'

The call sign was indistinguishable but the message clear enough. Echo One was in trouble.

Jim Young and Boyd joined the team and lurched onto the car park to see a bald headed van driver trying to hide beneath his van whilst a curly-haired Mercedes driver was aiming his handgun at everything that moved.

Boyd and Jim Young rolled from their car and hunched low with weapons drawn.

More shots followed and a middle-aged curly haired man in a French accent shouted, 'Get back….. Get back.'

'Jack!' screamed Boyd, singling out the Echo One detective. 'Jack are you okay?'

'Absolutely splendid, Guvnor,' came the reply. 'Jack has never been better and I do believe we may have the right man.'

Just what I need, thought Boyd, Jack Marshall: a comedian under pressure.

'Glad to hear it, Jack,' returned Boyd.

'And thanks for the call, Guvnor,' quipped Jack. 'Nice to be trusted by the boss but you can have control back. That's quite enough for one day!'

A bald headed man trying to bury himself further beneath the van was heard to shout, 'Drop it, Francis. It's over.'

Jim Young took a bead on the bald man and pleaded, 'Hands! Show me your hands!'

When two empty hands were thrust out from beneath the van, Jim cried, 'Now keep them there and don't move. Hear me?'

There was no reply.

'Hear me?' screamed Jim.

'Yes! Yes!' yelled the bald suspect.

Meanwhile, the Frenchman, Francis, decided to take his chances. He made his way to the Mercedes driver's door.

'Don't do it,' begged Jack. 'Please don't do it.'

Aiming deliberately at the detective speaking, the Frenchman stooped low, used the car door as a shield, and began to enter the vehicle.

Jack Marshall had a premonition and saw the Frenchman's finger curl around the trigger. As Francis fired a shot, Jack returned fire and rolled over seeking cover.

Two shots rang out when Boyd blew out the front nearside tyre before plugging two more bullets into the neighbouring offside tyre.

'Give yourself up,' advised Boyd. 'Throw down your weapon. It's not worth it! You're going nowhere.'

Two bullets fired in quick succession flew towards Boyd and missed him by inches. The first bullet took out a headlight and the second embedded itself in the radiator.'

The response was instantaneous when Jim Young, Boyd, and Jack Marshall returned fire hitting the target in the chest as well as the lower body mass.

A handgun fell with a clatter onto the tarmac and then a car door opened wide. The Frenchmen slid from the driver's area onto the ground in untimely tragedy.

'Target down,' yelled Jack. 'Target down!'

'Stay!' yelled Jim Young towards the man beneath the van. 'Stay!'

Weapon drawn long before him, Boyd moved towards the Mercedes shouting, 'I'm clearing…. I'm clearing….'

Not convinced of the man's immobility, Boyd stepped gingerly across the tarmac until he was directly above the Frenchman's body. With his foot, he kicked a gun away from the body and shouted, 'Clear! The target is clear!'

Bending down, Boyd felt the Frenchman's carotid artery and declared, 'He's still alive.'

Holstering his weapon, Boyd hit the mobile digits and relayed, 'Ambulance required at The Bent Daffodil car park, Bexleyheath! There's been a shooting and the suspect has been shot by armed police. Request senior supervision and uniform assistance. The area is clear and safe.'

When Boyd had finished on the phone, Jack Marshall lifted the Mercedes boot and announced, 'The Bellagoni, Guvnor! It's here. It's coiled up in a cylinder but it's the Bellagoni alright.'

Nodding as he pocketed his phone, Boyd directed his attention to Jim Young who was dragging the second suspect from beneath the van.

The bald headed suspect was a bag of nerves. He was shaking with fear.

'Go on,' suggested Boyd. 'Make my day. Tell me you've got a case full of money in the back of your van.'

Nodding profusely, the suspect revealed, 'Yeah, but I didn't know about the gun. I didn't know about the gun, Guvnor. Look, I'll do a deal with you on the Bellagoni but don't stitch me to the gun. I didn't know about the gun so I can't be an accessory can I?'

That sentence was enough to convince Boyd and his team that this wasn't the end of the Bellagoni affair. It was the start. Furthermore, the prisoner knew the way of the world. It wasn't his first time in police hands.

'Did you steal the painting?' enquired Boyd.

'No! I'm just the courier and so is he,' said the suspect pointing to the Frenchmen. 'He's just a money man. That's what he does. He carries money for the main man. You gonna do a deal with me, Guvnor? You're the boss man aren't you?'

'We'll see,' replied Boyd. 'We'll see.'

A liveried police van charged down the road followed by an ambulance with its lights flashing and its horn blaring.

Close to Caldbeck, Matthew angrily careered his Land Rover round another tight bend. Whilst both hands were on the steering wheel his mind rehearsed the conversation he predicted in the next few minutes. His level of resentment increased as he positioned himself to challenge Azzam.

Just because my daughter was in the wrong place at the wrong time doesn't give Azzam the right to push her around, he thought. No, he needs dealt with firmly and told about the error of his ways, considered Matthew. Yes, I'll tell him. Politely, of course, but I'll let him know in no uncertain terms that he can't push my family around and get away with it. He's not in Syria now or wherever it is he comes from. Culture or not, he's in England now. Indeed, if he gets stroppy at all, I'll punch him on the nose if need be. I can still do it. I'll show him.

Fingering the white collar band of his office, Matthew wished for a brief moment that he'd never left the army and had taken up boxing. Then he remembered his calling and decided that he needed to cool down. He snatched a lower gear and hurtled the Land Rover haphazardly round a bend narrowly missing an oncoming tractor.

There was a scattering of gravel when Matthew indignantly swung the vehicle into The Base and yanked on the handbrake at what appeared to be the main office.

'Azzam!' shouted Matthew. 'Azzam! Where are you?'

A rusted door hinge heralded the appearance of the commandant who appeared on the decking in front of one of the buildings.

'Ah! Vicar Lowther, what do you want?' challenged Azzam.

'Just a word, Azzam,' replied Matthew alighting from his Land Rover. 'I won't take up too much of your time.'

Towering above Matthew from his position on the decking, Azzam used his height to enforce a reply saying, 'That's good because I don't have much time. I'm busy.'

Suddenly, Matthew felt somewhat intimidated by the sheer height and size of the man. Suddenly, he felt his self-confidence diminish. Nervously, he began with a falsehood and explained, 'My daughter, Azzam. I came to apologise for her behaviour here. I understand you caught her trespassing. I assure you it will not happen again.'

Nodding, Azzam's bushy beard bobbled on his chest as he stepped from the decking onto the ground and extended his right hand saying, 'That is good, Vicar Lowther. Thank you. We shall shake on that, as you say, and then you may go.'

Declining his hand for a moment, Matthew began to chuckle and then took a step backwards. He laughed. Politely, at first, but Matthew burst into laughter and retorted, 'You can't be serious, Azzam. You have a way with the words that defies comprehension.'

Puzzled, Azzam withdrew the handshake offered and queried, 'I don't understand. I speak good English. What did I say that you do not understand?'

'Oh I understand you perfectly, Azzam. It's just the way you put things together, that's all. You don't seem to understand our way of life; yet in the village you told me you had learnt our language years ago in Syria.'

'Did I?' doubted Azzam. 'Then I apologise, Vicar Lowther.'

Gaining in confidence, Matthew regained tack and delivered, 'My daughter, Azzam, why did you push her to the ground?'

Azzam studied the cleric for a moment and then said, 'You will help me with the way of my words, Vicar Lowther?'

Considering his position for a moment, Matthew replied, 'If that's possible, yes, of course.'

Grooming his facial hair with long slender fingers, Azzam suggested, 'She was snooping. The girl was looking through the bedroom windows. She was looking for boys. It is not a good woman who looks for boys like that, Vicar Lowther.'

'She's not yet a woman, Azzam. She's nothing but a teenager.'

'I don't understand what you mean,' delivered Azzam.

'Susie is young and still learning the ways of life,' explained Matthew. 'She presumed you run a youth hostel of some kind and wondered if she could go paintballing too. That said, in all honesty, she wanted to invite the boys to a dance in the village this weekend. That's all. Susie meant nothing by it.'

Pondering for a moment, Azzam countered, 'Then she won't be back?'

'No, she won't be back,' promised Matthew.

'Good!' declared Azzam. 'That pleases me.'

'Tell me, Azzam,' insisted Matthew, more relaxed. 'What is this place now? If you don't mind me saying it looks a little dilapidated in comparison with what it once was. This place used to house the offices of a local mining company until they closed. Then it became a youth hostel.'

'It still is,' responded Azzam grooming his long beard. 'Of a kind! It is a Base for young people who come to enjoy the outdoor life and do some paintballing. We take young people in their late teens and early twenties who work in your bigger cities and are sent here to learn about teamwork.'

Listening carefully, Matthew swept a hand across his bald patch and probed, 'You said 'your bigger cities' not our bigger cities, Azzam. I can see you are not British but is this country not your home now?'

There was silence for a moment before Azzam replied, 'A slip of the tongue from a man answering too many questions from one who has no business to ask them.'

Matthew Lowther considered Azzam's response and replied, 'Now it is I that should perhaps apologise. Look, I can help you with the way you form your sentences if you can help me?'

'How would that work?' puzzled Azzam.

'Perhaps the youth of our village might come and paint your wooden buildings for you and spruce the place up.'

'No!' snapped Azzam emphatically. 'We are always busy. I will do that myself when time permits.'

'Busy?' questioned Matthew. 'I do not see any customers today, Azzam. Perhaps you only provide the facility for the followers of Islam. Am I right?'

The commandant leaned against the side of the Land Rover and said, 'And if I did, what is that to you, Vicar Lowther?'

'Interesting,' countered Matthew. 'Perhaps I could visit and speak of my God?'

'You sound like a missionary,' challenged Azzam. 'No, that would not be allowed. We have discussed this before. I am not interested in your Jesus Christ from Nazareth.'

'Pity,' replied Matthew. 'I came in peace as did our Lord but now it is time for me to go.'

Matthew opened the driver's door and climbed into the Land Rover. Catching sight of his reflection in the mirror he cursed himself under his breath for not speaking his mind as planned.

Realising, he needed to control the vicar and his errant daughter without causing problems, Azzam softened and enquired, 'And your daughter?'

Firing the engine, Matthew countered, 'Look, I cannot control the youth in the village, Azzam. I'm their vicar not a prison warden. They will do as they wish when they wish. I cannot stop them from snooping about if that's what you mean.'

Concerned, Azzam reluctantly suggested, 'I need to prevent your local children from sneaking into the Base when it is closed, Vicar Lowther. I am responsible for the belongings of my clients when they are not in the site, you understand. Yet I want to be their friend so that they know when to come and when not to come. Perhaps the youth of your village might want to play paintball on Sunday mornings when I can arrange my customers to be out walking on your mountains?'

'Sunday is the day of the Lord, Azzam. That wouldn't be possible, I'm afraid.'

'Well, perhaps, another day?' suggested Azzam.

'Yes, perhaps another day,' agreed Matthew.

'Good,' smiled Azzam. 'I shall arrange it. Where can I find you?'

'Most days I'm at my church, Azzam,' disclosed Matthew.

'I will arrange tickets and a piece of paper for a list of names so that I know who they are and where they live.'

'Yes, yes, of course,' replied Matthew. 'I shall look forward to hearing from you. You will come to my church even though you are not of my faith, Azzam?'

'For the list, yes,' responded Azzam.

'I see,' replied Matthew.

Apparently satisfied, Azzam nodded, smiled and offered a handshake.

Accepting Azzam's hand, Matthew shook it and pledged, 'May the Lord be with you, Azzam.' Then he drove off with his Land Rover tyres scuttling across the ground trying to find good purchase on an uneven terrain.

When the Land Rover disappeared from view, Azzam looked towards the mine shaft and simultaneously withdrew a mobile phone from his coveralls.

'Allahu Akbar, Vicar Lowther,' proposed Azzam quietly. 'Allahu Akbar! I know my language. It means my God is greater than yours!'

A voice spoke from the handset and Azzam quickly turned his attention to the call.

Suspicious! Yes, I am suspicious, thought Matthew as he drove away. I ought to be sceptical about this man, he decided. Why does he want a list of names and addresses of children in the village and surrounding area? What a bizarre man this chap has turned out to be! Matthew took another gear change and thought about the Arab he doubted was a Syrian. Here he is in the middle of nowhere running a paintballing site for young people! Yet he has no time for my religion, thought Matthew. He has no respect, no understanding of the Lord and his great works.

Come to think of it, he's right though, considered Matthew as he drove along the narrow roadway. Susie was trespassing and Azzam does have a right to protect his property. For goodness sake some of the local farmers are forever complaining about Fell walkers eroding the land and leaving farm gates open and the like. Why shouldn't Azzam decide to protect his own property from the youth of the village, proposed Matthew? Maybe, it's me that's bizarre and not him. Yes, perhaps I'm all Christian and don't have an understanding of how other Faiths deal with things. Oh dear! What shall I do?

Mind you, reflected Matthew, what nationality is he? Not Syrian, that's for sure. I think he might be Iranian or Iraqi but I cannot decide which. Dashed if I know! I wish I'd paid more attention to hair and skin colour in the army. Maybe he's a Jordanian, maybe not. I don't know but he's definitely an Arab, that's for sure. Then again, I didn't take to him, reasoned Matthew. Just something about him, he suggested to himself. What do I do now?

Glancing at a white business card wedged between the windscreen and its rubber surround, Matthew reached forward and snatched the card from its hiding place. He read the words.

Of course, that idiot policeman from London, thought Matthew. The mad runner who virtually head-butted my Land Rover! He was a counter terrorist policeman, wasn't he? Didn't he have something to do with catching terrorists? Some special squad, if I recall. Yes, there's a hotline number on his card. Should I?

Don't be stupid, decided Matthew. This man isn't a terrorist. Such people don't come to places like this and then fall out with the locals. It just doesn't happen that way.

Driving on, Matthew slung Boyd's card into the passenger foot well. Now who's bizarre, deliberated Matthew - The idiot Boyd who runs down Fells into my Land Rover - Or the idiot Azzam who offered to accommodate the village youngsters with free time at the paintball site? Yet here I am try to convince myself Azzam is a terrorist. Why? Yep, that's just what a terrorist would do, isn't it, thought Matthew. He'd run a camp for terrorists and invite the village youngsters to come and visit and get involved. Do me a favour? Get a grip, decided Matthew. Azzam is just short of a better understanding of our way of life, that's all. And me for that matter!

Climbing a slight hill, Matthew grabbed the gearstick, crashed through the gearbox into a lower cog, and shook his head, worried.

Azzam, thought Matthew. Was he currying favour in the hope of controlling access to the site? Or was he just trying to be friendly in his own kind of way?

Maybe! Maybe not, decided Matthew. He looked again at a discarded business card in the foot well and for the first time in many a year swore aloud.

'Forgive me, Lord,' spoke Matthew to the wind. 'I know not what to do.'

There was another awkward crunch in a gearbox when the man of God reached the summit of the hill and began his descent into the valley below.

In Commander James Herbert's office in New Scotland Yard, Boyd was listening and the commander was talking.

'Take a break, William. That's an order. You look tired and a tad jaded and I'm not surprised. You've dealt with two firearms incidents this week and I need you fresh and full of energy. Shooting criminals is not necessarily a regular occurrence and I want your mind clear, fresh and fully focused. You're no good to me when you're stressed out and ready for a break.'

Commander Herbert signed a couple of documents as he spoke and continued, 'You've done well but you need to rest. The French man has been identified as Francis Duval, by the way. He's a well-known Parisian crook and he specialises in being a bagman. He carries cash for Organised Crime so there's little doubt he was paying the van driver off on behalf of his masters when you upset the apple cart.'

'Have you heard how he is?' queried Boyd.

'He'll live, William. Now take a break and get some rest.' The ink flowed from the commander's pen and more paper flew from an in basket to an out basket.

'I've done all my paperwork for the incident, sir. I'm not stressed out at all,' countered Boyd.

'Take a break, William,' insisted Commander Herbert.

'I'm fine, sir.'

'That's an order,' twisted Commander Herbert reluctantly. The beginning of a scowl grew on the commander's face when he asked, 'Do you hear me, William?'

Boyd replied, 'Sir, I wonder if I could have a few days off to take a short break and recharge the batteries?'

'Of course! Granted, William,' declared Commander Herbert. 'You only have to ask but have you considered how busy you are at the moment?'

There was a brief silence and then Commander Herbert grinned before Boyd chuckled and replied, 'I hear you, commander. I'll make north as soon as possible. It will be great to get home and check on Meg properly. It's the downside of this job being so far from home.'

Nodding sensitively, Commander Herbert ordered, 'Away with you, William. Safe journey! I'll take over the Bellagoni enquiry and speak to Arts and Antiques. Your man is singing like a bird and they're as happy as Larry. The t's need crossed and the i's need dotted and then it's job done!'

'Thank you, sir,' offered Boyd. 'That's kind of you.'

'What's more the art gallery from which the Bellagoni was stolen is over the moon at its recovery. But before you go, and just to update you on matters in the north, Cumbria Police have charged the driver of the Volvo with attempting to murder you and Anthea, illegal possession of a firearm, and financing terrorism. I'd like you to cover all the bases at the remand hearing and liaise with our barrister, Sir Joseph Higgins, who will be handling the case when it hits Crown Court. Deliver our outstanding statements to him and visit Meg at the same time. I think they call it killing two birds with one stone, William. It might take you a few days!'

'Of course, sir,' agreed Boyd. On reaching the door, Boyd turned and said, 'Thanks, commander.'

Commander Herbert merely nodded. Charming as ever, he waved Boyd away with one hand whilst scribbling on his paperwork with the other.

'Come back refreshed, William,' pleaded the commander. 'And don't forget to give my love to your wonderful Meg as well as Bill and Beth.'

'Bill and Beth?' queried Boyd.

'The twins,' beamed the commander. 'They'll need nom de plumes until you decide what to call them.'

There was just a grin from Boyd but the commander continued, 'And you will wish to know that I have tendered papers relevant to my retirement, William. I do hope you and Meg will be able to attend my private function. I'll be sending out invitations soon. Until then the subject of my retirement will not be discussed. We are too busy to gossip about such irrelevancies.'

'But…' probed Boyd.

'Aren't we?' suggested Commander Herbert.

Boyd was half way through the door and on the way home as the Commander's pen raced across his legal documents.

'William,' shouted Commander Herbert.

Frozen in his tracks, Boyd reappeared in the office with, 'Commander?'

Still writing, head down, Commander Herbert instructed, 'Thames House, William! Whatever it is that you have Anthea doing over there make sure she's back soonest. As much as I love our colleagues in MI5 I have no intention of losing her.'

'Of course, sir,' replied Boyd.

Scuttling from the office without chancing any further conversation, Boyd wondered how on earth the commander seemed to know about everything that was going on, and what on earth they were ever going to do without the boss of all bosses.

Chapter Nine
~

The Caldbeck Fells.

Sir Joseph Higgins proved to be from a Manchester stable of learned barristers who appreciated a face to face case conference with one Detective Chief Inspector Boyd. Statements and additional evidence duly delivered, coffee taken, pleasantries exchanged, Boyd was at a loss for the day. Meg, not realising her husband had travelled north to surprise her, took a return coach trip to a health spa near Hexham for a few hours with a couple of girlfriends. A bit of harmless self- pampering would do her good, she had decided.

Typical, thought Boyd. Our communication skills are non-existent.

Parking his BMW off the road, Boyd adjusted his black bandanna, tightened his bum bag, and set off jogging along the track taking him high into the remote Fells of Cumbria. Wearing a strong pair of running shoes, Boyd also sported tracksuit bottoms and a Helly Hansen top.

Sunshine forced its way through the clouds and before long Boyd felt the rays prickling his skin. Furthermore, he became parched. Without stopping, he removed a glucose tablet from his waist bag and popped it into his mouth. There was an explosion of flavour and taste that abruptly dissipated his thirst. Climbing higher, he appreciated the phenomenon of freedom on the Fells and felt truly independent. He couldn't even see a mountain sheep in the area or a wild hare to startle.

But the wild Fells of North Cumbria could be a strange and unwelcoming place at times. To Boyd's left, the rays of the sun broke through the thin white clouds like spears penetrating the ground from above. To his right, dark heavy clouds moved in to challenge the splendour of a gorgeous day.

Unperturbed, Boyd shortened his stride, adjusted his technique, and ran higher and faster for over fifteen minutes. He knew then that he could crack twenty six miles in the weeks ahead. Boyd was alone in his mind, isolated with his body, and at one with the inner peace that only a long distance runner could ever explain.

The London Marathon, reflected Boyd. I wonder if I can run it in under three hours. Of course I can.

Checking his wristwatch, Boyd dug in deep and ploughed on when the terrain suddenly softened and remnants of a recent downpour made the ground muddy. Within a couple of minutes, Boyd found himself enveloped in mist and up to his ankles in mud.

A dark cloud overlooked the lone runner, his black bandanna, and a well-used pouch secured at his waist.

It must be a recent downpour, considered Boyd. Or did I run into a rain shower? It's characteristic of the high Fells, thought Boyd. One minute the weather is good but the next it is intolerable. Whatever, it's always fickle in this part of Cumbria, he decided.

The heavens open and drenched him before the sun broke through again and competed with the rain clouds gradually moving away to claim another victim.

Pulling himself onto a nearby rocky outcrop, Boyd sat, rifled through his bag, and produced a hooded waterproof which he quickly donned. Standing, he took in the valley below and decided it was time to play it safe and choose the lower ground. As the rain beat faster, Boyd traversed the side of the valley and dropped slowly into its belly.

Fifteen minutes later, Boyd found an exceptionally narrow path and headed for the valley floor, a quarry, and huts lying ahead of him. The narrow path proved a tributary to a much broader path wide enough for a vehicle to negotiate. Eventually, Boyd joined this path and trotted towards the quarry and a couple of abandoned outbuildings.

With the rain still incessant upon him, Boyd ran the remaining few hundred yards and found shelter close to one of the huts beneath the mangled remains of a slanted roof which had dislodged from a building during a recent storm.

The quarry buildings had seen much better days and were close to crumbling completely to the ground. Indeed, they were dangerous but the quarry walls seemed quite safe. Moreover, the shape of the quarry reminded him of a very broad horseshoe with the walls gradually encircling him. The walls were robust but did not tower above him. Perhaps they were old slate quarries that had been discontinued long ago. He did not know.

Crawling beneath the roof that lay at forty five degrees to the rest of the building, Boyd welcomed the dryness and a chance to take stock of things and rest his weary limbs. Exhaling in relief, he unzipped his waterproof, took a deep breath, and removed an ordnance survey map from the pouch. Spreading it out as best he could, Boyd charted his journey across the Fells.

Two miniscule squares on the map, lying in a valley bottom ten miles from the village, convinced Boyd of his location. Smiling, he knew precisely where he was. He was in the middle of nowhere. Oh yes, the broad track to the disused quarry could be distinguished on the map amidst the light brown contour lines of the ordnance survey map. Regrettably, there were few other features in the area that he could pick out.

Shielding his head with an arm for a moment, Boyd looked out and scanned the horizon. He studied the contours of the ground and observed an aeroplane flying in a patch of blue sky far away. The plane's wingspan and vapour trail suggested to Boyd that the aircraft flew at about twenty five thousand feet; it was a passenger vessel and it flew north towards Glasgow airport.

Has to be, thought Boyd, there's no other regional airport this side of the Pennines that will take a jet like that.

Benefitting from such knowledge, Boyd checked again his position on the map. If the aeroplane is flying northwards, which it is, then I'm probably here, decided Boyd. No problem, I'll lie up for a while, get my breath back, take in some glucose tablets, and a flagon of water, and then head down the valley floor. About ten miles, I reckon, decided Boyd. But next time, you idiot – he said to himself - pack the compass.

Shaking his head, he folded the map and replaced it in the pouch. That was when he saw the object in the mud.

Dumbstruck and convinced he was hallucinating, thanks to intrepid physical exertion; Boyd did not believe his eyes. Eventually, he crept from beneath his shelter and crawled on his hands and knees in the mud to study his find.

Prizing it lightly from the shallow mud, Boyd held an AK-47 shell case in his hand.

Boyd knew guns. He knew enough about firearms to pull a trigger and deliver a lethal shot if he must. Now he held a spent 7.62 x 39mm cartridge in his hand and wondered how on earth such a weapon had travelled to the middle of nowhere.

Ratching in the area, three more shell cases were found and Boyd secured them in his bum bag before considering his find.

What on earth is such a deadly piece of ammunition doing in the middle of nowhere? More importantly, how did it get here and who used an AK-47 in these parts? Not a farmer, that's for sure. They tend to use shotguns.

What do I know about such a firearm? An AK-47, thought Boyd, is generally accepted to be accurate to a distance of about one hundred yards. This means that if I discharged a cartridge from an AK-47 assault rifle here, at a point where I am now kneeling in the mud, the original target must be within a radius of about one hundred yards from where I am currently located.

Slowly turning his head, Boyd rotated full circle before selecting a low branch that had decayed and fallen to the ground from a substantial tree. It was the closest physical object and fitted the distance well. Walking over to the bough of the tree, ignoring the rain battering his body, Boyd examined the bark and realised what had happened.

This branch is quite huge, he decided. It fell from the tree in a storm no doubt. Someone came along with an AK-47 assault rifle, placed targets on the branch, and then walked back across the quarry floor about a hundred yards before shooting at the targets. Coke cans or bottles, I don't know what the targets were. That said I can sure as hell see where the branch of the tree and its bark have been scathed by those bullets. Obvious really, thought Boyd when he realised the quarry wall was some yards behind the broken branch. He presumed the solid rock bore the scars of the shooting range. Yes, the solid rock is the back stop for the improvised shooting range, determined Boyd.

Retrieving a mobile smart phone from his bum bag, Boyd photographed both the bough of the damaged tree, the shell cases he recovered, and the solid rock of the quarry wall.

Jogging back to shelter from the rain, he warmed his hands by wringing them for a few moments and then rubbed his legs and arms. It was important not to become complacent in bad weather, affirmed Boyd. Speedily, he donned another tee shirt and increased the layers covering his body.

Hitting the digits, Boyd transmitted a text to his office and attached the photographs he had taken. Sitting in the rain, sheltered beneath an old mangled roof, splattered with mud, Boyd waited in the middle of nowhere for a reply.

Entrenched in Thames House, Anthea rubbed her eyes and scored imaginary lines on her face with her fingers. She swung away from her computer screen and closed her eyes tight for a moment. This is pointless, she reasoned. I'm getting nowhere. There's absolutely no evidence we have a leak in our department. Moreover, there's nothing to suggest that this man Ryan is anything other than a hardworking civil servant dedicated to Her Majesty's Government. What's more no evidence to prove any inappropriate relationship with the media had come to light. It looked as if the Press had just been lucky enough to be in the right place at the right time and had taken advantage of the circumstances. Freelancers, she thought. According to her research it wasn't unusual for freelancing independent journalists to chance their luck. A good photograph of an incident on the motorway held a fair price in the modern age. Just another form of paparazzi, thought Anthea, but I must remember to tell Boyd of the result so far.

Anthea stepped away from her work station for a moment. Sauntering over to the window, she spent a short time thinking and watching the murky River Thames meander through the capital. Why do I bother? It's all a waste of time, she considered. God, why am I feeling so low? I must be getting tired.

Reluctantly, she took a deep breath and returned to the computer and a file of papers.

All these documents reflect the phone calls they've made; the duty diaries they've kept, and the expenses they've claimed, deliberated Anthea. Then there's a review of the cases they've presented. Nothing there to suggest something was left undone and no data to reveal any dubious connections with individuals or groups exerting undue pressure on any one individual.

Let me look at the meetings and conferences they've attended, considered Anthea. What about health records? Have any of these people been off sick for a period of time with a questionable illness? Is there any indication that one of them is stressed? If someone is on the take, who did they meet? Who has a hold on one of them and why? Where do they meet? If there's a payoff where does it take place? A financial enquiry and analysis reveals not one of these people has received an undue sum of money that would make anyone particularly suspicious.

Am I wasting my time, she wondered. Or do I look for a false bank account?

Unscrewing a bottle of mineral water, Anthea poured it into a glass tumbler. She took a long drink and returned the glass to the table. Lifting the telephone, Anthea dialled Antonia's extension and said, 'Antonia, I've been thinking outside the box, as they say. I have a proposition for you if you have the time.'

There was a moment's silence as Anthea listened before reporting, 'Antonia, I'm wasting my time. At the moment I've discovered absolutely zilch. Not a sausage! The Special Crime Unit appears to be whiter than white. If not, I'm missing something that might be so obvious I can't see it.'

The raid on the Building Society on the outskirts of Bamber Bridge, Lancashire, was well planned, swift, and violent.

Shell cases flew indiscriminately from the AK-47 assault rifles when marauders parked their getaway cars outside and dashed into the premises. Wearing tight black leather gloves, overalls and balaclava masks, four raiders aimed above their heads and peppered walls and ceilings with deadly fire.

When customers and staff alike cowered beneath office furniture, the leader: a tall man standing over six feet and quite broad according to witnesses, leapt aggressively over the counter and into the heart of the office. There was little doubt he knew how to handle his killing machine as he deliberately fired a warning salvo towards the customers.

Then, grabbing one of the cashiers by the hair, he dragged her into a back office, ignored her screams, and ruthlessly forced her to open a safe.

Whilst the gunmen in the counter area of the building society rifled the till contents, their leader emptied the safe.

More bullets flew; more terror, more mayhem when the armed robbers turned the screws and petrified their victims. There was a shriek of terror, the shock of unadulterated panic, and the pure horror of violent criminality as the plunderers acted out their well-rehearsed performance.

Four black holdalls were produced, unzipped, stuffed with banknotes, zipped tight, and carried to a waiting Porsche motor car.

Yet there was a bizarre brashness about the leader when he paused and aimed his rifle at a line of frightened customers.

'Down!' he ordered and then shot above their heads.

As the bullets slammed into the wall above them, a mass of plaster disintegrated and cascaded onto the floor covering the customers with dust, dirt and grime.

'Further down!' he shouted and promptly lowered his rifle. 'Flat on your bellies!

With the customers squealing in horror, they tried to shrivel into the floor as he raked fire only a matter of inches above their heads.

'Adam!' shouted one of the raiders. 'Leave it, Adam! Are you mad? Come on, let's go.'

Adam's rifle descended to his side and he joined his comrades. Hoisting one of the holdalls onto his shoulder, he responded, 'Target practice!' and let off a final barrage of fire towards the innocent when he burst into laughter and marvelled at his own uncaring disposition.

When the raiders stepped backwards out of the building, threatening everything in their sights, a police patrol car entered the street. The gunmen had no hesitation in turning their attention to the lone patrolling officer and fired off a welcoming salvo

The police woman threw herself from the driver's seat flat across the passenger seat when their attack blew out the car's windscreen and bullets slammed into upholstery behind her. She screamed in fear as a barrage of shells continued through the vehicle and exited the rear of the car via the boot and rear bodywork.

Grabbing the radio, she shrieked, 'Emergency! Bank raid Bamber Bridge....'

Radio operators never received the rest of her message in the hullabaloo that followed. All they heard was an unparalleled bombardment of ammunition exploding on the radio waves as the officer tried her best to survive the attack. Through the airwaves they picked up the screaming, heard the gunshots, and listened to the indistinguishable shouting.

Then there was silence when the wireless died.

On the streets of Bamber Bridge, the interior of a building society had been decimated and the occupants scared witless.

A stolen Porsche and a stolen Lexus roared away with tyres screeching and back ends twitching as they tried to find purchase on the dry tarmac. Within minutes the choice of three motorway routes opened up to the drivers: the M6, M61 and M65.

An eerie silence configured the aftermath.

The police patrol car's windscreen was blown away and lay in a thousand fragments on the tarmac. The car bonnet lay on the road side peppered with bullet holes whilst searing grey steam escaped from a riddled radiator. There was no blue flashing light on the roof of the patrol car. It was gone. Shot to pieces, no longer associated with the wireless aerial drooping hopelessly from the rear of the vehicle's bodywork in a wilted angle of redundancy.

A police car was wrecked but, miraculously, the female officer remained physically unhurt.

Sobbing, distraught, mentally brutalised, the policewoman pushed open the passenger door and stumbled onto the road where she promptly collapsed in catatonic shock.

Inside the Building Society, a man sobbed and a woman began an ear-piercing scream as she clasped a young child closely to her body. More plaster fell from the ceiling and splattered onto the floor. Another cloud of dust rose into the atmosphere and blurred memories forever for the luckless victims of a ferocious crime.

Boyd's mobile phone burst into life and he answered it immediately with, 'About time too! Who's speaking?' There was no deterioration in the rainfall and Boyd glimpsed a view of dark clouds above when he continued, 'Stuart! Good to hear from you. What did you make of my message?'

Listening intently, Boyd replied, 'Yes, AK-47 shell cases! It looks like I've stumbled across some kind of shooting gallery here in the Caldbeck Falls. Look, Stuart, I'm talking on my mobile phone obviously. Get onto the network and ping my phone. It's got GPS

– Global Positioning System – Get the exact location and plot it to an ordnance survey map. That way, we'll know exactly where I am and, more importantly, where this shooting range is. Got that?'

Stepping out into the rain, Boyd shrugged and quickly darted back beneath the shelter. 'What's that? Another bank robbery featuring AK-47's! Where?'

'Bamber Bridge, Guvnor, Lancashire! It's not that far from Southport,' reported Stuart. 'Things are still a bit sketchy because it's just come in over the wire. One thing is definite though; the raiders were armed with AK-47's. I understand it's only the second robbery ever recorded in the UK involving AK-47's.'

'Is that a fact, Stuart,' replied Boyd. 'I'm not surprised. Look, find Commander Herbert for me. Tell him what I've found and tell him I'm suggesting that we think about mounting an observation point and...'

'Excuse me, Guvnor,' interrupted Stuart. 'Did you mention a place called Caldbeck?'

'Yes, why?' asked Boyd.

'You'd better talk to Janice. She's taken a call on the hotline number for you.'

The phone went silent for a moment when Stuart passed the handset to Janice whilst Boyd waited patiently in the cold and rain.

'Guvnor!' queried Janice.

'I'm here,' snapped Boyd into his mouthpiece. 'Make it quick, Janice. I'm freezing and if I don't get off this Fell soon I'll be trapped all night.'

'A Reverend Matthew Lowther rang the hotline wanting to speak to you and only you. Apparently you met recently. I persevered and managed to get him to tell me that he's concerned about an Arab looking gentleman who has settled close to the village in a base for young people. Apparently the subject runs a paintball site in the area and your vicar thinks he's up to no good. Basically, he wants you to ring him and discuss this Arab chap. The Reverend Lowther tells me the Arab purports to be a Syrian but he thinks he's probably Iranian or something like that. All sounds a bit off the wall to me, Guvnor, and so does the vicar actually. He might just need reassuring. Unless, of course, they've moved the Khyber Pass to your neck of the woods?'

'Thanks, Janice,' cracked Boyd. 'What's his number?' Nodding, Boyd memorised the detail and declared, 'I'll call him. Just give me a moment please. Keep the line open for a second.'

Moving out from beneath the shelter, Boyd pocketed his phone for a moment, zipped his top as tight as possible, and then began to stride out away from the site northwards. But Boyd was mulling things over in his mind when he broke into a slow trot and said, 'Ask Commander Herbert to ring me, Janice. I'm going to put a surveillance team on this. There's something not right.'

Jogging slowly, Boyd began a slow descent towards safety as the rain pelted down upon him and he listened to Janice's Glasgow accent jingling in his ear.

Ryan came onto the phone.

'Chief Inspector Boyd,' announced Ryan. 'I'm with Janice listening to you on the speaker. That all sounds quite ridiculous to me if you don't mind me saying so.'

'How do you mean?' ventured Boyd.

'All too convenient,' suggested Ryan. 'You're up there in Cumbria taking a break from the rigours of work here and then it occurs to you that there may be an excuse to stay at home. Your wife is expecting, isn't she? This is the very thing I was sent here to uncover.'

'What on earth are you talking about?' probed Boyd.

Arguing, Ryan offered, 'It's ridiculous, that's all. The local vicar gets paranoid about an Arab in the Lake District then you find the same kind of bullets that were used in a bank robbery a hundred miles away. Put two and two together and there you have it, convenience!'

'Send me a surveillance team and stop messing about, Ryan,' suggested Boyd. 'I can do without the humour. Put Janice back on.'

There was a chuckle from Ryan who contended, 'Actually, Boyd, I wasn't joking. I'll make a note of the event in my diary for my report. The fact remains you are in the middle of nowhere. Anyone could have been shooting out there.'

'Not with an AK-47, Ryan. You can't buy such a weapon legally in this country,' explained Boyd. 'They're fully automatic weapons and they're outlawed under British law. The fact that I've found spent ammunition when there have been two robberies with such rare and prohibited weapons is significant.'

'AK-47's are certainly not rare, Boyd,' remarked Ryan. 'They're the preferred weapon of people living in Iraq and Afghanistan. Everyone has one!'

'But not in the north west of England, you idiot,' argued Boyd. 'Whoever is using these AK-47's assault rifles has some explaining to do. They're in deep trouble, believe me.'

'How's your wife?' probed Ryan.

'Fine!' delivered Boyd. 'Now put Commander Herbert on before I lose my temper with you, Ryan.'

The phone went dead and Boyd found himself running along the track shaking his mobile as if to reboot the conversation. The rain didn't ease off at all but the break did Boyd good and he eased down to a slow jog when he dialled the Reverend Lowther.

Once Matthew answered, Boyd slowed to walking pace, stuck the phone to his ear, and listened attentively. Nodding, agreeing, soothing and smoothing, Boyd pieced together the thoughts and concerns of the Reverend Matthew Lowther. With some reassurance, Boyd promised to check out the owner of the Base but in return he – Boyd – expected to be kept up to date in the coming days of anything untoward concerning Azzam.

Agreeing wholeheartedly, Matthew noted Boyd's mobile number. With pleasant aplomb they ended their call just as the rain stopped and a ray of sunshine penetrated the grey skies above.

Pocketing the phone, Boyd shook his head and increased his speed striding out towards the village and the comparative comfort of his vehicle. He was safe in the knowledge that a couple of AK-47 shell cases nestled closely together in his bum bag. But still his mind played overtime as he tried to fathom how such a weapon ended up in the middle of nowhere.

Boyd's phone rang again. This time it was Commander Herbert who seemed less than pleased at Boyd's recent conversation with Ryan: the man from the Treasury.

Commander Herbert opened up with a broadside. 'Did you have to call him an idiot, William? It's all rather childish if you ask me. I think the pair of you ought to grow up.'

'You're right, sir. I'll offer my apologies when I next see him,' responded Boyd.

'Good! I'm glad to hear you remain a gentleman and conscious of your position. But then, between you and me, William, you're right. Mister Ryan has obviously only recently returned to our shores and has not yet acclimatised to the current state of the western world.'

'He just needs reminding, sir,' suggested Boyd.

Commander Herbert continued. 'I'm up to speed on the hotline call, William. Have you spoken to the vicar yet about the Arab gentleman going by the name Azzam?'

'I have, sir,' confirmed William. 'It's a strange story.'

'Good! I'm glad you spoke to him because I've discussed events with detectives from Lancashire Constabulary. The raid at Bamber Bridge did indeed involve AK-47's and the robbers all wore ski masks. It's the second robbery with AK-47's. Do you remember the first at Southport when a policeman attending the scene turned out be an ex service man? He has revealed that one of the raiders used the term 'Kafir' which means 'disbeliever' in Arabic. But the main thing is people at the scene recall the leader of the gang in Southport was referred to by the others as Adam. I've asked for more information on the Bamber Bridge raid but they do seem remarkably similar.'

'Adam?' queried Boyd. 'Where does that take us?'

'In the heat of the moment, William, did the witness hear the name Adam or Azzam?' posed the commander. 'They are perhaps similar in pronunciation, don't you think?'

Boyd considered the challenge for a moment and suggested, 'Look, sir, I've only met the vicar once. I bumped into him recently - literally - and thought him a little bizarre. His behaviour, in some ways, is a little whacky for me. He is strong then weak; sensible then silly. He's like a straw in the wind. And as for his family! Well, the daughter is a typical horrid teenager that you really wouldn't put your faith in and his wife is a throwback to the Fifties. Forgive me, commander, but maybe you're just stretching things a bit too far. Did the Lancashire witnesses note an Arabic accent?'

'No, not to my knowledge,' replied the commander, 'Other than the word Kafir – hardly enough to make out an accent. But as you mention Arabic, William, I'm sure I don't have to remind you that Al-Qaeda when translated from Arabic means The Base.'

'Now we really are trying to cut the jigsaw pieces to fit the puzzle, commander,' suggested Boyd with a chuckle.

'Yes,' agreed Commander Herbert. 'But add the puzzle of Adam or Azzam to AK-47 shell cases and you've got the only lead worth investigating at the moment. A conundrum of your own making in some ways, William. My problem is that we still have an intelligence lead suggesting there are four Al-Qaeda terrorists in the country. Put simply, the commissioner wants to know if we're on the trail or not. Given that an AK-47 is the preferred weapon of a terrorist assault force I'm inclined to run with the notion that this lead needs hunted down and sorted out. But you're right, William. We need to keep our eye on the squirrel and focus on finding our four terrorists. Anyway, I'm sending you a small dedicated team.'

'Great,' responded Boyd. 'Let's find out one way or another.'

The commander continued, 'A couple of days should give you enough time to decide whether you're onto something or not. If there's worth in it we'll find the resources; don't you worry. Otherwise, we'll move on to more fruitful affairs. William, I'll send

Janice Burns, Stuart Armstrong and Terry Anwhari up to join you. That's three officers, three vehicles, and yours makes four. I'll even include Ryan as an observer. Look after him, won't you. It will do him good. We've nothing to lose, William.'

'Except our reputation,' delivered Boyd.

'William, if we worry about our reputation, we'll never leave the office; never investigate anything worthwhile, never make a decision, and spend the rest of our lives regretting not doing things we should have done. I've made my decision. I'll send you a team. You have ground control.'

'Toni, sir?' queried Boyd. 'Can you send...'

Interrupting abruptly, Commander Herbert reported, 'Antonia Harston-Browne will join you as soon as possible, William. She's tied up all day but I have spoken to Phillip Nesbitt: the Director General. He'll arrange her deployment. Good luck!'

As ever, Commander Herbert ended their call spontaneously leaving Boyd with a vision of the commander dominating a large walnut table covered with the articles of high office.

When the telephone settled on its cradle in the commander's office, Phillip Nesbitt offered, 'I know we planted Ryan with Boyd as part of our investigation, James, but if I were a politician right now I'd be asking why the hell we are sending a surveillance team to the other end of the country at a cost that defies a natural approach to intelligence gathering. The case for surveillance is rather flimsy and you're making these so-called clues fit. Adam and Azzam, indeed! Give me strength, James.'

'It will do no harm,' countered Commander Herbert. 'Our problem is we didn't plant these four terrorists that our friends in MI6 have reported.'

Shaking his head, Phillip contended, 'We have all our main and primary targets across the country covered with various forms of technical and electronic surveillance, James. Yet we are apparently allowing your man to play a set of wild cards. Is he a genius, a gambler or an odd ball who needs his head examined?'

'None of the above,' responded Commander Herbert. 'But to be precise, you're referring to individuals and groups we know about and who we consider are a danger or a possible threat to national security. That's why we have them covered with some form of analytical methodology. We should be more worried about people entering the country that we don't know about.'

'I take your point,' acknowledged Phillip.

Commander Herbert continued, 'The oddball you refer to is Boyd. The man performs better when given his head, Phillip, and - with respect - you planted Ryan. Why not wait for the seeds to germinate?'

A pager sounded and Phillip checked his device before advising Commander Herbert, 'I must go, James. I'm wanted elsewhere. Forgive me but it is a dangerous game we play.'

As the office door closed behind the DG, Commander Herbert said aloud, 'It is the nature of the beast, Phillip. We're fighting a war. I'm not expecting to sign an armistice.'

Up on the Fells of Cumbria, with the road finally in view, Boyd thought about how he might lead this investigation. Bit of a trial this one, he thought. I've got a quarry that looks as if it's being used as a shooting range; a paintball site ran by a suspicious Arab, and a gang of robbers armed with AK-47's plundering building societies whenever they want. My problem is both the shooting range and the Base are in the middle of nowhere. I think I'll get home to Meg as soon as possible and enjoy some quality time together. I know I'm going to get earache from her when I tell her how busy I am and that I'll have to return to London soon. But that's just the life we lead. It might be a long week, decided Boyd. But Toni, he wondered. What was Antonia Harston-Browne up to?

In a quiet but salubrious West End restaurant, Antonia leaned across the table and filled her companion's glass with more champagne.

'Bollinger?' came the query.

'Of course,' replied Antonia.

A waiter quickly appeared to assist but Antonia declined with a smile and offered, 'No, honestly. Thank you, but I can manage.'

Withdrawing, the waiter retreated into the shadows.

'He can help me anytime, Antonia,' whispered Jacquelina. 'Let him pour it next time, Antonia. He's so handsome.'

'And you, my dear cousin,' countered Antonia, 'Need to behave yourself. Don't you think it's time you gave it a rest.'

'Gave what a rest?' enquired Jacquelina.

'Men?' delivered Antonia.

'Mmm…. You are a spoil sport, my darling, Antonia. But now that we have enjoyed such a wonderful meal together perhaps you can tell me what it is that you want from me?'

'Soon,' responded Antonia. 'Soon!'

A trio of waiters wearing black tuxedos with coordinated handkerchiefs and bowties promptly appeared and began removing the abandoned crockery from the table.

Watched closely by Jacquelina, the waiters operated smoothly and swiftly and soon cleared the debris.

The head waiter then approached, bowed politely, and asked, 'More champagne perhaps, ladies? Or would you prefer a liqueur or a cocktail?'

'Nothing for me, thank you,' declared Antonia. 'Jacquelina?'

'Crème de banane pour moi, s'il vous plait,' chuckled Antonia's cousin before suggestively enticing the waiter with, 'Is there anything else on the menu, monsieur?'

'Crème de banane,' smiled the waiter, politely ignoring the customer. 'One! Thank you, ladies. I trust you enjoyed your meal?'

'As ever,' preened Antonia. 'Quite remarkable as usual, Pierre. Could I change my mind? Can you make it two Crème de banane?'

'Of course,' agreed the head waiter who grinned and added, 'One moment please, ladies. I shall return with your drinks quite soon, I assure you.'

'I know you will, Pierre,' offered Antonia.

Whilst Pierre withdrew to prepare their drinks, Antonia suggested, 'Your French is getting worse, Jacquelina.'

There was no response just a flash from Jacquelina's hazel eyes and the disparaging flick of a blonde curl.

Taking an opportunity to scan her surroundings, nodding and smiling pleasantly, Antonia acknowledged one or two faces seated in various parts of the restaurant. She even offered an occasional flimsy wave here and there.

Antonia's choice of restaurant had been carefully determined. It wasn't too posh and it wasn't overly downmarket either. It wouldn't necessarily be her first choice given her affluent tastes of luxurious grandeur. Yet the French eatery was perfectly positioned in the market place to impress Jacquelina without making her feel as if she were royalty personified. Moreover, Antonia knew that she needed her cousin on side for what she was about to propose.

The large glass frontage dominated the building's façade and the eating area was decked out in thick pile carpet decorated with a fleur-de-lis design. Indeed, the colour, vibrancy and pattern in the carpeting accentuated the Parisian theme and brought France effortlessly into the heart of the West End of London. Furthermore, the dining area exuded space and the décor was agreeable. Crucially, it was also warm and snug.

Wearing a long dark blue dress set off with a necklace and earrings, Antonia's appearance gathered even more refinement from a silver brooch she favoured. Yet, Antonia had been deliberate in her dress sense suspecting Jacquelina would seek to use her assets to the best of her advantage. As expected, her gorgeous cousin arrived by taxi for dinner and cocktails wearing a silver gown that dazzled onlookers with its glitzy sequins. More importantly perhaps, the dress beguiled male admirers by offering a deep cleavage and an intriguing split to the thigh. Undoubtedly, Jacquelina knew how to dress to impress and had done so.

Pierre arrived with the liqueurs promptly and retired with equal speed despite a squeeze of the hand from Jacquelina.

Antonia sipped her drink and pronounced it, 'Exquisite!'

Suddenly the mood changed when Jacquelina demanded, 'Wonderful meal, excellent champagne and liqueurs to die for, Antonia. Now what you want?'

'A man!' returned Antonia.

'Don't we all,' smirked Jacquelina. 'What is the bank up to this time?'

'The bank?' queried Antonia.

'My dearest Antonia, it is well known you work on a consultative basis for the banking sector in Canary Wharf. Investments and investigations come to mind. Who is he?'

Antonia removed a photograph from her shoulder bag and discreetly slid it across the glass top table. 'I need to know about this man,' she instructed.

Studying the image, but without touching it, Jacquelina remarked, 'Not quite a Pierce Brosnan lookalike if I may say. What do you know about him?'

'Everything except his true sexual preferences!' returned Antonia.

'What do you know so far?' enquired Jacquelina.

'He's married with two adult children at Cambridge and a daughter on a year out in Thailand. But I want to know what makes him tick not what he puts on his census form,' declared Antonia.

'Would such knowledge influence the banks decision to loan this man money, Antonia?'

'What the bank does with their money is their business, Jacquelina,' revealed Antonia. 'I want you to check with your girls. Is he a regular with any of them? Do any of them know him?'

'My girls!' responded Jacquelina. 'You make it sound as if I'm some kind of pimp, Antonia.'

'You are, Jacquelina,' smiled Antonia. 'You are the flirtiest, most raunchy lady south of the river. But you also have all your fingers in every pie there is south of the river. Your business extends from prostitution to massage parlours to vice clubs to…. Need I go on?'

'I can't deny that I have some business interests, my dear cousin, but I wouldn't describe them as criminal,' disclosed Jacquelina.

'A Judge might,' proposed Antonia. 'Look, Jacquelina, it's a favour, that's all. I need some answers quickly and previous arrangements between us have always proved advantageous for both parties. What do you say?'

Jacquelina looked again at the photograph and then collected it from the table. Turning the image over she read the address and offered, 'Swanky and somewhat upmarket, I'd say.'

Antonia took a sip of liqueur and demanded, 'Middle of the road and mortgaged to the hilt, I'd say. Well, yes or no?'

'What do I get out of this my dearest one?' enquired Jacquelina.

'My continued support,' proposed Antonia.

'And the banks?' probed Jacquelina.

Antonia leaned back in her seat, grinned at her cousin, and said, 'Jacquelina! You know as much about banking as I do about the services you offer to your male clients. That said, I suspect no-one knows you provide the top tier of private investigators in London with subtle and sensitive information relative to your clients and the clients of others in the Establishment. Now let's stop pretending you are the Madame of an expensive Soho brothel and get down to business. I need your discreet and judicious team of especially selected private investigators to find out all they can about this man. I want to know if there's a man in this man's life, or another woman other than his wife. I want to know if he has a habit of dressing up in female clothes. Is he a transvestite? I want to know all the things that I can't find out from running his national security number through the system. For that you get my continued support and your darling husband, Lord Cartwright, will remain forever blissfully ignorant of the true state of your private affairs. Is that understood?'

Palming the photograph, Jacquelina queried, 'Would seven days suffice?'

'Make it five!' demanded Antonia.

'Consider it done, Antonia,' smiled Jacquelina. 'Another crème de banane, perhaps?'

'Of course,' agreed Antonia. Then Antonia raised her hand to summons Pierre.

'Blessings to you, my darling. Blessings!'

'Tell me, Jacquelina,' offered Antonia. 'How is that husband of yours, Lord Peter Cartwright? You haven't mentioned him at all this evening.'

The photograph of a man called Ryan silently skated into Jacquelina's clutch bag whilst she replied, 'Peter? Enjoying himself in Brussels, I understand, Antonia. The work of a Member of the European Parliament is quite compelling from what he tells me. In any case, he's back for the weekend. I'll tell him you were asking after him.'

'Please do,' delivered Antonia.

More drinks arrived.

'Blessings to you, Antonia. 'Blessings!'

Elsewhere, at an airfield amongst the green fields of England, an RAF Hercules touched down and taxied to the cargo area at the far end of the runway. When its engines finally died the hydraulics whispered and a ramp at the rear of the aircraft steadily lowered.

The staff sergeant, stood, donned his hat with its slashed peak angling downwards towards his eyebrows, and addressed his men.

'Okay lads, let's take him home.'

Six uniforms straightened up. They were smart, elegant, the pride of their regiment with boots gleaming and sharp creases in both trousers and jackets.

But the soldier did not move. He was just a passenger travelling on an open passport.

The six approached the traveller, took hold at the appointed place, and swiftly hoisted his coffin onto their shoulders.

Obediently, they listened to the sergeant's whispered countdown. Pacing short steps they set off.

The sergeant stepped backwards down the ramp with his hand outstretched resting upon, guiding, reassuring the foot of the coffin as it angled downwards on the soldier's journey home.

'Steady, gentlemen,' he advised in murmured tones. 'Respect!'

With slow carefully measured steps, they reached the smooth tarmac, levelled off, and halted quietly in complete silence.

There was a whispered cool breeze hovering across the area; an air sock gently billowing at the edge of the field close by; a handkerchief dabbing a soft loving face.

A tear fell and a voice cried out.

Unruffled, the sergeant whispered his orders and the repatriation party marched quietly off again in slow time with their charge held high on broad shoulders.

The sergeant led the party.

Each careful stride was a regimental honour. Each measured footstep was filled with respect. Each beat of the heart meant an inch closer to home.

They reached the hearse parked on the tarmac.

The hearse was the first of the procession vehicles and the party escorted the soldier to his position in the rear. They lowered the coffin, found the runners, and slid him quietly into the depths of the hearse.

Preceded by a police motor cyclist and a patrol car, the cortege departed. Leaving the airfield, they journeyed to a village close to a motorway and the soldier's route home.

Slackening to a crawl, the cortege drove gradually and serenely through the village. It passed the massed ranks of people who turned out to pay their last respects.

There was a tear in an eye and a heavy heart. Union flags fluttered. Some were waved in the breeze and coloured proceedings red white and blue. There was a squeeze of a hand and a child lifted high and hugged close to a heaving chest. Flowers were thrown on the roadway in front of the cortege and onto the roof of the hearse.

The funeral cortege was a display not just of mourning, but of a celebration of a life lived.

People wept, sobbed, and remembered.

Prayers were spoken aloud. The sound of hands clapping together in gratitude of his service permeated every aspect of the village. Applause, in commemoration of his life, guided our soldier home.

The regimental flag lowered next to the standards of the Royal British Legion and a row of officers saluted when the coffin ambled by. And a large group of legendary motor cyclists dressed in leathers stood with heads bowed as the cortege moved on.

The village was silent, respectful, and sombre.

Where the soldier died was not on the lips of those who turned out to honour their hero. Maybe the soldier wasn't really a hero, they didn't truly know. Maybe the soldier had just been unlucky, they didn't actually know.

The crowd in the village did not know, had not been with the soldier at his time of death, and could not envisage the nature of his sorrowful passing.

But they knew why he'd been fighting and what was at stake. The man had fought and died for his country.

They saluted the soldier. He had arrived home.

A man in the crowd, perhaps in his sixties, perhaps more frail than he had once been in his younger days, gathered his scarf and overcoat around him and sensed his war medals jingling from the breast. They were from another era, another battlefield where the soil had been reddened by the blood of man.

Decorations on his chest tinkled quietly as he swayed on his heels. He knew why he was there. The veteran was one of many.

More importantly, the man from another service understood why people like Boyd, Antonia, Commander Herbert and Phillip Nesbitt, made the decisions they did, and carried them out in the manner that they often did.

Sometimes clever and intelligent decisions based on fact and reality made sense and proved the right thing to do. Other times chaotic haphazard questionable decisions without rhyme or reason were evident. It was in such times that leaders emerged. It was the nature of war.

The veteran turned and made his way home – until the next time.

At the going down of the sun, they would remember the soldier who had come home.

*

Chapter Ten

~

Heathrow Airport, London.

Stepping from the Lisbon flight, Khalid stood for a moment at the top of the landing and cast his eyes across the thriving complex that was Heathrow airport.

England, he thought, grey, chilly and uninspiring.

There was a huddle of people behind him. He made his way down the staircase onto the tarmac and into a bus that would take him the short ride to the arrivals area.

Standing in line, Khalid studied the movements of the people around him. He took in the uniforms of his enemy and heard their tongue properly for the first time. He admired the cut of their clothes, the cleanliness of the marble concourse, the lights, and the splendour of an international airport.

Officers made a note, scanned a passport, took a photograph of the visitor from the Middle East on covert equipment, and nodded dispassionately when the charlatan walked by.

Khalid was a warrior of special choosing. Already, his eyes were taking everything in as his brain dissected every action and compartmentalised life in England into its various boxes.

On strolling into the arrival lounge at Heathrow, Khalid suddenly appreciated how huge the airport actually was. There were people around him from all denominations and skin colour. Needing to reflect and catch his breath for a moment, he sought out a designated area to pray in the tradition of his culture and religion. As he strolled gradually through the international arrivals lounge, Khalid glimpsed the multi storey car park where he expected his onward transport to be waiting for him.

Then, inexplicably, he spun round and walked back the way he had come. In the twenty yards that Khalid stepped, his eyes penetrated every face, every slight movement, and every man or woman who might be following him.

Gradually, he re-joined the mass of people snaking their way through the corridors. Then he entered the prayer room and closed the door quietly behind him.

In a background to private worship, an aircraft took off from one runway whilst another landed close by. The stands were full and a glut of aircraft tugs, air start units, air stairs for aircraft, and various apron vehicles added to the hustle bustle of a truly thriving piece of machinery: an international airport.

Meanwhile, a murmured incantation gradually intruded on the energetic scene...

'There is no God but Allah and Muhammad is his Prophet....'

In an ancient church in a village in Cumbria, the Reverend Matthew Lowther addressed the altar in private communion with his God. Raising his hands in veneration, he spoke aloud and heard his lonely words reverberating from the cold grey walls when he read his preferred version of The Lord's Prayer.

'Our Father, who art in Heaven, hallowed be your name; thy kingdom come; thy will be done. On earth as it is in heaven. Give us this day our daily bread. And forgive us our trespasses, as we forgive those who trespass against us: And lead us not into temptation; but deliver us from evil. For thine is the kingdom, the power and the glory; for ever and ever, Amen.'

A footstep smarted on the gravel path outside and Matthew immediately bowed to the altar and made his way quickly to the entrance of the church.

There was a spine-chilling creak from the hinge of a giant wooden door when Matthew pulled it open and stepped outside. An unwelcome breeze infested the lobby, invaded the nave, and rushed towards the altar behind him

Standing tall, dressed in a bulky anorak covering his black overalls, Azzam offered, 'It's me! I have come to see you, Vicar Lowther. It is your church, yes?'

'Oh, goodness!' disclosed Matthew. 'You surprised me for a moment, Azzam. This is the Lord's church, Azzam, and it is the people's church too.'

Offering a handshake, Azzam radiated a smile that might fill a cathedral when he declared, 'I have come to offer my sincere apologies, Reverend Lowther. See! I know, Vicar Lowther that you are the Right Reverend Lowther and that is how I should address you.'

Accepting the handshake, Matthew replied, 'Actually, Azzam. My name is Matthew. Please call me Matthew if you would rather.'

'Of course,' responded Azzam. 'Matthew it is then.'

Look, why not take a walk with me?' suggested Matthew. 'I'll show you the graveyard and you can appreciate the architecture of the church. It really is a splendid example of a quintessential place of worship.'

'Yes, I would like that,' remarked Azzam.

As the men strolled, Azzam took stock of the exterior of the church and marvelled at the stained glass window. He broke away from Matthew and strolled towards the spectacle which depicted Jesus of Nazareth. It was Jesus Christ on the Cross framed within the stained glass.

'That is your God?' asked Azzam.

'That is Jesus and he is the Son of God,' disclosed Matthew making the sign of the Cross. 'He rose into Heaven to make us stronger.'

'I see,' revealed Azzam. 'Perhaps you can tell me why he is nailed to that wooden cross one day when I have more time, Matthew?'

Adjusting his vestment, Matthew offered, 'Yes! Yes, indeed, Azzam, I would like that very much. Perhaps you will tell me of your God and we can be friends and worship our Gods together?'

'Here in this church?' queried Azzam.

'If you wish,' suggested Matthew,

Azzam seemed taken aback for a moment. Unsure of how he might respond, he offered, 'Perhaps, but then again I am not of your faith and your God is inferior to Allah.'

'Perhaps?' queried Matthew. 'I take it you are a devout Muslim, Azzam, as opposed to merely a follower of Islam? This explains why you could not enter our church. It is not an unfriendly place, my son. Everyone is welcome.'

'I am not your son,' snapped Azzam angrily.

'The church of God is a family, Azzam. I wish to welcome you to my church.'

Suddenly Azzam interrupted Matthew and revealed, 'I have come to bring you this book back. It is your Bible.'

From beneath his anorak Azzam produced the Bible and offered, 'When we first met in the village you left this book on the back of my vehicle. It has your name on the inside.'

Taking the tomb with both hands, Matthew appeared delighted. He leafed through the opening pages and then responded, 'I could not remember where I put my Bible. I have searched all over the house for it, Azzam, how wonderful. I am so indebted to you, my dear Azzam.'

'No,' replied Azzam. 'It is I that am indebted to you, Matthew. I have also come to apologise for being hasty with your daughter. I have arranged free tickets for the paintball centre for the children of your village. Let me know what day you can bring the children.'

Surprised and delighted, Matthew responded eagerly with, 'I shall put this offer to the church committee and make sure it is accepted and sorted out, Azzam. That is so very kind of you and in return we will be able to make sure the children understand that is the only time they can go on the site because it may be dangerous at other times.'

'And no horses!' suggested Azzam with a sly grin.

Laughing, Matthew replied, 'And no horses, Azzam.'

Making a slow attempt at the sign of the Cross, Azzam then watched Matthew make the sign.

Azzam mimicked him and Matthew reacted by nodding is approval and adding, 'Your words are improving as well, Azzam.'

'I would like to make a contribution to the church, Matthew,' revealed Azzam, suddenly.

'Why on earth....'

'I insist,' interrupted Azzam producing a roll of notes from his wallet. 'It is for you and your church for keeping my place out of the bounds of the children.'

Matthew stepped back and refused to accept the cash but Azzam thrust half a dozen ten pound notes into Matthew's fist and said, 'Thank you, Matthew. I am pleased we understand each other now.'

Azzam turned on his heel and made for the gateway.

Matthew uncurled his fingers to count the cash.

Puzzled, perhaps naïve, he held sixty pounds in one hand and a newly returned Bible in the other. Shaking his head, he speculated on the events of the last couple of minutes. Is the money a bribe or a donation, he considered. He is obviously a devout Muslim because he would not enter the church, he decided. Yet he returned my Bible when he could have thrown it away. Doubtful now, Matthew worried on whether his telephone call to Boyd's hotline had been advisable given the benefit of hindsight.

Graciously, Matthew looked high towards the stained glass window before announcing, 'Forgive me, Lord, have I sinned against this man?'

Matthew's eyes fixed on the vision of Jesus in the stained glass window.

'Forgive me, my Lord. I know not what I do.'

On the gravel path Azzam clutched his anorak tight, dug his hands deep inside the pockets, and spat on a gravestone as he made for his vehicle.

Pulling open the gate at the entrance, Azzam mumbled, 'Infidel!' and slammed it shut behind him.

The village of Crosby on Eden, on the outskirts of Carlisle, Cumbria, is actually a combination of two villages: Low Crosby and High Crosby. There has been an airfield close to the village since 1941 when RAF Crosby on Eden was built as an operational training unit for pilots in the Second World War. Villagers now know it as Carlisle airport where a small number of privateers operate their own aeroplanes from the site.

It is to this rendezvous point that Janice Burns, Terry Anwhari, Ryan, and Stuart Armstrong arrive in convoy with their vehicles.

Standing in the car park outside the small airport complex, Boyd relayed to a man standing beside him, 'Here's your passengers, Alan.'

'It'll be two trips then,' replied Alan. 'It's a Cessna I've got, Billy. Not a Boeing 747!'

Janice stepped from her vehicle and approached Boyd with Terry, Ryan and Stuart in close attendance.

'Glad you could make it, guys,' announced Boyd. 'And on time too! Good journey up?'

Janice nodded enthusiastically and queried, 'An airport, Guvnor? Are you taking us on a pleasure flight?'

'No,' chuckled Boyd. 'He is!' Boyd gestured to the chap standing next to him. Introducing his friend who was dressed in a pilot's coverall, Boyd revealed, 'This is my close friend, Alan Grant. He is a retired police officer who served in both the traffic department and the drug squad. Now he's a pilot instructor and he is, indeed, going to take you for a pleasure flight.'

'Sounds good,' reported Stuart. 'I'm thinking your mate is going to fly us to the Caldbeck Fells, Guvnor.'

'I'm impressed,' replied Boyd. 'Why do you say that, Stuart?'

'Well, if I've read the map correctly, Guvnor, your GPS reading puts this shooting range in the middle of nowhere by the look of it.'

'That's right, Stuart,' admitted Boyd. 'Alan…'

Slightly overweight with long golden hair that flowed to his shoulder blades, the moustachioed Alan stepped forward and divulged, 'Yeah! I'm your guide.' He jerked his thumb towards the perimeter fence where an aircraft waited and disclosed, 'I've a Cessna 172 Cessna Skyhawk. It's a four seater, single-engine, high-wing fixed wing aircraft and your Guvnor here wants me to fly you all over the site you'll be working on. We'll split into two groups and move out as soon as Mister Boyd has completed his briefing. Now if you'd like to come to my office, we'll have a brew.'

'I'm all for that,' replied Ryan.

There was a screech of tyres when Antonia Harston-Browne swung her blue Porsche into the car park.

'Better late than never,' suggested Boyd.

Slamming the car door closed behind her, Antonia beamed a wonderful smile and declared, 'You mean you were about to start the party without me?'

'Wouldn't dream of it, Toni,' revealed Boyd.

They trouped into Alan's office where Boyd related the story about the Base for young people, the Paintball site, and the AK-47 shell case find. Then he plotted the locations on a wall map whilst briefing the team on the bank raids at Southport and Bamber Bridge.

Alan provided hot drinks and sandwiches whilst Boyd answered his mobile phone and took a call.

'Are you coming with us?' asked Janice when he'd finished.

'Me?' replied Boyd. 'No, I'm going to church and Toni is coming with me. Look after the choirboy for me, Janice.'

'The choirboy?' queried Janice.

'Ryan!' confessed Boyd.

If there was such a thing as a pure Scottish scowl, Janice found it and twisted a reply. 'Aye, Guvnor! The wee man will be safe with me.'

Coughing, Ryan explained, 'I'm purely an observer, miss.'

'Aye, make sure that's all you do then, Ryan,' advised Janice.

'Alan,' suggested Boyd. 'Any problems? Ring me.'

'Will do,' replied the pilot.

'Your car or mine?' queried Boyd.

'The Porsche,' decided Antonia. 'I'll drive. Where to?'

'Caldbeck! That call was the vicar again. Come on, Toni. I'll tell you what I have in mind on the way.

'And I'll tell you what I think,' offered Antonia. 'It'll be another madcap idea.'

Alan's Cessna Skyhawk fixed wing aeroplane overflew the nearby A689 with its passengers as Boyd and Antonia drove towards West Cumbria and the northern Fells of the Lake District.

Within the hour, Boyd and Antonia were drinking tea and snacking on ham and cheese sandwiches with Matthew, Elizabeth, and their daughter Susie. The atmosphere was more relaxed than Boyd anticipated and was undoubtedly aided by the well-mannered Susie who spent much of her time staring out of the window.

'Thank you for ringing our hotline number, Matthew,' revealed Boyd. 'We rely on people like you to provide information that we can act on. I'm here to thank you for your calls, seek your confidentiality, and assure you that we are looking into your concerns.'

'That's his problem,' replied Elizabeth. 'My husband no longer suspects this Arab chap and rather thinks he should apologise to you for wasting your time. Go on, Matthew. Tell, Mister Boyd and his friend what happened.'

'Really, Elizabeth, I can speak for myself,' snapped Matthew.

'I haven't come to arrest the man for terrorism, Mrs Lowther,' explained Boyd. 'I'm merely thanking you for your information and assuring you of our interest. There is no evidence to suggest your suspicions are well founded. We often follow up on suspicions and gut feelings but you shouldn't confuse that with hard evidence and a court of law.'

Susie moved from the table and glanced outside. Then she took her seat again and snatched the last sandwich from a plate.

'Susie!' scolded her mother.

'Sorry,' twisted Susie in an unapologetic manner.

'Matthew thinks he made a mistake, that's all,' explained Elizabeth.

'Yes, I do, I'm afraid, Mister Boyd,' remarked Matthew. 'It all started when Azzam challenged my daughter, Susie, and I took it too personally. I merely added suspicions of his behaviour and attitude to the bullying of my daughter and reached the wrong decision. I added two and two together and made five. I'd really appreciate it if you just forgot about my call and got on with some proper police work.'

Boyd exchanged concerned looks with Antonia.

Matthew continued, 'Did you know there had been some thefts from cars on the road to Mosedale, Mister Boyd? A mobile phone from one car and a camera from another apparently. Like I said when we first met, we never see the police in these parts. Now that you are here it might be time to do some police work and sort these crimes out. Perhaps you and your policewoman might uncover the thieves?'

'Perhaps,' agreed Boyd. 'But that's not what I'm here for. What has changed your mind?'

Matthew looked away for a moment but Elizabeth prompted her husband with, 'Tell him, Matthew. He's come a long way to see you. The very least you can do is treat the man with some respect and answer his questions!'

'I lost my Bible,' explained Matthew. 'I inadvertently left it in his Land Rover when we bumped into him in the village.'

'He left his Bible on the back seat of Azzam's car. Can you believe that, Mister Boyd?' interrupted Elizabeth.'

'I'll tell the story if you don't mind,' declared Matthew.

'Here we go again,' murmured Susie. 'I get wronged for snooping at the paintball site and trying to find some young people to come to the dance but it's all right for these two to argue with each other day in and day out.'

'Susie!' exclaimed Elizabeth annoyed.

Susie wandered to the window again where she remained.

'Excuse me,' proposed a somewhat irritated Antonia. 'Can we all settle down? Reverend Lowther, can you tell us, in your own words, why you have reappraised Azzam?'

Antonia's questions were accompanied by a gentle swish of red hair across her shoulders.

It was followed by a quiet moment of reflection before Matthew replied, 'As I said, Azzam returned my Bible which I thought was wonderful of him. He also revealed that he would allow the children to visit the paintball site and he would arrange it. Then he made a donation to the church and I realised I'd misjudged him?'

'How much, may I ask?' ventured Antonia.

'Sixty pounds!'

'You mean you changed your mind for a returned Bible and sixty pounds?' enquired Boyd.

'And agreement to allow the children to go to the site under supervision so that the privacy and security of the site might be respected at other times,' disclosed Matthew. 'He was so precise he even wanted a list of names and addresses of the children.'

'Interesting,' noted Boyd engaging Antonia's eyes. 'Passport control almost!' But then he said, 'I wonder why he wanted such a list? That worries me, Matthew.'

'And of course,' revealed Matthew, 'I reminded Azzam that it was the wish of our Lord that the world would one day come together as one irrespective of the various religious strains. He did not seem averse to such a prospect.'

Boyd nodded an acknowledgement but seemed to be mulling things over in his mind before he offered, 'I'm pleased you got your Bible back, Matthew. So very pleased for you! But I note he wouldn't enter your church. That tells me he has a sincere and heartfelt devotion to his religion. But I think you may have been a little naïve in the process.'

'In what way?' questioned Matthew.

Pursing his lips thoughtfully, Boyd proposed, 'Sadly, there are some of Azzam's culture and background who have a low perspective of the female form. I'd like Susie's views on this.'

'Susie?' queried Elizabeth. 'I'd rather you didn't involve our daughter, Mister Boyd. She's a little too young for this.'

Antonia leaned forward and suggested, 'As I understand it, Mrs Lowther, it was Azzam challenging Susie that started all this.'

'Yes, well...' offered Elizabeth, submissively.

Boyd penetrated the air with, 'Susie, I know you don't like me but can you tell me why you keep looking out of the window?'

Staring into the garden area, Susie did not offer an answer. She merely disclosed, 'Your wife has some car! Is that a Ferrari?'

'No!' grinned Antonia. 'It's a Porsche, Susie, and I'm not Mister Boyd's wife.'

'His girlfriend then?'

'No,' remarked Antonia. 'Mister Boyd is my work colleague.'

'Were you looking for boys at the Base, Susie?' queried Boyd.

'You know I was,' agreed Susie. 'It's how it all started. I thought there were boys in the huts or down the mine and the sod pinned me to the wall and then threw me to the ground like a rag doll. Bastard!'

'Susie! Your language,' warned Matthew.

Antonia held up a cautionary but reassuring hand and solicited, 'Go on, Susie. What did you really see through the windows?'

'Nothing! There were no boys.'

The conversation seemed to have reached an impasse but Boyd moved next to Susie and leaned on the window sill looking out towards Antonia's Porsche.

'One hell of a nice car that one, Susie, and it's a really attractive colour too,' suggested Boyd.

There was no reply from a slightly truculent teenager.

'Powder blue I think is the technical name of the colour. I'm not sure. I have a different type of car altogether. But I bet the horse power in a Porsche is even faster than your horse.'

There was no reply; not even an iota of recognition.

'Who would win a race over the Fells, Gabby or the Porsche?'

Still no response.

Boyd persisted. 'She's not my wife, Susie.'

'Mmm....' muttered Susie.

'My wife is having twins though!'

'What do you mean?' enquired Susie, intrigued.

'Meg! She's having twins.'

'Who is Meg?' asked Susie.

'Oh, sorry,' revealed Boyd, still looking out of the window in an apparently idle manner. 'My wife, she's pregnant and we're expecting twins.'

Susie spun to capture Boyd's deep blue eyes and snapped, 'Twins! Cool! Hey, how cool is that. Wow!'

Boyd raised his eyebrows slightly and suggested, 'Can I ask you something about your horse, Susie?'

'Maybe,' murmured Susie.

'Why do you call her Gabby?'

'It's a him not a her! I called him Gabby because Mum and Dad told me he would be called Gabriel after the Angel Gabriel. I called him Gabby to their annoyance.'

Laughing, Boyd said, 'Good for you. I like Gabby. It flows better than Gabriel.'

There was quiet for a moment before Susie offered, 'Would you like to ride Gabby, Mister Boyd?'

'Hey, that's a real cool offer but I've never ridden a horse before. I'd fall off. Anyway, there's more to life than horses.'

Susie turned and snapped, 'What do you mean?'

'Well, Susie, you're getting all grown up now and need to know about boys and stuff. I mean, you're not a kid anymore are you? You're a young lady really so you know how important it is for my wife and I that our children arrive on time and in good health. You know, stuff like that is important when you get older.'

'Absolutely,' remarked Susie. 'Yeah, I'm cool with that and you're right. I'm not a kid anymore. Do me a favour and tell my Mum and Dad that, Mister Boyd.'

Elizabeth and Matthew closed slightly but Antonia shook her head and used her eyes to suggest that they might just relax and leave it for a moment.

'Oh, I think you misjudge your parents, Susie. They're only worried that you might meet the wrong kind of boys, I expect. Hey, they love you dearly; it's just awkward I reckon. Still, I know where you're coming from in a place like this. It's the back of beyond and probably as boring as hell for a young lady like yourself.'

'Yeah, that's right. I can't even play loud music in my bedroom as it's the vicarage and we might upset the peace and tranquillity of the bloody village.'

Chuckling, Boyd shook his head.

Susie continued, 'I love living here but there's nothing to do except ride Gabby and go to the village hall at weekends.'

'But what beauty surrounds you, Susie. It's such a beautiful part of the world. You are so lucky and you don't realise it. I can't wait to bring Meg here and take my two children into the mountains when they are big enough.'

'Don't go near the mines, Mister Boyd.'

'Which mines?' enquired Boyd.

'At the Base, of course. I found a back way into the Base and before I knew it there was the old mine. We used to go there and play hide and seek when we first moved here years ago. The old entrance to the mine has stood open for yonks but now it's been blocked up with a crazy kind of door and a huge padlock.'

Matthew sat down suddenly and Elizabeth laid a hand on his shoulder as she stood behind him.

Boyd turned casually from the window and glanced at Antonia before suggesting, 'Hey, Susie. Do you think you could take my friend, Toni, up to the Base and show her the mine you are on about?'

'In the Porsche?'

'Of course,' replied Antonia. 'In the Porsche.'

'Yeah, real cool,' remarked Susie. 'Okay, but I'm not going on the site.'

'No need,' replied Boyd. 'But if you could point the way to the back entrance to the mine that's been locked up, that would be mega cool.'

'Mega cool!' mentioned Susie. 'Mum? Dad?'

There was a measured silence before Matthew replied, 'Of course,' announced Matthew. 'You're a young lady now, Susie. We just keep forgetting. I'm sorry.'

Boyd nodded to the sound of Antonia rattling her car keys. 'Come on, Susie. I'll drive. You can show me how to get into the back entrance.'

'Yeah, mega cool,' smiled Susie.

'Before you go,' responded Matthew holding his arms out wide.

Susie walked into her Dad's arms, cuddled him, and then embraced her Mum.

'Are you sure I can't drive?' queried Susie.

'I'm sure,' chortled Antonia. 'Come on. Maybe we'll see an aeroplane up in the sky.'

'You will,' agreed Boyd. 'I'll make sure Alan knows where you are. I'll ring him.'

Moments later, a front door slammed shut and a Porsche engine growled like a tiger. There was a deliberate screech of tyres and Antonia and Susie set off.

'Well, I never,' sighed Elizabeth in the silence that followed. 'I don't know what to say, Mister Boyd.'

'I do,' intervened Matthew. 'That mine entrance leads nowhere, Mister Boyd. The shaft was closed down twenty years ago and the entrance takes you into a corridor the length of the church aisle. Then you hit a stone wall because the mine has been made safe. It's a derelict site that's been abandoned and closed down properly by the mining company that previously owned it.'

Boyd nodded thoughtfully and declared, 'Yet the entrance is padlocked by the sound of it. Do you know the name of the company that used to own the mine, Matthew?'

'I can find out, why?'

Rubbing his chin, Boyd proposed, 'I don't know whether you are right or wrong about Azzam, Matthew, but I sure as hell intend to find out now.'

Half an hour later and Antonia and Susie returned. Pleasantries, promises, and agreements made, Boyd and Antonia bid their farewell and set off in the Porsche.

Thrusting the gear stick into third, Antonia swung the car at speed into a bend and asked, 'Alan overflew us and presumably positioned the mine on a map. Once we get back to Carlisle I'll ring the office and chase up the ownership of the mine. By the way, there's a blue Ford parked at the Base. I got the number. It's a hire car.'

'Good!' mused Boyd.

'What's on your mind, Billy?' asked Antonia.

Tapping his fingers on the dashboard, Boyd appreciated the Cumbrian countryside for a moment and then suggested, 'What to do next, Antonia? There's quite a few options.'

'Hey, Billy, I'm the MI5 operative who analyses intelligence and puts resources into your hands. I'm not the one who stands in the witness box giving evidence. What's going on in that complicated brain of yours?'

Easing himself into the bucket seat, Boyd itemised his problem. 'Part of me wants to take a sledgehammer to the mine entrance and find out what's in there. Another part of me wants to handpick some young detectives and arrange for them to try and undertake an undercover sabbatical at the Base.'

'That sounds like a good idea,' disclosed Antonia.

'Yes, but it's not practical at the moment,' revealed Boyd. 'Another chunk of me thinks we should sit on top of the shooting range where the shell cases were found and hope the shooters come back to practice. Another slice of me is still thinking.'

Braking for a sheep that suddenly appeared from a hedge at the side of the road, Antonia suggested, 'Should we do all three? What do you need to make it happen?'

'A satellite above Caldbeck that produces real time state of the art photography; a search warrant for the mine, and the SAS in the quarry waiting for the robbers with the AK-47's to turn up.' Boyd began to laugh and then sat upright in the car. He turned to engage Antonia and asked, 'What do you think?'

A sheep ambled safely across the tarmac. Antonia snatched a lower gear and gently squeezed the accelerator, shook her head at the animal, and replied, 'No chance, Billy! I couldn't even get the SAS for you on the strength of the situation so far. You'd have to persuade a strong presentation to my service to get anything. You might get a search warrant from a friendly magistrate but you're chasing a loose ball of string with a hunch and a gut feeling. Sorry, as much as I want to help, it's not on the cards. We haven't got enough.'

'We haven't got anything,' admitted Boyd. 'At least, not yet.'

At the crossroads above Caldbeck, Antonia swung right and headed towards Carlisle. The Solway coast came into panoramic view amidst the splendour of the northern Fells.

'Tomorrow?' queried Antonia.

'Tonight the team study the maps and put a face on the view they've had from the air today. Then I think we'll sink a few beers and relax. Hopefully, I'll bring Meg along for an hour or two. The break will do her good.'

'Yes, she must love it when you manage to work in your back yard, Billy.'

'Oh, yes, she does and so do I,' revealed Boyd. 'But tomorrow we'll cover access from Caldbeck to the motorway.'

'How on earth will you do that, Billy?'

'Let's suppose we give this man a very long leash and decide that he hasn't a clue that we are investigating him,' suggested Boyd. 'What we have got is a clear connection with two building society robberies involving the use of AK-47's. It's the only thing we've really got a hold on and the shell cases are a form of physical evidence. We don't know what's in the mine and we don't know enough about Azzam. We do know that the two robberies both happened close to motorways. The key isn't Caldbeck, Toni. The key to our surveillance operation lies on covering access to the motorway to and from Caldbeck.'

'Agreed!' snapped Antonia. 'By the way, I brought my fell walking gear. I might just go for a walk on the Fells if you're going to play with your cars.'

'Anywhere in particular?' posed Boyd.

Smiling mischievously, Antonia replied, 'Oh, I'll think of somewhere, Billy.'

'Yeah, I bet you will,' chuckled Boyd.

The Porsche growled deep in its belly when Antonia rounded a bend and powered the vehicle into north east Cumbria.

*

173

Chapter Eleven

~

The Motorway

Alan Grant's Cessna Skyhawk proved invaluable.

Boyd's colleagues subscribed to the notion that there was nothing worse than an interfering retired policeman who took pleasure in meddling in affairs that were no longer his concern. Quite the opposite in this case, Alan placed his aircraft at the Unit's disposal when Boyd arranged to hire the Cessna indefinitely. It made sense to Boyd. Cumbria boasted an air ambulance helicopter of some repute but Boyd decided the nearest Police Air Support Wing in Lancashire couldn't realistically guarantee full time cover given their many other duties.

By nine in the morning, the team were on the road having enjoyed a night in the bar and a good English breakfast. To crown it all, Meg enjoyed the evening and they'd enjoyed discussing names for the new arrivals. Nothing was sorted but all manner of names for the twins were up for grabs: from Bill and Beth to Jack and Jill, and then some.

Driving his dark blue BMW with Ryan as his passenger, Boyd didn't take long to park up close to the M6 motorway at Catterlen – interchange 41 – whilst Stuart parked his Ford Mondeo in a position to watch Skirsgill at interchange 40.

Meanwhile, Janice cruised west out of Carlisle on the A595 in her grey Seat and chose to position herself close to the carriageway in order to observe eastbound traffic.

Terry, in his silver Saab, made the longest journey and checked in on the radio when he reached the A66 junction close to the turn off for Caldbeck.

It was often joked amongst the unit that what they really needed was a permanent car salesman to recommend the cars.

With everyone in position, Boyd phoned Alan Grant at Carlisle airport. Moments later Pilot officer Grant, as the team had christened him, taxied the Cessna down the runway and took off at speed. With the city sprawling out beneath him, Alan flew west towards the Caldbeck Fells.

Antonia Harston-Browne also headed west into north Cumbria. Dressed casually in jeans and walking gear, Antonia gently urged her Porsche through the village of Dalston and headed towards Caldbeck.

Replacing his radio handset, Boyd poured two coffees from a flask and handed one to Ryan saying, 'Here, this might be a long day and you should know that I have a very bad caffeine problem when I get bored. Get that down you.'

Ryan accepted with a curt, 'Thanks!' and volunteered, 'I really enjoyed meeting everyone properly last night, Mister Boyd. Billy, isn't it? Anyway, it was a nice change to get out of the office and meet people.'

'Good!' replied Boyd. 'Just hope we get lucky or you'll be wishing you were back in the office by lunch time.'

'Ah yes, lunch! What happens then, Billy?'

'Nothing! We eat in here, in the car, beside the radio ready to go. It's what we do on this type of job, Ryan. I've some sandwiches and the glove compartment is full of chocolate bars, nuts, apples, and Kendal mint cake. Energy stuff! You'll get used to it.'

Unfastening the glove compartment, the lid dropped and Ryan feasted his eyes on the contents. 'Good God!' he said. 'So this is what you guys calls eating on the hoof?'

'Yep!' chuckled Boyd. 'Meals on wheels!'

'Do I get a gun like you guys?'

'Definitely not!' decreed Boyd. 'I'm told you know nothing about how to handle a firearm, Ryan, and, in any event, you're here to observe proceedings. If there's a trigger situation – that's a firearms related incident – You'll be with me and….'

'That's what I was afraid of,' voiced Ryan. 'You're a magnet for bullets!'

'Lots of policemen in this country do thirty years and never hear the sound of gunfire, Ryan,' explained Boyd. 'It depends what you do and where you're doing it. Unfortunately, this is the sharp end of the job but even then being shot at is not a daily occurrence, I assure you.'

'Pleased to know it,' uttered Ryan.

Boyd selected a CD and inserted it into the radio system.

'What now?' queried Ryan.

'We wait?' announced Boyd reaching for a bag of nuts. 'And enjoy the music.'

'You mean we sit here on some cockamamie hunch that one of the team will pick up either the hire car or this guy's Land Rover when he decides to leave the Base?

'Something like that,' nodded Boyd throwing and catching a peanut in his mouth. 'I love my hunches by the way, Ryan. I tend to base them on experience. Sometimes they work and other times they fail.'

'As I understand it from the briefing this morning, you've got the number of a hire car and a Land Rover from Antonia; no photograph of this guy Azzam, and not much else other than a handful of indications that would be better on a Cluedo board game than in real life.'

'Correct, Ryan. It's a long shot but things will happen today. Believe me!'

'If you say so,' countered Ryan shaking his head.

'I do,' confirmed Boyd.

'Mind you,' chuckled Ryan. 'When you translate Al-Qaeda from Arabic into English you end up with the word 'base'. Now that is just too much for me.'

'I'm not putting a lot into that, Ryan,' explained Boyd. 'We have all kinds of bases in this country. It's a very common word. I think that's just pure coincidence. Mind you, Ryan, you seem to know everything there is to know about Al-Qaeda.'

A mobile sounded before Ryan could counter the point. It was Alan in the Cessna who explained to Boyd that he was flying over the Base. The blue Ford hire car had left the location and was headed towards the village of Caldbeck. There appeared to be one occupant: a shadowy figure not clear from the skies above.

'Gender not known, Billy,' reported Alan.

Boyd acknowledged the call, updated his team on the radio, and drank his coffee.

'That aeroplane isn't ours, Mister Boyd. What do you expect the pilot to do?'

'Fly,' quipped Boyd obviously listening to a CD.

'You don't understand,' suggested Ryan. 'On whose authority was the aeroplane acquired?'

'Mine!' replied Boyd.

'Presumably you cleared it with higher command?'

'I am higher command, Ryan,' chuckled Boyd. 'But don't you worry Commander Herbert gave me ground control. I'll inform him in due course. This job does not yet meet the criteria for full time aerial surveillance from our air support wing.'

'Is that it?' queried Ryan. 'No further explanation or protocol necessary?'

'It's a war we're fighting, Ryan. You stand by and count the cost if you wish. I'm too busy making ends meet and getting to where we need to be. The commander knows how I work. He'll expect me to improvise and get the show on the road. If I fail he always has the option to replace me.'

'And if he does?'

'Then I won't need to worry about people like you anymore, will I, Ryan?'

Ryan turned away and looked out of the window for a few moments. He was obviously upset, perhaps annoyed at Boyd's arrogant attitude.

Fingering the volume control of the CD, Boyd played a saxophone piece from a Johnny Hooper album. The music was soft and soothing with just the right amount of energy and noise filtering into the car.

'What's that you're playing?' asked Ryan.

'Silhouette!' remarked Boyd.

'Aren't we all,' suggested Ryan.

'Probably,' agreed Boyd.

The music played on and the two men remained silent for a moment.

'What's next?' queried Ryan eventually.

'Now we wait to see which direction Azzam's hire car takes,' replied Boyd. 'We'll hold our positions until we're certain. I want to be sure the car isn't just going to a shop in the village.'

Ryan nodded and offered, 'It might be a decoy and you're presuming Azzam hired the car and he's in it. What if the Land Rover moves?'

A bag of nuts were attacked by Boyd who reflected on Ryan's remark for a moment before suggesting, 'Something else for your report, Ryan. Ground control equals dicey decisions based on what resources are available. Right now I'm relying on a second hand borrowed aeroplane, a retired policeman, a bag of nuts, a gut feeling, and a surveillance team strung out along the motorway like pearls on a string.'

'Is that it?' cracked Ryan.

'And Toni,' chuckled Boyd.

'Where is she?'

'Fell walking! Day off!'

Shaking his head, Ryan probed, 'Are you serious?'

A telephone rang and Boyd answered it quickly before closing it down once more.

'I'm always serious,' declared Boyd. 'That was Alan. The target is heading north towards Carlisle.'

A finger quickly ejected a music disc and the atmosphere changed abruptly. Collecting the radio in his free hand, Boyd

178

instructed, 'All units. The target is the hire car and we have movement towards Carlisle. Make ground, tighten the net.'

When radio call signs acknowledged, Boyd smiled at Ryan and offered, 'Take the Treasury hat off, Ryan, and join in. Relax a touch. It might do you good. Toni has a job to do and she'll do it well because she's a top operative. You enjoyed last night. Now try and get the best out of today.'

Nodding slightly, Ryan agreed with, 'I'll give it a go, Mister Boyd. But this is what I call a severe learning curve.'

Boyd offered a bar of chocolate which was accepted.

'Billy! Call me Billy, Ryan,' suggested Boyd. 'My team are all serving police officers and I like to think we acknowledge each other's ranks when we need to. It adds to the necessary discipline in a unit. You're not a serving officer so don't get too confused, Ryan. Billy will do nicely.'

Firing the engine, Boyd negotiated the slip road onto the motorway.

Looking down from the cockpit of his Cessna, Alan hit the digits of his mobile phone and updated Antonia Harston-Browne. Immediately swinging her Porsche into action, Antonia turned off the main road onto the byways criss-crossing the area.

Fifteen minutes later, the target hire car slid north onto the motorway as a surveillance team drove at speed to close the net on their subject.

Meanwhile, Antonia hit the Fells. She carried a medium sized haversack on her back and looked the part. Suitably dressed for the occasion, she plotted a route to the rear entrance of the Base.

On the motorway, the hire car travelled north from Carlisle at the entrance to the gateway of Scotland: Gretna. In the offside lane, the Ford cruised at seventy miles an hour with Boyd and company struggling to make ground from Penrith and elsewhere. But Janice kept the target in sight and fed the team speed and location as the action moved into the Scottish lowlands.

'Make ground,' radioed the Scot. 'Make ground, speed seventy miles an hour. I'm north towards Lockerbie on the M74. Speak to me people. Where are you?'

The radio was silent when Janice Burns sped north beneath the Gretna interchange bound for the heart of Caledonia.

Close to the Base, Antonia, gazed down onto the paintball site and took a compass bearing. Withdrawing an ordnance survey map and a tiny telescope from her haversack, she plotted her position on the map and tried to figure out exactly where she was. The surrounding terrain was unforgiving and, to the untrained eye, one Fell looked like any other. It was easy to mistake one dip in the land for one close by when they all appeared identical. But Antonia knew that precision was needed for she wanted to hit the rear of the Base first time.

Raising the telescope to her eye, she focused the device and honed in on the complex below. Eventually, she traced a lane from the main road into the complex where buildings were situated. Then she surveyed the terrain further and sought out the mine Susie mentioned. A vehicle suddenly approached the entrance to the Base and Antonia moved adroitly behind one of the boulders littering the Fell side.

Once the vehicle had trundled by, Antonia dropped onto her knees and used the cover of a boulder to prepare herself. Flopping onto her belly, Antonia used her telescope and scanned the Base; the buildings, and the path leading to the mines. Eventually, she located the two large oak trees spoken of and the old narrow bridge straddling the slender stream. More importantly, perhaps, Antonia followed the line of a barbed wire fence that provided a perimeter border to the complex.

Deserted, the Base seemed to be a ghost town.

An aircraft flew overhead when Toni's mobile phone rang.

'It's me,' revealed Alan Grant. 'I'm low on fuel but I can't see any movement down there. Be aware there's a Land Rover parked near the main building. That said there's no sign of life. I have to go now. Good luck! You're on your own.'

Antonia didn't reply but watched the Cessna drop a wing slightly and turn away from the area. She pocketed her telescope and selected a patch of land she believed would lead her to the rear entrance.

Moments later, Antonia began a slow and vigilant approach to the Base. Gingerly, she climbed over the barbed wire boundary to make her way downhill. Identifying the two old oak trees, she strolled quietly across an old wooden bridge spanning a narrow stream and then melted into the undergrowth for a moment.

Somewhere in the depths of Antonia's mind she wondered why she loved her job. Map reading! I should have tutored geography and topography in college, she decided with a smile to herself. No, I should have lectured on Greek Mythology at Cambridge or Oxford, she considered. Even teaching micro economics at Harvard would surely be more rewarding and profitable than this, she thought.

Catching her hair on a clump of gorse, Antonia reminded herself of a hair appointment she needed to make for the forthcoming country club event. If they could only see me now, she laughed. What would those fine friends of mine make of me now, she considered. Would they think me brave and patriotic as I work for the good of my country? Or would they call me a charlatan for never telling them the truth about my occupation?

Overhead, a Common Buzzard squawked a warning and interrupted her train of thought.

Seconds later, her hand glided over dry sheep droppings when she realised the entrance to the mine was a mere thirty yards ahead of her. Antonia studied the rusting narrow gauge railway lines that wandered towards the mine entrance and stopped suddenly at the behest of a padlocked wooden gate. Scrutinising the heavy close coupled padlock she speculated on why a bright new hasp had been affixed to a solid wooden frame. Intrigued, Antonia debated the state of the crumbling rock framing the gateway.

Why? What is the door hiding, she deliberated. What is so important that it has to be hidden in a mine shaft locked away from public view? Or is someone really just trying to block off a hazardous part of the land?

Stolen property, she deliberated. Works of art perhaps or expensive antiques? No, she decided. Surely those kind of articles needed special conditions in which to be kept: the correct temperature and humidity for example. Puzzled, Antonia reminded herself that there might actually be another building below ground. Conceivably she might be standing above it as this very moment. But then, of course, they might be hiding drugs, firearms, explosives, gold bars and foreign currency or….

'Get a grip,' she whispered. 'You've no idea so stop speculating and get on with the job.'

Antonia's belly hugged the land when she inched warily towards the mine's entrance. Pausing, she took a deep breath and held the sounds on the wind. The noise of weapons being discharged from the paintball site close by could not be heard. There was no tell-tale murmur of a Land Rover engine ticking over or bursting into life from its location near the buildings. There was nothing to worry about. She was alone. Wasn't she? The man they called Azzam drove the Ford hire car, didn't he? Damn this job, Antonia decided. Always too many unanswered questions.

Edging forward and then, from the corner of her eye, Antonia caught sight of a free-standing piece of timber sprouting from the land. She knew immediately what it was, why it was there, and that it was not alone. Holding her breath, she froze her very core to the ground and focused her eyes. Moving her head slightly, Antonia observed a fixture attached to the timber and realised it might be partly hidden by natural foliage. A careful study of the terrain led her to another free-standing piece of timber. Antonia deduced that both timbers had been battered into the ground by an unknown hand. The shafts of wood shooting from the harsh soil provided buttresses for a mechanism of active infra-red beams that supported an invisible weatherproof alarm system. It was sited immediately in front of her.

Riveted to the spot, Antonia's eyes tried to hypnotise the alarm system. She tried desperately to locate a battery that fuelled the device. Or was it solar powered? She did not know.

What she did know was that the safety catch on her handgun was in the on position and held in an ankle holster. Her fingers stretched down, removed the weapon, and eased it into the belt at the small of her back.

To move forward might lead to folly. To remain glued to the ground would not persuade progress. There was no point in ringing Boyd. He was probably too busy on the motorway. Who should she phone: the country club? She managed a sly chuckle as she considered her plight.

Only then did it dawn on Antonia that there might be close circuit video system recording proceedings.

Where is the battery pack? Where is the hidden camera, she wondered. Withdrawing from the area slightly, she removed her telescope again and settled down to carry out a three hundred and sixty degree search of the foliage.

Antonia began by focusing the tiny scope and holding it carefully to her eye. Then she scanned the flora and undergrowth trying to uncover the power supply and a hidden camera.

Her mobile phone vibrated and she knew it was Boyd.

Answering the call, Antonia spoke quietly and said, 'Speak!'

With the sound of traffic in the background coming through the mobile, Antonia heard Boyd report, 'We're off! The rabbit is running north into Scotland would you believe.'

'Ibrox!' suggested Antonia. 'Just a wild guess!'

'Who knows,' replied Boyd. 'How's the walk going?'

'I'm at the rear of the Base. There's no-one around but the entrance to the mine is covered with alarm beams and I'm just checking to see if there's a hidden camera anywhere. Otherwise, the weather's fine thanks.'

When the speedometer reached ninety five miles an hour, Boyd spoke into his hands free system saying, 'Are you carrying?'

Aware of the weapon nestling peacefully in her belt, Antonia replied, 'Correct! Where are you?'

'Good! We're about five miles behind, I reckon, with no radio reception and making ground as fast as we can. I hope we haven't lost Janice. If she turned off at the last interchange and we didn't hear the call then we are in big trouble.'

'The shoestring brigade strike again, Boyd. But have you considered that potentially she might also be in trouble. Ring her,' advised Antonia.

'We will if we don't catch up soon,' replied Boyd. 'Look, top of my head, Toni, Susie never mentioned beams or cameras and she was right outside the mine entrance. How close are you?'

'Not so close! Why? What's going on in that brain of yours, oh mighty one?' asked Antonia.

'Long shot for you,' replied Boyd concentrating on the road ahead. 'The alarm is on because the man is in front of me. It could be a new alarm system. Why wasn't it there when Susie was there? Or didn't she see it? When he was there with Susie he had no need for an alarm. But he's absent from the site today so he's rigged the beams and a camera so he can see if anyone is snooping about whilst he's away. Kids and nosey neighbours he can do without and deal with. It's people like you and me that will upset him. We've got a worried suspect, Toni! Is the mine entrance still padlocked?'

Antonia used the telescope and confirmed the presence of a heavy duty padlock.

Boyd replied, 'Good! Whatever he's got hidden in there is important to him. I'm going to stick my neck out and say that if there is a camera operating it will only activate when the alarm is triggered or interfered with and it will take a head on shot. Think about yourself putting the alarm system in. You'd want a good photograph of the intruder so I reckon the camera might even be inside the mine or in such a position as to get a really good photo of someone rattling the padlock before moving on. Does that make sense?'

'Perfectly,' replied Antonia. 'It might even be a video camera for all we know. I think I'll withdraw and take a look at the buildings instead. I don't want to spoil things at this stage of the game.'

'Agreed,' responded Boyd. 'Give it a wide berth, Toni. How's that sound?'

'Wonderful!' delivered Toni. 'I'll ring you when I'm clear of the site.'

'Roger that,' snapped Boyd.

With a silent phone Antonia began to retrace her steps. Once she'd made away from the mine entrance, she hitched the haversack onto her back and stepped towards the heart of the Base, an obstacle course, and a gathering of buildings that appeared to form both the main office and accommodation block.

Thinking aloud, Antonia said, 'I sure hope you're right, Billy Boyd, because if you're not there's someone probably following every move I make.'

Watching from a top story flat in Luton, Khalid gazed down on the morning traffic negotiating a roundabout and then peered deeper to the footpath below. He checked both ways and eyed the postman working his way along the street with a brown canvas sack slung across his shoulder. Khalid studied the young postman with his mop of ginger hair reaching towards his shoulder blades. Then he espied a green Ford reducing speed near a pedestrian crossing, pip a horn, and travel on.

Nervous, Khalid studied the people below.

They were as ants in fresh camel dung on an ascending pathway to the Spin Ghar mountain range, thought Khalid. Afghanistan's mother tongue – Pashto – referred to the Spin Ghar as the White Mountains, and Khalid longed to be there now. That long winding one hundred mile natural border between Pakistan and Afghanistan. Yet there were countless coloured skins and a chatter of sundry tongues irritating the streets below.

Kafir, wondered Khalid. Are they all disbelievers? No, some I see are like me. Not all of them and I do not think we share the same language. I cannot reach and touch these people. I may not shout and seek water or fruit for my dry lips and empty belly. I only have a pittance of an offering left on this larva infested table. Bread! Butter! Jam! Chocolate! And thick milk that smells like the entrails of a dead goat that has lain in the heat of the day. How do they drink this bilious liquid? It is surely the urine of an old camel struggling to climb to its knees as it chews on the last remnants of sward. This is not the food of heroes. This is merely a contemptible snack for a weary traveller waiting for the next phase of his journey. At home, in the mountains, I was their idol. I heard the incantations of my name when I walked out. Now I am hiding with ants in the hot brown shit of the infidel. I am nothing. When can I plunge my dagger deep into this black unbelieving heart? When?

Khalid shook his head free from thoughts of home. Catching his reflection in the window he decided he ought to stop complaining to himself. He fingered the scar on his face and traced its full course with a reluctant sigh. I am safe here, he decided, and I shall only be here a short time until I am collected for the final leg of the journey. I am secure because I can see what is going on in the streets below. It is as if I were sentry on a rocky outcrop, he thought. I can see all below me. I am free.

Standing back from the window, Khalid wiped his brow and checked his wristwatch before taking a seat by the table. It wasn't the heat that worried him. It was the cramped space he had been told to occupy. He'd remembered the address given to him when he changed aircraft in Paris. He'd committed it to his brain and made his way there by taxi shortly after arriving in England. Now he waited for instructions.

Unused to these claustrophobic conditions, Khalid began to sweat more. Within a short time, perspiration oozed from his skin and he pulled the collar of his tee shirt wider in an attempt to gain fresh air.

I should be cold, decided Khalid. My dear father told me I would be chillier in England at this time of the year.

Upon the table lay Khalid's mobile phone and a remote control handset for a television affixed to the wall. He stared at the phone, checked his wristwatch once more, and waited.

Suddenly, there was a singular blurt of hullabaloo emitted from the device before Khalid snatched it from the table and clasped it to his ear.

Listening for a moment, he contorted his face in anguish and furnished the caller with, 'I stay here? That is not what I was told.'

Khalid stepped again to the window and gazed down onto the streets. There was no sign of the postman only an excess of spellbound human ants intent on eating into Khalid's mind.

Nervously, Khalid retired into the belly of the apartment.

The call ended and Khalid angrily slammed his phone on the table.

Breaking bread with his hands, he mouthed a crust before spitting it out in disgust.

Studying the phone for moment, he allowed his fingers to trickle across the digits. Eventually, he picked up the device and rang the number.

Pacing his room, Khalid waited trying to control his rising temper. When there was an answer, his father, Abdul-Ahad, spoke quickly from the mountainous wastes of the Afghanistan – Pakistan border.

'Why do you telephone me at this time of day?'

'Father! We are told not to move. It is dangerous.'

'Father?' queried Abdul-Ahad, 'I am but a poor goat herder walking a stony path looking for those that might be lost. I have no son. My son left long ago.'

'Father, it is I Khalid. What should I do? I need your help.'

With the soft dust of a desert compound creeping across his open-toed sandals, Abdul-Ahad, spoke quietly but powerfully when he replied, 'When a goat is lost on the mountain it will try and find its own way down. Yet when the goat herder calls out to the goat, the animal will merely wait on the mountain path until it is gathered into the fold once more.'

'Sit tight? Do you want me to sit tight?'

Abdul-Ahad suggested, 'I am but a goat herder walking the path for my lost herd.'

Closing his cell phone, Abdul-Ahad looked down to the floor with a heavy heart and then gradually re-joined his company.

Khalid held the phone, realised his hand shook, and spoke aloud, 'Once I was an ant now I am a goat but I must stay here and wait.'

An electronic pulse activated the wall-mounted television. Khalid sat on the only armchair available, rested the remote on the arm, and settled down to watch a dose of western entertainment.

Back on the motorway a crackle of static informed Boyd they were gaining on Janice. A short time later, her grey Seat came into view and Boyd radioed, 'In your mirror, Janice. We are with you!'

'Och! About time too! Thank God for that,' radioed Janice. 'I'm peeling off. He's yours.' An interchange came into view and Janice signalled a nearside turn and began to leave the motorway.

There was no acknowledgement when Stuart Armstrong swept through and took up the lead position.

Mile after mile followed as the surveillance team ploughed north into the heart of Scotland tailing the Ford Focus and its occupant. Eventually, Glasgow was upon them and the convoy reduced speed as traffic became more congested.

In an off road parking area near Caldbeck's radio mast and transmitter station, Antonia sat on the tailgate of her Porsche and removed her boots. Massaging her feet, she connected with Boyd on her mobile and then checked her camera's product. Digital cameras are first rate technology, she thought, whilst she sat in the sunshine inspecting snaps of the buildings she'd taken at the Base. Flashing though the photographs, she returned again to a couple of snapshots of the mine entrance and studied them once more.

Her mobile sounded again. This time it was Anthea.

'I've got a result,' she announced from her computer console in the Thames House office.

'Good! Well done,' replied Antonia. 'Who's the leak?'

Anthea responded with, 'Sorry, I'm nowhere nearer to that than when I started. No, I mean the ownership of the mine.'

'Goodness,' gasped Antonia. 'What have you got then, Anthea?'

'Details concerning the owners of the mine!' delivered Anthea.

'You've been reading my mind,' suggested Antonia.

'Of course,' laughed Anthea. 'I'll leave a message on Boyd's mobile. He can listen to it when he has time. Anyway, the mines were owned by Northern Fells Mineral Deposits Ltd. They operated the mines for over thirty years until extracting the deposits became unviable. They sold the mine to a charitable organisation. Not surprisingly, I can't trace any of the previous owners of the mine but I have got into the charity.'

'Interesting,' proposed Antonia.

'Yes! The mine, buildings, and surrounding land inside the boundary are now owned by the Shamama Muslim Educational Trust. It's based in the Midlands and is a very highly respected institution.'

'Shamama?' queried Antonia.

'The word means 'forgive',' explained Anthea. 'The Trust is a registered charity and has a very good long standing reputation. There's nothing suspicious recorded about the organisation.'

'Ah well, it was worth a try,' counselled Antonia.

'Oh I haven't finished yet,' declared Anthea. 'I decided to check out the individual directors and Trustees of the charity. One of them, Abd-Al-Rashid, is on the CIA's terrorist watch list.

'Is he really,' gasped Antonia. 'Bet you don't know what Abd-Al-Rashid means, Anthea?'

'Servant of the Rightly Guided,' chirped Anthea. 'I cheated and looked it up by the way. Tell me, Antonia, does being on the CIA watch list mean that you guys have the subject under surveillance?'

'Not necessarily,' replied Antonia. 'It depends on the subject and the intelligence used to place the individual on the list. It could mean anything from be aware of to monitor closely. We're mainly interested in people like that when they are travelling across international borders. Either way, we'll chase that one up with our American allies. '

'Oh, I've already done that. I went through the appropriate channels here in Thames House and eventually spoke to the American Embassy here in London. I got blanked to start with but eventually got to the right man from Virginia. Abd-Al-Rashid is on the CIA watch list because he was mentioned in an intelligence report eight years ago. Apparently, it was alleged he was involved in sending members of an extreme Islamic sect to Pakistan for training in terrorism.'

'You have been busy,' encouraged Antonia. 'I'm impressed, Anthea. I'd thought you'd have enough trouble keeping on top of the intelligence newsreel but I was wrong. No wonder, Boyd wants you as his inspector. I think I'd better get back to my desk or I'll be losing my job. '

'Ha-ha,' replied Anthea. 'Good one! No, I wondered if your service might be on him but we needed an answer so I chased it to the end. The problem is there's nothing substantial in this. It might be fact or it might be hearsay. The trace to the servant of the rightly guided is inconclusive.'

Antonia considered for a moment and then offered, 'If it's fact then we need to be very wary. If it's hearsay from primary or secondary associates that are in the melting pot then he's running with the wrong people so we need to be vigilant. Either way, he's just earned a huge red interest marker from me. What else did you discover, Anthea?'

'The Trust exists to provide schooling and educational opportunities for those affiliated to the Muslim religion,' explained Anthea. 'But I haven't actually discovered when this particular individual became a member of the Trust.'

'Anything else on the corruption investigation?'

'Nothing, but I've a note from Chief Inspector Boyd asking for a timeline analysis of our friend Ryan.'

'And?' queried Antonia.

'There's a gap every Tuesday morning for about two and a half hours.'

'How do you know that?' asked Antonia.

'He's always out of the office. His mobile and office phone show no use and it's habitual. Every Tuesday without fail; he disappears to who knows where!'

'Fascinating,' offered Antonia. 'Let me think about that one and I'll get back to you. I have an iron in the fire.'

'That's fine. I'm struggling a little. Boyd is with Ryan at the moment. Do I ring to tell him or let it ride for the moment?'

Antonia advised, 'The melting pot is getting quite big now, Anthea. No, let it simmer for a while. Indeed, wait until today's surveillance is over.'

'Will do, Antonia. I wonder how they're getting on.'

The surveillance team pressed north along the M8 motorway with Renfrew on its offside and Paisley on its nearside. Stuart led the convoy reporting position and speed as well as informing the entourage of each and every monument that came into view. Suddenly, Stuart radioed, 'Boss car, there's another monument coming into view. Take closer order, guys.'

'What do you see?' requested Boyd a mile or two behind.

'Glasgow airport!' expressed Stuart.

'Departing or meeting arrivals?' asked Boyd.

'I wouldn't like to say,' offered Stuart. 'But the target is reducing speed and moving to the nearside. It looks like he's going flying, Guvnor.'

'Keep tight, boys and girls,' instructed Boyd. 'I'll make a call.'

The driver of the blue Ford swung casually to the nearside and waited for the slip road to appear. Moments later, an indicator began to flash and the Ford drifted from the motorway and headed towards the airport complex.

Meanwhile, Boyd arranged for CCTV coverage to meet and greet the target, and keep him company during his visit.

But Boyd shared Stuart's concern and wondered if the target intended taking a trip abroad, or was he meeting a visitor.

Stuart allowed a suitable gap between himself and the target to form and then he held in behind other vehicles as they made their way to the long stay car park.

'Tail end Charlie, hold the back door,' radioed Stuart. 'He's looking for a parking space. Janice and Terry with me. Boss…!'

'You have control. I have the back door,' revealed Boyd on the radio. 'Give me photos and confirmation of the target.'

As the surveillance team wandered into the airport, Boyd manoeuvred to cover the static Ford should the driver return suddenly minus his followers.

'Aren't you going with them?' enquired Ryan.

'No, Stuart has the tab. He has convoy control.'

'Isn't he a bit young? What's he going to do if the man takes a flight?' queried Ryan. 'I mean, Stuart is in control?'

'There's only four of us,' reminded Boyd snatching the radio. 'Where are we and who have we got?' radioed Boyd.

'Stand by,' quipped Stuart. 'We're in the check in area for…. Wait one….. Yeah, we're in the check-in for international departures and the description fits Azzam. Stand by!'

Good man, thought Boyd who answered the hands free mobile on the dashboard.

'He's not joining the queue, Guvnor!'

'Interesting,' relayed Boyd. 'So what's he doing at the airport?'

The commander's voice rattled in Boyd's ear.

'William, Commander Herbert! I have the Head of Strathclyde Counter Terrorist Command on the other line. I've told him you are in control, not to panic, and to render you all possible assistance. What's going on?'

'Our man has gone walkabout at the airport, sir,' reported Boyd. 'Stuart has convoy control and we have the back door covered. CCTV ought to be on our side and I have confirmation that the target appears to be Azzam. Some holiday snaps will be on your desk some time later today. Other than that, there's nothing to report.'

'Is the suspect engaged in a terrorist attack?' probed Commander Herbert somewhat anxiously.

'Possibly,' replied Boyd. 'But actually I think we've just got a stooge at the moment. He's not up to anything illegal as far as I can see, sir. I'm watching and waiting to see what he does and if he presents his passport at control I'll ask the locals to move in and do a routine detention. Other than that, I'm giving him plenty of rope.'

'I'm on my way to the operations centre, William. I'll be in radio contact. Keep me updated. I'll alert Strathclyde as to the unfolding situation.'

The call ended and Ryan tapped Boyd on his elbow saying, 'That was quick!'

A liveried police car cruised into the entrance and discharged four heavily armed officers who proceeded to filter into the building in support of colleagues.

Boyd studied the gradual unrushed characteristics of the armed officers and radioed, 'This is Boyd. The locals are in the process of supplementing and strengthening security in the immediate area. Keep your eyes on the target and don't approach the triggers.'

'Is that wise?' enquired Ryan.

'I want their eyes on our target not the locals,' revealed Boyd. 'And it's too easy to saunter over, introduce yourself, and then blow your cover.'

As the radio call signs acknowledged, Janice chipped in with, 'I have some good head-on photo shots. He's stopped for coffee at one of the kiosks. Our man is just taking everything in. He's not going anywhere and if he's waiting for a friend then that's a no show.'

'Agreed!' from Stuart.

Little happened for quite a while; Azzam drank his coffee, walked the full length of the concourse, visited the gents toilets, and sat watching the queues gather at the check in desk of the various flight providers with yet another coffee. Eventually, Azzam slid the empty carton of coffee into a litter bin and made his way to a wall map.

Stuart and Janice held their ground but Terry Anwhari stood close by and realised the map showed the road system between the nation's airports. Convex in shape, the well illuminated map stood out and displayed all the arterial road routes between the sites. Close to the wall map a hire car kiosk was open for business. Azzam advanced to the counter, produced something from his wallet, and waited.

The attendant busied herself with paper work but Stuart radioed, 'Target is doing business at a hire car kiosk. Stand by!'

Azzam spun on his heel suddenly and approached the exit. Timing the revolving door, Azzam stepped from the warmth of the building into the chill of the day. It was all in a flash.

'I have a temporary loss on the subject,' radioed Stuart. 'Guvnor!'

On the zebra crossing at speed Azzam walked towards the car park and his Ford Focus with the followers lingering some way behind.

Boyd sensed the move, took control, watched the Arab come into view and radioed, 'Easy does it. I have him. Terry and Janice come through. Stuart hold and tidy the concourse until the wheels move. Recover the coffee mug. I want his fingerprints and I want to know what happened at the hire car spot.'

'Consider it done,' radioed Janice. 'The coffee mug is already in my bag by the way!'

'Gold star!' delivered Boyd impulsively. 'Okay, the subject is approaching the Ford. Standby!'

With Ryan reading a newspaper and Boyd pouring from a flask, Azzam strolled right past the two men, head down, collar up, and made for the Ford.

'What's he doing?' whispered Ryan sliding down his seat.

Studying the rear view mirror, Boyd replied, 'Act naturally, Ryan. Be yourself or you'll give the game away.'

'Sorry,' offered Ryan. 'I forgot.'

'Not to worry, I don't think he's made us,' suggested Boyd watching Azzam through the rear view mirror.' Well, well, he's walked right passed the Ford Focus.'

Boyd snatched the radio and said, 'All units, the target has ignored his wheels. He's still on foot in the car park. Eyes peeled everyone.'

Thirty seconds later Azzam dug deep into his trouser pocket, produced a key fob, and got into a purple Vauxhall Vectra. He fired the engine and reversed into the traffic flow at the same time as Boyd rattled out the information on the radio.

Out of sight of the target, Janice made her way to the hire car kiosk whilst Terry and Stuart quickly strode towards their vehicles.

On Boyd's surveillance log, another page turned and another chapter commenced as a purple Vauxhall Vectra driven by a man called Azzam cruised past on his way out of the airport.

'I have control,' radioed Boyd. 'He's out of the car park and headed for the roundabout. Come through.... Come through.... Back to the M8 motorway and into the southbound lane.'

'Guvnor,' radioed Janice. 'Our man has abandoned a hire car but collected a prepaid hire car from another company. It's hired in a different name. He's probably using a dodgy driving licence.'

'Understood,' snapped Boyd who threw an aside to Ryan, 'Get the Commander on the phone, Ryan, please.'

Ryan punched the digits as Boyd wrestled the BMW into a good position. Within minutes Azzam's purple Vauxhall was down the slip road and straight across the carriageway into the offside lane of the M8 motorway.

'He made me,' suggested Ryan. 'He picked me up when I ducked down thinking I was doing the right thing. It's my fault, chief inspector. I've put my foot in it. Look, he's flat out and making a run for it.'

The BMW hit ninety miles an hour as Boyd squeezed his foot on the accelerator and barged his way into the fast moving traffic.

'I don't think so, Ryan,' explained Boyd. He's got half a mile on us, that's all. Keep your eye on his motor and don't lose it.'

Engaging the radio, Boyd instructed, 'Make ground and come through, team. Our man has a heavy foot. We're south on the M8 at ninety miles an hour.'

The team rattled acknowledgements as Boyd spoke to Commander Herbert on the hands free.

'I'm monitoring your radio, William,' revealed the commander. 'I've arranged for the locals to finalise the enquiry at the hire car kiosk and my counterpart in Strathclyde has despatched a small surveillance team to monitor any movements of the Ford Focus that our man has left behind.'

'Excellent,' responded Boyd. 'This morning we were a blip on the map and now we are the map. What brought that on?'

Commander Herbert chuckled and queried, 'I'll let you into a secret shortly but tell me, William, you've enough to arrest Azzam now. At least one of those hire cars must have been acquired on a stolen or false driving licence. I'll wager your target has a double life. The thing is if you arrest him there's an opportunity to search the mine and his compound at Caldbeck. You'll get a search warrant once he's in custody. A recovery there might just tip the scales and add to the charges. What do you say?'

Checking his rear view mirror, Boyd became conscious of the team catching up. 'I say we give him a little more rope and see where he takes us, commander. Don't you agree? I mean, he's not going anywhere. He's half a mile ahead of me heading for Carlisle…. No…. No, he's moving over. He's eastbound towards Edinburgh. The plot thickens, commander.'

'Oh it's a thick plot all right, William. This operation really began when we received an intelligence report indicating that four Al-Qaeda operatives were headed for the UK. The source of the intelligence is electronic: a mobile phone. Apparently, the phone hasn't been used since but a short time ago our intelligence newsreel reported that the phone had been activated once more.'

'And?' probed Boyd.

'The telephone that instigated the hunt for four inbound terrorists spoke from the Afghan – Pakistan border to a cell phone in Luton earlier today. The national threat level has been increased and the Security Service has the lead. We've notified the locals and sent two enquiry teams to Luton to shake the cage and see what comes out. The notch has been turned, William. I'm withdrawing some of the routine work and I'm doubling up on some of our counter terrorist operations. Phillip and I both agree you have a good lead there. The DG is right behind you. What do you want in the way of manpower?'

'One full unit, one inspector, a sergeant and ten,' requested Boyd. 'Ours! All armed! And a booster to the radio signal.'

'I'll set the wheels in motion, William. You'll have a full unit with you tomorrow. I'm sure we can get the tech guys to boost our radio signals from the Caldbeck transmitter. What about air support?'

'I've got all I need at the moment, sir.'

'All done! Anthea wants a private word with you, William. Are you alone?'

Boyd collected the hands free and held it to his ear, 'Anthea, I've missed you. What have you got?'

'A timeline with four hours missing every Tuesday morning and a lecture for Ryan at the Training Centre at Hendon on Tuesday afternoon. I think that's what you wanted to know, Guvnor.'

Relaxing visibly, Boyd offered Ryan a smile and spoke into the telephone, 'Tell me, Anthea, what do Hendon want Ryan to lecture on?'

'The radicalisation of an Islamic terrorist!'

Dropping the phone to his chest, Boyd engaged Ryan and queried, 'Can you manage that, Ryan? It's a lecture at Hendon on Tuesday afternoon?'

'Of course, I'll take the train back in the morning if that's all right with you, Mister Boyd. I do feel I've made a mess of things and I'm going to get in the way.'

'Not at all, Ryan,' smiled Boyd. 'You came to see what we do and you've been fine. Now you can pour yourself into an intake of young recruits. It's important you share your knowledge with them.'

Nodding, quietly pleased and proud, Ryan stole a glance at the Glasgow skyline as the convoy powered east towards Edinburgh and the surroundings began to gradually adopt a more rural setting.

'He'll be there, Anthea,' reported Boyd. 'Perhaps you'll make all the arrangements necessary on our behalf. I'd like things to go smoothly and without any complications.'

'Arrangements…. 'Anthea paused, almost faltered and then heard Boyd repeat, 'All the arrangements, Anthea. I'd like to help you with this and I'm sure Antonia would too if she were there. Are you following me?'

Sometimes people who work together over long periods develop a sixth sense. Something of an acute awareness of what the other was thinking. Anthea replied, 'Of course! Leave everything with me.'

The call ended with Boyd reducing speed and moving into the centre lane giving way to Janice, Stuart and Terry as they roared through in pursuit of Azzam.

But there was no question in Azzam's mind of escaping the clutches of law. Unfettered, he enjoyed the open road and drove at speed because he could, not because he needed to avoid capture. A two and a half hour drive later revealed he'd bypassed Edinburgh and Dunbar, skirted the east coast route, and found himself on the A1 approaching Newcastle airport.

A quick check in his mirror revealed no following traffic and Azzam slid quietly from the A1 dual carriageway towards the airport.

By then, Alan Grant in his fixed wing Cessna flew across the interchange, circled, and radioed to the team below that the subject was entering the airport's long stay car park.

They closed round Azzam like bees round a honey pot and watched a repeat performance as he eyed the concourse, studied the lay out, drank coffee upon coffee, and then strolled to another hire car kiosk.

By close of play that night, the surveillance team returned to Cumbria with Azzam still in their sights. But Boyd recognised there was a mystery bursting at the seams now.

Talking to Commander Herbert on the phone, Boyd explained, 'Azzam drove that day from Caldbeck to Glasgow in a Ford Focus which we suspect was delivered to the Base by a local hire car company earlier that day. At Glasgow airport Azzam left the Ford and drove to Newcastle airport in a Vauxhall Vectra. So far so good, but he abandoned the Vauxhall in a parking space at Newcastle and returned to Caldbeck in another hire car: a grey Renault Megane.

'What do you make of it all, William?' probed Commander Herbert.

'So far he's planted two cars in two airport car parks for two of the four individuals expected to invade our shores, commander. I think our man Azzam is setting the skittles up.'

'If you're right, William,' suggested Commander Herbert, 'Let's hope we're there when they need knocking down.'

'Indeed,' replied Boyd.

'Tomorrow, William, what are your plans for tomorrow?'

'The target makes the plan, sir, as well you know. For myself, I expect to watch him plant two hire cars in unknown airports. I might be wrong but I'm surmising our man is in cahoots with our four unknowns that detailed in the intelligence newsreel. No disrespect intended but I presume we're all over airport arrivals?'

'Oh yes, William,' delivered Commander Herbert. 'We certainly are.'

'Wonderful, Commander, but right now I need a night watch when we wrap this one up later. Can you help?'

'I'll arrange a late watch, William. Probably local, leave it with me.'

The telephone call ended and Commander Herbert rested his hand on the phone cradle. Behind him staff in the operations centre worked into the night checking and double checking every passenger scheduled to enter the United Kingdom in the next seventy hours.

There are approximately forty significantly sized airports situated in the United Kingdom capable of handling international arrivals on a daily basis, acknowledged Boyd. But there are hundreds of smaller airports and aerodromes operating throughout the nation who are equally capable of accepting smaller craft on their landing strips. The list of passengers ran into many thousands. It wasn't that the named passengers hadn't been checked at the time of booking via the advanced passenger system. It is the case that the information given is correct and the governance, integrity and honesty of the provider are beyond question, isn't it? I mean, thought Boyd, would a provider willingly submit false information? Indeed, suggested Boyd to himself, would a State sponsor such activity by aiding and abetting the provision of false information. Yes, decided Boyd. State sponsored terrorism is not a new concept in the terrorist handbook. Yet Al-Qaeda has no geographical State and no international borders, considered Boyd. So how extreme is Islam? And how far will Al-Qaeda's friends and associates go to support Islamic extremism?

Well, sighed Boyd, we surely have one hell of a haystack in front of us. And somewhere inside there's four needles to find. Every piece of straw needs to be turned over, decided Boyd.

I'm missing something, thought Boyd. We're watching a guy plant cars here, there and everywhere for four suspects that our intelligence system tells me are coming to the UK to cause mayhem. But one of them is already here? Azzam is surely going to take us to Luton tomorrow. You mark my words. But there's something that must be done before I lose track of the evidence. I must prove that the man we are following is Azzam. Moreover, who on earth is Azzam? What's his real name? Will the fingerprints on the coffee mug help me prove his identity or will they just confirm he's a foreign national and the system has no trace of him?

Pinching his tired eyes, Boyd closed down for the night and made his way to bed.

Elsewhere, a man drove north on a dual carriageway through the night. The stars watched over him and guided him towards his destination. The stars were his friends, perhaps his only friends in a land where his enemy slept. His eyes grew accustomed to the dark. It was as if he were on horseback negotiating the mountain passes of his homeland. He picked his way carefully through the traffic as if they were pieces of gorse or a rock or a bush on a mountain path.

The man drove alone. He'd been let loose in a declaration of war from his inner self. There was no route back for the individual. His name was Khalid and he was a killer of men.

*

Chapter Twelve
~

The Service Station.

Yawning, Terry Anwhari pulled up at his observation point on the A66 Penrith to Keswick road. Close to the Caldbeck turn off, near Mungrisdale, he yanked the handbrake on and reached into the rear seat for a vacuum flask. Time for a coffee or three, he thought as the night watch drove off to their beds.

Minutes later, a grey Renault Megane turned left out of the Caldbeck road and headed towards the motorway at Penrith. Terry recognised the driver as Azzam, ignored him as the Renault drove past, and took a drink of coffee.

As the Renault disappeared from view over the crest of a hill, Terry wound down his window and emptied his coffee cup. Casually, he fired the engine of his silver coloured Saab. He slid the vehicle into gear and gathered speed as he approached the crown of the road. Ahead of him, possibly close on a mile by now, the grey Megane motored downhill with the village of Skelton closing to its nearside.

Engaging his wireless, Terry smiled, shook his head, and radioed, 'Good morning, Cumbria! Game on. I hope you all had an early breakfast because we have a contact. Our man is up and away with the early birds. A66 towards the M6 motorway, speed about six zero. I'm on him. Anyone want to join in?'

Terry carried a vision of his teammates quickly disposing of cups, mugs, chocolate bars, newspapers, and a host of trivia as the news of an early movement whistled across cyberspace.

In no time at all, they were onto the motorway southbound at a steady seventy miles an hour with the grey Megane leading the way and Terry Anwhari controlling the surveillance convoy as they headed for the heart of England.

Janice screeched in broad Scots, 'It's nae right, mon. I've no had ma cuppa. I cannae be on wid this!'

'Tallyho! Tallyho! Tallyho!' radioed Stuart, assuming a pompous English accent. 'The fox is jolly well running and the Bassett hounds are on the scent!'

'My goodness, Antonia,' cracked Boyd. 'I've suddenly got a happy squad. I can feel it on the airwaves.'

'About time too,' chuckled Antonia. 'It must be in the water.'

Seizing the radio, Boyd said, 'Good shout, Terry. We are closing with you. Be advised, you'll meet Jack Marshall's surveillance team heading north. They're on their way to strengthen our squad.'

Before Terry answered, a degree of static buzzed across the frequency and a voice announced, 'Jack Marshall and his team are waiting for you at Tebay services. We're holding here. Keep me advised as to direction and speed.'

'Morning, Jack,' acknowledged Boyd recognising the voice.

They were on. The commander had been as good as his word when another unit supplemented Boyd's squad and gradually filtered into the system as Jack Marshall's team took over the lead. Antonia had joined Boyd as passenger whilst Ryan headed for London by train with a series of lectures to prepare.

By midmorning, Azzam turned from the M6 and followed the signs for Manchester airport. This time Boyd knew what might be expected and plotted his crew ahead of Azzam anticipating his every movement.

As predicted, yesterday's manoeuvres repeated themselves when Azzam reconnoitred the international departure lounge, drank copious amounts of coffee from a carton, and then surreptitiously planted another hire car in the long stay car park.

Boyd placed the vehicle under surveillance and joined in the long uneventful drive home.

Uneventful that is until Janice radioed, 'I'm refuelling at Charnock Richard service station. I'll catch you guys later.'

As part of the surveillance team followed Azzam north on the motorway, Janice drifted onto the slip road knowing part of the team would not join her on their journey north. It is the way the team refuelled. Everyone dropped off and took their turns to fill up. At all times, at least fifty per cent of the team were half full of fuel.

Suddenly, a message transmitted across the national radio network.

'All units! Approximately five minutes ago an armed robbery on the Standish to Chorley road occurred at a building society. Four males armed with assault rifles are wanted in connection with this offence. Dressed in black coveralls, they were seen leaving the area in a dark blue Ford Galaxy …. Part registration PJ10BK…'

Janice looked twice but there was no mistake. It was there, in front of her, pulling up on the service station car park. It had to be them: the bank robbers, thought Janice.

The Galaxy came to a standstill. Three men on board alighted from the vehicle and approached the boot. Removing overalls, gloves and head gear, they hauled bulging holdalls from the boot and waited for their driver to join them.

Pulling into the nearest car parking space, Janice snatched the radio and interrupted the wireless broadcast with, 'Four men debussing from a dark blue Ford Galaxy with a similar registration number at Charnock Richard service station on the northbound carriageway.'

'Say again,' snapped the radio controller.

Her heart beat loudly and adrenalin zipped its way round the bloodstream when Janice repeated her message and then rattled out, 'Boyd! Trigger! Trigger! Trigger! Charnock Richards northbound!'

Hearing the call, Boyd responded immediately. 'Units north of the services continue with the target. Units south of the services attend…Break… Break…. Break….'

Pressing his foot to the floor, Boyd snatched a view in his mirror and then swung the BMW across the carriageway clipping the hard standing and bouncing onto the grass verge as he made for the parking area. There was a blare of car horns from passing drivers annoyed at the madcap detective's infringements.

'Steady on!' screamed Antonia grasping a handgrip.

Boyd stood on the brakes and slowed the vehicle trying to assume a sedate gentle pace into the service area.

The driver of the Galaxy stepped out of his vehicle at the same time Boyd's BMW lurched over the kerb and bounced onto the tarmac.

'Who's that?' he asked pointing to the BMW.

'Shit!' swore Janice grasping the radio again, 'He's made us. I am engaging… No choice!'

Pushing the driver's door open, Janice stepped from the Seat and used the roof of the car to assume a shooting position. Shouting, 'Armed Police! Standstill!' She thrust her handgun in the direction of the Galaxy's driver.

Two of the suspects were visibly stunned and froze immediately but one of the men ducked to the opposite side of the Galaxy, out of sight, and rummaged in his holdall. Meanwhile, the driver dived back into the Galaxy and reached into the passenger well.

'Hands! Let me see those hands!' snapped Janice.

Acknowledging the drama, Boyd quickly slammed the accelerator to the floor and powered the BMW to the scene. He yanked on the handbrake and spun the steering wheel slewing the vehicle to a broadside. 'Go!' he shouted and sensed Antonia roll out of the vehicle with her handgun drawn.

The preferred weapon of the Special Crime Unit is the subcompact Glock 26 designed specifically for concealed carry and favoured by plain clothes officers in the Unit. When fixed with a factory magazine the handgun holds 33 rounds of ammunition. It is no match for an AK-47 despite its fearsome reputation.

'Hands! Hands! Let me see your hands!' repeated Janice, yelling at the top of her voice. The sweat poured from her brow and her heart thundered spurred on by cold fear but she held on relentlessly again yelling, 'Hands!'

In the background, travellers emerging from the refreshment area realised what was going on and either ran to their vehicles or stepped back inside to hide from the melee. There was a flurry of activity when a young child stepped from the shelter of her parents towards the Galaxy.

Snatching the child to safety, Antonia threw the girl to one side when she pointed her weapon at the two subdued suspects.

The driver reappeared with a sawn-off double barrel shotgun retrieved from the Galaxy's interior. He levelled the weapon and discharged two shots towards Janice. Some of the slugs peppered the Seat's door but others tore into Janice's shoulder. Simultaneously, she dropped her handgun, screamed in agony, and hurtled backwards towards a cement litter bin.

Boyd snapped two shots off from his Glock towards the Galaxy's driver who took the full force in his chest and careered backwards dropping the shotgun at his feet.

Searching for cover, Boyd dived behind a litter bin and then dragged Janice by the shoulder with him.

Screaming in agony, blood gushed from Janice's shoulder as individuals screamed and ran for safety in the ensuing mayhem. One of Antonia's captives suddenly bent down reaching for his colleague's shotgun whilst another of the robbers salvaged an AK-47 from his holdall and jerked off a rambling salvo of ammunition across everyone's heads.

As two of the robbers turned their guns on Antonia, the red headed MI5 lady from the cloisters of a quintessential country club in the south of England, let rip with a barrage of fire from her Glock. One man fell, hit in the chest, as Antonia hunched to one knee, speed loaded with another clip, and promptly wounded another assailant in the chest area.

With the air alive with screaming people, the nauseous smell of cordite, and the distant sound of a lone police siren, Boyd engaged the man with the AK-47. Standing astride Janice, protective of his colleague, Boyd pulled the trigger of his handgun and loosed off round after round from the Glock.

A wild staccato response rent the air as the full power of the assault rifle came into play and ripped chunks from the cement bin and tarmac close to Boyd.

Throwing himself to the ground, Boyd minimised himself as a target, rolled onto his stomach, and aimed two shots at the aggressor.

Whilst AK-47 shell cases flew into vacant air, one of Boyd's bullets lodged in the gunman's knee causing the gunman to stumble agonisingly to the ground. The assailant's AK-47 seemed to falter for a moment but then the gunslinger raked the area with a bombardment of firepower which saw Boyd rolling beneath the Seat dragging Janice possessively behind him.

Screaming in pain, eyes rolling, blood spurting from her shoulder, Janice used her good arm to limply point her Glock at one of the gunmen. There was a clatter when the gun dropped to the ground when she was unable to retain control.

The AK-47 exploded in rage and tore into the environment. Fragments of metal rained from the vehicle, tarmac exploded into a dozen or more dark bundles of shrapnel, and a posse of surveillance cars suddenly appeared travelling the wrong way down the hard shoulder and into the service area.

The robber with the AK-47 ignored the excruciating pain in his knee. Dragging himself towards the Galaxy he heaved himself into the driver's seat. At every juncture, he turned, loosed off a fusillade of gunfire at anyone and everyone and then powered the car engine.

He slammed the Galaxy into gear whilst simultaneously discharging the weapon from an open car window.

Stuart Armstrong and Jack Marshall rolled from their vehicles and returned fire.

Terry Anwhari had other ideas. Slamming the accelerator to the metal, he deliberately rammed his vehicle into the Ford Galaxy and effectively blocked any escape route.

There was a sickening crunch of metal grinding harshly into metal when the two vehicles entwined and the driver of the Galaxy smashed through the windscreen and flew through the air landing on the vehicle's bonnet.

A second later, he was surrounded by the plain clothes officers holding him at gun point.

Taking control instantly, Boyd unearthed himself from beneath the Seat, pulled Janice into an open space and began applying pressure to her wound.

'Weapons!' shouted Boyd as he bore down on Janice's shoulder and high chest area.

There was a quick check of the gunman and the sound of 'Clear!' 'Clear!' 'Clear!' as the team made their prisoners' weapons safe.

'Who's down?' shouted Boyd.

Antonia replied quietly, 'Looks like we took two out with two badly injured. How's Janice?'

'Not good!' sounded Boyd. 'She's losing a lot of blood. Terry! Call it in! We want ambulances and a helicopter evacuation.'

Grasping the radio, Terry Anwhari rattled of the situation and requirements to the control room.

A liveried Lancashire Constabulary car skidded to a halt close by and two uniform officers ran across.

'Anyone hurt?' shouted one of the officers.

Terry Anwhari shouted, 'Two dead, three with gunshot wounds.'

Grasping Boyd's arm Janice demanded weakly, 'Did we get them, Guvnor? Did we get the bank robbers?'

Still delivering direct pressure to her shoulder, Boyd cracked, 'Yes, Janice. You did well.'

Janice closed her eyes and began to slip away with Boyd pleading, 'Don't you dare, Janice Burns. Stay with me, girl; stay with me. That's an order. Do you hear me, girl?'

Five minutes later an air ambulance arrived on the scene and gently lowered to the ground before tending to Janice and the other casualties.

The service area was closed for six hours as crime scene investigators and a coroner's officer combed the area interviewing witnesses and securing evidence for court. But within the hour, the gun battle was national news and all over a dozen or more social media sites. Modern technology captured every second of the police response to the armed robbers and Facebook and twitter were soon bouncing with the news from Charnock Richards. No-one could recall the last time there had been such a horrendous fire fight involving the police and criminals on British soil.

That same day the Independent Police Complaints Commission was appointed to fully investigate the incident.

Boyd's unit was temporarily delayed whilst they underwent an ordeal of questions and answers with the investigators.

At the hospital later that night, Janice was stable and, although she had lost a lot of blood, a smooth recovery was on the cards.

When Boyd and Antonia walked away from Janice's bedside into the outside corridor, Terry and Stuart approached.

'How is she?' asked Stuart.

'Badly hurt with a heavy blood loss but she's going to be alright,' revealed Boyd. 'She's asking for her family and they're on the way. But she wants to see you too, Stuart.'

Stuart nodded and then stepped into the ward.

'Did we lose him, Terry?' queried Boyd.

'No,' disclosed Terry. 'Two of Jack's team were so far north of the services they just continued with the target. They housed him at Caldbeck a short time ago and I stood them down. The night watch has him. There's no reason why the target should suspect us. He was long gone from the services when the shooting started.'

'Yeah, well you guys did well,' offered Boyd. 'I don't know what we'd have done without you.'

'Word is you probably saved Janice's life, Guvnor,' suggested Terry.

'He did,' confirmed Antonia. 'Janice would have taken more shots if the boss hadn't dragged her out of the way.'

'Don't be ridiculous,' promoted Boyd. 'I was using her as a shield that's all. Look, we need to get back on track here.'

Antonia smiled at Boyd's dry humour and said, 'Really?'

'Actually,' reminded Boyd. 'Janice is the heroine. She engaged the crooks without taking one step backwards. I think we'll put her forward for a medal.'

Terry responded with, 'I'm sure she'll appreciate that but there's something you should know, Guvnor.'

'Go on,' suggested Boyd.

'Two of the deceased bank robbers have been identified as Libyans from Birmingham. They have links on the intelligence data base to Ansar al-Sharia: an extreme Islamist group that supports the establishment of Sharia law in Islamist States. The patron of Ansar al-Sharia is Al-Qaeda.'

'What about the two we have in custody? Is one called Adam by any chance?'

'No, but one of the deceased carries the name Abdul. There's no Adam and no Azzam if that's what you're looking for. I'm guessing the witnesses misheard what was said in all the noise and confusion. They're Pakistanis from Birmingham, Guvnor! By the way, Commander Herbert is under pressure. Someone in the Home Office has got it into their head we've just solved the case of four terrorists intent on a bombing campaign in the UK.'

Exchanging looks with Antonia, Boyd replied, 'They're criminals for God's sake. Just armed robbers with high powered weapons! Time and investigation might prove some or all of the money was stolen to fund terrorism but that's for the locals to pursue initially. It's Lancashire's enquiry. We've done our bit by responding to the call. We were in the right place at the right time and got lucky, that's all.'

'To put it bluntly,' interrupted Antonia. 'Janice was in the wrong place at the wrong time. She's the one with the battles scars.'

'Isn't she just,' admitted Boyd before continuing, 'Terry, look after things here and make sure Janice and her family get whatever they need. Antonia and I need to go and see a vicar.'

'No problem,' replied Terry. 'Safe journey, don't stop for petrol.'

'But think on this problem, guys,' remarked Boyd. 'We're supposed to be looking for four terrorists. So far, Azzam has planted three cars in three airports. Is he the fourth who's been here for some time or are we one short? Have we missed someone?'

There was a stunned silence and a shake of heads.

'I'm open-minded on that one, Boyd,' declared Antonia. 'But I'll let you into a secret. I need to reply to my cousin's text. In fact, I think I'll ring her on the way.'

'Your cousin?' queried Boyd as they made their way to the hospital car park.

'Jacquelina!' disclosed Antonia. 'She's a private investigator of sorts. I have an agreement with her which is mutually beneficial.'

'I daren't ask,' delivered Boyd. 'What is she privately investigating for you?'

'The Royal Flush!' delivered Antonia. 'Amongst other things.'

'The Royal Flush?' queried Boyd.

'Albert Charles Henry Ryan!'

'Does your DG, Mister Phillip Nesbitt know of this arrangement?' asked Boyd.

'Of course, we discussed it quite recently over coffee in his office. Now get this wreck of a BMW north and we'll take my Porsche. Your team needs four new cars or a whole lot of sticky gum to block the bullet holes.'

'I'll requisition three new Aston Martins shall I? I'm sure the Commander will just sign the papers without a care in the world.'

'I doubt it,' chuckled Antonia.

'Well, I could always try your mob. Your boss has a bottomless pit, hasn't he? I mean, you could put a good word in for me when next you're having a cosy tête a tête with him. Three Aston Martins – Blue ones please!'

'Can it, Boyd. You're getting on my nerves,' cracked Antonia.

Three hours later they were in Caldbeck with the Reverend Matthew Lowther and his family.

'Thanks for seeing us at such short notice, Matthew,' began Boyd. 'This actually won't take too long.'

'Well, it's late but we understand why,' revealed Matthew.

Removing an envelope from his pocket, Boyd produced a photograph and probed, 'Is this the man you call Azzam?'

Matthew looked at the surveillance snap and passed it to Elizabeth and Susie saying, 'Oh yes! No doubt! I take it you've been following him.'

'We're making extensive enquiries, Matthew,' admitted Boyd. 'I just needed to be completely sure that we are on the right man.'

'You two are heroes,' whispered Susie.

Antonia smiled and said, 'Well, I think that's all we came for unless you've anything we should know.'

'You were on the television earlier,' divulged Susie. 'It was like a wild west film. You were on television and they were shooting at you and you were shooting back.'

'Were we really?' asked Boyd. 'Well, these things rarely happen but it's over now. Look, Matthew, thanks for your time. We just needed to know that your Azzam was our Azzam, as it were, and you have.'

'I'm glad we could help,' revealed Matthew.

'Anytime,' confirmed Elizabeth.

'Are you going to shoot Azzam?' questioned Susie.

Antonia stepped in and said, 'Look, Susie, one day when we've more time we'll take a drive in my car again and discuss this. You see, we don't like shooting people and try really hard not to but every now and again these things happen and we have to protect ourselves.'

'Who was the lady you protected, Mister Boyd?' asked Susie.

'Just a friend,' replied Boyd.

'I'm glad you're my friend, Mister Boyd,' suggested Susie. 'I've never had a hero as a friend and I watched you on You Tube. You saved that lady's life.'

'I think the doctors at the hospital did that, Susie, but thanks,' acknowledged Boyd.

'Stay for coffee, why don't you?' invited Elizabeth.

'No, thanks,' replied Boyd. 'We have to be in London tomorrow morning.'

'Who will watch that man?' asked Susie.

'Colleagues,' explained Boyd. 'Now don't go worrying yourself, Susie. Everything is under control.'

'How long?' probed Matthew.

'Soon, Matthew,' revealed Boyd. 'I appreciate your patience and your discretion but all I can say at the moment is soon.'

Matthew nodded and opened the front door amidst handshakes and a farewell.

The Porsche powered up and set off down the drive.

Leaning on the window sill as Boyd and Antonia disappeared from view, Susie quietly whispered, 'I didn't like that man Boyd once but he's a hero now.'

*

Chapter Thirteen
~

Tuesday, London

Anthea drove the taxi and listened to a tale of the motorway antics of Antonia and Boyd before finally remarking, 'Just my luck. I end up pushing buttons on a computer whilst you guys end up with all the action.'

'What you got for us today?' probed Boyd. 'A Royal Flush by any chance?'

'Oh Ryan's unofficial codename,' suggested Anthea. 'Well, I'm driving and you're on the camera, Guvnor.'

'And what's my role?' asked Antonia.

'To buy us all a drink if we're on a wild goose chase,' suggested Anthea. 'Look, I'm hoping we're going to sort something out once and for all today. Ryan's timeline shows a gap every Tuesday morning when he just disappears. According to our data, there's no phone calls and no meetings. No trace of what he does each and every Tuesday morning.'

'Toni?' probed Boyd.

'I'd suspected he was having an affair with someone,' intervened Antonia. 'A man possibly as there's no evidence of him buying flowers and chocolates for a woman. Anyway, my ace source tells me there's nothing to report. Not one iota of sexual deviation. Either that or he's abducted by the aliens every Tuesday morning.'

The front door of a large semi-detached house closed and Ryan walked down the garden path, opened the gate, and got into his car to the distant accompaniment of Boyd's camera.

Moments later they were into heavy traffic heading for the Thames and central London.

'Heading for the Yard?' queried Boyd.

'Why hasn't he taken the tube?' queried Antonia.

'Beats me,' cracked Anthea. 'By the way, you asked me to set this up so I did. I'd appreciate it if you stopped asking questions and kept your eyes on the target. I don't know where he's going and I don't know why he's not using the tube. Maybe he'll park up soon. I don't know. What I do know is that you're only as good as your last job. Yesterday you were heroes but today you're observers. So kindly observe please.'

'Whoops!' offered Antonia.

'Point taken,' replied Boyd.

The operation continued with Anthea's black taxi secreted amongst a dozen others as they made their way into the capital's heart during rush hour.

'Here we go,' suggested Anthea. 'He's taken the lane for Tower Bridge and the A11.'

The camera snapped again capturing Ryan's vehicle changing lanes. Stop go traffic interrupted a smooth drive but before long Ryan was crossing the Thames and then onto Whitechapel Road heading east.

'I have a bad feeling about this,' delivered Boyd.

'Me too,' admitted Antonia.

Reaching the borough of Tower Hamlets, Ryan drove through the narrow streets into Brick Lane.

'What do you see?' asked Boyd shooting more photographs.

'Mosques everywhere,' replied Anthea. 'And a multitude of nationalities.'

'Precisely!' remarked Boyd. 'Where are we Bangladesh or Pakistan?'

'We're in multi-cultural England,' suggested Antonia. 'Just about every nationality you can think of from Somalis, Chinese, Vietnamese, Indian, Pakistani, Black African, and Caribbean. It's the most deprived area in the United Kingdom and successive governments have neglected it. Now they're about to feel the backlash because English is the second language here and if you look around you'll see synagogues, mosques, a Buddhist centre and a Hindu temple.'

'Welcome to London,' offered Boyd.

'Where are the Pearly Queens and the cockneys?' asked Anthea.

'Moved out long ago, I suspect,' remarked Boyd. 'Look, maybe our man caught religion after all.'

'Do you think so?' queried Antonia.

Boyd replied, 'It reminds me of what the vicar once said. It is the wish of our Lord that the world will one day live together in harmony.'

'Well,' observed Antonia. 'If the Lord is chairing the debate, he's got all the religions at the same table here.'

'Has our man caught religion though?' repeated Boyd.

Ryan locked his car and walked away passing a Buddhist centre before turning into a street of terraced houses.

Boyd's camera worked overtime.

'I think we are about to be enlightened,' remarked Anthea.

Guiding the taxi into the nearside kerb, Anthea switched the engine off and watched Ryan who knocked on one of the doors. Smoothly, she raised a pair of binoculars to her eyes, observed the house number, and then announced, 'Guvnor, the address is well known to us.'

'I know the street name but you'll have to remind me why I should know the house, Anthea,' proposed Boyd working his camera.

'It's the home of a Quadi,' declared Anthea. 'An Islamist judge who presides over a Sharia court. This particular Quadi is a doctor in the area.'

A stunned silence shrouded Boyd and Antonia before Boyd replied, 'Yes, of course it is. I seem to remember some intelligence report or other. Last year was it?'

'Eighteen months ago you had the bright idea of trying to work out who was running these courts in case there was a relationship to the radicalisation of individuals. You wanted to determine if there was a connection to Islamist extremism and terrorism,' explained Anthea. 'The unit investigated who was who

217

and what the role of the Sharia courts might be but it didn't go any further.'

'Because there was no threat of terrorism from the Islamic legal system as I recall,' disclosed Boyd.

'That's the way it was then,' confirmed Anthea.

'Yeah, well, the Cold War ended,' offered Boyd. 'We made peace with the Irish Republicans and then Al-Qaeda and the Taliban got in on the act and took the spotlight.'

'And they've managed to keep it,' remarked Anthea under her breath.

'But why is Ryan visiting a Quadi?' probed Boyd.

'No idea,' replied Antonia. 'Except we have another interesting man in the street; do you see him, Boyd?'

A male walked from the far end of the street. His gait was strong and purposeful for he was tall and self-assured in the manner of his deportment. There was no swagger in his step, just a sure and certain movement that spoke volumes about the character and personality of the individual who came into focus in Boyd's camera lens. The guy seemed strong and erect, full of assumed confidence.

'I see him,' responded Boyd. 'But I haven't a clue why I'm photographing him, Toni. You'd best explain.'

'Wait one,' replied Antonia. 'I want to see where he goes. Come on Billy Boyd, get your memory working. You're having a bad day. Do you want a starter for ten?'

She knew him, recognised him from afar, and considered it her job to be able to recognise such people. Apart from that, Antonia Harston-Browne knew the individual personally. He was still handsome, she thought. Oh yes, rather suave and sophisticated in some ways but then quite down to earth in others.

'Funny,' quipped Boyd. 'The great thing about this camera is its zoom facility, Toni. I know this man. We've crossed swords before but if I remember right, he's on our side.'

'Sometimes,' suggested Antonia. 'He's on his side all of the time.'

The man wore dark brown leather slip on shoes with matching casual trousers, a polo neck sweater, and a dark brown jacket. He rapped his knuckles on the door of the Quadi. There was a handshake and he entered.

'Ismail Benjamin Cohen,' announced Antonia. 'He's a lawyer working out of an office in Kensington but he's allied to the Israeli Embassy in Palace Green.'

'That would seem to be a good enough reason for him to be here surely,' suggested Anthea. 'What's wrong with a lawyer visiting an Islamic judge?'

'Except he's a member of the Israeli Security Service,' stated Boyd. 'Am I correct, Toni?'

'Oh yes, you remember him too,' delivered Antonia. 'Yes, we met Ismail some years ago when he tipped off MI6 about an arms cache on its way into Tilbury docks bound for members of the PLO: The Palestinian Liberation Organisation. It's a long time ago but he's been on the board a few times since.'

'Is he Mossad?' queried Anthea.

'Every inch,' replied Antonia.

'But I thought they were on our side,' proposed Anthea.

'It works like this,' insinuated Antonia. 'MI6 plays its game in a highly educated manner. It's almost like a gentleman's club in some ways but it's probably one of the best secret intelligence services in the world sitting proudly next to the CIA and Mossad. Its method of recruiting agents all over the world is second to none. The problem is that Mossad often harbours twisted ideals that personify a self-centred character. They have little respect for human life in some cases. It has been known in the past for them to mount a campaign of ruthless assassination of its enemies and that doesn't always sit well with us. You see, you take a chance to some degree if you trust them because their interest will always rise above the others. They're a good team player but only when they win and when it suits them to win.'

'You make it sound like a dangerous game,' proposed Anthea.

'It is,' agreed Boyd. 'But what have we uncovered here?'

'Enough to put Ryan with Mossad and an Islamic judge in the middle of the Islamic Republic of Tower Hamlets,' remarked Antonia. 'What do you make of it, Boyd?'

'I think we need to take it to our commander and the DG,' advised Boyd. 'This is partly a police matter because of Ryan but it's also something that might infringe on national security.'

'What does Ryan know that ought to worry us?' asked Anthea.

'He knows all about British policy in Afghanistan, Iraq and the middle east,' said Boyd. 'He once told us how he advised diplomatic staff and ministers about the Arab world. I'm not sure he has access to real secrets but it worries me that he might be talking to the wrong people about inappropriate things. Makes you wonder why we got him.'

Silent, thinking, wondering, Antonia turned things over in her mind as Anthea tapped nervously on the steering wheel and Boyd lowered his camera for a moment.

'The commander works in strange ways,' offered Anthea thoughtfully.

Boyd engaged Anthea's eyes and then studied Antonia before saying, 'Of course! Well done, Anthea.'

'Well done for throwing Ryan into the pot and making a bigger mystery than we had before? Is that what you mean?' suggested Anthea.

'No,' replied Boyd. 'For working out why Commander Herbert and Phillip Nesbitt planted Ryan on us.'

'Exactly,' agreed Antonia She was a little shocked when she continued, 'They suspected Ryan all along but didn't want to commit national resources to go up against our friends in Mossad. They don't want to upset the relationship with the Israelis. You know what that means don't you?'

'Ryan is talking to the Israelis or the Arabs. Probably both! He can't be trusted.'

'That's what I think,' agreed Antonia. 'They wanted us to find out what was going on without Phillip Nesbitt having to commit a large scale surveillance and enquiry operation that might have drawn out our people to the Israelis. That means there's something else. They've already got their suspicions.'

'Of course, there is an alternative,' suggested Anthea.

'You're in the driver's seat, Anthea,' smiled Boyd. 'What's on your mind?'

'Oh nothing much,' offered Anthea. 'You two observers have forgotten the basics. Have you considered for one moment that your Mossad man – Ismail – might be covertly financing the Quadi via the Sharia Law court system in order to penetrate Muslim extremism? I mean, you said Mossad is mainly interested in its own problems.'

Lost for words for a moment, Boyd glanced at Antonia and suggested, 'Anthea, you're in the wrong job. You should be with MI6. You've had a good day. Listening to you, we haven't got a corrupt detective on our books because they're all above board. Yet we have got a dubious civil servant working with us. Come on, let's go and drop this one on the commander's lap.'

Later, in an office at Thames House, Commander Herbert merely smiled and replied, 'William, I can't for the life of me think what is going on in your complicated mind. To suggest we planted Ryan on you as a deliberate ploy is quite astounding. Are you really suggesting that we covertly placed you in a position whereby you were obliged to investigate a member of staff to ascertain whether or not he could be trusted?'

'Yes, you and the Director General of MI5 didn't want to get your hands dirty. Or, to be precise, someone smelled a rat called Ryan snuggling up to the man from Mossad – or was it the man from the Sharia Court first – and you needed to know what was going on without upsetting the balance of our nation's relationship with the Israelis. Now is our man Ryan talking to Mossad or the Quadi?'

Commander Herbert stood, nodded to Boyd approvingly, and invited Phillip Nesbitt saying, 'Phillip, you wanted a job done. I think Antonia, Anthea and William deserve an explanation.'

The two ladies and Boyd waited whilst Phillip removed a red file from a wall safe and placed it on his desk. Opening the folder, Phillip leafed through some papers and revealed, 'Albert Charles Henry Ryan has been taken into custody by the Ministry of Defence Specialist Intelligence Unit a short time ago. This occurred as a direct result of your information linking Ryan to a Quadi of historic suspicion and Ismail Benjamin Cohen. Briefly, diplomatic staff abroad recently formed the belief that Ryan was visiting a centre where 'Radicalisation' was taking place. It was suggested he might be receiving regular doses of extremist literature and media, whilst he was abroad, that was likely to change his outlook and radicalise him to a level not acceptable to Her Majesty's Government. Indeed, he was posted back to the United Kingdom so that a closer inspection of his lifestyle could be undertaken. It soon became apparent that his life revolved around his work and yet it worried me that our colleagues in MI6 pointed the finger of suspicion at him. You are correct, Chief Inspector Boyd, we are aware that our allies in Mossad are working hard on British soil to penetrate the Muslim extremist target here in London. They have been for some time and our relationship with them is occasionally somewhat strained as you have correctly ascertained. I asked your commander for assistance and he recommended your team. I decided to deliberately plant Ryan with you so that you might become suspicious and commence your own enquiries. It is not my intention to apologise to you all for the decision I made. It is the nature of my calling to preserve the security of our nation by any means possible. That will always be my prime concern.'

Phillip glanced briefly at the commander and disclosed, 'Commander Herbert tells me you are rather tenacious in your endeavours, chief inspector, and I have to agree with him. When you trailed Ryan to see the Quadi today there is little doubt Ryan was being radicalised by people not normally held in the high esteem of our friends in the British Muslim society. Ismail was merely a by-product of your enquiry and a confirmation of Mossad's involvement against terrorism here in the UK. The point is that Ryan can no longer be trusted in his role as a government advisor and we are taking appropriate action to remove him from his office of employment.'

'Has he breached the Official Secrets Act?' queried Boyd.

'Perhaps, we are unsure at this stage but appear to have lanced a boil that was likely to fester in the months ahead. As you know it is not a criminal offence to be radicalised but where it does occur we need to be on our guard to ensure we are able to deal with it accordingly. I expect Ryan to be removed from his office of employment forthwith. We must uphold the integrity of our national security at all costs. Ryan is merely collateral damage I'm afraid. It is a sad affair ended by a timely intervention.'

Boyd pursed his lips and winked at Anthea

Closing the file, Phillip Nesbitt declared, 'Thank you!'

'I wonder if….' pursued Antonia.

'I'm sorry. I have nothing else to tell you at this time,' confirmed Phillip. 'Perhaps in the future.'

Boyd nodded and said, 'Oh, don't worry about it, sir. We knew right from the start Ryan was a plant, didn't we folks?'

Smiles and a slight chuckle followed.

Straight-faced, Anthea suggested, 'Forgive me, gentlemen, but you could also disrupt both Mossad and the Quadi by turning Ryan to our advantage and allowing him to become a double agent. Why not run him into the system and see what you can find out?'

Neither Phillip Nesbitt nor Antonia responded but Commander Herbert ventured a sly smile when Boyd declared, 'Anthea, you're definitely in the wrong job.'

Boyd's pager vibrated and he checked the screen saying, 'Excuse me.'

Stepping away from the desk for a moment, Boyd punched the digits on his mobile phone and said, 'Stuart, it's me. What you got?'

'The vicar has been on the hotline again, Guvnor. Apparently Azzam has issued an open invitation to all the kids in the village and surrounding area. They're invited to the Base tonight at eight o'clock. Free paintballing by all accounts.'

'That man Azzam is intent on inviting those kids to the Base. Anything to get close to the vicar it seems. Anything else?'

'The operations centre has identified a number of flights into Glasgow and Newcastle carrying individuals with passports that are worth close scrutiny upon arrival. The system is identifying people who are not regular travellers and who are of Arab origin. It's not brilliant but we have to start somewhere.'

'Where are the flights from?' asked Boyd.

'They're travellers of Middle Eastern origin but they're arriving from Brussels and Amsterdam.'

'Okay, nothing wrong with that but you're right, Stuart. Ask the locals up there to carry out a specific inspection of anyone travelling on such a passport. In fact, better still, fly to Glasgow yourself and take ground control of the passport section. Tell Terry I want him in Newcastle airport doing the same job. I'll ask Commander Herbert to liaise with the local heads. I feel it in my bones. Something is on. Those hire cars have been planted for a reason and they're not going to sit there in a car park for weeks on end.'

Closing the call, Boyd turned to Commander Herbert and said, 'I'd like to take Anthea and Antonia to Cumbria, sir. I'm deploying my unit to cover the airports in question and bolster surveillance on those hire cars.'

'Of course, William, fly if you must. I'll speak with Manchester, Strathclyde and Northumbria. It must be autumn.'

'I beg your pardon,' puzzled Boyd.

'Plants, William! They seem to be everywhere this week.'

Frowning, Phillip Nesbitt watched Commander Herbert shake hands with Boyd, Anthea and Antonia saying, 'Good luck.' The Director General then approached the group and said, 'God speed and good luck.'

Boyd replied, 'I think you got your seasons wrong, commander. My book says it's spring.'

'Spring?' queried Commander Herbert.

'Weeding time!' declared Boyd.

Chapter Fourteen
~

Northern England.

Lakeland's slate grey mountains climbed towards a blue cloudy heaven to remind Khalid of home. The Fells weren't as sky-scraping as the Afghan-Pakistan border but they did reveal mottled patches of green pasture offset by blotches of yellow gorse and thriving moorland heather. Here and there traces of dry stone wall seemed to pencil the Lakeland canvas and divide the land on a journey across its landscape. Khalid wondered if an artist might have mixed the colours on display and then splashed them across the geography in a haphazard manner. Observant and intrigued by the scenery, he realised the Fells were not scattered with a thousand goats belonging to the infamously brave Mullagori tribe. But the area was infinitely better than the damp squalid apartment in Luton where his eyes constantly looked down on a swarm of human ants below.

Reducing speed, he pulled into the side of the road, checked his map, and then accelerated away again. When the signpost appeared, he veered over the centre line and turned into the road that would take him from the A66 towards Caldbeck. For the first time in a week, Khalid actually felt happy. He enjoyed the freedom these mountains offered and a scarcity of population that was apparent in England's most northerly corner.

Checking his mirror, Khalid knew he was alone when he twisted his way through the attractive hamlets of Mungrisdale, Mosedale, and beyond. The single track road seemed to be the same width as the Khyber Pass, he thought, except it was flat and threaded its way carefully through the patchwork quilt of meadowlands and pastures.

Twenty minutes later, Khalid turned a corner and finally appreciated the wooden sign set close to his destination. The sign read 'The Base – A Retreat and Adventure Base for Young People.'

Changing down into a lower gear, Khalid gently negotiated the lane towards a collection of buildings.

In airspace above north east England an aircraft cleared a patch of turbulence, latched onto the glide path, and began its descent into Newcastle airport. An Iranian, Al Harith, tugged at his collar and writhed for breath. Not wanting to draw attention to himself he was reluctant to make a fuss but grudgingly pressed the button in the console above his head. At last he felt a gust of fresh air blow down upon him. Oh, how he disliked the claustrophobia of travelling in an aeroplane. Seated towards the rear of the cabin he stole a glance through a cabin window at England's green and pleasant land whilst simultaneously fidgeting for possession of his travel documents. Twenty odd thousand feet above the surface of the earth his mind focused solely on the task ahead. One last time, he thought; one last time to recite my new name, place of birth, and date of birth. I shall not let myself down. I have come to do a job and once I have stepped foot on the lands of the infidel I, Al Harith of Iran, will be at war with the Kafir.

Close by, in a neighbouring air corridor, the Egyptian from Aswan – Rafid – carried out the same mental procedure. Suddenly he was interrupted by the stewardess who tapped him gently and pointed to the sign above the seat. It was time to put his seat belt on. The descent into Glasgow has started, she explained, and a little turbulence might be expected when they negotiate the airspace above the Scottish lowlands.

Rafid nodded his thanks, smiled, and sought his seat belt. A passport dropped from his hands and fell awkwardly into the central walkway. He felt a surge of cold panic sweep over him.

The stewardess bent down, retrieved his passport, and handed it to him with a pleasant smile.

Sweating, cold, I am so nervous, thought Rafid. Then he closed his eyes in private communion with Allah as the engines changed pitch and the plane dropped slightly on its final approach.

Above Bristol the man from Sana'a in the Yemen slept. Saleem spoke to his God in his dreams, saw the gates of Paradise ahead, and waited patiently to land at Manchester airport.

Saleem bore no nerves. A leader of men, a destroyer of adversaries and competitors alike, he did not court friendship with his fellow man. Experienced in the capabilities of his enemy, his proficiency in dealing with unexpected problems was legendary in the frontline of war torn streets where he was a predator etched in the folklore of his calling. Saleem had flown from the heart of Al-Qaeda and intended to penetrate the very nucleus of his enemy.

It was time. It was their time. The four archangels of death gathered in readiness for their planned campaign. The long journey was over but it was also just about to begin.

On the Fells above the village of Caldbeck, Susie rode her angel: Gabriel.

'Come on, Gabby,' she whispered when she clicked her heels into the stallion's sides. 'We're going to take a ride. Show me what you can do. Come on!'

Gabby galloped where Khalid and a trillion other visitors to the Lake District once looked on high and appreciated the stunning beauty of Cumbria and the Caldbeck Fells. Where pastures changed from a deep green to a hazy yellow, the land rose suddenly and blurred with the slate grey Fell tops to look down smugly on the valleys below. A church steeple; a ribbon of a stream, a pair of Buzzards dominating the atmosphere, a source of pure fresh water oozing mysteriously and suddenly from the side of a Fell, and not a human being in sight. This was Susie's land: her playground in the sun, her back garden.

Breaking Gabby down into a canter, Susie reined the stallion downhill towards the Base. Below her stretched the paintball site sitting next to a narrow stream, a wooden bridge, a mine entrance, and an assortment of buildings making up the Base.

No! Turn away and leave it to the police, Susie thought. It's nothing to do with me. My mum and Dad have sorted it all out with Mister Boyd and the red haired lady, Antonia.

'Come on, Gabby,' said Susie turning in another direction. 'Let's go, not today.'

In the distance, she recognised Azzam walking from one of the outbuilding. He jumped into his Land Rover, fired the engine, and drove off towards the main road. At the T junction, Azzam turned towards Caldbeck and soon disappeared from view.

Patting Gabby's neck, Susie spoke to her horse and said, 'Okay, he's gone. Come on, Gabby. Let's see if the mine is open. We can help our Mister Boyd if we're lucky. He deserves a hand from people like us. Let's go.'

Susie clicked her heels and guided Gabby towards the two oak trees that heralded the hidden path into the rear of the site.

A touchdown at Manchester airport revealed Saleem grooming his dark grey beard as he shuffled from the cabin of the airliner and made his way cautiously towards the arrivals lounge.

In Newcastle airport, Al Harith, suitcase in hand, short and stocky, walked from the airport terminal and took a courtesy bus to the long stay car park. His yellowed teeth and stubbly chin stood shameless to his venture when he clung to a strap for the short ride.

Rafid managed to decipher the Scottish tongue at Glasgow, smiled politely, produced a passport, and then nodded when it was returned to him after inspection. Tall, also quite broad, and with a slight limp from an old bullet wound to his right leg, he made his way across the road to a car park. He did not drag his limb as if it were a burden to him. Not for a moment did Rafid feel such a hindrance. Neither was it a symbol of heroism or a badge of honour. The bullet wound was no more than an inconvenience in the life that he led. Warily, he approached the car park with his eyes darting from left to right in their quest for reassurance and safety.

Here and there, an operation began when a CCTV camera panned and zoomed. A surveillance officer tightened a seat belt. A radio frequency zipped into life. A bottle top was screwed tight and thrown into the rear of a car. A toffee was devoured or a mint selected. In their own individual way, Britain's finest honed in on Al-Qaeda's bearers of doom.

One by one the archangels of death approached the hire cars planted days earlier by Azzam and began their journey to the new frontline.

Stuart Armstrong took convoy control at Glasgow, Terry Anwhari at Newcastle, and Jack Marshall pulled the strings in Manchester. The men of the Special Crime Unit were specialist surveillance officers. They overshadowed their counterparts of higher rank and enjoyed a reputation in the job that was second to none. For the specialists, it was time to specialise.

Saleem powered up his hire car and motored slowly away from the parking place. He was two minutes into his journey when he stopped, pulled into the kerbside and feigned a breakdown. Astute, he pulled the handle on the hood, got out of the vehicle, and pretended to examine a presumed fault in the engine. Ingeniously, he bent low and watched each and every car that drove past him. Occasionally, he wrote down the registration number of a vehicle he was unsure of. Perhaps such a vehicle carried only two men or a driver speaking on a mobile phone. It did not matter to Saleem. There were no hard and fast rules as to who might be innocent and who might be suspect. He'd spent months learning how to evade suspicion, how to check and double check if he were being watched, how to be living proof that an Al Qaeda operative could survive on the infidel's soil. Saleem felt no fear in his belly. He had no fear, could not taste it, dare not smell it, and failed to understand its very concept. He had come to give his life to the cause of Islamic dominance and vowed long ago not to be captured. In any event, he knew he would not be taken alive. It was not the way of Al-Qaeda to fall into enemy hands. He was the chosen one in this country. He was safe, healthy, whole, and flawless, just like the translation of his name suggested.

Closing the bonnet, Saleem fired the engine and drove off towards the roundabout where he made two circuits before choosing a route to a nearby hotel. Parking outside the hotel, he allowed the traffic to pass him by as he listened to the engine idling. Again, he watched the comings and goings of traffic around him for a while before selecting first gear and re-entering the traffic flow. This time, he took the second option and began a slow drive north.

From a walkway leading to the Radisson Blue hotel, above the road system, one of Jack Marshall's men lowered his petite telescope and radioed, 'Okay, the target is off again. Filter out slowly and take the second option at the exit roundabout. Give this guy plenty of room. He's looking for company and he's good.'

Jack acknowledged with, 'Thank you, Jimbo. Acknowledging your transmission – Give this guy plenty of room - Move out slowly, team, and watch for his next trick. Make ground, Jimbo. Make ground.'

There was a register of acknowledgements as the unit finally powered up and began the follow.

In Glasgow, the story was not dissimilar when Stuart Armstrong took the lead, tucked in behind Rafid, and ordered some of his team to overtake the target in order to cover the road ahead. When translated, Rafid means 'Support'. He didn't have any but he'd arrived in the country to provide support to his colleagues. Carefully, eyes everywhere, darting in between traffic at various speeds, Rafid played cat and mouse as he headed towards England and a date with his demonic destiny.

Sweat poured from Stuart's brow as he wrestled with speed and distance in an effort not to get caught out by the Egyptian maestro.

Stuart recognised the problem. Every time one of his team settled in behind the target Rafid simply slowed right down and secreted himself between two heavy goods vehicles. Within the space of ten miles, two of Stuart's team were obliged to sail past and peel off at a suitable junction. Potentially, Rafid was identifying and burning the surveillance team using the oldest and easiest trick in the book.

'Get it together,' rattled Stuart. 'It's not a bloody race. The target has a brain and he's using it. Think, guys! You can do better than that. Think! He's going to make bloody fools of us.'

The airwaves returned silence before Stuart cursed to himself when he realised he was a part of the problem. Relax, he scolded himself. Sit back and get those eyes working and the team together. Then he remembered the importance of team work when he radioed, 'Okay, guys, I'm sorry. I need to get it together too. Look this guy is jumping about like a frog on heat. Let's put him inside a bubble. Front and rear and both sides when we need to. Let's go!'

The story was different again in Newcastle. Al Harith collected his luggage and the hire car planted for him by Azzam. Abruptly, he took off from the car park at high speed, swung round the roundabout, and headed directly for the A1 dual carriageway almost leaving Terry's surveillance team standing still in the starting blocks. With vehicle velocity mounting, Al Harith simply decided to out run anyone who might be watching for him. Foot hard to the floor Al Harith powered down the A1 towards Newcastle. Close to the west end he turned onto the A69 and headed in the direction of Carlisle with a frenzied surveillance convoy struggling to stay in touch. Al Harith, 'the plowman', ploughed through traffic narrowly avoiding a collision with a thirty two tons articulated wagon and an ambulance carrying a patient to Newcastle Royal Victoria Infirmary.

'Come through and make ground,' radioed Terry. 'Keep up! This man is flying. Make ground team and keep in the picture!'

Problems set in when Terry Anwhari realised some of his team were still negotiating traffic between the airport and the A1 turn off. The plowman was up and away, and he was gradually increasing the distance between himself and his followers.

In Cumbria, Boyd listened to the reports coming through, punched his mobile phone, and called Alan Grant into the air from Carlisle airport.

On a wooden bridge across a narrow stream, Susie guided Gabby towards the entrance to a mine shaft. She tethered Gabby loosely to a branch and looked towards the accommodation area of the complex. The Base appeared deserted. Confident, self-assured, determined to help her newfound heroes, Susie bent low and crept towards the entrance. Looking into the Base she saw the distant paintball centre, the assault course with its high walls and netted obstacles, and then advanced to the mine. Narrow gauge railway lines came into view and led towards the mine's entrance.

Keenly, Susie followed the line of the tracks and realised the gate was open. The shiny padlock was missing and the grass at the lintel of the gates folded over and wilted towards the ground. But the gate was open inviting access to the mine and the secrets it held.

Cautiously, warily, Susie stepped into the mine to find herself gradually enveloped in darkness. One step, two steps and on the third step a rat or a mouse scuttled between her legs. She screamed and then laughed on turning round to see the creature rush into the daylight. Exhaling loudly, Susie sighed and ambled deeper into the mine. A long narrow corridor sloped gradually downwards into the heart of the mine and then morphed into an L shape. On negotiating the first bend, a light grew from within and the darkness of her first steps began to disappear with each pace.

There was the sound of footsteps behind but when she twisted a hand grabbed her around the waist whilst another clamped her mouth closed tight.

Kicking out, Susie swung her head and used her free hand to try and scratch the unknown assailant. Struggling for all she was worth she tried to scream, tried to escape, tried to break the hold of the man who fought to possess her.

Suddenly, darkness invaded her eyes when an object of some kind smashed into her head and her body flopped into surrender.

Another rat scurried up the incline to freedom casting a long eerie shadow on the dimly lit wall. The figure reached down, grasped Susie beneath the armpits and dragged her deeper into the mine.

In the skies above Cumbria Alan Grant guided his Cessna north and then circled above the Scottish border with his eyes observing the traffic below.

A radio burst into life and told of three vehicles under surveillance roughly heading towards Cumbria. The surveillance teams dominated the airwaves with their commentary when Rafid, Al Harith and Saleem powered their cars craftily towards their destination. Was it the case that the suspects were aware they were being followed? Or was it that they were merely exercising extreme caution as instructed? Members of the Special Crime Unit didn't know for sure either way, but the operation continued with Alan contributing in a never ending circle of aerial reconnaissance.

Then, without warning, the three suspects all stopped within minutes of each other. Saleem cruised into Burton Services on the M6 Cumbria-Lancashire border. Al Harith parked up at a Little Chef restaurant close to Haltwhistle on the Cumbria-Northumbria border, and Rafid drove into Gretna services on the M74 close to the England-Scotland border.

Within minutes the surveillance radio died and mobile phones became the preferred option. The questions and answers were similar. Why had they all stopped within minutes of each other? Had the surveillance teams been rumbled? What was the next move?

Saleem bought a coffee and took a seat where he could watch the front entrance to Burton Services. Meanwhile, Al Harith stepped into the café and browsed a selection of magazines whilst

Rafid parked next to a telephone box, a row of fuel pumps, a bus stop and a travel lodge.

It was a waiting game, thought Terry Anwhari, but why were they waiting? Seizing the moment, the Unit across the board gathered their number, reorganised, and melted into the landscape as best they could.

Meanwhile, Boyd was making plans and studying his maps with Anthea and Antonia but as they turned into the vicar's driveway the charts were folded into the glove compartment.

Anthea yanked on the handbrake and the trio got out and approached Matthew and his wife.

'Thanks for calling the hotline, Reverend Lowther,' remarked Boyd. 'I understand from your call that Azzam has invited all the children to the Base. Do you know the precise details, sir?'

'Of course, chief inspector, but who's your new driver?'

'I do apologise to you both,' offered Boyd. 'This is Anthea Adams. She's a sergeant with the unit: my second in command actually, and Antonia you know, of course.'

Handshakes followed before Matthew explained, 'It's just that since we reported our suspicions you don't really seem to have done much, chief inspector.'

Boyd grimaced and opened his mouth to reply but Elizabeth interrupted rather haughtily and said, 'Hear my husband out a moment won't you, Mister Boyd?'

Caught slightly off balance, Boyd flustered, 'Yes, of course, Mrs Lowther. Okay, Matthew, what's upset you this time?'

Rubbing his chin in thought, Matthew fidgeted with his jacket before imparting, 'We keep getting promises from you that the police are doing something and it would help if we just kept quiet, remained patient, and allowed you to get on with whatever it is you are up to. But, with respect, Mister Boyd, nothing seems to be happening and now I am told by some of my parishioners that Azzam has issued a number of children in the village with free tickets to the paintballing site. Indeed, he's even written me a note asking me to attend and discuss allowing him to join our Christian Brotherhood'

'Has he indeed?' remarked Boyd. 'Persistent, isn't he?'

'And it's not the first time I've mentioned this, chief inspector.'

'Correct,' admitted Boyd, 'But it is the first time I've been made aware that the invitations were coming directly from Azzam.'

'Well don't take our word for it,' suggested Elizabeth. 'He's put a poster up on the village noticeboard. You can take your children along tonight at half past seven. The event is free and so is the ice-cream apparently.'

'That's right, dear,' offered Matthew to his wife. 'What's more, Mister Boyd, I think, given your capacity not to progress this matter at a suitable pace, it is time to forget the entire issue and revert to my previous desire to befriend our multicultural neighbour and let bygones be bygones. I'm sorry I telephoned you. Now if you'll excuse us…'

Raising his hand Boyd relied, 'I detect you are unnecessarily belligerent, Reverend Lowther, and I am regularly confused by the signals you put out. One moment you are suspicious of everyone but the next you want to befriend the whole world. Oh how I wish life was so simple. But I have to tell you, sir, that it isn't normal practice to discuss our investigative methods with the general public and complainants such as yourselves…'

'Complainants?' queried Matthew intervening. 'We've never registered a complaint of crime with you but I am minded to consider registering a complainant about your inactivity with the powers that be at Scotland Yard. Would you suggest I start with your superiors?'

There was a sudden movement at the side of the house, a swish of grass, and a horse trotted into view.

Startled for a moment Boyd suggested, 'If this is Gabby I suggest you start with asking where your daughter is, Matthew. It is your daughter's horse, I presume?'

'Gabby,' prattled Elizabeth rushing to gather the reins. 'Where's Susie?' Searching beyond the stallion Elizabeth shouted, Susie! Susie where are you?'

An air of panic invaded the atmosphere when Matthew tried to ease the clerical band collar from his neck and delivered. 'No! No! Please God no! Where is she? Where is our daughter?'

In a telephone kiosk a hand lifted a phone and dialled a number.

The caller waited patiently before being rewarded with a voice disclosing, 'I am at the border. I have journeyed alone and unseen to break bread with you. But when shall we break bread?'

A voice in the kiosk replied, 'It is safe. Come, tonight we break bread and drink wine. Tomorrow we shall pray together.'

The telephone dropped to the cradle. Azzam made two more identical calls and then stepped from the kiosk to return to his Land Rover nearby.

In Burton services, Saleem replaced the handset and walked to the doorway of the building. For a moment he paused, studied the driver's faces of the vehicles parked on the car park, sought out those who might be his enemy, and then stepped consciously towards the hire car. In his mind, it was the last leg. He was safe and he was on his way.

Close to Haltwhistle, Al Harith pocketed his magazine, replaced the telephone, and walked to his car. Almost simultaneously, Rafid stepped from the kiosk towards his car and bade farewell to Scotland.

They were on the move again. The suspects set off and plotted a final course as their shadows let out the leash and followed on behind.

In Caldbeck, Boyd was asking questions.

'Where do you think Susie went riding?' he asked.

'Who knows,' offered Matthew. 'The Fells were her back garden. She could be anywhere.'

'Would she be alone or with a friend?' asked Anthea.

'Alone, I expect,' revealed Elizabeth. 'But if you come into the house with me, Anthea, I'll ring some of her friend just in case.'

Boyd nodded as Anthea headed indoors and Antonia asked, 'Did she have any particular routes that she especially enjoyed?'

'No, yes, I don't know,' answered Matthew. 'I'm sorry. I'm not much help am I?'

'Look,' said Boyd, 'Let's just presume that Gabby has thrown Susie or Susie has just fallen off somewhere and is unable to get back home. She could well be just holed up in a difficult place slightly incapacitated. Now there must be some particular places that she spoke of. It's important, Matthew, because I can arrange for an aircraft to make a quick search of the main areas. Do you understand what I'm saying?'

'The Mill!' suggested Matthew. 'The old Bobbin Mill was one of her favourites and then there's the stream of course. She often used to follow the stream.'

Boyd's mobile rang and he answered it. He listened intently to what was said and then instructed, 'I agree. They're on their way here, Terry. Jack will bring one of them up from Mungrisdale and I expect you and Stuart will follow the other two and come on in by the northern route. These are very narrow roads and not a good place for surveillance. Let them travel in under their own steam. Let's not clog the system but use Alan and his Cessna to confirm the destination.' Boyd listened again and said, 'That's precisely what I have in mind, Terry. Let the unit know and form up on the common near the radio station.'

Closing the call, Boyd looked up to find Anthea reporting, 'Guvnor, Elizabeth just spoke to some of Susie's school friends on the 'phone. Susie said she was helping a Mister Boyd today. She was riding to the mines to find out what was going on because Mister Boyd is her hero and....'

'The mines!' remarked Boyd interrupting. 'Good Lord!'

Punching the mobile digits Boyd connected with Commander Herbert at the same time as Antonia rang Alan Grant.

'Commander?' queried Boyd. 'We've three suspects heading into Cumbria in hire cars provided by Azzam. The three suspects are all travelling on documents that don't match hire car details. I think we have three ringers. Three suspects all living under false names aided and abetted by Azzam who appears to be the host and organiser. I think they're all coming to Caldbeck. My problem is compounded by the fact that Azzam has put posters up in the village and probably elsewhere inviting all the local kids to free paintballing at the Base tonight. Given the locality and the neighbourhood I've neither the time nor the teams to go round telling everyone not to go. And why Azzam wants children there when he's expecting guests is not worth thinking about, commander.'

In the Operations Centre Commander Herbert had the call on speaker for the benefit of Phillip Nesbitt and countered, 'That's on the presumption your targets are bound for Caldbeck, William. Let's not read too much into this unless we have to.'

'We have one kid missing already, sir,' reminded Boyd. 'How many do you want?'

In Thames House, the commander's hand swept through his head of white hair and came to fidget with his beard before he replied, 'In view of what you say the Director General and I are considering requesting the attendance of the Special Air Regiment, William. On the supposition that this is a terrorist training camp we need to be mindful that other terrorists are not already there. I don't want you rushing in feet first without thinking things through. The three suspects your units are following may meet another thirty three terrorists for all we know. Remember, we have the ability to deploy Special Forces if need be.'

Boyd responded immediately. 'No, sir, I don't think they're coming to a terrorist training camp in the Lake District. Furthermore, aerial reconnaissance doesn't support the theory that the place is awash with people. I think our suspects are already highly trained in various surveillance and anti-surveillance

239

techniques – as well as despatching terrorism in lethal doses - and I'm really wondering why they're all making for the middle of nowhere because I'm as close to the middle of nowhere that you would ever want to be. The way I look at it is that the suspects have been told to watch out for people watching them. They've learnt their lessons well but the reality is that whilst they've led us a merry dance they haven't actually managed to shrug off any of our teams. I'm pretty sure they haven't a clue we're following them. But what I really need you to understand sir, is that the vicar's daughter has gone missing and we believe she's making for the Base. I'm not minded to wait for the cavalry, commander.'

Antonia tapped Boyd on his shoulder, walked away, saw the Cessna high above, and spoke directly to its pilot.

Commander Herbert replied, 'You have ground control, William, and I have operational control as ever. This is a difficult one but I'm going to arrange the deployment of the SAS as a precaution. It will take them a couple of hours to reach you so do what you need to do prior to their arrival. One thing, William, are you sure the girl is heading for the Base?'

Pausing briefly, Boyd confirmed, 'Yes, the Base, commander. I think she may have fallen from her horse somewhere close to the area of the Base. On the other hand, I really don't know. I'm just trying to second guess the world as usual. It's young Susie: the vicar's daughter. What's more, I'm monitoring the surveillance radio channels and I reckon we have three suspects making for the same area. It's a recipe for disaster, sir. When my three units arrive, I'm going to hit it hard and fast and find out what the hell is the big secret there. I'm going to arrest them for obtaining vehicles by deception – false driving licences – entering the country illegally – anything that fits. I suspect we'll prove the passports are forged or stolen and I'm sure something else will come to mind between now and then. But obviously I've got my eye on the big one: Conspiracy to commit acts of terrorism!'

Commander Herbert declared, 'It's done, Phillip is on the phone to the barracks. Special Forces are deployed. The clock is ticking, William. Good luck! You've a couple of hours at the most.'

'Yes, sir,' replied Boyd. 'I'll keep you posted.'

'Boyd,' interrupted Phillip. 'We're declaring a no fly zone over the Caldbeck area. Only the Cessna and Special Forces' helicopters have permission to overfly. In addition, in exactly one hour's time, the mobile telephone network will be taken down. There will be no media coverage and no wireless transmissions. This will effectively prevent Azzam and his people communicating with each other and anyone else in their organisation. Let your team know because your phones will be down too.'

'Will do, sir, thank you!'

When Boyd ended the call Antonia offered, 'I've spoken to Alan. There's no sign of Susie but there's another car turned up at the site. I've checked the database. The vehicle is a hire car from Luton. I think we've found number four, Boyd.'

'Number four?' queried Matthew. 'What the hell is going on? What four are you talking about, Mister Boyd.'

'Matthew, I'm going to mount a raid on the Base and see if we can find Susie. It's time we sorted this out.'

'My daughter! I'm coming with you,' implored Matthew.

'I'm sure you will and I'm not going to attempt to stop you although I really ought to try. But here's the deal.'

'What deal?' enquired Matthew.

'If you're coming with us I want Elizabeth to stay here just in case we've got it all wrong and Susie returns unexpectedly. If Susie reappears I want her Mum to be here for her.'

There was a swift exchange of looks between man and wife before Elizabeth responded, 'Agreed, good luck, Mister Boyd.'

Spreading a map out on the BMW's bonnet, Anthea appealed to the gathering with, 'Toni tells me there's a back entrance, Guvnor. Where is it?'

'Toni?' delivered Boyd.

Antonia Harston Browne turned with the telephone in her hand and said, 'I'll be with you in a minute. I'm talking to Alan again. I have a plan.'

'A good one I hope,' suggested Boyd.

'Of course, it's just a fly by, Boyd. Nothing to worry about; now then the rear entrance, where's the map?'

'We need Janice,' offered Anthea. 'We could really do with her now.'

'Well, that's not possible,' remarked Antonia. 'So we'd better make this one count for her.'

The trio clustered over the map and plotted the raid.

Elsewhere in Cumbria, three Al-Qaeda terrorists deviated from the motorway and journeyed towards the Caldbeck Fells.

It didn't take long to establish the worst of their fears. Saleem, Al Harith and Rafid drove into the Base ahead of the surveillance teams who made for a car park near Caldbeck's wireless transmitter.

Boyd confirmed on the radio with Jack Marshall that he was close to the Base hidden in the hedgerow watching the entrance then he turned to brief the thirty officers gathered before him.

'Let's get ready,' instructed Boyd. 'First thing to do is improvise. We've no fancy briefing room; no chalkboards, no photographs pinned on a wall like they have on the telly, and no clipboards with operational orders. It's an open air briefing so gather round because the acoustics are pretty bad.'

'There was a mild chuckle from the group before Boyd snapped, 'Weapons check! Kit on!'

Matthew was horrified. 'No, chief inspector, you're surely not looking for a gun fight. Someone is going to get hurt.'

'Just making sure my people are safe, well protected and adequately armed, sir. If you've a moment to give us a prayer then please do but, generally speaking, if things get rough we won't be throwing Bibles at them.'

Matthew glanced away unsure of his place. Fidgeting with his clerical collar, he pulled at the white band constraining his neck. He wondered for a moment if the time had come to admit that the collar was perhaps constricting his very mode of life. He'd long wondered what it would be like to challenge a man of peace going to war for all the right reasons. Or were they the wrong reasons, he couldn't decide for sure. Or was Boyd simply another Roman centurion planning to go over the wall and invade the lands of the Caledonian Picts with his marauding unruly cohorts? How could I ever know the truth about another man, thought Matthew; I am just a man of God. What do I know of men like Boyd?

When the briefing ended a mass of car boots opened. A bullet proof vest was donned and a magazine slotted into a Glock pistol. A Viking shotgun was broken, loaded with slugs, closed with a snap, and shouldered ready for action. From a hidden compartment diced headgear was dusted off and pulled tight over the scalp. And someone somewhere took a quick glance at a crumpled photograph in a worn out wallet before joining the party. Across the car park the men and women of the United Kingdom's counter terrorist command made ready.

'May I?' interrupted Matthew.

'Of course,' sidestepped Boyd.

'Ladies and gentlemen,' pleaded Matthew. 'Many years ago in a different life as an army chaplain I learnt this prayer. I'd like to end your briefing with the following words. Please join me in a moment of reflection.'

Here and there a cap was doffed and a firearm pointed to the ground.

Beneath a radio transmitter on expansive grassland of the Caldbeck Fells, Matthew Lowther found his place at last, responded to his calling, and prayed aloud proudly saying. 'Finally, my brethren, be strong. Be in the Lord and in the power of His might. Put on the whole armour of God that you may be able to stand against the wiles of the devil for you do not wrestle against flesh and blood but against principalities, against powers, against the rulers of the darkness of this age, against the spiritual hosts of wickedness in their heavenly places. Therefore take up the armour of God that you may be able to withstand this evil day, and having done all, to stand once more free men. May God be with you.'

Lowering his head, Matthew made the sign of the cross and felt Boyd's hand on his shoulder.

'Thank you, Matthew,' offered Boyd. 'That was very kind of you and I am sure it will strengthen our resolve in the coming hour.'

Turning to the team, Boyd delivered, 'Okay everyone. This is what we train for. This is why you were selected. Let's go.'

A car engine burst into life and the team moved out.

In the skies above England, four black helicopters carrying the world's most proficient Special Forces journeyed north following the Pennine Chain from central England.

Inside the armoury at the Base, surrounded by handguns, rifles, a ton of ammunition, and three devout followers, Azzam faced the east, slumped to his knees, and prayed. 'There is no God but Allah and Muhammad is his Prophet.'

*

Chapter Fifteen
~

The Base

Dug into the undergrowth, Jack Marshall peered through the foliage and found a line of vision available to him. A twig of thorns prickled his arm and he glowered at the bush wishing that it might wither to its roots.

A mile away Antonia and Anthea got out of Boyd's car and made for the rear entrance to the Base.

Raising the telescope to his eye once more, Jack scanned the Base and radioed, 'Wait... Wait... Wait.'

The land was bare. Only a handful of empty vehicles displayed themselves. Taking his time, Jack surveyed the entire area and advised the approaching convoy, 'Wait.... Wait... Wait... Okay, boss car, there's no movement outside. My last positive sighting locates Azzam plus three males in the third building on the offside as you enter the complex. Beware there are two storeys with windows at both levels... Wait and prepare... Ready.... Down to you, boss car...'

Boyd replied, 'All received, making an entry now. Go!'

Passing the wooden sign at the entrance, Boyd led the convoy into the complex at a sedate speed. Terry Anwhari broke right and shepherded his team to the rear of the outbuildings. Stuart Armstrong broke to the nearside to cover the paintballing site and assault course whilst Boyd drove quietly towards the outbuildings travelling at less than fifteen miles an hour. He was ever watchful and studied the doors and windows on the approach.

At the rear of the site, Antonia checked her mobile phone and realised there was no signal. The network was down as promised. As the other units fanned out in a slow and careful attempt to encircle the Base, Antonia looked skyward and whispered, 'Now, Alan!'

The silence was abruptly shattered when a Cessna Skyhawk plunged from the clouds and swooped low across the Fells. There was a huge wave of grass rising to greet him from the swaying meadowland as Alan flew low and hard. Then he blipped his engine as it roared across the complex. Banking harshly in the skies Alan exposed the Cessna's underbelly before throwing his plane back at the Base. The rocketing aircraft whipped up an enormous cloud of dust as he swooped towards the rooftops once again.

The Antonia and Alan conspiracy had its desired effect when an unnerved Azzam, Al Harith and Saleem rushed from the building and stared into the skies.

A wide eyed freaking Saleem ducked low when Alan guided his Cessna a matter of yards above the earth, pitched upwards, and then audaciously wiggled his wings in an act of pure impudence.

With all three suspects intimidated and exposed in the open air, Boyd's voice boomed from a loudhailer.

'This is the police. You are surrounded. Stand still and wait for my officers to approach you.'

To Boyd's rear Matthew and a number of officers appeared but any desire that such a plea might lead to conformity soon dissipated when a confused Azzam backed away shouting, 'Go away! What do you want? Go away!'

'We have legal power to search these premises, Azzam,' boomed Boyd. 'Stand still!'

'Allahu Akbar!' yelled Saleem as he sprinted into the building closely followed by Al Harith. Rafid scuttled along almost dragging his injured leg as he tried to keep up with his colleagues.

Azzam walked backwards towards the building shrieking, 'Keep away! Keep away from us!'

Allowing the loudhailer to drop to his side, Boyd took a step forward and said to Azzam, 'Come to me, Azzam. This is not the way.'

Matthew Lowther could contain himself no longer and bellowed, 'My daughter, Azzam! Have you got my daughter?'

'Guvnor!' screamed Jack across the radio. 'Get out of there. They don't want to know.'

'We needed to try,' replied Boyd as he turned and grabbed hold of Matthew. Unbalanced, Matthew stumbled backwards as Boyd dragged the vicar to the shelter of his car.

Simultaneously, Saleem appeared at the entrance to the building with a sub machine gun in his hands. There was a rattle of gunfire when Saleem responded and stated his case. Seconds later, Rafid and Al Harith appeared at the windows. The sound of breaking glass preceded a crescendo of shooting.

Stuart's team engaged Saleem and returned fire whilst Boyd hurtled Matthew into the rear of the BMW and hid behind the car door.

Meanwhile, Al Harith climbed the stairs to the top storey, smashed a window with the butt of his gun, and used the height to pick out his targets.

There was a rush for cover by Stuart when a volley of bullets clustered close to him and precision firing became the order of the day.

Throwing himself behind the assault course wall Stuart reloaded. Aware of lethal bullets zipping around him his team returned a barrage of fire. Regaining his composure Stuart took a two handed grip on his gun, espied his targets in the building, and let off another barrage from the cover of solid brickwork.

Jack Marshall approached, unclipped a stun grenade from his belt, and lobbed it into the entrance. There was a loud explosion and an almighty flash which drove Azzam and his associates further into the building.

In less than a minute the sombre Fells of Caldbeck morphed into a battlefield.

At the rear of the building, Terry's team made contact with Al Harith and Rafid trying to escape. There was a brief exchange of gunfire before the two terrorists melted into the building once more.

Slipping from his car door, Boyd sprinted across the divide and flung his spine against the building line. Withdrawing his Glock, Boyd inched towards the doorway. Shots fired from within and without the building as the exchanges continued and a stray bullet ricocheted from the door jamb close to Boyd's head. Kneeling down and peering inside, Boyd saw an open cabinet holding rifles and boxes of ammunition.

More gunfire dominated the atmosphere when Stuart engaged Al Harith who had made his way to the front door only a matter of inches from Boyd.

From the rear of the BMW, Matthew screamed his daughter's name but realised his call was drowned in a barrage of gunfire. More shooting occurred. Another stun grenade exploded and a barrage of bullets peppered half a dozen cars.

Al Harith ran out of ammunition and dropped back into the building to reload.

Seizing the moment, Boyd made a grab for the gunman, caught him by the arm, and hauled him from the doorway.

With gunfire raging, Stuart raced across open ground and pointed his gun into the entrance as Boyd struggled to subdue the Al-Qaeda man and remove him from the melee. Moments later, the butt of a gun landed on Al Harith's skull and ended the tussle.

There was another barrage of shooting from the building

'Looks like we've found a hornet's nest,' remarked Boyd.

'Take cover,' screamed Stuart.

Saleem threw a grenade towards the cars and then ran out of the building towards the rear of the Base with Azzam hard on his heels.

There was another huge explosion when Terry Anwhari pitched a stun grenade into the rear of the edifice and then followed up by throwing himself through a ground floor window to catch Rafid cold. With his pistol nestling close to Rafid's skull Terry simply enquired, 'Your choice! I'd drop the weapon if I were you.'

On the narrow bridge, close to the oak trees, Antonia and Anthea advanced carefully into the complex. Ahead they could see the smoke of the stun grenade, the flash of bullets fleeting from the muzzle, and they could smell the faint odour of cordite wafting towards them

Hurrying towards the pair, Azzam and Saleem made for the entrance to the mine. When Antonia and Anthea gradually closed the distanced with their adversaries, they realised the wooden gate to the mine stood open. Narrow gauge railway lines coursed towards the mine, stopped outside, and then seemed to begin again just inside the mine's entrance. Loose earth above the gateway threatened to tumble to the ground and litter the entrance.

Saleem had no regard for his puny female enemy. He'd been brought up in the belief that a woman's position in life was slightly higher than that of his father's cattle. Yes, Al-Qaeda recruited warrior women to its core in some places, thought Saleem, but here in the United Kingdom these irrelevant bitches were merely servants of man.

Firing from the hip in a haphazard manner, Saleem let loose a salvo from his machine gun. Bullets splayed everywhere.

At a distance of about seventy yards Antonia and Anthea held their ground. As bullets ripped up the earth close to them, Anthea adjusted her profile, presented the left side of her body, and carefully drew a bead on the approaching Saleem. Instantaneously, Antonia withdrew her Glock, stood square and unyielding, flexed her body, and took a deep breath. Judiciously, Antonia threw away her mantle of ostentatious flair and brought her weapon to the business level.

Sixty yards, thought Anthea. A handful of shots flew by her shoulder and smashed into the foliage behind. Part of a branch fell from one of the oak trees, destroyed by a charging Saleem.

Fifty yards, reckoned Antonia. The ground in front of the MI5 lady exploded in a mini volcano as Saleem missed his target and peppered the land.

Suddenly, Saleem found a rational mindset and realised his chaotic slapdash attack needed immediate refinement. Continuing to shoot, he raised his weapon from the hip to the shoulder and fired continuously as he rushed towards his enemy. Spitting bullets from the barrel, chipping sods of earth from the target area, Saleem blasted his way forward.

Forty yards, decided Anthea.

A bullet tore through the cloth at the elbow area of her jacket. Unperturbed, she raised her weapon and curled a finger around the trigger.

'Death to the infidels!' screamed Saleem as he took aim.

In the micro second that followed both Anthea and Antonia exhaled slowly, steadied and rectified their aim, and then firmly squeezed the trigger.

Somewhere inside the Glock the trigger mechanism activated the hammer action which exploded and propelled a succession of bullets along the barrel and into the atmosphere.

When the various rounds entered Saleem's head and upper body mass they stopped him in his tracks and perhaps signalled to him, in the finality of his death, that the United Kingdom has women warriors too. A carefully targeted series of deadly projectiles dispatched by Antonia and Anthea brought an end to the life of Saleem from Sana'a.

The assassin from the Yemen was thrust backwards when the bullets smashed into his being. His machine gun flew aimlessly into the air still surrendering its final chaotic slugs as he hit the ground. Saleem's backbone wriggled for a moment, determined to aspire to a longer life, and then capitulated to total surrender when Anthea took two steps forward and finished the job.

'Sorry, Toni,' offered Anthea. 'He's a dangerous little fish!'

'Did you notice his yellow teeth,' remarked Antonia.

'Nope!' replied Anthea. 'But we weren't far from smelling his breath!'

'Job done!' exclaimed Antonia.

'Where's the other one?' asked Anthea.

There was a gush of wind when Azzam ran into the mine and steadied himself against the side of the wall. Then he descended gradually into the core of the pit as he followed the incline downwards towards the secrets of Al-Qaeda's treasure in the Caldbeck Fells.

Boyd arrived, breathless, with his Glock held skyward and his mind intent only on one thing. 'Where is he?' he demanded.

Anthea lowered her handgun, reloaded, and offered, 'Glad you could join us, Guvnor. He went thataway.' She pointed to the mine entrance.

Looking down at Saleem's body, Boyd revered, 'Good grouping. Let's go.'

He hurried towards the mine entrance. Again, he flung his backbone against the rock close to the entrance.

'On me,' he signalled to the ladies.

Anthea and Antonia fell in line behind Boyd and drew breath.

'Well done, ladies,' responded Boyd. 'If I don't make it tell Meg to look after the twins.'

'Tell her yourself,' suggested Antonia. The redhead shrugged, waved her handgun, nodded Boyd forward, and readied herself.

'On three,' declared Boyd. 'High and left, high and right, and low in the centre. Ready… One… Two…'

On three, Boyd flung himself across the blank divide to the far side of the mine wall and thrust his handgun into the darkness prepared to fire. Antonia slid round the corner and complimented Boyd whilst Anthea threw herself onto the ground and felt her belly hug the soil. Low and lethal, Anthea's red hair finally settled on her shoulders as her eyes sought a target in the dim light.

'So far,' inspired Boyd.

There was a sudden rush of cold air as the trio advanced warily down the narrow passage.

Thirty feet below ground Azzam sorted through the available arsenal and mentally selected his preferred option. Turning to

Khalid, Azzam said, 'This is not what we planned, Khalid, but I say to you now that it is time.'

Withdrawing an enormous sword from its scabbard, Khalid smiled and countered with, 'This finely honed blade is my message, Azzam. Its jewelled handle grants me Prophet Muhammad's great wisdom as well as his strength to accomplish the task ahead. The venom from my razor-sharp blade grants me the power of supreme conviction. You called me forward, my great and honourable leader. I came to kill the infidels and kill the infidels I shall.'

There were approximately a dozen boxes of hand grenades, four score of rocket launchers, crate upon crate of handguns, and a long stacked row of over one hundred AK-47 assault rifles and associated ammunition carefully arranged in the depths of the mine.

Azzam ignored them all and dragged his chosen suicide bomb jacket from a row of twenty or more such devices.

'Make your father proud,' offered Azzam to Khalid. 'By dawn tomorrow we will be all over the media. Our names will be forever revered in the history of Jihad. Paradise awaits us, my true friend. Allahu Akbar!'

They embraced and then Azzam donned his suicide jacket and stepped towards the incline leading to the entrance.

His eyes accustoming to the dim light, Boyd edged down the narrow passageway with Anthea and Antonia supporting him every inch of the way. Suddenly the giant that was Azzam appeared before them. Immediately, Boyd realised his opponent was somehow misshapen. Moments later, a cog in Boyd's brain fell into place and he lowered his gun, turned, and yelled, 'Run! He's a suicide bomber. Run!'

Retreating quickly, Anthea took aim but then Antonia touched the barrel of Anthea's weapon and advised, 'No! You'll bring the roof down.'

Lumbering slightly from side to side Azzam climbed the slight incline shouting, 'There is no God but Allah and Muhammad is his Prophet.'

The trio of law enforcement officers were racing at full pelt now with passages from the Koran echoing in their ears. Their endangered dash for freedom witnessed the three of them galloping up the slope when daylight beckoned them to the entrance.

To their rear, Azzam bounced from one wall to another in pursuit as he bellowed, 'Kafir! Kafir! Kafir!'

Bursting into sunlight Antonia and Anthea ran straight into Matthew trying to enter the mine.

'No!' screeched Antonia. 'Run, Matthew! He's a suicide bomber!'

Shrugging off Antonia, Matthew sidestepped Anthea and stepped into the darkness only to be rugby tackled by Boyd who tumbled over the vicar's body. Catching hold of Matthew's jacket Boyd yanked the vicar away from the entrance.

Azzam appeared at the entrance roaring 'There is no God but Allah and Muhammad is his Prophet.'

Firing haphazardly underarm Boyd wasted a couple of shots in a poor attempt to dissuade Azzam.

'Susie!' screamed Matthew.

'Run!' hollered Boyd suddenly realising that Terry, Stuart and Jack were approaching the scene. 'Run, everyone!' he shouted.

'My daughter,' screamed Matthew above the chaos. 'Have you got my daughter, you bastard?'

Erupting into the daylight, Azzam appeared in all his terrifying glory laden down in his suicide bomb jacket. Laughing at Matthew, Azzam sniggered, 'Vicar-man! I came to kill the infidels!'

As Azzam snatched the jacket's ignition cord, Boyd pushed Matthew backwards into the stream at the same time as Antonia and Anthea reached the narrow bridge.

Azzam detonated his jacket with an abrupt tug.

Boyd dropped his Glock before he and Matthew hit the surface of the stream and sank below the water line. Instantaneously, Antonia and Anthea dived to the ground at the same time Terry, Stuart, Jack, and a dozen officers, backed away.

The explosion blew Azzam into a thousand pieces.

Amongst Azzam's flesh and muscle sinew flying through the air a collection of ball bearings, nails, screws, bolts and glass hurtled towards the infidels.

Boyd felt a huge thud when he surfaced and a ball bearing embedded itself into his bullet proof vest. A shower of nails and bolts rained down into the water beside him.

'What's that?' screamed Matthew.

'Shrapnel!' shrieked Boyd. 'Get under water!'

The two men took a deep breath and submerged once more as the explosion gradually subsided and an uncanny silence penetrated the atmosphere.

In the distance a squadron of black helicopters came into view. Ropes dangled from the helicopter bellies like umbilical cords and troopers in blacked out gear carrying weapons stood on the helicopter running rails. They were about to abseil into the danger zone.

There was a dash for freedom when Rafid tried to escape the clutches of the law. He jumped into the nearest motor vehicle, fired the engine, and set off towards the road.

Terry Anwhari dropped to one knee and fired a succession of bullets into the front car tyres and engine block. To no avail, Rafid bypassed Terry but then suddenly veered out of control and smashed into the side of a building. The car embedded itself in the brickwork and the windscreen shattered. The horn sounded long and noisily when Rafid's unconscious body slumped over the steering wheel in final surrender.

Emerging from the stream, Boyd yanked Matthew onto the bank and they tried to shake themselves dry like young puppies in the rain. Anthea and Antonia followed suit before Boyd collected his weapon and suggested, 'Ladies?'

Signalling to the mine entrance, Boyd led the way and quickly stepped into the narrow corridor. He followed the broken intermittent narrow gauge line downwards into the pit to the corner. Angling his head forward, Boyd stole a glance around the bend and espied a laptop computer linked to a video camera standing on a table. A mobile phone lay close by. But it was worse than that, realised Boyd. The scar-faced Khalid was about to behead Susie.

The blindfolded vicar's daughter sobbed uncontrollably when Khalid dragged her from the dark recesses of the mine and forced her onto her knees. It was then that Boyd acknowledged that both her hands and her ankles were tied.

Khalid withdrew his sword and grasped tight its bejewelled handle.

'Shit!' exclaimed Boyd. 'It's my worst nightmare!'

'What is it?' snapped Matthew from the top of the incline close to the entrance.

Boyd declined an answer, glimpsed again, and shielded his eyes when Khalid flicked a switch and lit up the area.

A blast of light suddenly invaded the mine shaft and Boyd's eyes took in the long scar that disfigured Khalid's face.

Switching on the video recorder, Khalid began the public decapitation of an innocent girl.

Anthea and Antonia moved closer but Matthew galloped down the incline shouting, 'Susie!'

Alerted, Khalid glanced up and saw Boyd watching him from the corner of the L shaped corridor. Withdrawing the sword to his rear, preparing to swing, Khalid shifted balance and began reciting the Koran in all its glory and divine wisdom.

'No! I beseech you, no!' screamed Matthew.

Another verse, another incantation from the great Prophet Muhammad echoed and bounced eerily from wall to wall as Khalid revealed his Jihadist message to Matthew and the entire world.

'Not like this,' screeched Matthew. 'What would your parents think of you, for God's sake?'

'My father will be proud of me,' snarled Khalid.

Jewels on the handle sparkled in the light as Khalid inched further backwards to the extremity of his swing.

Susie screamed, 'Dad! I love you, dad!'

'For a shimmering dawn,' barked Khalid as he commenced his gargantuan swing.

Khalid's wrists twisted slightly as he gripped the handle tighter. There was a sparkle of light on the bejewelled handle, an ostentatious streak of rainbow coloured evil flashing in the half light, a twinkle of vivid iniquity on a finely honed blade, and a bulge in a bicep as human power came into play.

Nearby, a tear fell from Susie's eyes and splashed an unseen rivulet of water in the dust. A scream wedged in her terrified throat; a young girl's neck dropped and her chin touched her chest.

A perilous cutting edge began its journey through the musty mildewed atmosphere of Caldbeck's mine.

'Muhammad!' bellowed Khalid loudly and emphatically.

Boyd's finger squeezed the trigger and a bullet exploded from the barrel winging its way through the thin diluted air towards its target.

A race of bullets stormed the air space when Anthea and Antonia joined in the riposte but a venomous blade carrying a fourteen centuries time-served antediluvian message scurried on its journey.

'Susie!' screeched the vicar; his white collar band greyed from the dust and dirt of the mine and all that had gone before.

The first bullets thundered into Khalid's left temple and burst his skull open.

But still the murderous sword glided on lugging its evil memorandum.

Still firing one-handed into Khalid's physique, Boyd threw himself at Susie and took the full force of Khalid's sword on his bullet proof jacket as Anthea and Antonia delivered a barrage of gunshots to Khalid's perishing body.

The barrage had been enough to severely weaken the strength in Khalid's swing and Boyd screamed aloud in cold fear when he felt the sword glance from his back as he shunted Susie off target and felt her body beneath his.

There was an unobtrusive swish of a failing blade when Khalid staggered forward as the shots continued to hit his body. Nerve ends deep inside his frame twitched in a spasm of death as a death defying reluctance bit into his brain when it fought to accomplish its task.

But suddenly, his being surrendered and his body fell to the ground in bitter surrender.

Khalid's three foot sword clattered to the ground and then rolled inconclusively before it finally redeemed itself and came to rest at Antonia's feet.

In agony, Boyd stood up and enquired, 'Girls, how bad?'

Anthea moved forward, sunk her fingers into the Kevlar vest, probed, and said, 'Two ball bearings, a couple of nuts and bolts and an eighth of an inch deep cut across the main area of your back. Lucky man, I would say. If you'd been nearer to Azzam when he exploded he'd have ripped you to pieces and if the female section of the unit hadn't been here to provide extra fire power at the end you'd have been mincemeat ages ago.'

'I'll second that you bloody fool!' muttered Antonia.

'I'm not going to stand up properly for a week, pronounced Boyd. 'Good stuff that Kevlar but I can feel every inch of pain, I can tell you.'

Susie gurgled and Anthea and Antonia immediately dropped to their knees to untie her.

Matthew rushed to his daughter's side, cradled her, looked up and said, 'How can I ever thank you.'

'Oh, you could pray for me at the discipline proceedings,' revealed Boyd. 'They'll hang me out to dry for endangering you.'

'The Lord is my shield, Mister Boyd. I was never in danger. My God protects and guides my every move. You were merely angels carrying a message.'

Boyd chuckled and suggested, 'That's where it all started and went wrong, isn't it? With God! Everyone thinks theirs is the best. And me, an Angelic messenger, I thought that was Gabriel?'

'Whatever,' remarked Matthew lifting Susie to her feet.

'On the other hand you might try not to knock me over next time I'm out running,' offered Boyd.

'That's not quite as I remember it,' countered Matthew hugging close his daughter.

Susie wept the tears of England deep in Caldbeck's heart.

Antonia examined Khalid's laptop and remarked, 'He's not online. He was making a recording.'

'Well, we'll need to identify him and the others here,' suggested Boyd. 'Can you manage the lap top and I'll take this for now.'

Picking up Khalid's mobile phone, Boyd remarked, 'I suppose we'll find his name in here or at least a good lead to it. Look, why don't you take this as well, Toni? Your team is likely to make something of this and the names and numbers it contains.'

'I'm sure it will be useful,' replied Antonia taking the phone.

'Well, this little lot is going to take some writing up,' offered Boyd. 'Where to start, that's the question?'

'Leave it to me,' said Anthea. 'I'll do it.'

'Are you sure?' asked Boyd.

'The experience will do me good,' conceded Anthea. 'But apart from that you need some attention to your back: a hospital or a doctor for instance.'

'Thanks, Anthea,' uttered Boyd.

'Let's go and see the cavalry,' proposed Antonia. 'I can hear the helicopters above.'

As the group emerged into the daylight a contingent of SAS troopers' abseiled into the complex and were approached by Anthea.

Boyd and Antonia walked back to the car amidst the shimmering sunshine of Cumbria.

'It's not a terrorist training camp then,' revealed Antonia.

'No, it really is a Base for young people, Toni. It's just that Azzam was running it as a rendezvous point and an armoury for Al-Qaeda.'

'By the look of the weapons and ammunition in the mine, this is some find,' advocated Antonia. 'Some find, indeed.'

'Yes, but I wonder what their real target was?' submitted Boyd.

'I expect we may never know,' suggested Antonia.

'Time to relax,' revealed Boyd. 'How are things with Phillip?'

'He's a very good boss,' indicated Antonia.

'That's not what I meant,' stated Boyd.

'We have a dinner date very soon.'

'Dinner for two?' enquired Boyd.

'Of course,' replied Antonia.

They walked on oblivious to the clear up operation now taking place.

'Pity really,' said Antonia.

'What is?' asked Boyd.

'You could have had me once but you chose Meg instead. Remember?'

'So I did, Toni, but I that's because I knew you needed someone like Phillip.'

'Is it really?'

'Of course, would I ever lie to you, Toni?'

There was silence for a moment before Antonia hit the car roof, smiled and said, 'You're the best friend I ever had, William. But Phillip, do you think I should…'

'Yes, Antonia,' interrupted Boyd. 'I do. He is your destiny.' A helicopter landed and whipped up a ground swell of debris as the men and women of the Special Crime Unit took stock of the situation.

'Well, we have a date tonight if I make it back in time,' smiled Antonia.

*

Chapter Sixteen
~
Retirement

When they gathered to pay their respects to the outgoing leader of the Special Crime Unit Commander Herbert invited his guests to a suite in the Operations Centre. His family and closest friends congregated when he opened the large cabinet behind his desk to display a fine array of wines and spirits from around the world.

'Another ritual, James?' enquired Phillip.

'But of course,' replied the commander. 'Bearing in mind that we have visitors from all over the world we have a collection of police cap badges and military insignia that will beat any private collection across the globe.'

'And your own vineyard,' suggested Phillip.

'Indeed, it's customary for visitors attending on business to bring either a bottle of whiskey or a bottle of wine of their choice,' explained Commander Herbert. 'We end up with produce from all over the world. Everything from champagne to vodka to American beers and, of course, as you might expect, gallons of Irish Bushmills and the like.'

'And you keep it for posterity?' queried Phillip.

'No, we keep it for occasions like these. Red or white?'

'I'll take a small red if I might,' replied Phillip. 'What about you, Antonia?'

'Oh, I'll leave that to the commander,' smiled Antonia. 'I'm sure he remembers my favourite.'

'But of course,' chuckled Commander Herbert. 'That will be Champagne then.'

'Thank you,' replied Antonia.

'Yes, a Bollinger, I understand,' mentioned Phillip.

A pair of smiles transmitted through space and met in the middle.

'Here, let me be the waiter,' interjected Boyd observantly. 'Meg and I are very good at this, aren't we, Meg?'

An increasingly pregnant Meg appeared at Boyd's side and remarked, 'We certainly are and I'm sure I can manage the champagne. But we do need some help. Are there any spare hands available?'

The door opened and Stuart entered with Janice by his side.

'Och… I heard that,' revealed Janice. But dinnae you worry, I've a spare hand but the other is out of action at the moment.'

There were chuckles and cheers all round as Janice accepted a small glass of bubbly, turned to Commander Herbert, and said, 'Happy retirement, sir, and lang may yer lum reek.'

'How wonderful to see you, Janice,' beamed Commander Herbert. 'Err, pray tell me, what does that mean?'

Boyd leaned across and whispered, 'It means live long and be happy, sir, or, to be precise, may you always have a warm fire.'

'Oh yes, yes, indeed, Janice. I'll give it a try,' acknowledged the commander. 'Tell me how long will you need to wear a support?'

Easing the shoulder support slightly, Janice chuckled, 'Until it's strong enough to lift a crate of champagne, commander. I've to wear it for a while and go back to outpatients in due course. I'll be off a while until I'm stronger and fully recovered but I'll be back. Och aye, I'll be back.'

'You'd better be back soon,' suggested Commander Herbert. 'You and Boyd and the team have been awarded a stack of medals. Anthea has received a recommendation for a promotion to Inspector and we're hoping to move Chief Inspector Boyd a notch higher in coming weeks. What a wonderful time to bow out from the job I love. I'm so pleased for you all.'

Turning to Anthea, Janice enquired, 'Did you ever find that leak to the Press you were on about?'

'No,' replied Anthea. 'It really was just coincidence on the part of the Press paparazzi. No, the only leak was Mister Ryan who has been removed from office.'

'Oh well,' sighed Janice. 'All's well that ends well. But can you tell me if those robbers in the motorway services shoot out had anything to do with the terrorists we were looking for? The news isn't very good when you're in hospital.'

Boyd engaged Janice with, 'No, they were just criminals, Janice, but I think we'll find that the weapons and ammunition were supplied by Azzam to the bank robbers. The problem is, of course, Azzam is dead and our prisoners aren't the most talkative on the block. Time and forensic analysis will tell in the end. The fact is that whilst we know a lot we also know very little. We still don't know why the four Al-Qaeda men came to England and we don't actually know who Azzam really was.'

'Stuart told me about Azzam wanting the names and addresses of all the local kids in the Caldbeck area,' mentioned Janice. 'Was that the target?

'No,' replied Boyd. 'I think that was just Azzam gathering a little bit of intelligence for future use. But if he'd ever got all the village kids down that mine I shudder to think what might have happened. Realistically, we don't know what the Al-Qaeda target was. All we can say for sure is that we thwarted an attack of some kind.'

'And that wee lassie, Susie, and her family?' enquired Janice.

'The Lowthers have taken some friendly advice and taken a holiday,' smiled Boyd. 'In fact, I think they're planning to visit Spain soon for a fortnight to get away and relax.'

'Great, I don't blame them,' revealed Janice. 'But, Guvnor, there's one more think I need to say.'

'What's that?' asked Boyd.

'Thank you! Och I can still hear the bullets whistling across ma heed and I can still see the tarmac exploding. Thanks, Guvnor.'

'No, thank you, Janice,' replied Boyd. 'You are an inspiration to us all.'

Antonia offered, 'You certainly are, Janice. Well done! Your family must be so very proud of you.'

'Aye, but they used to think I was a check out girl at the local supermarket,' chirped Janice.

They laughed but as Boyd guided Antonia to one side he asked, 'Toni, you and Phillip?'

'What about Phillip and I?' asked Antonia.

'Are you… You know are you two…?'

'Don't be ridiculous, Boyd,' snapped Antonia.

'Well,' explained Boyd, 'I just thought…'

Antonia walked away but then returned and said, 'Billy, do you think Phillip….'

'Don't be ridiculous, Toni.'

Boyd walked away, looked over his shoulder and winked at Toni, and then took Meg's arm saying, 'How's the champagne going?'

Antonia smiled and watched Boyd go before turning her attention to Phillip Nesbitt who offered her another glass of champagne.

The evening wore on with a succession of corks pulled from bottles and the sound of laughter penetrating the corridors outside. Ultimately, the time arrived for speeches and Phillip paid tribute to the commander for his many years of dedicated service. Then Boyd took centre stage and made an eloquent and compassionate speech on behalf of the Unit before presenting Commander Herbert with a photograph album. Littered with dozens of photographs spanning the commander's career over the decades the final pages contained snaps of the entire Special Crime Unit past and present.

When the applause died down, Boyd invited the commander to make a speech.

With his family close by, Commander Herbert stood, nodded, and addressed his company.

'I suppose taking stock of a photograph album in which you all appear is like taking stock of the life you have just lived,' chuckled the commander. 'So I will share these thoughts with you who have been kind enough to support me for so many years and those of you whom I have only been fortunate enough to know for a much shorter period.'

The commander lifted a retirement card from a pile on his desk and reflected, 'Your card wishes the boss a happy retirement. But I'd like to remind you that you never worked for me although you always called me boss. You worked for your families and our country. Your boss lies within your soul and guides you on the path you have chosen to take. I was just there to make sure you made the best possible decision and be in the right place ready to catch you if you fell. For me, a good boss is someone who can lead by example and support those who look up to him for leadership. At the same time a good boss needs to be able to stand up to those above him and represent those with whom he serves. I have tried my best to accomplish that task. Ladies and gentlemen, friends, it has been an honour and a privilege to serve with you... Thank you...'

To thunderous applause Commander Herbert strolled towards a small wooden shield on the wall. It was the image of a Bell, Book and Candle exposed upon a crest.

The Commander touched the shield and said aloud, 'Ever vigilant.'

Commander James Herbert took hold of his wife's hand, embraced his son and daughter, and then hugged Boyd saying, 'I'm so glad you could all make it, William.'

Finally, with a wave as he sat down, he retired.

In the following days, a shimmering dawn broke the morning on the Afghanistan-Pakistan border. The sun rose high giving both light and life to the population below. Suddenly, an unexpected thunder storm moved in from the west when the fist of God smote down his wrath on the grey mountains of the Spin Ghar range.

The heavens opened and drenched the ground beneath. There was almost a five hour time difference between the border and the United Kingdom where it was approaching midnight.

In a room at the joint RAF - American Operations Centre, the Director General of the Security Services, Phillip Nesbitt, and Antonia Harston-Browne shook hands with the squadron leader before Antonia removed Khalid's mobile phone from her shoulder bag. She handed it over to the officer.

The squadron leader interrogated the device, checked a number, and handed the mobile phone to an American colleague close by. He then invited Antonia and Phillip to step forward and inspect the television screens and control room that was functioning as normal.

On the Fells of north Cumbria, a row of red aircraft warning lights clinging to Caldbeck's radio mast readied themselves for another night's work as the structure stood tall and proud over the glories of Cumbria.

From their home on the Moor, Meg held Boyd's hand whilst they sampled the glories of the northern Fells and the static omnipresent lights of Caldbeck's mast.

At the RAF station a finger pressed a digit on the keypad of a mobile phone whilst a television screen played in the background revealing nothing but a mountainous desert landscape.

In a church in the Caldbeck Fells a reverend's voice proudly intoned, 'We separate him, together with his accomplices and abettors, from the precious body and blood of the Lord and from the society of all Christians. We exclude him from our Holy Mother, the Church in Heaven, and on earth. We declare him excommunicate and anathema. We judge him damned with the Devil and his angels and all his reprobate to eternal fire until he shall recover himself from the toils of the devil and return to amendment and to penitence.'

The Reverend Lowther made the sign of the cross and gazed into the stained glass window above the altar.

Inside a fort situated in the foothills of the Afghan-Pakistan border a mobile telephone rang unanswered for half a minute or so. Eventually, Abdul-Ahad stepped away from his friends and followers, looked into the window display, and recognised the number. He lifted the phone to his ear, grinned broadly, and said, 'Khalid! Khalid, my son, is that you? Hey, everyone, it's Khalid!'

In the skies above, the belly of an unmanned drone opened and swiftly deployed a missile towards the target below. Flying through the air at a phenomenal speed, the missile honed in on the signal, penetrated the roof of the fort, and exploded in a deafening display of firepower killing the occupants instantly, rocking the ground for miles around, and rejecting the shimmering dawn.

Far away, Matthew approached the altar and made the sign of the cross. He rang a bell, closed his Bible with an abrupt 'snap', and then deliberately snuffed out a candle. He then knocked the candle to the floor with all the might he could summons.

Stepping back, Matthew took hold of Susie in one hand and Elizabeth in the other, bowed to his God and intoned, 'So be it!'

'So be it!'

~

Author's Note

~ ~ ~

The phrase 'Bell, Book and Candle' refers to a method of excommunication for one who had committed a particular grievous sin. Apparently introduced around the late ninth century, the practice was once used by the Catholic Church. In modern times, a simple pronouncement is made. This antediluvian ceremony involved a bishop with twelve priests reciting an oath to an altar.

'We separate him, together with his accomplices and abettors, from the precious body and blood of the Lord and from the society of all Christians. We exclude him from our Holy Mother, the Church in Heaven, and on earth. We declare him excommunicate and anathema. We judge him damned with the Devil and his angels and all his reprobate to eternal fire until he shall recover himself from the toils of the devil and return to amendment and to penitence.'

After reciting this the priests would respond 'So be it.' The bishop would ring a bell to evoke a death toll, close a holy book to symbolise the excommunicate's separation from the church, and snuff out a candle or candles knocking them to the floor to represent the target's soul being extinguished from the light of God.

The image of the 'Bell, Book and Candle', is found on the badge of the Metropolitan Police Anti-Terrorist Branch, S013, - now restructured as Counter Terrorist Command - along with some of the poignant words from the method of excommunication...

'Bell, book and candle' lives on...

Paul Anthony....

~

The UK ANTI-TERRORIST HOTLINE

~

If you see or hear something that doesn't sound quite right, don't hesitate. You may feel it's nothing to get excited about but trust in your instincts and let the police know.

Remember, no piece of information is considered too small or insignificant.

If you see something suspicious – tell the police.

'Suspicious activity could include someone:

... Who has bought or stored large amounts of chemicals, fertilisers or gas cylinders for no obvious reason...

... Who has bought or hired a vehicle in suspicious circumstances...

... Who holds passports or other documents in different names for no obvious reason...

... Who travels for long periods of time, but is vague about where they're going...

It's probably nothing but... if you see or hear anything that could be terrorist-related trust your instincts and call the Anti-Terrorist Hotline on 0800 789 321.

The UK Anti-Terrorist Hotline
0800 789 321

~

Welcome to Paul Anthony's book shop.
~

I am a retired British detective who has served extensively throughout the U.K and elsewhere. In the past I've been published by a Vanity House and a Traditional Publishing House but I'm currently an independent self-publishing author with my own publishing imprint and editorial services business. I've written both television and film scripts either on my own, or with the award winning screenwriter Nick Gordon. Paul Anthony is my pseudonym. Born in Southport, Lancashire, I'm the son of a soldier whose family settled in Carlisle before I joined Cumbria police at the age of 19. As a detective, I served in Cumbria CID, the Regional Crime Squad in Manchester, the Special Branch, and other national agencies in the UK and elsewhere. I have an Honours Degree in Economics and Social Sciences, a Diploma in Management and a Diploma in Office Management. The Chairman of a Registered Charity, 'Champ's Camp', I support the Dyslexia Foundation UK who selected 'The Fragile Peace' to be the first book in their audio library. Additionally, I actively promote the 'United Artistes Casting Agency' which works to provide job opportunities for ex military and police in the acting field, often providing both 'extras' and people with 'specific' military and police skills required by film and television production companies. When not writing, I enjoy reading a wide range of works, reviewing same, and playing guitar badly. I like running, Pilates, kettlebells, athletics, keeping fit, dining out and dining in, keeping Koi carp, and following politics, economics and social sciences. Married, we have three adult children and five grandchildren. I'm a former winner of the Independent Authors Network Featured Author Contest and was a Featured Author at the 'Books without Borders' Event in Yonkers, New York, 2012. In earlier years I was a Featured Author at the Frankfurt Book Fair, Germany. I am also a member of the writer's circle.

This is the current Paul Anthony Collection. You will find all these books in print and kindle. I recommend Lulu for the cheapest print

versions and Amazon for the eBook versions. Thank you for visiting the book shop. I hope you enjoy your visit and would like to thank you for supporting the works of Paul Anthony.
… Paul Anthony

*

Paul Anthony
'One of the best thriller and mystery writers in the United Kingdom today'.… Caleb Pirtle 111, International Best Selling Author of over 60 novels, journalist, travel writer, screenplay writer, and Founder and Editorial Director at Venture Galleries.

Paul Anthony is one of the best Thriller Mystery Writers of our times! … Dennis Sheehan, International Best Selling Author of 'Purchased Power', former United Sates Marine Corps.

'When it comes to fiction and poetry you will want to check out this outstanding author. Paul has travelled the journey of publication and is now a proud writer who is well worth discovery.' … Janet Beasley, Epic Fantasy Author, theatre producer and director - Scenic Nature Photographer, JLB Creatives.

Paul Anthony is a brilliant writer and an outstanding gentleman who goes out of his way to help and look out for others. In his writing, Paul does a wonderful job of portraying the era in which we live with its known and unknown fears. I highly recommend this intelligent and kind gentleman to all.' … Jeannie Walker, author of the True Crime Story 'Fighting the Devil', 2011 National Indie Excellence Awards (True Crime Finalist) and 2010 winner of the Silver Medal for Book of the Year True Crime Awards.

'To put it simply, Paul tells a bloody good tale. I have all his works and particularly enjoy his narrative style. His characters are totally believable and draw you in. Read. Enjoy…. John White, Reader

*

Behead the Serpent
Published by Paul Anthony Associates, February, 2013
THIS BOOK IS #3 IN THE DAVIES KING 'stand alone' series, where each book has a separate stand alone tale involving the detective, KING, his detectives, and British Intelligence.

Genre: Fiction / Thriller / Espionage / Murder /Mystery / Tension / Suspense
Synopsis:
Compromising photographs discovered in a vacant office in central London are not immediately connected to a ferocious attack on Davies King. But when the campaign against the chief of detectives and his closest friends turns to blackmail, it becomes personal. A series of horrendous bomb attacks and brutal shootings convince Davies to discharge himself from hospital and confront the two 'most wanted' criminals in the United Kingdom. Disillusioned with a temporary chief constable, and anxious to relieve a stressed out bomb disposal officer, the chess playing detective joins forces with British Intelligence to challenge the megalomaniacs who are holding the nation to ransom. Her Majesty's Government announce a Tier One threat level as the lights across the south of England are extinguished and parts of Europe and North America face the reality of the first stages of society's breakdown - Dystopia.
It's a simple question for the obstinate detective to answer. Does the country pay the ransom or do the lights go out? It's not rocket science, but who makes the decisions, and why?

Could a cyberspace war really happen? Read this fascinating novel and you realise, yes it could! Detective Chief Inspector Davies King

flies by the seat of his pants taking everyone along with him as he tackles the problem threatening society... 'Another cracking 'unputdownable' read from Paul Anthony.'
Pauline Livingstone, Editor...

Another fast-paced, action-packed thriller from Paul Anthony. Davies King, the hard-nosed chess master detective, needs all his cunning, skill, and nerve to play a megalomaniac and a terrorist at their own game. When the very fabric of not only his personal life, but that of society as we know it, is threatened, Davies has to be at his masterly best. The consequence of failure is disaster on an international scale..... A real page-turner from start to finish
Meg Johnston, author.

REVIEW: This tale is so up to date it is unbelievable. Part mystery, part spy adventure, always a thriller, and at a time when the world's hackers have carried out the biggest ever DDOS (Distributed denial of service) on the world wide web, Paul Anthony's typical multi genre work pre-empts reality with a fascinating story that penetrates the very essence of life in the world of Intelligence. A brilliant piece of fiction aided and abetted by some classic characters.
Dan, Reader... Grange Over Sands...

Review: Five stars awarded - A well written, bang up to date or even ahead of its time plot, written by an obviously knowledgeable, well informed author.... Peter Baxter, Reader

*

Moonlight Shadows
Crime / Espionage / International Chase Thriller
Published Spring, 2012
THIS BOOK IS #2 IN THE DAVIES KING 'stand alone' series, where each book has a separate stand alone tale involving the detective, KING, his detectives, and British Intelligence.

Book Description

When Conor is betrayed, he spends the night hidden in the bracken surrounded by security forces. As moonlight shadows flicker, he realises who is responsible. With his unit destroyed, Conor sets out for revenge. But dark unspoken forces are at work and the track goes cold. A decade later, a displaced British Intelligence Agent produces a mysterious piece of software and demands reinstatement. The enigmatic software, threatens to destabilise the world's economy should it fall into the wrong hands. Pegasus returns only to be plunged into a breath-taking international chase involving terrorists, spies and criminals. Greed, corruption, dishonesty and mistrust are uncovered in the most powerful of places as the need to secure an enigmatic memory stick dominates proceedings. Only Davies King, a chess playing, hardnosed detective, and his team, seem capable of bringing sanity to a cyberspace driven society. Is there a traitor? A traitor of the worst kind! And there's only one... Isn't there?

Review: Paul Anthony builds tension into every page. His characters are so real you will feel as if you know them, and believe me, some you will never want to know... A cracking read...
Pauline Livingstone, Editor and Book Critic.

A Review from Scott Whitmore, former US Naval officer, sports journalist, freelance writer, and author... A bit of a genre-mix, part international espionage Moonlight Shadows features interesting and well-drawn characters, exciting bursts of action, multiple storylines, and more than a few well-placed plot twists. I enjoyed it immensely. The reader is swept up into a world of international intrigue in Japan and Amsterdam as well as common-sense policing in London and the English seaside town of Crillsea. The plots come together soon enough, and along the way the reader gets to spend plenty of time with Detective Chief Inspector Davies King, newly promoted but saddled with a green and ambitious "political" type. Joining the chess-playing Davies are most of the wonderful cast of characters introduced in The Conchenta Conundrum including the proper and ultra-efficient office manager Claudia, who is - as everyone who works there knows - the glue that keeps the Crillsea "nick" running, as well as Archie, a Crillsea fixture not afraid to add a pint or two to the tab of DCI King. Other returning notables include larger-than-life Detective Chief Superintendent "Big Al" Jessop, Detective Sergeant Ted "Barney" Barnes - whose days in the Royal Ulster Constabulary (RUC) prove very useful - and Detective Inspector Annie Rock, who I hope Mr. Anthony finds a larger role for in the future as her confidence and competence made her a favourite of mine. Those familiar with Mr. Anthony's biography, which includes stints as a detective in local, regional and national police agencies in the United Kingdom, including the Special Branch (now known as Counter Terrorism Command, will take special interest in the "behind the scenes" aspect of this story. There is a sense of utter authenticity to the proceedings; no extra drama needed. Finally, as I've noted before I'm an Anglophile so the settings and dialogue were just the icing on a very tasty and satisfying treat of a story.

THE CONCHENTA CONUNDRUM
Murder Mystery/Crime/Detective
THIS BOOK IS #1 IN THE DAVIES KING 'stand alone' series, where each book has a separate stand alone tale involving the detective, KING, his detectives, and British Intelligence.

Book Description
Two beautiful and mysterious women are murdered in the same week. The local police chief believes both killings are the work of one man and instructs his officers to bring about a swift conclusion to the investigation. Davies King, the hardnosed, chess playing detective, reckons the game is much more complex and refuses to accept an apparent checkmate. With the odds stacking up against

him, Davies tries to shuffle all the pieces and capture the guilty party before an innocent man is wrongly arrested. But the clock is counting down, there's a bomb explosion imminent, and he's running out of time.... With enigmatic characters that are credible and authentic it doesn't take long to become engrossed in a well-crafted and gripping plot. Paul Anthony's mesmerizing conspiracy carries the reader all the way and skilfully builds to an exhilarating and explosive finale.

'My favourite detective novel so far from a most remarkable novelist, gripping to the last...'
Nick Gordon, International award winning screenwriter

Review: One of the best books I have ever read. The story is well written and holds you from start to finish. I really like the character Davies king and would love to read more books with this character in it... Susan Murray, Reader

If you're a fan of the PBS series "Mystery" then "The Conchenta Conundrum" by Paul Anthony is a must-read. Even if you're not, buy this book: I enjoyed it immensely. Several parallel stories involving murder, larceny, politics, organized crime and high finance intersect in surprising and delightful ways. A thoughtful, engaging protagonist in Inspector Davies King who is dedicated to solving crimes by using his intelligence, wits and experience -- but who is also not afraid to throw a punch or come up with a shortcut to the truth. A great "supporting cast" of unique and well-drawn characters on both sides of the law. I highly recommend "The Conchenta Conundrum" to anyone looking for an intelligent, well-written and fun-to-read mystery... Scott Whitmore, Freelance writer and author of 'Carpathia'

Review: I thoroughly enjoyed reading `Bushfire', another of Paul Anthony's books, so my expectations of `Conchenta Conundrum' were extremely high. I was not disappointed. 'Conchenta Conundrum' held me from the very first page, keeping me engaged to the last. The pace of this exciting book is fast and gives the reader a real appreciation of what the police force do behind the scenes during an investigation. The story centres around several cases on which the principal character, Davies King, and his team are working that include two murders and a series of robberies at jewellers in their jurisdiction. Apart from the criminal cases, there are other plots running through the story concerning the careers of Davies, his friends and his colleagues. I really related to and empathised with the characters as they are involved in the politics and the management mind games in the organisation. The `Conchenta Conundrum' gave me an insight into the working life of a policeman. Additionally, I learnt that, like all careers, there are those in the police force that work with, and for the team, and those that concentrate on developing their own careers and advancement at the expense of others. I rate this book very highly and recommend it to all.... Elizabeth Marshall, Best Selling author of 'When Fate Dictates' and the Highland Secret Series

This is what murder mysteries are supposed to be.... Dennis Sheehan, author of 'Purchased Power'... The Conchenta Conundrum sets the standard for murder mysteries. You can get the sense that the author is a real life detective, civilians wouldn't have the insight nor the technical know how to write like this. Once you start reading you won't be able to put it down. I highly recommend this book.

THE LEGACY OF THE NINTH
Espionage Thriller/Crime/Historic Fiction
THIS BOOK IS #3 IN THE BOYD 'stand alone' series, where each book has a separate stand alone tale involving the Cumbrian detective, Boyd, and his Special Crime Unit.
Book description

Packed with action, stacked with intrigue, and sprinkled with ingenious conspiracy, The Legacy of the Ninth is a whirlwind thriller of bitter conflict and religious mystique, echoing through the centuries of time from the desert wastes of the Roman Empire to the luscious green valley of the River Eden and the land of the Lakes. Behold, the noble Domitian: a valiant Roman Centurion who witnesses an appalling act of mass suicide in the Negev desert, and Hussein who plunders a Jewish artefact from its rightful owner. Centuries later, Boyd, the detective, tries to find out why events in Masada are now so closely linked with nearby Hadrian's Wall. Indeed, against all the odds, Boyd realises that the links are so strong that prospects of peace in the Middle East are in danger of collapsing...Things can't get any worse, can they?

'Full of intrigue, espionage and cold-blooded murder; the action is on-going, the descriptions vivid....'
The Keswick Reminder

'A thriller mixing fact and fiction, stacked with intrigue.'...
The Cumberland News

The Legacy of the Ninth takes the reader on a breath-taking journey, following the traces of a certain ancient artefact all the way from the desolate deserts of the devastated by Romans Judea to the modern day Britain and the Middle East. Victorious Roman legions, fierce ancient Scots, British and Israeli Intelligence, terrorists camps in Lebanon, undercover police officers, drug dealers, fishermen - you get to meet them all, while the action never slacks, never let you relax and pause for breath. You finish this story breathless, unable to let the book go before you know how it ends. This novel is very well written and deeply satisfying. It analyses all aspects of human nature, never turning to the easy solution of the good and the bad. The multiple points of view are astounding. Every angle of the unfolding story fascinates you with its different points of view, which exploring the inner worlds of various people of various cultures. The depth of the historical research is amazing and reminds us that life was brutal and cheap through all times, the modern days included. A very rewarding, enjoyable read that I would recommend to anyone. Zoe Saadia, Eminent Respected Author of The Cahokian.

I began reading The Legacy of the Ninth thinking that it was a story of the Roman Empire, but was not disappointed when it morphed into present day England where an artifact carried there from the Middle East by the Ninth Legion is uncovered. Its discovery becomes the catalyst for a new battle in the continuing conflict between Arabs and Jews. Paul Anthony populated this story with a host of three-dimensional characters engaged in the conflict from different venues, England, Istanbul, Lebanon, and Israel. One in particular, a British policeman reassigned from undercover work in London to leading Bobbies in Cumbria, faces the daunting task of reigniting pride in a group that has been allowed to languish in mediocrity. This challenge alone would be sufficient foundation for a good story. In The Legacy of the Ninth, it is but one facet of a complex tale with plots within plots. Lastly, I was pleased with the author's style. Thank God, I read it on Kindle and had a copy of the Oxford Dictionary built in to help me with the language (I am American and don't speak English). That aside, Paul Anthony varies his pace, lingering on details to establish the milieu, and racing ahead with action to make it exciting. Yes, I can recommend this one without reservation… Jack Durish, Vietnam War Veteran, business consultant, and Venture Galleries Author

Review = An intelligent exposition of historic fiction at its very best. A quite brilliant and well crafted multi genre tale that takes the reader on an incredible journey from the Ist century to the 20th century. Set in Masada, in the Middle East, the author tackles issues of religious conflict from the days of King Herod to the present day problem of Islamic extremism, and carefully weaves the work into the 20th century before leaving the reader breathless: This is a slow burner that gradually explodes - page by page - A master craftsman at work.... Five stars.... Dan, Reader, Grange....

*

BUSHFIRE
Espionage Thriller/Historic Fiction/Terrorism/Crime
THIS BOOK IS #2 IN THE BOYD 'stand alone' series, where each book has a separate stand alone tale involving the Cumbrian detective, Boyd, and his Special Crime Unit.

Book Description
A terrifying thriller of greed and deceit.
The action spans the oceans; from Northern Ireland, to Portugal, from Colombia to the British Isles, and is set against the inferno of a raging drugs culture. Cumbrian undercover detective, Boyd, working with two Portuguese investigators, a determined female British Intelligence officer, an American drug-busting legend, and the covert power of the State, battle against globally organised crime syndicates unaware that some amongst them have different plans... Private and personal revenge...

'A gripping story.... Take a bow...' The Cumberland News

'A fast paced, expertly written, brilliant tale of crime and suspense. The plot is clever, multi layers, detailed and precise. The writing has great depth which makes the reader feel as though they are right there, in the middle of this dangerous world of crime. This book is captivating and filled with adventure, excitement and drama. In a nutshell, this story has all the hallmarks of a Martina Cole book, but the big difference between the two is that what Paul Anthony has created in 'Bushfire' feels real, raw and grown-up. It opened my eyes to the world of organised crime and those who bravely fight it.

It tackles deep social issues and forces your mind beyond the normal bounds of society into the terrifying underworld of drugs and terrorism. I found myself connecting with the main crime fighting characters, routing for them, supporting them and wishing I could get into the book and warn them of dangers only the reader could see. The criminals terrified me as I glimpsed the inner workings of a world I didn't know existed. The very darkest side of human nature – greed, illicit drug trafficking, organised crime and terrorism. It is a story of a world only few can really understand.

This is a book that will keep you on the edge of your seat from the first page to the last. I have only ever read one crime thriller which felt absolutely real – 'Bushfire' by Paul Anthony….
Elizabeth Marshall, Book Reviewer, Travel Critic and International Author of 'When Fate Dictates'…

"Bushfire" by Paul Anthony is about the illegal drug industry in 1990's spanning Ireland, Portugal, and across the ocean to South American connections. This complex, well-written crime story follows layers of characters, from the criminals, the law enforcement, and the go-betweens as they make plans and interact with each other, making a non-stop story that is almost impossible to put down. I highly recommend this novel to readers that enjoy being pulled into the dangerous, intense world of international crime fighting. Five stars!
C.C. Cole, Award Winning Author of the 'Gastar' Dark Fantasy series.

I could not put the book down. It was fast and moving. Even in the midst of the mayhem that this story produced, Paul Anthony managed to use pleasing language to describe the surroundings. It seemed that when he described a beautiful spot, it got marred by the incidents surrounding it. I found that appealing in that it gave me a contrast between "normal" life and the lives of criminals and the havoc they reek on society… Sonia Rumzi, International Best

Selling Author of 'Simple Conversation', 'Caring for Eleanor' and many others works of 'Woman's literature'.

What an excellent book. I thoroughly enjoyed it.
This story has held me more and interested me more than the last two Clive Cussler books I have read and that is saying something as Clive Cussler is one of my favourite authors. I do believe I have found a new favourite author. The plot is brilliantly gripping and the characters are vividly real. It has an excellent pace and is crammed full of adventure, suspense and twists.
Andrew Brown, Book Critic and Reader.

Paul Anthony has written a winner with Bushfire. He takes the reader into the dark and dangerous world of narcotics trafficking and terrorism. The realism is in every page because the author moved in this world as a British detective investigating these crimes. The story centres on a group of British detectives attending a Europol conference in Portugal. They are led by Detective Inspector William Boyd, a dedicated and seasoned police officer. During the conference, Boyd goes for a run and spots a terrorist. This leads to a joint investigation with the British detectives, Portugal authorities and DEA... ... Bushfire is action filled and gripping. A must read if you like action/adventure novels.
Mike McNeff, Arizona Highway Patrol Academy; the DEA Narcotics Commanders' School, the Arizona Law Enforcement Academy, the Chandler/Gilbert Law Enforcement Academy, former Deputy County Attorney and Prosecuting Attorney...... and successful author of the GOTU series.

I found this an amazingly well written book. The author really did his research on the drug organization and the Justice system. Mr Anthony is a brilliant writer. The book just flowed when reading it. Bushfire is a fast paced, on the edge of your set book. I had a hard time putting it down. Need to know what was going to happen next. I feel in love with the main character of the book. The characters seemed so real that you felt you where there with them. You wanted to try and help at times. I'm hoping to see more of the main character in books to come. Just could not help liking him. I love thriller books and this was sure one thriller with a lot of twists and turns. I would recommend this book. Need to keep an eye on this author. He is going to go places with his writing.

Georgia Girl, Amazon Reader

*

THE FRAGILE PEACE
Historic Fiction/Thriller /Love Story/Crime/Espionage/Terrorism
Kindle version Published Spring, 2012
THIS BOOK IS #1 IN THE BOYD 'stand alone' series, where each book has a separate stand alone tale involving the Cumbrian detective, Boyd, and his Special Crime Unit.

The Fragile Peace reached #1 in its genre in March, 2013, in the Amazon Kindle store.

Book Description:
The Fragile Peace is a thriller of violent prejudices and divided loyalties. This Ulster novel reaches to the very roots of sectarian life and death. Written by a member of the security forces, it reveals a human landscape that is unknown, yet startingly believable. It is a world where sworn enemies may exchange confidences over a game of snooker; where a kneecapping operation turns into a deadly vendetta fuelled by sexual jealousy and where the fate of the United Kingdom could rest in the hands of one punch-drunk bruiser with a dangerous addiction. Everything is here, from the glamour of hi-tech intelligence work to the despairing pub-talk of men locked in the past. Trace the origins of these relentless tit-for-tat killings, often starting in childhood and see how the lives of vastly different

people may be mysteriously linked forever against the fatally beautiful backdrop of Northern Ireland.

'A powerful novel... A hard hitting tale of intrigue and suspicion, treachery and tension...'
The Keswick Reminder

A remarkably balanced piece of fiction... Gripping...'
The News and Star

'Selected in 2011 as the first audio book in the Dyslexia Foundation UK audio Library...'
Steve O'Brien, The Dyslexia Foundation UK

'A book that has accompanied me around the world. A great read, time and time again...' Eddie Lightfoot, Book Critic and Reader

REVIEW:
This gripping thriller puts a human face on Irish "Troubles". "The Fragile Peace" by Paul Anthony is an excellent read, and one I highly recommend. Don't worry if you don't know the background going in: "The Fragile Peace" isn't a history lesson or alphabet soup of group names. There is a very human face put on the "Troubles" in the form of Liam Connelly, a Provo soldier, and Detective Inspector Billy Boyd, two men who find themselves on opposite ends of the battle but connected by their love of someone else. Beginning in 1970, the early parts of the book, probably to the halfway point, set the stage for the exciting conclusion in 1995 after a tenuous ceasefire -- a temporary halt to the violence that factions on both sides distrust -- was put in place. I won't spoil the finale with too many details, but it is gripping and I stayed up into the early hours this very morning to finish it. Early glimpses of the development of Liam and Billy are seen in vignette, at critical crossroads on their way to finally meeting. Some may find this

jumping around in time a bit confusing, but for me it felt just right; the key players are introduced and the missing pieces of information are provided in a very natural way. The motivations of players on both sides of the conflict are muddied; while the "soldiers" of Active Service Units believe they are serving a great cause many Provo leaders earn big money running drug and protection rackets. In a similar way, some RUC and British police fight based on strongly held beliefs of right and wrong while others let ambition and ego colour their actions. The authenticity and sure-handedness of the tale are no surprise given Paul Anthony's resume: "Working as a detective, he served in the CID, the Regional Crime Squad in Manchester, the Special Branch, and other national agencies in the UK."

Scott Whitmore, former US Navy officer, freelance writer, copy editor, sports journalist and successful author of 'Carpathia.'

REVIEW:

The Inside Story of "The Troubles", The Fragile Peace is an important book if you have any interest at all in the war between the Catholics, Protestants and the British Government in Northern Ireland. The setting of the story is from 1969 to 1995. As the reader, you not given a tutorial of the war, you are dragged into the middle of it. You are the IRA man, the RUC patrol, the informer, the British intelligence agent, the anti-terrorist detective and the victim. It is quite evident that the author, Paul Anthony, lived this story in his former life as a member of a Scotland Yard anti-terrorist team. It is a work of fiction, but the book is so vivid and realistic there can be no other explanation. The way the book written makes the reader feel like a part of the story. I highly recommend the book. I read the original edition and I understand it has been rewritten because Paul Anthony has learned much about writing since he first wrote The Fragile Peace. As a writer, I did see some technical flaws in the first edition, but the story is so powerful, it is easy to overlook those flaws.... Read it. You will not be disappointed... Mike McNeff, Arizona Highway Patrol, Attorney, Law Enforcement Officer, and acclaimed author of the 'GOTU...' series.

REVIEW:
5.0 out of 5 stars Storytelling at its Best 21 Feb 2013
By Dan - Published on Amazon.com
Format: Hardcover
"The Fragile Peace" is an excellent read. I remember the times recalled by the author very well and anyone reading the book will come to realise the traumas borne in the "troubles" which are still in living memory and therefore, not all that long ago.

The characters are believable and are brought to life by some very descriptive writing.

An excellent novel with a thrilling climax. Storytelling at its best.

*

SUNSET
POETRY COLLECTION

Book description
Sunset is a collection of poetry tracing the life of a relaxed carefree teenager in the Sixties to a man at the dawn of the Twenty First Century. The journey captures an age of experiences; peaceful and pleasant, violent and murderous. The voyage from one century to another smoothly results in a unique portrayal of the era in which we live. From love and romance, war and peace, sorrow and surrender, to private fears and unknown tears, Paul Anthony delivers a roller-coaster of poetic emotion in his third book, Sunset.
'From boy to man in seventy seven poems...'
The Cumberland News

'A very touching and wonderful collection of poetry from an author who has experience and has worked with teenagers and adults alike. Paul Anthony does a wonderful job of portraying the era in which we live with its known and unknown fears. The author uses his expertise as a crime-fighter to depict the diversity of emotions both good and bad that we all share in common with one another. I encourage all to read it when you get a chance...'
Jeannie Walker, author of the True Crime Story 'Fighting the Devil', 2011 National Indie Excellence Awards (True Crime Finalist) and 2010 winner of the Silver Medal for Book of the Year True Crime Awards.

'This was a wonderful read. I really enjoyed it.'
Arlena Dean, Reader...

Scribbles with Chocolate
Published Spring 2012
Short Stories
Welcome to Scribbles with Chocolate. A collection of short stories, poems and extracts to be read at leisure time and especially designed for use during a break, or when travelling from a to b. Lots of poems and short stories - From murder to mayhem from ghosts to romance and back again.

~

Monsters, Gnomes and Fairies (In my Garden)
Published January 2013
In March, 2013, this book reached #5 in its genre in the Amazon Kindle store.
Written with Meg Johnston, this is a quite wonderful collection of short stories for children aged between 4 and 11. The stories are written by a couple of grandparents who have recounted these tales to their children and their children's children. And oh what fun we had writing them. So if you have girls who like fairies, boys who like

football, and a granddad who talks to a garden gnome..... This is for you....

*

PAUL ANTHONY

http://www.independentauthornetwork.com/paul-anthony.html

Printed in Great Britain
by Amazon